The Last Seal

BY
RICHARD DENNING

Written by Richard Denning

© Copyright 2010 Richard Denning

First Published 2010

This paperback second edition published 2011

ISBN: 978-0-9568103-3-5

Published by Mercia Books

A catalogue record for this book is available from the British Library.

Book Jacket design and layout and Hourglass Icon

by Cathy Helms www.avalongraphics.org

using Artwork by Andreas Resch (Image of London in flames)

www.andreasresch.at

Internal Artwork and Map by Gillian Pearce

www.hellionsart.com/

Copy-editing and proofreading by Jo Field.

Author website:

www.richarddenning.co.uk

Publisher website:

www.merciabooks.co.uk

For Jane, Jean, John and Margaret.

The credit for producing this new edition falls firstly to the encouragement of author, Helen Hollick and the hard work of my superb editor, Jo Field. I am also grateful for the three artists who contributed to the cover and to the internal artwork.

The Author

Richard Denning was born in Ilkeston in Derbyshire and lives in Sutton Coldfield in the West Midlands, where he works as a General Practitioner. He is married and has two children. He has always been fascinated by historical settings as well as horror and fantasy. Other than writing, his main interests are games of all types. He is the designer of a board game based on the Great Fire of London.

By the same author:

Northern Crown Series
(Historical fiction)
1.The Amber Treasure
2.Child of Loki (Coming 2012)

Hourglass Institute Series
(Young Adult Science Fiction)
1.Tomorrow's Guardian
2. Yesterday's Treasures
3. Today's Sacrifice (Coming 2012)

The Praesidium Series
(Historical Fantasy)
1.The Last Seal
If you enjoyed this book please join the fan page on
www.facebook.com/TheLastSeal

The City of
London 1666

N
W E
S

Artillery Grounds

Smith Fields

Moor-Fields

Holbourne

Bishopgate

Moorgate

Cripplegate

Aldersgate

Grub Street

Guild-Hall

Newgate

Cheapside

Ludgate

St. Paul's

To Westminster

Royal Exchange

Cornhill

Aldgate

Poor Jewry

The Tower

Thames Street

LONDON BRIDGE

THAMES

Southwark

Key

H Location of the Six Seals

1. Tobias' House
2. Freya's Stable

Chapter 1
London 1380

The warlock, Stephen Blake, released the demon, Dantalion, from the Abyss on the fifth day of July in the year of our Lord thirteen hundred and eighty.

Just before the hour appointed for the service of Lauds - the sixth past midnight - a short figure stole down Ludgate Hill and out through the old city gate to a small church that lay beneath the shadow of St Paul's Cathedral, which brooded over London like a mother hen protecting her clutch of chicks. With his cloak wrapped tightly around him to keep out the chill of an early morning mist, he slipped unnoticed between the gravestones and stopped at the side door. Blake paused to glance behind, his wary gaze probing the shadows along the road and around the indistinct bulk of nearby houses.

Somewhere in the city lurked the one man who could prevent him doing what he planned. This moment had been long in the preparation and he did not want it spoilt by the interference of the *Praesidium* Order, or their leader, Cornelius Silver. Blake took one last look and, satisfied he was alone, opened the door, wincing slightly as it juddered and creaked on rusty hinges.

Inside, he glanced at the altar, the font and then the main doors. A smile that was more of a sneered grimace curled one side of his mouth. This was once a place of worship: a hallowed sanctuary for the parishioners who would have come here to find peace, comfort and protection from evil, but those days were past. Looking around him, Blake considered the paint peeling off the mould-covered walls, the cracked dilapidated windows, a patched altar cloth and the chipped stonework of the pillars. The local people and even God himself had apparently abandoned the place. Only an aged, half blind priest came here faithfully each day to carry out his offices.

Blake crossed to the lectern, where a musty bible lay open, and bent his neck so he could read some of the words.

"Nam et si ambulavero in medio umbrae mortis, non timebo mala, quoniam tu mecum es," he recited, his lips moving but the sound coming almost as a whisper. He then stood in silence pondering the verse for a moment.

"For though I should walk in the midst of the shadow of death, I will fear no evils, for thou art with me."

He laughed and the sneer snaked further across his face. Those very people who had abandoned this church would soon run from the shadow of death and Blake himself would be the one to bring them fear. No – much more than fear – in a few hours he would bring them terror!

Blake heard footsteps approaching along the stones that lined the path outside. Quickly he moved to lurk behind the door and reaching inside his cloak clutched his fingers around his dagger, holding it up, so the early sunlight filtering in through the grimed windows danced along the sharp steel blade. He waited. The door opened. The old priest stood on the threshold, his almost sightless eyes squinting as he sensed someone was within his church and that he was not alone. Delight flooded his tired old face as he stepped inside and saw Blake move.

"Welcome, welcome my son!" the priest said, followed by a look of puzzlement and concern, then a cry of fear as Blake stepped forward, placed a hand over the old man's mouth and as panic came into those ancient eyes, slashed the blade across the exposed throat. The priest stumbled onto his knees, one hand trying to stem the gushing blood the other reaching out, imploringly, towards the crucifix that stood on the altar. Then he was dead.

Wiping his dagger on the old man's stained vestments, Stephen Blake tucked it back beneath his cloak before taking the priest's own communion cup and using it to collect the blood. His blood: the blood of a holy man slain on consecrated ground. He mixed it with the dried hawthorn and yarrow leaves, crushed poppy seeds and bruised eaglewood root that he carried in the pocket at his belt, stirring the ingredients into the bronze cup, which he set with care and reverence upon the altar. A single candle heated the mixture releasing a plume of noxious fumes that permeated the church with foul smoke. Blake stood, motionless and upright within one of two circles he had drawn in the old priest's blood on the worn flagstones. Head back, arms stretched upward as if in devout prayer, he recited the incantations that would summon the demon.

As he spoke, a ring of flames sprang up around the second circle – rising higher and higher until they started to lick the timbers of the roof above. With each word he uttered, the air burned and crackled about him. Intense heat singed his hair, turning its silver-grey colour to a charred black – his skin becoming scorched and blistered – but he was aware of none of it. On and on he recited, chanting the words, unbroken, and undisturbed: words contrary to the laws of God, of goodness, of Light – contrary to the very rules of the Universe and existence. The world was shuddering and shaking as reality twisted, distorted and buckled around him – but still he chanted, ignoring the cacophony of screeching so shrill that his eardrums were close to bursting. Then in triumph he shouted the last few words and, with a suddenness that startled him, there was utter silence as the completed spell tore a hole from his world into the Abyss: into the other world, the world of the demons.

Since the day of his birth, Blake, a warlock, had been raised for this moment. He and his forefathers had worshipped and studied the demons for one reason, one purpose: to rule alongside them, just as his distant ancestors had done when demons walked this earth beside man millennia before. Blake had longed for this day. He had imagined the pride he would feel at mastering the Words of Power. He had dreamt of the wealth he would earn as well as the domination he would gain over other men and had revelled in the thought. None of those dreams and longings had prepared him for the intensity of fear that suddenly swamped his senses. Only now did Stephen Blake realise the terrible risk he was taking. In a few moments he might be as dead as that old fool of a priest. Once exposed to the fury of the creature he was about to free, in an instant he might be left a bloody corpse or nothing more than a pile of blackened ashes.

The intense white flames encircling the second circle roared around the rift Blake had created. For a moment he could see nothing inside that fire. Then, Blake felt his heart thumping as he realised he was no longer alone. Something had come through the portal: something vast which stood amidst the furnace the warlock had created, utterly oblivious to the heat. Slowly the flames died until Blake gazed upon the beast in all its terrifying clarity.

As it emerged, the giant form of the demon, Dantalion, roared: a sound that shook the earth from far below the foundations of the church to high above, indeed to the very vault of the sky.

Towering fifteen feet above him, Dantalion wore the form of a human – although Blake was aware he could take many others if he so wished. The demon's skin was a ruddy brown colour devoid of hair. The eyes, which stared at Blake empty of compassion or emotion, were a glowing red as if fire blazed within. He wore britches and a leather breast plate covering a powerful and muscular body. His limbs ended in appendages that were more like claws than feet or hands and which bore talons as sharp, long and as vicious as daggers. He carried no weapons, for he needed none, but in his right hand he clutched a book that looked to Blake - standing, mouth open, too scared to move, blink or breathe - as if it were a large leather-bound bible. The creature stank. Blake's eyes watered and his guts heaved as he was assaulted by a vile stench of decay and sulphur fumes.

Dantalion took a single step forward and as his foot left the enclosure of the circle and landed on the ancient flagstones, the church shook, shuddering as if Blake's tremendous fear was permeating the walls of this defiled sanctuary. The demon reached a claw towards the warlock's neck, the dreadful talons dripping with what resembled oozing pus.

With a cry of terror, Blake stumbled, tripped and fell. The creature took another stride and the terrified man scrabbled backwards, a scream of terror locked in his throat as the beast stood like a colossus over his cowering figure. As the claw swung back in readiness to slay him, the warlock found the desperate courage to raise one trembling arm to stay the blow, and begged for his life.

"Spare me, Master Dantalion! Spare me!"

The beast grunted and tilted his head, hesitating, eyes narrowing in puzzlement.

Blake took his chance, thinking and speaking quickly, "Lord of demons, Great Duke of Hell, it was I who brought you here to rule this world. All I ask is that I may be granted the honour

5

to serve you." Shaking in fear and feeling his heart thumping, Blake waited through the long seconds that might be his last on Earth. Incongruously, he wondered if it would hurt to be slashed apart by those wicked talons; whether it would take long to die.

Lips rolled back to reveal sharp, yellowed teeth, Dantalion extended his claws, his muscles taut in eager readiness to finish this grovelling worm. For a moment, his nostrils distended, he studied the small insignificant warlock at his feet. The moment dragged on as if the demon were enjoying the pleasure of smelling this fool's terror. He growled; a low rumble that again shook the church walls, then reached out, placed one hand on Blake's head and caressed the man's ash-white face almost tenderly. Then the fire within his eyes flared.

Blake screamed as searing pain shot through his skull, as if white hot needles were being forced into his brain. He squirmed as the agony continued for an eternity until, suddenly, Dantalion released him, stepped aside and stood glowering, his expression one of contemptuous appraisal.

"I have searched your soul, human, and it is black," the demon said, his voice rumbling like the drums of an approaching army. "You are loyal to no one and serve only your own interests."

"No, Master, I swear I am loyal to you, I ..."

Dantalion dealt a savage blow with the back of his hand, splitting Blake's lip and flinging him backwards, his head striking hard against the flagstones.

"NEVER lie to me! Never!" Dantalion's harsh voice boomed and echoed along the nave, bouncing from stone wall to stone wall, dislodging dust from the arched rafters above.

Despite his agony, Blake realised with incredulous wonder that the demon was not going to kill him.

The beast gave a slight nod of his monstrous head. "Yes, you may live ... for now. My race knows the value of black hearts and black souls. Feeble men who care only for themselves make good allies for us against their own kind."

He moved away, took two steps then paused, turned back to Blake.

"Come, follow me. I command it." Without waiting to see if the warlock obeyed, he strode down the nave, and with a deafening boom, burst through the front wall, smashing stone and wood as if they were mere fragile parchment.

Stunned and shaking, Blake scrabbled to his feet, wiped the sweat from his brow and ran to follow his master. Outside, the sun was climbing in the sky and the warlock was dazzled by the sunlight pouring in through the shattered walls and windows. Eyes watering, he stood coughing and spluttering within the rubble and clouds of dust as the falling masonry came to rest. The terror that clutched London when the creature had erupted with a deafening boom from the church had manifested in a profound silence. It lasted only a moment. In the mass of terrified people gathered at the entrance to the city a child screamed, then a woman. A man shouted and pandemonium spread faster than wildfire.

Blinking as his eyes adjusted to the bright light, Blake could make out the morning crowds clustered around the Ludgate; the road filled with carts piled high with goods waiting in line for the gates to open. In panic, the drivers abandoned their vehicles and the rearing plunging horses and mules, and fled towards the gate. A prior leading his monks on pilgrimage to the Cathedral, stared open-mouthed at the demon and raised a crucifix towards Dantalion, futilely trusting that the holy symbol would protect him. Hawkers of food and drink, who normally offered refreshments out of their carts to anyone with the coin to buy them, left their goods without a thought and now fought each other to be first through the gate. Two guardsmen armed with billhooks were moving towards the source of the commotion, but then stopped and looked up at the monster bearing down upon them, their faces betraying their fear as well as their uncertainty at what to do.

The first to die was a man who had been selling oysters from a barrel. One-handed – for in the other he still clutched the great book - Dantalion took hold of him and casually tossed him over his shoulder. Screaming, the man smashed into the church tower and fell dead to the ground next to Blake. The warlock glanced down at the bloody mess that was once a man and took a deep breath as he felt the exhilaration of having unleashed this power and destruction on the city.

The demon, his foot the length of a man's leg, stamped down on to the barrel, pulverising the oyster shells. He took two strides towards a group of merchants gathered round a cart piled high with cloth. They had been trying desperately to unload bolts of expensive red and gold velvet, but now turned at the sound of the demon approaching and froze, terrified. Dantalion pointed one talon at them, spoke a few arcane words and instantly a searing ray of heat burst forth and incinerated them all, men and cloth, to a smoking heap of ash.

The guardsmen still stood in the middle of the road staring at the demon in uncomprehending shock. To Blake it was as if Dantalion grew a little with each kill. Now taller than the houses that lined the street, the beast smashed both fists down on the roof of one, sending timber and thatch tumbling on to a family that huddled against its wall. One of the guards recovered and charged the beast, his billhook aimed high in an effort to reach the demon's belly. The blade snapped on Dantalion's hide and while the guard stared stupidly at the ruined weapon, the demon scooped him up with one hand and simply bit off his head, dropping the bleeding corpse into the ruins of the house.

Dantalion roared and the crowds on Ludgate Hill quailed at the sound and then – screaming in panic – they started to scatter, running any way they could to escape the horror.

8

Dantalion possessed more than immense size and strength, and more than mastery of the arcane elements. His words held power: power that could seize men's minds and influence, command and compel them.

"Stop!" he boomed. Instantly, people stopped running and turned to face him.

To Blake, it seemed that the demon's appearance had changed subtly. The fire had left his eyes and his features had softened. Was he perhaps a fraction shorter? And surely his talons had dwindled in length? The odour of death and decay was gone and a sweet smell of spring blossoms drifted along the road. When the demon spoke again his tone had also altered and was filled with charisma and seduction.

"I am Dantalion. I am your Lord. You will love me and obey me. Bow before me!"

Monks, merchants, vendors and guards, women, children – everyone bowed low, Blake too. Dantalion stood by the city gate and looked down upon them all. Then, with a laugh of delight, he turned to the warlock.

"Witness, my lieutenant: witness as the first subjects of my Kingdom honour me. From here we will conquer all, and all will see me and love me, worship me and obey me!"

Blake nodded and smiled to himself, scarcely daring to believe that he had achieved his dreams. This was the secret his forefathers had guarded and passed on: the knowledge to free the demon and through him to rule England, Europe - the world! It had taken generations to learn the litany and magicks required, but now he paid his ancestors honour by fulfilling their destiny. He, Stephen Blake, had mastered it!

He laughed and above him Dantalion also laughed. Together, as partners, they strode off, down through the gate and on towards St Paul's. There, between the rickety wooden houses, Blake could see the vast Cathedral: taller by far than any other building in the city, with its square tower topped by a magnificent spire – the largest in the land. A place of pilgrimage for the thousands who flocked here: folk like the Prior and his monks who had come here to worship in the holy place and who now trailed along behind their new master – their new god: Dantalion. It was there, walking down Ludgate Hill, that Blake realised something was wrong. The feeling crept up on him as if a dark mist was choking his soul. Suddenly, Dantalion gave a cry of frustration and panic. Blake searched around for the source of the threat and saw it. There! Over there standing by the south wall of the Cathedral was the man Blake had feared would come: Silver! Cornelius Silver!

Blake clenched his fists, anger spilling into him with the force of a flood tide. Silver: the one man who could interfere; the one man who, with his sanctimonious meddling could ruin everything. "*Praesidium* filth!" he spat.

Cornelius Silver, the white sorcerer, was robed in his monk's habit and stood, straight and still in the road in front of them, his expression that of determination with not a sign of fear. With a shudder of apprehension Blake, the warlock, could see dedication there. Silver's tonsured head was a pale contrast to well-trimmed brown hair and his clean-shaven chin. In one hand he held a stone tablet, the other was outstretched towards Dantalion. This was a man who believed utterly in his purpose, who would sacrifice himself without thinking to oppose the evil Blake served; the one man who *could* oppose him.

From the tablet Silver carried, a soft ethereal glow emanated, which rapidly grew brighter. Casting a quick glance at Dantalion, who was standing motionless in the road staring at the monk as if paralysed, Blake chanted a counter invocation.

The sorcerer's attention snapped across to fix Blake with an intense glare of contempt. Ignoring the demon, he pointed at the warlock, spoke three short, sharp words and a bolt of fire hurled at Blake, who leapt with a gasp of alarm to one side and rolled away to avoid the fire bolt. With a mind-numbing

10

explosion it impacted on a cart standing behind him in the road. The wooden vehicle erupted into flames, the ferocity of the blast stunning the warlock's senses.

The violence of the arcane blast halted the jostling crowd of people trailing along behind their new master. A man at the front of the crowd shouted out in agony as the flames bathed his arm and the skin burnt and blistered in the heat. The other followers stirred from their trance, took one look at the demon, another at the sorcerer and scattered in all directions fleeing in terror; even as a second explosion rocked the street behind them.

Dantalion, meanwhile, responding to Blake's chant, was advancing on the sorcerer his claws open and ready to bring death to this mortal who opposed him. Silver turned back to the demon and continued to recite his incantation. The tablet glowed brighter; tendrils of silver light flowed out of the stone, weaving in and out of each other as they curled along the street towards the horrendous creature. Dantalion snarled and started backing away from them, fear now etched on the ancient creature's features. Cursing, Blake dragged himself to his feet and staggered towards his master He had to oppose Silver – had to!

"No, I will not go back! No! No!" Dantalion bellowed his anguish, lashing out in fury at the tendrils emanating from the white sorcerer's stone tablet. One talon caught Blake, raking down his side; with a scream of pain he fell dazed and bleeding to the ground.

The demon retreated, using the great book he carried as a shield, but the tendrils were rampant, dozens of them twirling, twisting, entwining, clutching at his feet, his ankles, his legs, reaching for his arms, binding those slashing talons in skeins of light. One grasped at the book, then another, and another, tearing at the leather binding, rustling through the pages and ripping it from his clutch, sending it spinning across the dusty road.

Roaring his fury, Dantalion attempted to break free; tried desperately to reach for his book, but he was being pulled inexorably towards the implacable monk. As he was dragged along, so his size diminished along with his strength. Dantalion struggled and cursed and his hands sent forth flame and light, but the words the sorcerer monk chanted were too old, the power they held too potent. Screaming his pitiful terror and anger, the ancient beast was lifted off the ground and was tumbling and spinning in the air, his great size and power shrinking and shrinking as the tendrils pulled him nearer and nearer to the stone tablet that held such immense power. With a crack of sound louder than thunder he vanished, drawn right into the stone.

Confined; entombed; less than an hour after being freed the demon was trapped in a new, stronger prison.

Aware of a stabbing pain, Blake opened his eyes and groaned. His side was a mass of congealed blood and aching, but that did not matter; the hollow feeling of defeat inside him was worse. He had been so close to triumph, but he had failed. He dragged himself to his feet, one hand holding his bloody side, and glanced around. This street – usually one of the busiest in London – was empty and silent. The crowds having fled in terror had not returned, although the cause of that terror was gone. Silver too had vanished. Carts and spilled merchandise lay scattered around; one still billowing black smoke; another being cautiously nosed by a mangy cur. A dead mule and a few bodies sprawled around it were already attracting blowflies. There was nothing else to show for the horror that had happened here.

Blake briefly considered repeating the summoning rite, but knew he could not. The components needed for the spell were rare, the preparation took hours, this was not the place, the time – and even if he had all of that ready, the void where Dantalion had been held before was not where he was now.

Forty centuries before, when the demons had attacked the first civilisations, the sorcerers of that ancient empire had learnt how to bind the monsters in stone slabs that bore their inscribed incantations. One of those slabs the *Praesidium* sorcerer had used today: that was where the demon was once again trapped and there was nothing Blake could do about it.

Still groaning, he leant against a wall and winced at the pain in his side. He must find Silver. Somehow he must find a way to release Dantalion again, but he was tired and he was hurting. How could he go through all that again? How could he start all over? Maybe by passing what he knew down to his son and his grandson, and so on? Ah, but then it would not be *his* triumph would it? Not now. He closed his eyes, suppressed the anguished cry of failure; stood there, bereft, his bruised body pressed against the wall, fighting the grief tumbling through his black soul. He had failed! He had failed!

To start again: that was his only choice. Start again. Wearily he pushed himself away from the wall, took a few stumbling steps, halted when he saw an object lying in the entrance to an alley way. What was that? It looked familiar ... his eyes widened as he recognised it. The book! Dantalion's book! Eagerly, heedless of the pain in his side, Blake reached for it. Pages were torn, the leather binding was cracked and spoiled, but what secrets did it hold and what powers could be gained from studying it?

Eagerly he lifted it, and hastily dropped it with a cry of dismay. It weighed as much as an oak chest. Nearby was an upturned hand cart. Blake righted it and with difficulty and much grunting heaved the book into it. Hurrying, he pushed the cart down the deserted Creed Lane towards Blackfriars and the river. He would find a boat to ferry him across the Thames and travel to some place where he could recover and study the

13

book. It might take a lifetime, perhaps many lifetimes, but one day the knowledge in Dantalion's Tome would reveal itself.

Blake smiled at the thought, and disappeared into the shadows.

Chapter 2
The Truant and the Thief

London, Saturday 1st September, 1666: late morning

Thwack! The birch cane struck Ben's thigh, sending a jolt of pain down his leg. He bit his tongue to avoid crying out and then, when no further blows came, opened his eyes and blinked to clear the tears the pain had brought.

He stood in the yard outside his dormitory, his head bent forward in an attempt to avoid the terrifying and almost Medusa-like stare of the Headmaster, Dr Busby. Ben's own tutor, Wilkinson, stood beside Dr Busby, glaring with frustration at the boy. Behind them the entirety of the teaching faculty loomed, and further back, Ben's classmates watched the proceedings with a mixture of horror and excitement on their faces.

Ben returned his gaze to the forbidding form of Dr Busby who, having now completed the punishment began his customary lecture.

"Boy, you will learn to be obedient and follow the rules!" Busby said, dark eyes glinting and cheeks puffing as he spoke. "No pupil, and I mean *no* pupil, will abscond from any activities at this school, and certainly not my Saturday morning assembly or this afternoon's debate. Do you understand?"

Ben's legs were still throbbing with a burning pain. This was his penalty for being caught hiding in his room, rather than being in the hall enduring two hours of his classmates reciting passages of Plato. Despite, or perhaps because of the pain, there was an edge of defiance in his voice as he replied.

"But, Sir,"

"Do not 'but Sir' me, boy! Everyone has to attend the debate!" Busby roared and even the teachers winced at the noise.

"But, Sir," Ben tried again, "I know it all already," he replied, "isn't there anything more interesting I could do?"

That brought gasps of surprise and shock from pupils and teachers alike. Busby's cheeks reddened in indignation. A pupil daring to make such a statement was unheard of. Ben knew this too and part of him wondered what was getting into him. He also knew he was in deep trouble and yet another part of him did not care.

"More interesting? You come here to be educated, not entertained. Know it already do you? Oh do you indeed!" Busby said and smiled at the assembled ranks of his teachers. Ben shivered, suspecting that expression could not bode well for him.

"Please educate us, young man; who wrote *The Carmen Saeculare*?"

"Horace, Sir," Ben answered with a smile. Busby nodded.

"Very good and what are the opening words?" the Headmaster asked. The smile was wiped from Ben's face.

"Er, I don't know, Sir."

"I see; well, let's try another question. According to Plato, how old was the philosopher in the *Apology of Socrates*?"

Ben's mouth moved, but he was unable to reply. He dared not look at the teachers, but he could sense them watching, listening and judging him and he could feel his face beginning to burn in embarrassment under their gaze. A few sniggers at his discomfort reached him from the pupils. In front of him he saw Busby's lip now curling in contempt.

"I thought you knew it all already, boy," he sneered.

Ben squirmed, desperately wishing he was somewhere else and he did not care where it was. There was no escape, however, and showing no mercy, Busby asked another question.

"In *The Iliad*, who does Homer say is the father of Diomedes?"

Ben's mind was blank. What was wrong with him? He should know all this.

"I don't know, Sir, I'm sorry."

There was total silence, punctuated by a gentle swishing sound as the Headmaster waved the birch cane back and forth through the air. Fearing it would be used on him again, Ben tensed in anticipation of the blow. Busby looked rather like a kettle into whose spout someone has pushed a cork before placing it on the fire: boiling hot and likely to explode at any moment. In the end, though, Busby spoke softly, but in a tone that made Ben wish the Headmaster had used the cane on him.

"Your behaviour and attitude is unacceptable for a boy at my school as is your impertinence and arrogance. You are confined to your room as of this moment. On Monday, I will see you again and decide whether to write to your uncle and inform him of my intention to have you removed from this school forthwith on suspension. Whether I do or not is entirely in your hands. Do you understand?"

Anxious to escape from the attention of the Headmaster, Ben nodded in apparent sincerity, but he knew he was lying. He was already making plans for an expedition of his own for this very afternoon.

With a final glare at Ben and with his robes billowing behind him, Busby marched away towards the refectory and his midday meal, followed by the other tutors hurrying along in his wake like a naval squadron in line behind their flagship. The pupils marched off as well, but not before several had met Ben's gaze and sniggered at him. Finally, he was alone with Wilkinson, who now studied the boy for a moment while he appeared to marshal his thoughts. At last he spoke.

"I don't know what to do with you, boy. The change in you since last year has been marked," his tutor said. "You never used to be a poor student: quite the opposite in fact. I'd say you were by far the most intelligent and able pupil that has been to this school in many years. You can – and you and I both know you can – read and write Latin better than a Roman. All those questions the Headmaster asked: you knew all that and more in the examinations last year – why not now? You used to be able to quote all the writers of antiquity with effortless ease. Heavens, but there was even a point last year when you started correcting errors I had made!"

Ben said nothing. He felt angry and not only at his tutor, but at everything and everybody. The pain of the punishment was not the source of his dissatisfaction, although it hardly helped his mood, and he could feel the anger twisting inside him like a knot, but terrible as it felt it was better than the other feelings it had replaced: feelings he did not want to and could not deal with at present. The anger helped him cope, so he just stood there in a cloud of misery, a glazed expression on his face, looking at the tutor and waiting for the discussion to end, but not really caring what the outcome would be.

"You are late handing in work. What you do hand in is poor and shows almost no sign of effort. You hardly pay attention in class and you are surly and bad tempered. You don't seem to talk to your classmates any more or join in with their activities. I am aware that your parents died recently and I sympathise

18

with your loss, but you must know that many of the boys in the school – aye, and the tutors too – lost some of their relatives last year," Wilkinson grimaced and added, "the plague in '65 was the worst in living memory, yet they bear their losses bravely and although the circumstances are different, so must you."

He waited for Ben to say something, but when the boy remained silent Wilkinson glowered and pointed towards the dormitory. "Get out of my sight," he shouted then turning on his heel, stomped off after Busby towards the teachers' entrance to the dining hall.

Ben took a few steps in the direction of his room and reached out to grasp the door handle. Then he stopped and watched his tutor depart. He knew Wilkinson was trying to help and that the Ben of a year back would have responded with enthusiasm, but that boy seemed buried and far away. It was with a sense of futility that he now endured each school day; every activity seemed pointless and every moment spent a resented waste of time.

All at once his temper rose to a peak, the muscles in his arms and legs suddenly tensing, hands curling into fists. He let out a howl of rage, opened the door and without entering, slammed it shut. Still feeling a need to vent his anger, he kicked the door frame for good measure. Breathing fast, he stared at it for a few moments then turned away from his room and set off towards the front gate. He knew there would be trouble when he was found missing, but he did not care. With a furtive glance at the refectory, Ben sneaked out of the school and walked northwards towards the heart of London.

****

Standing on Fleet Bridge, the thief counted the miserable few coins yielded by the sale of a shirt and a pair of stockings stolen earlier off a washing line in Holborn. A fat-looking merchant, passing by on a cart loaded with barrels of ale, glanced over and noted a splash of red hair and unwashed hands, scruffy britches riddled with holes, shoes with soles that flapped and gaped and a wide-brimmed hat that shrouded most of the thief's face. The merchant's haughty sniff clearly dismissed the figure as a vagabond, beggar or a good for nothing lad best avoided. This was a common reaction and meant that few folk came close, and that suited the thief just fine. If a vagabond lad was the role to be played to keep living, then so be it.

Below the thief, on the banks of the ditch running beneath the bridge, was the Rag Fair. The poorest came here each day to pay copper coins for a few pathetic clothes stolen in tenements or stripped off the dead, linen taken from the beds of plague victims and then washed in urine in an effort to cleanse the contagion, or wigs pulled off the heads of passing pedestrians on Cheapside by enterprising boys hanging out of first floor windows.

Children played on the narrow shore barely inches from the decaying body of a dog that floated downstream through the stinking filth that was the River Fleet. A brief gust of wind from the north brought more noxious smells, this time from scores of huge brass and iron vats standing along the water's edge and perched on top of fires that threw a dense cloud of smoke and fumes skyward. The vats produced a hundred wares: vinegar, glue, cured leather and soap, or were used to bleach cloth or boil the fat off animal skins. Further up the river, butchers smoked animal carcasses and the refuse from this and all the other trades was thrown into the water or littered its edge. The smell was unbelievable and sickening, but here, in rotten wooden huts overlooking the ditch, the poor just endured.

The thief's nose wrinkled: time to move on perhaps; towards Newgate, drifting through lanes lined with the tottering two- and three-storey wooden houses that made up the city of London. The top floors leant out so far that in some places it was possible for folk in one house to shake hands with those living opposite. The streets below were in permanent gloom, overshadowed by the buildings and the unremitting clouds of smoke that covered the city.

A cry of warning rang out from above and the thief darted forward, dodging the torrent of excrement from someone's chamber pot tipped out of a high window. A lawyer walking down the lane towards the Inns of Court, was not so lucky and let out a shout of outrage as his fine clothes were ruined. The thief chuckled and moved on.

Just outside Newgate, country women were selling nosegays from the side of the road. The ale merchant had stopped his cart at Pie Corner to buy one and now held it close as he drove on through the gate. From the way he screwed up his face the thief guessed it failed to disguise the fetid stench that escaped the jail built into the gatehouse, where the condemned and accused alike had to endure rats and gaol fever, and the open sewer that ran through their cells.

"Have pity on us, Sir," croaked a voice from a barred window built into the jail at ground level. "Please, Sir; do you have any food, any coins?" The inmate pushed a desperate hand through the bars for anything passers-by might give him. The thief knew prisoners were not fed in the jail and survived by begging or buying food, and on the charity of friends. Many died in that dank hole. The merchant, his mouth full of pie, turned his head away, but the thief went over and dropped one copper coin into the outstretched palm, enough perhaps for a meal.

"Bless you, lad," the prisoner said and the thief nodded, thinking that ill fortune might lead any man or woman to be needing help in that terrible place one day.

Passing through the city wall, the thief entered the Shambles, where blood and offal from freshly butchered meat dripped on to the ground and ran off downhill. All round the

21

market, hawkers sold candles, beer, mussels, honeyed nuts and cane rods; the latter for the punishment of children. Beggars, prostitutes and pickpockets plying their trade were all noticed and expertly avoided by the thief. Some were moving stealthily and in disguise, snatching coin pouches off belts or food from baskets. Others drew attention to themselves by first having scratched and cut their own skin, or that of their children, before rubbing mud - or even blood spilt by the butchers - over themselves to exaggerate their pitiful appearance. Then crying for alms, they lay on the ground in the street.

Concluding that this place was just a bit too occupied by those who shared a less than rigid adherence to the law and as such, given the competition, the chances of profit were probably limited, the thief decided to move on. The objective was easy enough: to survive another day. To creep along looking for an opportunity: a dropped coin, an inviting money bag, or perhaps a valuable object left unguarded by a careless shopkeeper. Maybe a piece of fruit would find a place inside the thief's tunic along with a crust of bread. On a good day a bottle of beer might join it.

After the hell on earth that was the Fleet Ditch and the poor pickings at the Shambles, the thief decided to head for richer prospects; somewhere where one theft would pay for a week or two's food. Yes, that was the plan: just one risk, one chance and then the easy life for a bit. Where to go though? Somewhere like ... somewhere like ... ah yes, just the place.

"Lambs to the slaughter!" the thief muttered with a smile and slunk away, eastwards.

Chapter 3
Gabriel and Artemas

London, Saturday 1ˢᵗ September, 1666: noon

The sun was now at its zenith. Outside the shelter of the school, the humidity of the day was already stifling and the heat intense. Within a few minutes of setting off, sweat was trickling down Ben's face. He dragged the mortar board off his head and used it as a fan to try cooling himself, and running a finger around the inside of his collar muttered, "Will this summer never end?" Still not content, he undid the buttons and pulled open his shirt, revealing a silver pendant hanging from an iron chain. As was his habit, he touched it with his right hand, his fingers rubbing the engraved symbol that looked like a steel gate or a portcullis, his eyes becoming distant as though the feel of it took up all his thoughts.

After a moment he let go of it in order to wipe a bead of sweat off his brow. He felt as if he was roasting in the day's heat, so he took off his robes. Rolling them up and stuffing them in his satchel, he walked along in shirt and britches, while peering guiltily back down the road towards Westminster School, half expecting old Busby to be chasing after him. The Headmaster insisted boys wear collars buttoned up, mortar boards on their heads and black robes at all times when both inside and outside the school, and if he was seen, Ben could expect another thrashing at the very least. Then he shrugged: he was playing truant and the penalty would be far worse than that if he was caught. The thought made him turn his head again, but the school was now out of sight, although the Abbey still loomed in view. He hurried on past White Hall, turning his eyes downwards in case someone in the court saw him. Suddenly he laughed out loud, causing a few passersby to frown at the noise and stare at the thin, gangly figure, who appeared to be all elbows and knees. Ben could not help it, for the unlikely image of the King or his brother, the Duke of York, keeping an eye open for errant schoolboys had popped into his mind.

The spontaneous laughter made his spirits soar, his black mood lifted with each step he took away from the school and he felt his tension easing as he enjoyed the unusual freedom. This was why he was escaping after all: it was dry, sunny and warm as it had been all that long summer and he was going to explore the city and try to take his mind off other thoughts.

Westminster had its own shops and in Westminster Hall there was a market. The boys at his school would often go there and spend their pennies on books, sweets, trinkets and toys. Ben had been many times and even the decapitated head of Oliver Cromwell, mounted high up on its roof, did not interest him anymore. Although it had been a curiosity of morbid fascination when he had first arrived at the school, he had seen it so often that he barely glanced at it now. Ben had a more distant destination in mind in his search for something distracting.

The heart of London, at least as far as the shops and merchants went, was the great Royal Exchange to the east on Cornhill. It was a couple of miles away, the other side of St Paul's, so Ben swept back his black hair, bent forward and stretching his legs, picked up the pace, wincing slightly as the bruise from Busby's cane tugged at his thigh. He had missed lunch and, with a few coins jangling in his pocket, planned to have some on Cornhill.

Ben reached the Royal Exchange a little past one o'clock and stopped for a moment to take in the sights. The huge building loomed over him, dominated as it was by a tower over the front entrance. He screwed up his eyes to look up at its pinnacle where the sunlight reflected off an iron statue of a green grasshopper.

He passed through the arched gateway and on into the central courtyard. This was occupied by statues of kings and queens of England, which seemed to glare almost disapprovingly at the chaotic scene in front of them. Ignoring the decorum and solemnity the statues were originally intended to create, the yard was full of hundreds of people bustling back and forth about their business. Some he heard gossiping about the Duke of York and his latest mistress, while others were speculating on the war with the Dutch from where any day news was expected of a naval battle. Others cared nothing for all that and perhaps, like Ben, had minds set on no more than buying pastries, bread and fruit for lunch from carts dotted here and there.

He was standing at one of these deciding what to buy, when he was distracted by a loud voice booming across the courtyard. It came from a man standing outside a bookseller's stall.

"I say to you that the time of judgement is at hand. Yea, even soon it comes to this city of sin: this city of greed and corruption. This Sodom and Gomorrah will suffer at the hand of the Angel of Judgement and he shall not stay his hand from the unworthy. I know this, for he has spoken to me and I hear the voice speaking for the Lord of Hosts. Yet, it is not too late: there is still time to repent."

Ben glanced over at the speaker. He was a wild looking man, probably in his late forties, with slightly bulging eyes that did not seem to focus quite right, a florid complexion, yellow teeth that leaned this way and that, and thinning black hair streaked with grey. He was dressed in plain puritanical dress – rather out of fashion these days since the return of King Charles and his court had swept away the dreary years of the Commonwealth and brought colour back to the city. The merchants and their customers frowned and hurried on by.

Feeling uncomfortable with what the man was saying, Ben turned back to the cart owner, selected some bread, cheese, an apple and a meat pie, handed over some coins and then moved away from the preacher. He stood munching on his food and looked about. On either side of the courtyard there were covered walkways on two floors where well over a hundred merchants set up their stalls: if it could be bought or sold it seemed, then it was here.

Ben walked along the stalls, peering into each in turn. One was selling swords and firearms for hunting; next to it, exuding a heady mix of exotic aromas, was a stall piled high with a hundred different spices from the Far-East and India. Beyond that was a goldsmith's with candlesticks, plates and goblets reflecting the sunlight, and further along still, an apothecary advertising cures from all illnesses, sold in small glass bottles at a penny each.

He paused at the next shop, the bookseller's. Above the door the owner's name, 'G. BARLOW', was written in black letters on a painted blue sign. Underneath the name were two symbols. One was an open book, which was no surprise, but it was the other that caught Ben's attention. It appeared to be a gate or perhaps a portcullis. His hand went automatically to the pendant hanging on its chain at his neck, his fingers finding the engraving and rubbing across it, feeling the lines. Curious about the apparent coincidence, Ben approached the shop.

The shelves outside were lined with news sheets. Most told of the latest naval engagements between Prince Rupert's fleet and the Dutch, and others of atrocities that, the sheet said, the enemy had inflicted on a Suffolk fishing village. A few discussed the recent expedition against the Barbary pirates. There was news from the North American colonies and of a witch trial in Northumberland. Mixed in with these were religious tracts and pamphlets as well as some copies of the *London Gazette*.

Venturing inside the door Ben saw more shelves – this time occupied with books; rather more than he had ever seen on offer from the book hawkers of Cheapside or Westminster. Still further back were rolled up parchments and stacked manuscripts. He scanned the spines of a few volumes and saw they were mainly the writings of the ancient poets, similar to those Busby had so recently questioned him about. Bored, he moved deeper into the shop in an effort to find something new, different and exciting to read.

****

Standing at the gateway into the Exchange, the thief was suddenly spun round by a pair of hands placed heavily on both shoulders. The thief's head swam for a moment before being able to focus on two boots, which were planted firmly on the dusty road outside the Exchange. The boots belonged to a captain of one of the trained bands – the local militia that could be called out to defend London and acted as the City Watch as well. The expression on the captain's face was not anger, but frustration.

"I thought you promised me to stay away from trouble?"

All that got was a non-committal shrug from the thief.

"I warned you before, if you carry on the way you are going, all you will get for your trouble is a couple of feet of rope, a dangle on Tyburn triple tree and an unmarked grave. You are what, fourteen, maybe fifteen?"

Silence again.

The captain sighed. "Look, when your mother was dying last year I promised to look after you. You go and get hanged and I have got your death on my conscience. Do you want me to feel guilty?"

The thief did not care one way or the other. At fifteen you don't remember much of a father who left your mother when you were only three, but it certainly gave you little reason to trust people. As for Mother, well, dying of the plague last year she had left an orphan with no skills or hope and only wits and guile to live on.

The captain seemed to read some of these thoughts and his face softened a little. "Look: go home and later tonight I will bring some bread and ale for you. Is that all right?"

Not wishing to upset the only regular source of food and drink in this harsh city, the thief nodded and turned away back down Cornhill, watched by the captain until out of his line of sight.

What the captain did not see was the small figure sneaking back a few minutes later and then passing behind him into the courtyard.

****

Clutching his mortar board under one arm, Ben was leafing through a book he had picked up, when he became aware that he was not alone in the shop. Looking up, he saw a man studying him suspiciously. He was barely in his forties, Ben guessed, heavily built and bordering on fat, the result perhaps of too much wine, judging by the red glow to his cheeks, or too many pastries, as evidenced by the cake he was munching on even now. His already thinning black hair was streaked with a smattering of grey. The academic-style robes he wore were worn and dusty, but so similar to Busby's that, for a moment, Ben feared a tutor he did not know had followed him from the school.

"Can I help you, lad?" the man asked. "Are you sure you know what you have there?"

Realising that it was only the shopkeeper, Ben relaxed and nodded in response, lifting the book in one hand. "The account by Scipio Africanus of the final defeat of Hannibal in the Punic Wars – it makes interesting reading, don't you think?"

The shopkeeper's eyebrows rose in surprise, and then he smiled. "Impressive. Where have you studied the ancient writings?"

Ben hesitated a moment before answering and the man spotted this. "Ah, perhaps you should still be there then?" He laughed. "Don't worry, boy, I won't be telling tales on a potential customer."

Relieved, told the shopkeeper about his school.

"Westminster, eh? Imagine that – I went there you know. Tell me, who is the Headmaster now?"

"Dr Busby."

"Hah!" the laugh came out like an explosion, "Busby? Good lord, Old Rusty is still the Head? Mind you he was pretty new when I was there. Bit of a terror back then. How is he now?"

"Not much better. But Rusty? Why do you call him that?"

"Oh, I don't know, I think it was because he seemed ancient, like a rusty old gate."

"In which case, I would say he is even rustier now!" Ben replied and the shopkeeper chuckled. Despite his usual gloom, Ben smiled too.

The shopkeeper reached out a hand for Ben to shake, "The name is Gabriel, by the way."

Ben shook it, "Mine's Benjamin."

"Well then, Benjamin, what are you after today?" Gabriel smiled, moving forward to help.

Ben found three titles he would like, but he had little money and books were expensive. He shrugged, "These - but I cannot afford your prices."

Gabriel's smile dropped and he appeared to be about to argue, but as he opened his mouth to speak he happened to glance down, catching sight of the pendant at Ben's neck. His eyes narrowed and for a moment he stared at it in silence, then his gaze moved up to study Ben's face. Finally, just as Ben was beginning to feel uncomfortable, he broke into a smile again. "Tell you what, boy, pay me for that one book." Gabriel pointed at the book on the Punic Wars, "and you can owe me for the other two. I think I can trust you ... and if you don't turn up I can always tell Old Rusty!" he added with a wink.

Suddenly, his smile vanished to be replaced by an expression of fear and perhaps even of shock. Now, though, Gabriel was not looking at Ben, but at a man who had come into the shop.

Curious, Ben eyed the stranger: he was short and slight, his pale, pasty skin disguised partially by a finely trimmed goatee beard and a luxurious moustache which, like his hair, was a hazelnut brown colour. The hair on his head was long and curled, on the top of which perched a wide-brimmed hat decorated by a peacock's feather. He wore an expensive green tunic embroidered with silver patterns and his legs were clad in matching trousers. Around his neck was a fancy lace collar and his hands were encased in lace-cuffed, kidskin gloves. The outfit was finished off by enormous brown leather boots, which reached above his knees, and a sword hanging from an ornate belt. Ben hid a smile. The man's apparel was strangely old-fashioned: he wore no wig and there seemed an excessive amount of lace, even in comparison to the flamboyant style of the courtiers who strolled around Westminster. In fact, aside from his small stature, the stranger reminded Ben of the caricature of that famous Cavalier, Prince Rupert, which hung in Busby's study.

"Gabriel, old friend," the man drawled with a smile, his languid voice coming slowly from his mouth, rather like honey dripping off a spoon. "You don't look, um ... pleased to see me."

This was certainly true; Gabriel in fact looked very alarmed, which made Ben wonder who this elegant stranger was.

"Artemas ... I th ... thought ..." Gabriel stammered.

"You thought you had run so fast we would never find you? You should know better than that. I knew you had to be here in the city somewhere. The *Praesidium* – or what is left of you – would hardly leave it undefended."

"What do you want?" Gabriel demanded. "Am I to die to make your triumph complete?"

Ben started to feel uncomfortable. He sensed a crackle of energy in the air between these two men and it was not pleasant, nor was the look in the eyes of this Artemas. His words were spoken softly and seemingly agreeable, yet there was a threat hanging there that made the heat of the lingering summer vanish. It was as if a cold wind had rolled down from the frozen northern seas and blasted through the Exchange. Ben shivered and sidled into the shadows.

The stranger shook his head. "Not yet, and perhaps not at all. Rumour has it that you have been searching for something." He glanced around the shop taking in the books, maps and prints. "The scroll: do you have it?"

He stepped into the shop, his boots tapping noisily on the tiles underfoot, his gaze flicking across the shelves. "Is it here, perhaps?"

"Artemas, I don't know what you are talking about," Gabriel replied.

31

Ben had no idea what either man was talking about, but something in Gabriel's voice did not quite ring true. It seemed that Artemas noticed it too for he pointed at the shopkeeper and then waggled his hand back and forth.

"Tut tut, old chap. Somehow I don't believe you, but let's change the subject a moment. Nice shop you have here. You have done well for yourself," he picked up a book and flicked through it.

"Fascinating things books: you can learn so much from them. Still, there are risks in your choice of business. Books are so expensive and so ah ... flammable," he added with a nasty smile. Then for the first time he noticed Ben.

"Hello, young man. That's an interesting selection of volumes you have there. Perhaps it would be best if you make your purchase and leave. Gabriel, here, and I have some, ah ... matters to discuss."

Ben nodded, passed Gabriel the pile of books and his coins and then held his satchel open as the shopkeeper, his back turned to Artemas, dropped the books into it. Glancing at Gabriel, Ben was about to say something, but with a slight shake of his head, the bookseller said quickly, "You run along, Benjamin. As the gentleman says, we have some things to discuss. You can come back another day and pay me for the others."

****

The goldsmith almost missed the robbery, occupied as he was selling a fine platter to a court flunkey. The thief always waited for just such an opportunity and moved in quietly – just out of the eye line of the goldsmith – picked up a stunning gold goblet and moved noiselessly away. It was the height of misfortune that the weapon smith happened to enter the stall at this moment, looking to borrow some coins from his neighbour to give a customer change.

"Julian, you have a thief!" he bellowed and the goldsmith, the flunkey and half the crowd in the courtyard turned at the noise. The thief ran towards the weapon smith, dodged an outstretched arm, leapt over a basket of fruit, rolled head first between the legs of a tall man eating a cake, and sprinted on in the direction of the bookseller's.

****

Emerging from Gabriel's shop, his satchel hanging over one shoulder, and a new volume of *Caesar's Gallic Wars* open in the other hand, Ben did not notice the thief running towards him. The two collided then fell over in a tangle of arms and legs. Up first, the thief spun round and bounced away to the pillars that lined the colonnaded walkways. Ben watched in amazement as the figure, moving with the ease of a spider, used iron lamp hooks embedded in the pillar to climb past the windows of the first floor and then carried on up, finally disappearing over the roof top.

Suddenly, Ben felt a hand on his shoulder. He turned round quickly to see the goldsmith and the weapon smith – the latter now armed with a cutlass and pistol – glaring at him.

"Got you, you thieving rat!" the goldsmith said with an unpleasant grin that revealed badly cracked black teeth.

"What?" Ben gasped.

"You, boy: you're a thief. That vagabond up there stole my goblet and passed it to you. Planned it all, the two of you, did you? Very clever you thought yourselves, no doubt.

"Goblet? No!" Ben looked down and saw that he was indeed holding a goblet and that his satchel had fallen off his shoulder and spilled its contents on the ground, "But ... I ..." he stammered, not sure what to say.

The weapon smith cut him off with a snort. "I bet you figured we would not search a young gentleman and the pair of you could sell it later, eh?"

"No!" Ben protested. He shook his head and dropped the goblet then crouched to pick up the books. Among them was a roll of parchment. It looked like an old scroll, although this one had a gold ring keeping it rolled up. 'That's odd,' he thought fleetingly, 'I didn't buy that.' Then, seeing the grim faces around him, he decided it was best not to comment. He scooped up his books and robe, thrust them and the roll of parchment into his satchel and slinging it over his shoulder he looked around for his mortar board. It was nowhere to be seen; he must have dropped it in the scuffle.

Standing, he eyed the goldsmith. "No, you've got it all wrong," he said. "I just bought these books. That thief crashed into me as I was coming out the shop and we fell. I ..." he tailed off as he took in their angry expressions of disbelief.

"Well, we will catch the other one soon enough. As for you, it's Newgate lock up and then a noose in the morning, my lad," the goldsmith leered and reached out to grasp Ben's collar.

Ben's eyes widened in panic and his throat went dry. Quick as thought, he ducked, turned, stumbled towards the pillar and grabbing the iron hooks, heaved himself up.

"Stop him!" a dozen voices called. The weapon smith took aim and fired his pistol. The bullet hit the pillar just next to Ben's head. He swallowed hard but carried on climbing. Breathing quickly now, he reached the first floor and then screamed in shock as a hand shot out and grasped his wrist.

"Got 'im!" A triumphant voice cried from inside the window, but Ben just bit down hard on the hand, then spat as he tasted stale beer and tobacco. With a yelp the hand's owner pulled it back bleeding and the boy carried on up. There was another sharp crack of gunfire: this one deeper sounding than the first and coming from a musket. Ben felt a sudden pain in his shoulder as a bullet grazed him, but he managed to hold on. Two more shots were fired in quick succession, but he was moving again now and they sailed wide.

Following the same route the thief had taken Ben crested the roof and slid down the other side. He could hear angry voices shouting orders to find him and knew he had to keep moving. Below him was a long drop into Castle Alley, which ran alongside the Exchange, but he spotted some sacks of grain piled up against the wall of the building. He slid off the roof to land on one, but the fall winded him and he sat on the sack for a moment forcing the breath down into his lungs.

"There he is!"

The call came from the Cornhill end of the alley, so jumping down to the ground Ben ran in the opposite direction into Threadneedle Street. He dashed out between two hackney carriages, but misjudged the gap forcing the second cab driver to haul on his reins and to then swerve to the left to avoid him.

"Watch it, idiot!" the driver shouted as he hurtled on by. But, by then, Ben was across the road and sprinting into the graveyard behind St Christopher's Church, his shoes clattering hard on the path. He could run no more and wheezing slightly, he collapsed behind a gravestone.

A moment later, he heard footsteps scuttling past on the other side of the headstone and he froze in renewed terror at the sound. Then there was silence again and he lay still for several minutes, listening anxiously for the noise of pursuit. None came, but he became aware of soft, slow breathing beyond the gravestone.

Goose pimples appeared on his skin and he felt his throat tighten almost in anticipation of the hangman's noose. Were his pursuers toying with him, letting him think he had escaped before jumping over to seize him? Well if so he would have none of it. Throwing caution to the winds, he leapt up.

"Just what are you playing at, I ... oh!" he tailed off as he saw not the black teeth of the goldsmith, nor the pistol and blade of the weapon smith, but the short squatting figure of the thief.

"Oh it's you! Look, you caused me a lot of trouble. Just look at this shirt: it's torn and filthy from crawling across that roof. I might have been caught and hanged," he shuddered at the thought, "all because of some scruffy little thief from the gutter."

The thief jumped up at the sound of Ben's voice and for the first time he got a close look at the cause of all this woe. The face was dirty and smeared with mud, the clothes untidy and the cap pulled down firmly, but now that the thief was staring at Ben from only a foot away he could see from the look in those deep, green, intensely fierce eyes, the curve of the face - and indeed, the shape of the body - that the thief was ... well it had to be ...

"But, you're just a girl!" Ben said, his eyes widening with surprise and indignation.

The green eyes glanced downwards and before he could move, Ben felt a sharp point pricking at his throat.

"No, not *just* a girl ..." the thief answered softly, "a girl with a knife!"

Chapter 4
The Map

London, Saturday 1ˢᵗ September, 1666; early afternoon

"What was that you were saying about the gutter?" the girl asked. Her tone was polite, even sweet, yet the cold, hard glare she subjected him to made Ben sweat. The pressure on the knife point increased slightly.

"Now, let's just try and calm down. I was a bit worked up after being chased so I got a little carried away. I was wrong, all right? No need to make it worse."

"Well, I suppose cutting your throat wouldn't help things much," she mused.

"No; leastways not for me!" Ben replied.

The girl nodded and withdrew the knife. It disappeared inside a sleeve in a moment, as quickly as it had appeared.

Rubbing his throat, Ben turned to see where the chase had brought him. The graveyard they stood in was bounded on the west, north and east sides by a tall brick wall, which was crumbling and leaning inwards slightly in some places. One five-foot section of the wall to the west had collapsed completely and he could see into the alleyway beyond. The church itself, and the path by which they had entered, lay to the south, just off Threadneedle Street. Ben could hear the bustle of hackney carriages, coaches and carts and even the eternal babble of London's immense population, but in stark contrast, here in the graveyard they were quite alone.

"I don't suppose you kept hold of the goblet?" The thief asked, hopefully, scratching absently at her nose when he shook his head. "Got anything to eat?" Her tone was now friendly and her manner quite different to that of a few moments before.

Unthinkingly, Ben pulled an apple and some bread out of his satchel where he had placed them when entering the bookshop. These were snatched away by a pair of grubby hands, and the bread thrust into her mouth. He watched her eat for a few moments and then, thinking about it for the first time since he had left the Exchange, he drew out the scroll and held it – still rolled up – in his right hand while he pondered what it was.

The girl looked him up and down as she ate. "Those are fancy clothes you're wearing. Your old man well off is he?" She spoke in a muffled voice around mouthfuls of bread.

Ben frowned for a moment and then, without taking his gaze from the scroll, shook his head. "My parents are dead," he said simply.

"Oh," she said, "mine too. Leastways me ma is. The old man shoved off when I was young. That's what she said anyway. Might not have known who he was, of course," she added.

"Sorry to hear that," he replied, not looking up.

Now it was the girl's turn to frown, "Why're you sorry then? It weren't nothin' to do with you." A moment later her face cleared again and she bit into the apple and chomped it. "So, what they die of?" she asked, juice running down her chin to leave a clean line through the grime.

Still looking absently at the scroll, Ben was silent for a long time as a suppressed memory stirred. His hand went unbidden to his pendant. In his mind he could smell smoke; he saw a red and yellow light, felt heat and heard a crackling, roaring sound. Then he recalled a scream and being lowered from a window; landing with a bump that winded him. 'Mother', he had shouted and, 'Father ...' and then he had passed out.

He felt the bile rising in his throat and swallowed it down, shoving the images away lest he disgrace himself with tears. Becoming aware the girl was still waiting for an answer, he glanced at her and shrugged, "Six months ago there was a fire ..." was all he said.

It was commonplace; there were often fires. She just nodded, her cheek bulging with apple.

After a moment, Ben spoke again. "My uncle is a lawyer at the court and he took me in after they died, but most of the time I'm at the school in Westminster. He's kind enough, I suppose, but I don't see much of him ..." His voice tailed away as he looked at the thief, suddenly surprised at what he was telling her. This conversation was the longest he'd had with anyone in six months. "What about you then? What did your mother die of?"

"The plague, last year," she answered, taking a last bite from the apple and tossing the core away.

Ben took an involuntary step backwards and the girl stopped eating and looked him over. "Don't worry, lad, I've not got it."

"Sorry, I never saw the plague much in Westminster when it started up, and Father took me back to our house out in Surrey when it began spreading, and then, after the fire, I was at my uncle's. I only came back to the school during the summer. But I heard things ... Was it bad?"

The girl stared at him like he was an idiot. "What do you think?

"Well I, er, I don't know."

"Look, I was with my ma every day till she died. First she got a fever and grew weak. Then her skin sprouted these 'orrible sores and boils. Then ... then she just wasted away and died." The girl's face took on a reflective expression, "Know what her last words to me were?"

Speechless, Ben shook his head.

"'I'm sorry, love.' That was it. Then she was dead." The thief's eyes grew moist. She grimaced and with a small shake of her head irritably dashed away a tear as though it were a fly landed on her face.

"The next day them plague searchers came," the girl continued, "all official like in their black robes and carrying white rods. They just barged in, saw Ma was dead and called in the bearers. Know what they did?"

Again, Ben did not answer.

"Well they came in with these long metal hooks and used them to heave her out of bed and thump her on to the floor." The girl's lip trembled and she slammed her fist into her palm, "No ceremony. No respect. The bastards just dragged her outside like she were a sack of corn. Then they dumped her into a cart and took her away."

"They left you there on your own?" Ben asked in a hushed voice.

The girl gave a hollow laugh. "I tried to go with her. I pleaded that they let me see her buried. The bastards said nothing and just forced me back into the house and nailed the door shut. I screamed to be let out but no one answered!"

Drawing in a harsh breath she looked down at her feet and shrugged. "Guess no one dared take the risk in case I had the plague. Weren't any good Samaritans in London last year, I can tell you. In the end I broke through the boards on the windows out the back and escaped. I later heard that my ma had been tipped with dozens of other corpses into the plague pits they dug just outside the city walls – never found out which one."

She paused, looked up and glared at Ben, "So, of course it was bad, you daft sod."

"Sorry," he mumbled.

"There you go again saying you're sorry. Why should you be sorry? You were in your palace in Surrey when it happened."

Ben shook his head, "It wasn't a palace, just a house."

"Well it wasn't a slum in Blackfriars, was it!" she snapped. "Nor a flea-infested stable loft by Cripplegate, which is what I live in now."

He did not reply. He was reminded that this was not his world, and again he was surprised to still be talking to her. Scruffy and dirty as she was though, there was a fire in her eyes that spoke of a world outside the books and chalk of his own and in some strange way he was drawn to her.

"So what's your name then?" she asked in a calmer voice, stuffing the last of the bread into her mouth.

"Benjamin, but most folk call me 'Ben'."

"Well, Ben, thanks for lunch," she said, and winked at him before wandering off towards the path.

"Wait a moment, what's your name?" he called after her.

She turned and looked at him and appeared to notice for the first time the scroll in his hand. A parchment, brown with age, rolled and held by a gold ring. She stared at it and retraced her steps.

"What's your name, I asked," Ben repeated.

"Fred," came the vague reply.

"Fred?"

"Yes, what about it?"

"Well, it's hardly a girl's name is it?"

The girl winced. "Well it's what folk call me because I don't like my real name."

"So what is your real name?"

She hesitated for a moment and looked about, perhaps to see if anyone was listening. Other than a crow sitting on a gravestone, its head tilted to one side, there was no one. She gave the bird a suspicious glare and said, "It's Freya; Freya Miller."

"What's wrong with that? I think it's a nice name."

Freya shot him a look that seemed to suggest his opinion was irrelevant. "Well, it just sounds a bit strumpy to me."

"Far from it; now let me see. Freya – Anglo-Saxon goddess of fertility," Ben recited as if from a book.

The girl's eyes narrowed, "Eh? What of what?"

"Never mind," he blushed, but Freya was looking at the scroll now and did not pursue it.

"What's that?" she asked.

"Don't know. I found it in my bag when we collided. I had planned to take it back but ... well."

She grinned, "But, you don't want to be hanged do you? So anyway, what's the gold bit?"

"Just a ring holding the scroll," he replied, pulling the ring off and passing it to her. She stared at it eagerly then gazed with astonishment at the boy who so readily handed over a gold ring worth a few weeks' food to her.

Ben hardly noticed; he was more interested in the scroll. As he unrolled it, it creaked and cracked with age. He scanned the graveyard and found what he was looking for: a tombstone that had fallen over and now lay on the ground. He ran to it and kneeling down flattened out the parchment. Holding it flat with one hand, he tipped out the contents of his satchel and used the other books to hold the scroll in place.

It was a map - a map of the city of London, covering the whole of it, from the Tower to a little west of the Fleet, and from the Thames to the old city walls. Within the walls were laid out all the recognisable streets: Cheapside, Threadneedle Street, Cornhill, Tower Street and many others. Outside the walls not many roads were shown. This was a map that dated back some few hundred years before Westminster and London had grown together, and before the northern suburbs outside the walls sprang up. Alongside the streets were the famous landmarks represented by little buildings: St Paul's of course and the Tower, Baynard's Castle as well as the Guild Hall and dozens of churches, but Ben noticed that the Royal Exchange itself was missing. That meant the map dated before – Ben had to think now – before Queen Elizabeth's time at the latest.

"That's pretty. It's London, isn't it? Looks old," Freya said, catching him up to peer over his shoulder.

"It is," he replied, his voice edged with an old feeling of wonder; a feeling he had once known but had not felt for a long while. "Two or three hundred years at least I would say."

"So, is it worth much, you think?"

Ben shrugged. "To the right person maybe ... but what is this?"

He had now noticed some writing running around the edge. He rotated the map to find the start of the script, which had a larger illuminated letter 'H' depicted as a gate. He studied it for a moment. *'No,* he thought, *'not a gate, but rather, a portcullis!'* With a sudden shock he realised the shape was identical to that on his pendant and also the sign above Gabriel's bookshop. Coincidence surely – but Ben was not so sure. He bent closer. What was that tiny shape behind the portcullis? He squinted and it came into focus. Ah, it seemed to be the image of a man, although the face was distorted in rage and anger. Fascinated, he now began silently to read the writing.

It was mostly in Latin - and a very old version of it - mixed with some Greek words and others he did not know. This combination struck him as odd, but not as odd as what he noticed next. As he struggled to make sense of the words they seemed to twist and move on the paper. It was as if they were sleeping beasts stirred into life by some disturbance. Ben dismissed this fanciful notion, but as the lines flowed and swirled under his fingers, his head started to throb a little and distracted, he rubbed at it.

"You all right?" Freya asked.

"Yes – it's just hard to read the writing. It's silly."

"Why?" The girl now squinted down at the parchment, but did not seem to see anything odd. She shrugged in disinterest; as if for her reading and writing were irrelevant to her daily struggle to survive and no part of her world. Doubtless, Ben mused, she never thought about well off folk like him stuck in their dusty rooms reading stuff written by long dead people, while the poor like her just tried to find the next loaf of bread. Then he caught Freya staring at him with a bemused expression and shaking her head. He realised that something of the fascination, the curious sense of wonder and awe he was experiencing, which this scrap of parchment elicited in him, must be reflected on his face. He expected her to say something scathing so when she did speak, her question surprised him.

"Can you read it to me?"

He blinked and glanced at her, oddly pleased at her interest, smiled slightly and then nodded. "Very well," he said, "but it's not in English. You won't understand the words."

"I don't care. I'd like to hear what it sounds like. You can tell me what it means."

He nodded again, and taking a deep breath, he began. "*Hostis humani generis*," he started, reading the words without pause or hesitation. As he did so he became aware that the headache had gone, and although the words did still move under his gaze, this time it was rather pleasant and almost like a dance. Ben was enjoying reading the script, the first person to do so, perhaps, for hundreds of years. He noticed Freya was smiling at him, but it was not an unkind smile. He returned his gaze to the parchment and was soon lost in the words. As he read, the letters seemed to light up as if on fire and then the

44

paper glowed. His lips tingled as they moved and a powerful warmth - far hotter than this, the hottest summer he had known – swept through him. Suddenly he knew what he had to do. He pointed at the map of London as he shouted the final word.

"*Ostendu!*"

Freya looked shocked by the outburst. She glanced at the path and grinned, clearly relieved to see no one was there. "Hush boy, they might still be about!"

Ben, however, did not respond. He was staring at the map, his eyes wide in amazement. Freya looked at it, and her jaw dropped open.

"Did you do that?" she asked after a moment.

He shrugged, and they both examined the parchment. The map was still visible looking much as it did before, beautiful in its detail and calligraphy. Now, though, six of the buildings around the city were prominently displayed, not just outlined or bigger than the others, but they appeared to be three-dimensional, standing up out of the map. The thief reached out a hand to touch one and her finger passed through it. When she pulled her hand back in surprise, the building was still standing up off the parchment.

"What do you think it means? Freya asked in awe.

"I don't know, but I want to find out," Ben replied, his voice shaky.

A sudden thought seemed to occur to her, and she jumped to her feet. "Heh, are you a witch or something?"

"What?" he asked astonished.

"I don't want anything to do with black magic and all that jiggumbo. It's not right," she continued, backing off.

"Don't be stupid," he replied, squinting up at her.

"Who're you calling stupid?" she snarled and in a flash the dagger was back in her hand. Before he could stand, she advanced on him.

"Come now, children, have you no respect for the dead?" called a voice.

It came from behind Freya, and looking that way Ben saw they were no longer alone. Standing at the corner of the church were about a dozen men. The speaker, Ben recognised. It was Artemas, the stranger Gabriel was afraid of: the man who wanted a certain scroll so badly he had threatened the bookseller's life. Could it be the same scroll? It seemed likely. Ben realised he was not yet ready to hand it over. Still on his knees, he crouched over the fallen tombstone to hide what he was doing, hastily retrieved the scroll and his books and pushed them all into his satchel, lastly grabbing up his robe.

When he stood up, Artemas, whose gaze was fixed on Freya, appeared not to have noticed, but Ben's heart seemed to miss a beat when he saw that another man was staring right at him. He looked vaguely familiar, and then Ben remembered that it was the wild looking preacher from the Exchange. He glanced at the man's advancing companions; most likely the same ones who had stood in the crowd around him, outside Gabriel's store. They, like the preacher, were short-haired and dressed in fairly plain clothes with a notable lack of ornament or decoration, which contrasted curiously with the cavalier flamboyance of Artemas.

The preacher got to Ben first, "So, boy, will you now tell us where the scroll is?"

"What scroll?" Ben bluffed.

The man licked his lips and pointed at Ben. His hand shook a little. "You jest with us and waste our time. My sacred mission is urgent and I cannot wait for your jokes. Come now, boy, tell me where it is, and even now your soul can be saved."

Freya glanced at Ben and rolled her eyes in an exaggerated manner. "Man's crazy!" she muttered.

46

Ben nodded and attempting to school his expression to one of injured innocence, said to the preacher, "Where what is? I have no idea what you're talking about!"

As Ben was speaking, Freya had stepped back a few paces and now stood next to him. He noticed she had moved her arm so that the dagger, still held in her palm, was out of sight of the men. "So, who are your friends?" she asked out of the corner of her mouth.

"No friends of mine! That one," he pointed at Artemas, "I just met, but I don't know what he wants. It must be a mistake."

Artemas' lips lifted in a menacing smile, "Well, you are right about one thing."

"Oh yes? What's that then?" Freya said shifting her feet apart ever so slightly. Planting them firmly she leant back a little as though ready to spring at him.

"There has been a mistake, and you two have made it," the little man said as he raised his arm. He was holding a pistol, and with his thumb he now pulled back the flintlock hammer to cock it. Then, he took aim, the barrel now pointing directly at the girl.

Chapter 5
Rival Societies

London, Saturday 1ˢᵗ September, 1666: early afternoon

"Get ready to run," Freya whispered.

"Eh?" Ben answered, his gaze still fixed on the pistol.

"Run," she hissed, "to your right. You do learn how to run at that fancy school of yours, don't you?"

Ben flicked a glance over to the gap in the western wall and then back to Artemas, whose attention had been momentarily distracted by the preacher. He felt his throat tighten and his heart began pounding hard.

"Artemas," the preacher was saying, "we need to know where the scroll is. You know that! Don't kill them yet. They will stand before the wrath of the Angel of Judgement as will all the unworthy."

Artemas shook his head, his gaze never left Freya and the pistol remained pointed at her chest. "I think I will just do the angel's work for him. If one dies it might loosen the tongue of the other, and we only need one of them, Matthias."

The older man seemed to consider this for a moment and then nodded. "Very well," he said and then looked at Freya.

"This is your last chance, child of sorrow. Speak or my friend will kill you."

"He can try!" she spat. Like a snake striking its foe, her arm came up and her concealed blade flew towards Artemas. The Cavalier's eyes widened and he swung his body to one side, firing his pistol as he did so.

"Now!" Freya shouted diving to her right and, without waiting for Ben, she was up and running towards the wall. Her dagger had missed Artemas, but struck one of the other men in the leg and he fell with a yelp of pain. The pistol shot clipped Freya's ear, but by then she was away and before Ben had even started moving, she was past him and bounding across the graveyard, her ear streaming blood.

It all happened so fast that for a moment everyone stood frozen in shock. Artemas moved first.

"Get them!" he roared and pulling out his sword advanced on Ben.

Still rooted to the spot, Ben's legs felt like lead and his brain was struggling to catch up with what had happened.

"Come ON, boy!" Freya yelled, glancing over her shoulder.

Suddenly his brain snapped into focus. He took in the approaching Artemas and the murder written on the Cavalier's face, blade raised high ready to strike. He saw the men running towards him, spreading out to surround him, and he saw Freya sprinting away. Finally, Ben started to run.

Haring after her towards the gap Ben was suddenly aware of a figure closing quickly from his left wielding a vicious-looking dirk. The man thrust it at Ben, who dodged instinctively to his right, only just avoiding the long deadly blade as he hurtled past, his satchel bumping against his hip. A moment later and a hand grasped the robe still clutched in Ben's fist and he was pulled backwards with a jerk. Panicking now, he let go of the robe. The man who had seized it lost his balance, fell back against a tombstone, tripped and with a cry of alarm tumbled over it.

Ben had reached the gap in the wall. He jumped to clear it, his feet landing with a thump on the packed dirt of the alleyway. There was nobody immediately behind him now, but he could hear shouting. He glanced to his left and saw that the passageway, which headed towards Threadneedle Street, was bordered by a wooden fence. He decided the lynch mob might be coming from that direction to cut him off and was best avoided, so he turned right.

The alley ran straight for twenty yards and then bent west again. He was just in time to see Freya disappear round a corner. So far, the little thief seemed better able to handle the situation than he did, so he hurried after her. As he ran, it occurred to him that although he had craved relief from his boredom, all this was perhaps just a little too much excitement! The irony of the thought almost made him smile.

When he reached the corner he glanced behind. The man armed with the dirk had emerged from the gap and was shouting over his shoulder, pointing towards Ben. Artemas came through, drew another pistol from his belt and assayed a shot that splintered the fence behind Ben's head missing him by an inch. Gulping, Ben ran on. The alleyway exited into a yard filled with piles of timber. Freya was running into a warehouse on the far side and Ben followed. Reaching the door he jumped inside and looked around, letting out a strangled cry as a grubby hand slapped on to his mouth from behind.

"Hush! We've got to be quiet and hide," Freya hissed, removing her hand and pulling him away from the door.

Ben saw that the large warehouse was full of barrels. Freya had scuttled to crouch down behind two of them, so he joined her. His breath came in quick gasps as he fought to calm himself and stifle the sounds before he betrayed their position.

A few moments later there was a tapping on the wooden planking of the warehouse floor, followed by the clatter of a score of boots stomping across it. Ben peeked between the two barrels. Artemas was standing ten feet away from them facing into the room, but not looking in their direction. There were at least nine of his group in the building. They came to a standstill and gathered behind Artemas, listening. There was no sign of Matthias or the others.

Thrusting the spent pistol into his belt, Artemas pulled out another and began to reload it, talking all the while, his voice pitched loud enough to be heard anywhere in the warehouse.

"So then, young lad ... ah, Benjamin, is it not?" He poured in the powder from a horn he carried at his waist. "This is silly," he drawled, removing shot from a pouch also on his belt and popping it into the gun barrel. His movements were slow and measured; his voice hypnotic, and Ben, like a rabbit confronted by a stoat, stared transfixed.

"There are twelve of us and two of you." Artemas rammed the ball home with a small rod, which he replaced in a groove under the pistol barrel. "There is no way out of here except through that door." So saying, he cocked back the flintlock and stood with the pistol held lazily in his right hand, tilting it to point at the entrance they had all used. "We are armed and unless your little friend has any more blades, you are not."

Afraid to draw breath, Ben tore his gaze away and flung a questioning glance at Freya, disappointed when she shook her head. Wondering if there was another way out he looked about him, but from where they were it was impossible to see. Maybe they should sneak around the barrels and find out. He shuffled a few inches, but a firm hand on his shoulder pulled him back.

'They will hear us,' Freya mouthed. He nodded that he understood and slumped back down onto his heels.

On the other side of the barrels, the tapping steps came a little closer. "So then, why don't we all make this easy for

52

everyone? I want the scroll. I know you have it, Benjamin, for I could, ah ... feel you reading it. Does that not astound you? What did you read there? Was it something that surprised you?"

The voice went on, its tone languidly seductive. The tapping of the Cavalier's boots became almost like a very slow musical beat. So long was the interval between the beats that Ben almost screamed in anticipation before the next one came, relieving the tension but signalling the start of another long pause. Were it not for Freya's restraining hand he would have jumped up; anything to stop this torture.

"Do you want to know what you read there: perhaps to understand it? I can make it happen you know. Just come out lad and we can talk."

Benjamin's thoughts wandered. The scroll had been something quite extraordinary – quite remarkable in fact – but the sensations he had encountered had been even more intoxicating and he realised that he did indeed wish to learn more. It would be easy to stand up and find out what he wanted to know. His need to assuage the wonder and longing, which had gripped him since he read the words on the map, was irresistible. He started to rise.

With a violent shake of her head, Freya dug her fingers into his shoulder and pushed down hard to hold him still while she peeked out between the barrels. Ben felt her go rigid beside him and give a slight gasp. Artemas seemed to be looking straight at them. Then he turned his head away and Freya let out her breath in relief.

Artemas glanced sharply towards the barrels and smiled slightly. "Or perhaps, I am mistaken and the scroll means nothing to you." He spoke softly now, almost wheedling, "Is it not just a worthless piece of parchment? Maybe you are right, but a man I know will pay much for such detritus. I will, right now, give you two pounds and two more when I can get hold of the coins. What do you say?"

Freya's mouth fell open and she looked at Ben, her expression one of wistful yearning. Catching sight of her face, he knew exactly what she was thinking and couldn't blame her. Two pounds! Why, that was maybe a year's wages for Freya, and with four pounds she could buy clothes and rent a place, instead of having to live in a flea-infested loft above stables near Cripplegate. Still, could Artemas be trusted? That was the question. Would he pay once he had the parchment? Somehow Ben doubted it, yet what did Freya have in her life worth preserving at present? Was it not worth a gamble to change this? Clearly Freya thought it a risk worth taking, for now it was she who started to rise.

Ben grabbed her arm, "Wait a moment, I think it's a trick," he whispered softly, but not softly enough. Artemas gave a shout of triumph and stepped towards the barrels. Then, he was there, standing above them, pistol waving back and forth between the two of them. Ben saw that Freya had closed her eyes, perhaps expecting the pistol shot. He put his arm around her and stared up at the Cavalier in defiance, anger outweighing his fear.

"Enough talking, give me the scroll now, boy!" Artemas growled, his finger beginning to tighten on the trigger.

Suddenly there was a huge BOOM and everything erupted in a brilliant flash of light.

The blast came from somewhere near the door and threw Ben over onto his back. He hit his head and for the moment lay stunned; all he could see was a bright white light. Above the ringing in his ears he heard the snap-crack of Artemas' pistol, followed by a cry of pain from Freya. All was confusion: men crying out; the crack of a musket then another and footsteps coming towards him. He blinked and the white light began to clear. Then he felt a rising sense of panic as it was replaced by

54

blackness. He could see nothing at all: he was blind! And he could smell burning.

"I ... I can't see!" Ben shouted in terror, "Oh my God, I can't see. Fire! I can smell fire. Someone help me, please!" He felt a pair of hands clasping his shoulders, lifting him to his feet.

"Hush, boy, I've got you," said a man's voice. It sounded vaguely familiar, but Ben's head was still spinning and he could not identify it. "It's just spent gunpowder you can smell, Benjamin, there's no fire. Quickly now, we must move. Can you walk?"

About to answer 'Yes, if only I could see,' Ben heard Freya say, "I think so. I feel dizzy."

"Not surprised," said the voice, "the shot grazed your scalp and you've lost some blood, but we must get the boy out quickly. My flash blinded him."

"Blinded me?" His panic vying with relief that Freya was alive, Ben cried out, "Wait, who are you? What have you done to me?"

"Calm down, lad, you'll be fine in a few minutes. Now come on!"

Ben felt himself being dragged forward and he tried to get his feet moving, stumbling in an effort to keep up. He felt for his pendant, comforted to find it still there. Remarkably, so was his satchel; he could feel it dragging at his shoulder. The stranger was at his side, leading him along. Ben's eyes were watering, tears running down his cheeks, but his vision was clearing and he could see they were now outside in the yard. Gabriel – for it was Gabriel, the bookseller – was supporting him on one side and Freya on the other, pulling him along by the hand. He blinked away tears, looked at her and gasped. She had lost her cap so that for the first time he could see she had red hair. It was matted with dried blood, which was also crusted over one ear, and she was holding a hand to her head.

It was bleeding profusely, fresh blood trickling down her arm, the bright red in stark contrast to the pallor of her skin.

"What're you staring at?" she snapped, letting go of his hand.

"Sorry, nothing, I can see now, I'm fine," he said, transferring his gaze to Gabriel, "But how did you ..."

"No time for that now," the bookseller cut across his question, "we must move quickly, they will soon recover and be after us!"

As if to emphasise the need for haste there came a shout from the warehouse. Ben glanced back; one of Artemas' men was staggering in the doorway and pointing at them. The man levelled a musket and fired, but it was a poor shot and the ball missed them, smacking into an adjacent pile of timber. Artemas was outside now and running towards them. Then he stopped, turned and shouted something across the yard. All of a sudden Matthias and the other men came jostling round the side of the building from where they had been guarding another exit – an exit that Ben could now see, but which Artemas had said did not exist.

"Run!" Gabriel said, and the three of them fled into the alleyway. Soon the bookseller had led them out on to Threadneedle Street, but their pursuers were coming up fast from behind with Artemas in the lead.

"Over here, quick!" Gabriel shouted, leaping into the path of an approaching hackney carriage and waving both arms.

Swearing at Gabriel, the driver heaved on the reins and the horses skidded snorting to a stop. Freya, whimpering in pain, got in and slumped down on the seat. The bookseller pushed Ben in after her and then hopped in himself, shouting up to the driver, "Ludgate Hill, if you please!"

Artemas was now just ten yards away and appeared to be pulling out yet another pistol, this time from his tunic. He was too late: the driver cracked his whip and with a lurch the carriage was away.

Risking a peek behind, Ben saw the Cavalier glaring after them before turning away, presumably to search for another hackney. At that point Ben's own carriage swerved sharply around a slow moving cart laden high with sacks of grain, and he lost sight of Artemas. He sat back on the seat, breathed out heavily, looked at Freya and then grimaced. She was still losing blood from the wound on her temple and had apparently passed out. Her hand, which as they ran had been staunching the wound, now hung limp at her side.

Biting his lip, Ben covered the wound with his own hand, pressing down hard in an effort to stem the flow of blood. "Gabriel, we must do something: she needs help quickly."

The bookseller nodded, "We are doing something. I am taking you to a man I must see who also happens to be a physician, Dr Tobias Janssen. He can help her. It is not far – just off Ludgate Hill outside the wall. If only this confounded traffic would ease up!"

The hackney carriage slowed down as they moved down Cheapside: the busiest road in London. Carriages and carts crawled along in both directions as they tried to navigate the busy intersection with Bread Street to the left and Milk Street to the right. Increasingly anxious Ben leaned across Freya to look behind.

The grain cart was just behind them and it was hard to see past it at first, but a moment later it moved slightly away from the edge of the road and Ben spotted Artemas and two of his men pushing through the crowds only fifty yards back. Ben ducked, jumping back into his seat, his breath catching in his throat. "Gabriel, they are following on foot," he panted, "not far behind. We have to get away!"

The bookseller nodded and then leant out of the window to shout up to the carriage driver. "We are in a hurry. This girl is wounded. I don't care how you do it – but get us to Ludgate Hill in five minutes and I will give you twenty shillings!"

There was a pause, and then a sudden crack of the whip. Ben gave a yelp of surprise as the driver swerved his horses into the middle of the road, hurtled through the chaos of carriages, strings of pack animals piled high with goods, loaded wagons, hawkers with handcarts, swaying sedan chairs, single riders and startled pedestrians. Clamping his jaw to stop himself from biting his tongue, Ben hung onto the seat with one hand and Freya with the other as their hackney turned sharp left across the front of an emblazoned coach - whose liveried footman shook his fist and with a few choice expletives shouted after them that they were mad - and careered into Bow Street.

In front of them now was a large wagon being loaded with a bed. It was almost completely blocking the street leaving only a walkway on one side. Without hesitating, the carriage driver plunged his vehicle through the gap with barely an inch to spare, scattering pedestrians like a flock of pigeons. One man fell backwards through the open window of a house and Ben, despite his anxiety, snorted with laughter as he saw the unfortunate fellow being chased back outside by the mistress of the house, wielding an iron skillet.

At the next junction the driver turned to the right down the narrow Watling Street and out into St Paul's churchyard, the carriage bouncing and rattling across the cobbles. As they passed the huge building, Ben chanced another look behind and was relieved to see they had lost Artemas. Freya groaned, her eyelids were flickering and her face was the colour of dough. He glanced at Gabriel, who was staring at the girl, his brow creased with anxiety.

"Not far now," Gabriel whispered, as if to reassure himself as much as Ben.

Beyond the churchyard they came to Ludgate and now had to slow down as they joined the queue to go through the narrow old city gates. Once through, Gabriel called up to the driver and pointed to a house on the corner of Ludgate Hill and Old Bailey and the man turned his sweating horses off the main road and pulled in. Ben got out and staggered slightly, feeling just a bit nauseous. It had in fact taken six minutes, but Gabriel placed a guinea in the driver's outstretched hand and brushing aside the man's gratitude, he lifted Freya out of the carriage and carried her up to a bright blue front door. "Give it a knock for me, Benjamin," he puffed.

As Ben rushed to do as he was bid, Freya stirred in the bookseller's arms and opened her eyes. "It's all right, lass," Gabriel murmured, "I've got you. Lie still now."

After a moment the door was opened slightly by a sour-faced servant. "The doctor has just finished with his last patient of the day, come back Monday," the servant said and began to close the door.

"We cannot come back," Gabriel shouted, "this one will die if she is not seen immediately."

The servant peered round the door at Freya and said, "I am sorry, but the doctor gave strict instructions. The hospital is only just a few streets away, take her there."

The door was almost shut when Gabriel pushed his foot inside. "Tell Dr Janssen that it is Gabriel, and I have a girl with me who's been shot by Artemas – you just tell him that," he growled.

Hovering on the step, Ben heard the sound of a door opening inside the house and the low murmur of voices. A moment later the front door was pulled wide and the servant, looking flustered, beckoned them in and stood to one side.

It seemed odd to Ben that this doctor friend of Gabriel's apparently cared not about the wounded girl save only that she had been shot by one particular man. Why? And who was this Artemas that his name should have such an immediate effect?

Chapter 6
Dr Tobias Janssen

London, Saturday 1ˢᵗ September, 1666: mid-afternoon

Freya's head was pounding as Gabriel set her on her feet and helped her to walk. Her vision was impaired by the blood that trickled into her right eye, but with her left eye she glanced around the hallway and stared in amazement. Her own house – when she had lived in one – had been the single room she had shared with her mother, used both for cooking over the hearth and for sleeping. Her mother had kept it clean enough, but it was very meagre and other than the shared narrow bed, a stool, chair and table were the only furniture they had owned. Half a dozen cooking utensils, a skillet, cook pot, three cracked plates, two cups and the garments they stood up in, plus a single change of clothes, were the sum of their possessions.

This hallway contained more wealth than her whole house put together. A rich red carpet covered the floor – the *floor* mind! Freya gaped; she had never seen anything like it. In her own home the floor had been of packed earth; their landlord had possessed a carpet, but like most rich folk she knew of, he only ever hung it on his wall.

There were four doors leading off the hall, as well as a set of stairs that promised even more rooms above. The walls were not the bare unfinished timber she was familiar with, but were neatly plastered and with several paintings decorating them. There was even a small polished table supporting a vase of freshly cut flowers, and with a chair on either side. Freya shook her head in wonder, and then wished she hadn't as it stabbed with pain. Despite it, she began the careful appraisal of a professional thief as she eyed the various ornaments and considered what small, portable but expensive items she might slip into a pocket.

The nearest door was opened by the servant and they were shown in to meet the master of the house. The room they now entered was a study, judging by the shelf of books against one wall. They appeared to have Latin titles; Ben would no doubt know what they were, Freya thought. One book was resting on a brass book stand and was open at what looked like a drawing of the muscles in a man's leg. A couch was pushed back against the wall behind the door and beside it was a table. Above this a shelf was filled with sealed jars and bottles of brightly coloured liquids. Freya wrinkled her nose; the room had a faintly medicinal smell. Opposite the door was a fireplace, although with the heat outside no fire would have been lit for months. To their right, under the front window, was a large desk. A man, who could only be the doctor, stood behind it with a face like thunder.

Tobias Janssen was younger than Freya had expected, mid-twenties she judged. He was very tall, but unlike Ben, who combined height with a schoolboy's clumsy gangly body, this man was strong and muscular with broad shoulders and handsome, albeit tense, features. His eyes were blue and his hair a light auburn colour. What spoiled this otherwise attractive appearance was the angry glare he was directing towards Gabriel.

"What in God's name are you doing here, Gabriel! I told you never to come back and you turn up dragging a spotty brat and a gawping tramp along with you. You've got a bloody nerve," the man said by way of welcome.

Gabriel looked down at his feet. Exchanging glances with Ben, Freya knew that, like her, he was assessing which of them was the spotty brat and which the gawping tramp. Not sure which was worse, Freya gave a groan and grabbed hold of Gabriel for support as she felt another stab of pain in her temple.

Ben, burning with indignation at being called a 'spotty brat' - for he surmised he could hardly be thought a tramp - looked at the thief with sudden anxiety, surprising himself that he was concerned about her at all, but realising that she had become the only constant in this topsy-turvy day. He clenched his fists and glowered at the doctor, "So, are you a physician or what? Are you going to look at her?"

Tobias Janssen sighed and came around the desk. "I suppose I'd better," he said. Despite his earlier anger his arms were gentle as he took Freya from Gabriel, led her to the couch and helped her on to it. Then he looked back, the fury returning to his face as he glared at the bookseller, "After I do this, you and I are going to have a chat and what you say had better impress me!"

Gabriel and Ben sat down at the doctor's desk and waited. Behind them Tobias examined Freya's scalp. Then he called to his servant for water and washed the blood away. Laid out on the table beside the couch were the tools of his trade: a gruesome assortment of instruments of iron, copper and shining steel. Selecting a probe and a pair of tweezers, he examined the wound and a few moments later gave a little chortle of triumph, holding up a bloody fragment of shot, which he dropped into a jar on the table. Next, he cleaned the wound and dressed it, finally winding a bandage around

Freya's head and securing it, before letting her rest back against a cushion. Throughout the entire time the girl had not made sound. Dazed, she looked up at him as though unsure where she was and then closed her eyes.

Tobias returned to his desk and stood for a moment looking thoughtfully at his patient before turning his attention to Gabriel, who raised an eyebrow in enquiry.

Pursing his lips the doctor nodded, "She has lost a lot of blood, but now I have removed the debris from the wound and it is clean she will live, though she may have a terrible headache for a while. It will be necessary to change the dressing in a couple of days and I'll give you some ointment to stop it festering. If she develops a fever you should bring her back to me. "

"Thank you, Doctor," Ben, smiled with relief.

Tobias shrugged, "It's nothing," he said modestly, and although he did not return Ben's smile, his expression appeared softer and kinder than it had before.

"Yes, thank you, Tobias," Gabriel inclined his head. "Doubtless you will tell me what I owe you. Now, though, I sense you want to know about Artemas, no?"

Doctor Janssen's face grew hard again and he leant forward, his fists on the desk. "It is the reason I let you in, wounded girl or not," he answered. Then, sitting back in his chair and crossing his arms, he nodded to the bookseller, "Go on then, tell me where Artemas is to be found then I can go and kill him."

The statement came as a shock to Ben, who gasped in surprise, but Gabriel just stared at the doctor, a sadness showing on his face. "I am truly sorry about what happened with your father, Tobias," he said in a mournful tone, "but you must believe me when I say if I could go back and change anything that happened that night I would do so."

"But you can't, so don't waste your breath with apologies. My father is dead and he is not coming back. All I can do is kill the man who murdered him."

"You could do more if you would help me rebuild the brotherhood. You would honour your father's memory in taking on his duties," Gabriel suggested and Ben, who was trying to make sense of what he was hearing, noticed his voice was tentative, as if the subject had been broached and rejected before. When Tobias spoke again Ben had no doubts.

"I warned you last time not to talk to me about this nonsense. It was his belief in this rubbish that led lunatics like Artemas to track him down and kill him. But tell me about today: what happened today? Why did Artemas turn up after a year and what is he after?"

Gabriel hesitated a moment and then turned to Ben and held out his hand. "The scroll you have, boy. Bring it out and show us."

Ben was reluctant to do this. He had unanswered questions about that scroll and had hoped to study it later, perhaps take it back to school and read it tonight. But then, as soon as he had the thought, he realised he did not intend going back to school yet. For one thing it was still only mid-afternoon and he hoped to avoid Busby - and whatever punishment he had in store - until the morning at the earliest. For another thing, something interesting was going on here. Dangerous too: there was no doubt about it, for the wounded Freya, who seemed to become more at ease and peaceful as she dozed on the couch, was evidence of that. Above all, whatever was going on was new and exciting, and Ben wanted to know more. He opened his satchel, retrieved the scroll and then rolled it out on the desk.

"You have opened it before?" Gabriel glanced sharply at Ben.

He nodded. "In the churchyard near the warehouse, and when I read it and saw ..."

"*What?*" Gabriel interrupted, his eyes widened in anticipation and surprise, "You were able to *read* it?"

"Yes, and a strange thing happened: some of the buildings seemed to ..."

Tobias cut across him with a loud wrap of his knuckles on the desk. "What nonsense is this? What is this scroll? It looks like a map of London. What is so special about it?" he asked, squinting at the document.

Gabriel, who had been eyeing Ben, his face animated with excitement, turned back to Tobias and held up his hand. "To answer that I must ask you to humour me. Lay aside your doubts for a moment and tell me what you understand about the Order your father belonged to." Seeing Tobias' face darken, he raised both hands and added, "Please believe that I ask it only because it is relevant."

Tobias grunted. "What about the boy being here? I thought your Order was secret."

Gabriel studied Ben for a moment, and his gaze seemed to flick down towards Ben's pendant. "It is, but I suspect the boy has discovered something already and it may be that he can tell me things I don't know. I also think ..." he hesitated, "but please, Tobias, first tell me what you know. It is important."

"It had better be!" The doctor let out a deep breath then said, "Oh, very well! My father was a Dutch merchant. He traded in cinnamon and nutmeg from the East Indies and imported them to London. My mother was English and they met, married and lived here in this house. Mother died when I was young, and it was then that Father started his obsession."

Intrigued, Ben leaned forward, "Obsession?" he asked, aware that Gabriel had become tense in the chair next to him.

If Tobias noticed too he ignored it, "Well it seemed so to me, let's put it that way. There were secret meetings he would not tell me about. I thought at first it was something to do with the war: that perhaps he was a spy for the old King Charles, or

66

something like that, sneaking about the city finding out secrets – what with London being held for Parliament after all, it seemed likely. I was only eight or so and I lived in fear that one day Cromwell's or Essex's men would come for him.

"But even after the war ended and Cromwell was made Lord Protector, the meetings carried on. Sometimes Father would take me out with him when he took his cart to the docks to collect goods, and once or twice he would stop on a street near St Paul's and leave me watching the cart while he went inside a church. He was often gone for quite a long time and I was curious - he was not given to praying much after Mother passed away. So I asked him once what he was doing and he said he would tell me when I was older, which of course made me all the more curious."

"And did he?" Ben asked.

"Well no, we did not discuss it again until I was a little older than you are now and wanting to study medicine. I had just been asked to enter an exam for a scholarship to university and I was excited and came and told him. He looked surprised at that and said I could not go because I needed to take over his role. I said I was not interested in being a merchant, but he said that was not what he meant and that I needed to be near him so I could take on his duties when the time came."

Tobias got up and strode across the room to the fireplace. On the wall above it was a portrait of a man who looked a little him, although an older version. He took it down and held it in both hands for a moment.

"I was confused and asked what he meant. Then he told me this wild, incredible story. He told me that a demon is imprisoned somewhere in London and that he, my father, belonged to an Order whose role was to make sure that this ... what was his name, Gabriel?" he asked looking up from the portrait.

Ben's mouth fell open and he looked sharply up at the doctor. Had he really just talked about a demon in London?

"The name of the demon is Dantalion," Gabriel answered casually, as if he was reading the date of a famous battle or the description of a flower from a botany book and not talking about an infernal creature. On the mention of the name, Ben felt a chill run down his spine accompanied by a sensation of inexplicable fear, and something more than that. It was a feeling of being watched. He turned and looked around the room, but other than the reclining figure of Freya, there was no one else present. He shrugged off the sensation and turned back to listen to the conversation.

"Yes, that was it ... Dantalion," the doctor said. "My father was a member of an Order whose role, so he told me, was to prevent this evil creature and others like him from being summoned or emerging or rising: those were his exact words. Dantalion was supposed to have been buried or trapped somewhere under the city a few hundred years ago, and the man who did it had arranged that his Order keep a watch over him forever. They called themselves the '*Praesidium*'."

"The guardians," Ben muttered, almost to himself as his mind raced to keep up with a conversation that felt a bit like a runaway cart. He'd heard that word once before today, but where. He cast his mind back; yes, that was it: Artemas had used it this morning when he was threatening Gabriel in the bookshop.

"Well, something like that," the doctor agreed. "He also told me there existed a group of men trying to find and free this demon – for the power they would gain through him. They were called *Liberati* or some such nonsense to do with freedom."

"The liberators, I think," Ben corrected, still bemused.

"Smart boy; well I never believed him of course, and told him so. It led to a row between us. I ridiculed his belief, and he stubbornly refused to allow me to study the medical arts. So I just left. I walked out on him. I had my scholarship and that gave me enough to get by on. I went off to university and did what I wanted. That was seven years ago now. I did not speak to him again until I finished and was ready to set up in practice somewhere."

Tobias hung the picture back on the wall and returned to his seat. "Just over a year ago I returned to London and came to see him hoping for reconciliation. If anything the rift had grown with the years. He told me that a dangerous time was coming, and that the *Liberati* were on the move. They had found a spell to free Dantalion in some ancient writings, and were going to use it. My father was going to summon his Order to confront and oppose them. Well I still did not believe a word he said, and I remember asking if he would forget all about it for my sake. I still recall his words and always will ..."

Tobias broke off and looked across at the portrait, silent for a moment. Ben, hanging on his every word, waited impatiently, relieved when the doctor resumed.

"He said that he was doing it for my sake, and for everyone else, but to remember that he loved me. I called him a fool and he just looked at me with this terrible sad face. It was the last time I saw him."

There was a long silence. Ben shifted awkwardly in his chair and glanced at the bookseller. Grimfaced, Gabriel said nothing, but to Ben's eyes, his expression seemed tinged with guilt.

With a heavy sigh, Tobias repeated sadly, "I think he knew he might die and I had called him a fool ... the next thing I know, there you are, Gabriel, bringing me his body. He had gone to his confrontation, fought his battle and died for some load of superstitious nonsense that folk like you and he believed in. Was it worth it? You tell me."

Ben, who had been holding his breath without realising it until now, let it out with a gasp. His hands were sweating and he wiped them on his breeches.

Looking uncomfortable, Gabriel cleared his throat. "Your father believed that it was worth it, Tobias."

The doctor snorted, "Clearly. That's my point," he said. "Well anyway, there it is, that's my story." He folded his arms and glared again at the bookseller, "Now tell me, why did you ask me to go over that again?"

Chapter 7
Theft

Gabriel scratched his head thoughtfully before he replied. "So that I could see where the gaps were," he said. "Firstly, imagine for a moment that it is all true. Dantalion is a demon with horrific powers and supernatural abilities and completely evil. He is a member of a race more ancient than you can imagine, which dwelt in our world long before mankind. Our Order overcame their strength and drove them away, but there are those who try to bring them back, seeing in that awesome power a chance for their own glory."

Tobias leaned forward and opened his mouth to speak, but bit back whatever he was about to say.

"You have a question?" Gabriel said.

"It doesn't matter,' Tobias shook his head. "For the moment, I will let you have your fantasy; go on."

"Well, someone did summon Dantalion once, but he was banished by a member of my Order. Not back to the void where the demons live but, because it was all he could manage at the time, into a tablet of stone, which he then hid somewhere in the city. Since then, the *Liberati* have been trying to free him.

The night your father died, they thought they had found a way to locate the stone at last, after all their years of searching. There was a battle and my Order was destroyed."

"Apart from you, Gabriel!" Tobias said bitterly.

The bookseller nodded sadly. "Yes, apart from me. The *Liberati* were stopped, though. Many were killed and the rest scattered. They had failed to free their demon. They had, however, learnt one thing. They had discovered that the stone was shielded from the spells they were using, by seals or a kind of lock that collectively protected the place where Dantalion was trapped: a slab of stone we call 'The Last Seal'."

"Accepting all this for a moment, where is this leading to? And what does this have to do with it?" Tobias fingered the scroll that had partially rolled itself up on his desk.

Ben, who had been listening enthralled, was the one who answered. "It is a map showing the locations of the seals," he burst out, his eyes sparking with excitement.

Tobias raised one eyebrow. "How can you know that?"

"Like I said, I read the words and when I did, some of the buildings grew up out of the page," Ben said.

Spreading it out again, Tobias held the edges down and examined the scroll. "Pah! You have too vivid an imagination, young man. It looks like a perfectly ordinary map of London to me," he said, not troubling to hide his contempt. "Too old to be of any practical use," and lifting his hands, he let the parchment snap back into a roll.

"Well it's not," said Ben. "Let me read the words again, and you will see."

Gabriel shook his head. "No, Ben, better not ... or at least not yet. Artemas could sense it and track us here. Both he and I felt it before – though I did not know what it was at the time – and it led us to you; me a little belatedly, unfortunately, but that is how I found you and saw what was happening at the warehouse."

"Well thank God you did! How did you create that great bang and extraordinary white light?"

"I'll tell you another time. More important just now is to tell me if you can recall where the buildings were that you saw standing out of the map?"

Ben thought for a moment, "Maybe."

"Well, try to remember. We must write the locations down in case we fear to use the scroll."

"I can see you both believe this nonsense," Tobias looked thoughtful. "Presumably Artemas does too. I imagine that is why he turned up looking for it?"

"Yes," said Gabriel, "I think so. What I do not know is how much Artemas knows about the steps and the precautions that Brother Cornelius – the man who created the seals – took."

Gabriel hesitated a moment and then, reaching into his clothes, pulled out a locket hanging on a chain round his neck. He opened it, removed a folded up piece of parchment and laid it on the desk. Peering over his shoulder, Ben could see it bore a few sentences and was written in Latin.

"I should keep this secret, but I cannot do this alone so I must convince you to help, Tobias, and I will just have to trust you." Gabriel held out his hands to the doctor. "Please, I beg you; won't you suspend your disbelief, at least until such time as we have contained the threat from Artemas?"

As though judging the bookseller's sincerity, Tobias looked at him for a long moment. Meeting his gaze without flinching, Gabriel waited; his face tense and drawn.

Watching them both, afraid to break their silence, Ben could hear the distant sounds of traffic filtering into the room. Freya seemed to be sleeping peacefully still and he wondered if the doctor had given her a draught of some sort.

"Very well," Tobias said at last. "What can I do?"

Withdrawing his hands, Gabriel smiled in obvious relief and leaning forward, unfolded the scrap of parchment. "My Order

73

has passed on this script that Cornelius wrote just before he died. He gave it to his successor as the Order's Record Keeper, who passed it on to whoever came after him, and so on. Down through the years each of us has kept it secret in case it was ever needed. Read it to us, Benjamin."

Ben picked it up and looked at it and then translated the Latin into English as he read it.

"*Three secrets I leave that tell of the seals that bind Dantalion.*" Ben paused, cleared his throat and glanced up at Gabriel, who nodded encouragement. "Go on."

"*The seals number six but a seventh and last there is. The seventh cannot be found while the six remain. The locations of the six I leave on a map in the hands of the Archbishop who knows our secret. The location of the seventh I record in my journal here at the Priory. Finally, one secret remains and that is the words that free Dantalion. That secret I am loath to impart and I take it to my grave.*"

Tobias snorted, "Well, that is as clear as the skies in a thunder storm," he muttered.

"Not really," Gabriel said. "It is not as hard as all that. The map we already have. The Archbishop of the day left instructions that it be kept forever in the archives at Canterbury and, although it took time, I was able to find it. Alas I had to ask a few questions and Artemas must have heard that I was investigating."

"Is he one of the *Liberati*?" Ben asked.

"Yes indeed. He is also a man who is greedy for power at whatever the cost."

"What about Cornelius' journal, do you have that?" Ben asked, feeling his pulse quicken as this mystery unfolded.

"Cornelius lived his last few years in a monastery near Badersley Compton and that is where I expect the journal would have been left. There is one problem that he did not foresee ..."

"The Dissolution?" said Ben.

"Precisely. Cornelius could not have known that a couple of hundred years after his death the monastery would be closed and its lands confiscated when old King Henry sold all of them off. The library itself was valuable and the King gave it and the land to a Sir Robert de Windley some years later."

"*Gave* it? Rather a large present, don't you think?" Tobias said.

"Seizing the monastery lands when he broke from Rome was not exactly popular! King Henry needed political support to get it through parliament. He rewarded those who helped him with land." Gabriel gave a bark of laughter, but there was no humour in his tone as he explained, "Sir Robert's son and grandson turned out to be devout Catholics and later actually used the place to hide priests who were being hunted down and persecuted by the Protestants. Ironic when you think about it."

A question occurred to Ben. "How do we know the library is still there?"

"Sir Robert's collection was famous at the time and he passed it on to his successors. Scholars would and still do visit it at times to study the old parchments. The Manor is still there and so I think that is where we will find the journal."

"What of these 'words that free Dantalion'?" Tobias asked, the expression on his face betraying his interest despite a mocking tone.

"That secret is lost I'm afraid. If indeed Cornelius ever did impart it, then one of his successors must have died before they could pass it on. But in a sense that is not important to us now: our main aim is to prevent Artemas finding the seals and to do that I need to know where they are."

"Do you not know? You are *Praesidium*, aren't you?"

"I was the Record Keeper for the Order. I organised meetings and kept everyone in contact, but I did not myself know where any of the seals were. For safety's sake, no one man knew where everything was in case one should fall into the hands of the *Liberati*. But I did have this," and Gabriel indicated the parchment in Ben's hand. "Thank you, Ben," and taking it back, he folded it and put it away.

"So, I looked for the scroll. It took a lot of effort to track it down. Artemas was also searching for it and, as I said, he must have eventually heard that I was too. Today he turned up with new followers, including a man I do not know – that Matthias man – so, he is looking for it and, because of that, for you, Ben – and now Freya. He does not yet know you are here, which is good, but I imagine he will soon guess. He must have known his shot wounded Freya and that she would need a physician, and he knows of my past association with your father, Tobias. It would not be hard to put two and two together, but even had he not the wit for that he will pay handsomely for news of you, Ben, and our precipitous journey here will not have gone unnoticed." Gabriel sighed, "We, of course, don't know where he is, nor do we have any way of finding out."

"I think I do, or I can find out," said a female voice.

Ben swung round. He had been so engrossed he had not heard Freya move, but now she was sitting up and clearly had been listening; he wondered for how long.

"I know my city. He won't be hard to find," she said, smothering a yawn.

"I will need to know where he is that is certain," Gabriel said. "Would you do that for me?"

Her hand straying to her bandage, Freya nodded. "Of course, for a few shillings," she replied and seeing Gabriel's face darken, added, "you surely don't expect me to do it for nothing?

"Freya!" Ben exclaimed, "Gabriel here just saved your life."

"So? Got to earn to live I have and we aren't all folk with a mission like you and him."

76

Tobias frowned now and came rushing round the desk. "You should not be sitting up. Lie down and rest," he instructed pushing her back onto the couch. "I will fetch you something to eat." He strode for the door, beckoning Ben and a reluctant Gabriel out of the room. "Come to the kitchen. I will have Owen get you some food before we talk anymore."

He led them out of the room and along the hall, down a short staircase and into a large, stone-flagged kitchen, where he indicated they were to sit on a bench pulled up to the scrubbed oak table that took up the centre of the room. As they took their places, he summoned his manservant. The room was intensely hot, even though the fire had been damped down in the huge fireplace. Sweating as he watched the servant emerge with a tray of food from the pantry, Ben was aware of his stomach rumbling. Embarrassed, he grinned and looked around, but neither Gabriel nor Tobias paid him any attention. His mouth watered as bread, cheese and meat were set down before him, followed shortly by a jug of small beer, which the servant poured frothing into three pottery mugs.

"Thank you, Owen. That will be all," Tobias said. "Please, help yourself," he said to Ben as the servant shuffled away.

Ben needed no second bidding; he reached for the food and tucked in.

Back in the doctor's study Freya got up stiffly and moved across to the desk. The scroll was still lying on it. Unrolling it, she could see that Tobias was right and that none of the strange changes she had seen were visible. Had she imagined it? Perhaps it had been a trick of the light. She picked up the scroll and considered her actions, holding it this way and that.

The door opened, and hurriedly she replaced the scroll and made to return to the couch, but before she could move Tobias was already inside laden with plates of food and he, taking in the situation in an instant, nodded at her.

77

"You are a thief, aren't you?"

Freya went to shake her head, thought better of it and winced. Before she could speak, the doctor pre-empted her.

"Oh, don't bother to deny it. I can see what you are thinking: while the room was empty you meant to take the scroll, sneak out of the door, find this Artemas and sell it to him, didn't you?"

"No! I swear it!" Freya put a hand to her head and squinted up at him.

"No? Well, I was hoping that is what you'd be thinking, because that is why I got rid of the fanatic and the dreamer," he said in a milder tone.

Freya's mouth dropped open, "Eh?"

"You and I are down to earth and more realistic. I propose a simple deal. You take the scroll, find Artemas and sell it for what you can get. Then you return to me and tell me where he is and I will double your money."

Eyes wide, Freya stared at him then frowned as suspicion overtook surprise. Thrusting out her lower lip she said, "Not sure I can trust you. You want me to sell it, after all you have just heard? Don't you believe any of it?"

"Why? Do you? Or perhaps you believe more in this?" He tossed a silver coin at her. Forgetting her throbbing head she caught it deftly in mid-air and looked at it thoughtfully.

He smiled, "It's all sleight of hand and tricks of the light, superstitious nonsense and hocus pocus. You and I, Freya, we are different. We believe in the real world. Money is all that matters, money and revenge. Find me the man *I* want and you will have all the money *you* want. It's as simple as that."

Freya's eyes glittered as she thought it over. Then, without saying a word, she pocketed the coin, picked up the scroll, rolled it up tighter and tucked it inside her clothes. She stepped to the door, turned back and helped herself to a handful of bread and cold ham, stuffed it into her mouth and took another handful.

"I will delay your friends to give you a head start, but be sure to come back," Tobias said. "If you don't, rest assured that I shall find you and I can promise you it will not be pleasant when I do."

Freya shrugged, not impressed. It would entirely depend on how much she could get for the scroll, but she was not about to tell the doctor that. Her mouth full, she said with some difficulty, "I will be back as soon as I can." Still chewing, she glanced up the empty hall then turned towards the front door and resisting the temptation to stuff her pockets with ornaments, quietly left the house.

She walked down to Blackfriars first, to visit a scruffy old man she knew, who ran a fence operation selling stolen goods out of a rundown shack only a couple of streets from her old house. They haggled for a while before settling on a price for the gold ring, which had held the scroll and which she had secreted into her clothes when Ben had apparently forgotten all about it. The price was a few shillings more than the old man wanted to pay but a little less than Freya had hoped. Nonetheless, she left the slums with more coins in her money pouch than she'd had for many a week. She next purchased a new dagger, which she slid up her sleeve, and then bought a replacement cap. She tugged it gingerly onto her head, both to disguise her appearance and hide the bandages. It was late afternoon when, with an eye open for the Captain of the Watch, she directed her steps back to the vicinity of the Exchange, being careful not to enter it or talk to anyone who owned a shop there. In a few days it would be safe enough to enter, maybe with a change of clothes, but this morning half the shop owners had chased her with the intent of seeing her hanged, and as discreet and invisible as she tried to be, someone would be bound to recognise her.

She drifted into the shops and taverns on Cornhill and Threadneedle Street, using her new wealth in bars and taverns to buy more than a few drinks, and as the grateful merchants drank, she asked about Matthias and a Cavalier called Artemas. No one could recall seeing the latter, it was as if the man was invisible. But many had seen Matthias. The itinerant preacher had turned up a couple of weeks ago and started giving sermons on street corners about the approaching day of judgement.

"Just two nights ago I was coming back from the river, when there he was on the corner of Gracechurch and Lombard Street," a leather merchant, enjoying a cup of ale after a day's trading, told her. "He had found a barrel and stood on it. He was a bit mad looking if you ask me and if truth be told I swerved across the road to avoid him. But the old fool saw me and pointed at me, shouting in a great booming voice he was, so everyone stopped to look, 'Will you be safe when the Angel of Judgement comes and all the unrighteous are swept away like the chaff they are?' he said, and then, 'Do you not know the year, man: it is 1666 and surely even you know the significance of that?' I was right annoyed, I can tell you, lad."

The merchant took another swig of his ale then noticed his tankard was empty and looked hopefully into it, until Freya ordered another drink and passed a few more coins over the bar.

"You were saying about the year, Sir?" she prompted.

"Oh aye: the year. Well it was the 666 bit he was talking about. You know, from the Bible." He paused and grinned at Freya, "Don't mean nothin' to you, eh? Well to be truthful I was a wee bit rusty on the detail too and I think the old fart could see my confusion so he quoted me chapter and verse: from the Book of Revelations he said it was. Now how'd it go?" The merchant scratched his head, "Oh yes, I remember: '*Let him that hath understanding count the number of the beast: for it is the*

80

number of a man; and his number is six hundred threescore and six.'
Seems to me he was suggesting some great beast or the Devil or
something would come this year," the merchant laughed and
sipped some more beer.

Freya laughed too for Matthias was clearly another lunatic,
like Gabriel with his stories about Dantalion. Still, this was all
to the good as far as she was concerned. If Artemas believed all
this stuff he might pay more for the scroll. The merchant went
on talking.

"Well, I must admit, crazy or not, he was captivating and
quite difficult to break away from. He went on about the
wickedness of the world for a while and then he said that he
was entrusted with a glorious task, that task being to assist the
coming of the Angel of Judgement. He was calling for followers
to join him in the divine quest he was embarked on."

"Did he say what you were to do if you wanted to join
him?" Freya asked tentatively for this was the information she
sought.

The merchant screwed up his face in concentration for a few
moments. Then he smiled.

"Yes, I remember now, it was the Old Bull: that tavern out
on Bishopsgate Street, just this side of the wall. He has rooms
there and asked that anyone who wanted to join him come to
him there. Well I nodded and got away quickly. There was
something frightening about him, or maybe his followers, that I
wanted to avoid."

"I think you made a wise move," Freya muttered and
tossing the barman another penny said, "More drink over here,
landlord!" She winked at the merchant who smiled drunkenly
back as she walked to the door.

Chapter 8
Words

London, Saturday 1st September, 1666: late afternoon

Matthias Archer knelt in prayer in the private rooms Artemas had taken for them in the Old Bull Inn. He disapproved of the establishment of course, as all godly men must, but Artemas had argued that it gave them a good base to search for the scroll. The scroll was the last step in freeing the Angel of Judgment. On that day of wrath the unworthy and ungodly would perish and he – Matthias, the instrument of the Almighty – would be vindicated at last.

He thanked God that he had purpose again after so many years of despair. He felt the same fire in his soul that he had when he stood on the battlefields of Edgehill and Naseby alongside his brother and father, and had known with utter conviction that they fought for God and against the evil influences that poisoned his enemies. Upheld by this faith he had fought bravely against the King and had delighted in Parliament's victory.

That should have been the start of God's Kingdom on earth: a new world run on godly principles. A purer religion and a fairer way of running the country with the common man having his say: but it did not happen. Cromwell became Lord Protector of the Commonwealth, and his army cronies, the Major Generals, soon swept away the rule by Parliament and eventually even the oligarchy went as Cromwell was offered the crown. He refused it, but became a dictator in all but name and Matthias remembered how his father and brother had become angrier and angrier at the betrayal.

One day they went to speak out against Cromwell's latest draconian action. It was by sheer chance that Matthias was not with them; he had been laid low by a bout of pestilence on that day. They were arrested and later executed on some drummed up charges. Stricken with grief, Matthias had watched as they were strung up, helpless to do anything lest he go the same way. Then, a year or two after this, Cromwell died and the new King returned with his gaudy court. After that, all that Matthias had fought for had gone – swept away by a wave of popular demand. The country rejoiced at the end of the Commonwealth and for them the happy times were back. Matthias, still grieving for his loss and seeing a world falling into sin, had sunk into deeper depression.

He was at his lowest point when, a year ago, Artemas had found him. Had he been in his right state of mind he would have had nothing to do with him, for this fancy-dressed stranger was blatantly a Royalist; the kind of man Matthias had fought against so hard. But despite his misgivings, he had been tempted when the Cavalier had shown him the huge leather-bound book he carried, which contained words that Matthias, an educated man, could not understand. Artemas had said it was written in the language of angels and that he could talk to one through it. All he had to do was to place his hand on the book. To humour him, Matthias had done so, but then, to his amazement, he had heard the voice in his mind.

"Matthias, my name is Dantalion. I am God's Angel of Judgement and you are my instrument. Together we will burn

84

the ungodly from this world and it will become pure. Will you serve me?"

The voice was majestic and strong, and Matthias at once found a purpose to his life and burning hope again. In time he learnt that evil men had trapped Dantalion through black magic and sorcery and, driven by a compelling zeal to free the angel, Matthias went out and found others who felt rejected and betrayed by a dark, uncaring world or were sickened by its depravity. They heard his message and his words convinced them.

Now they were so very close to success. The scroll was what they needed and that boy and girl had it. They would have been captured, but for the intervention of that bookseller Artemas had called 'Gabriel'. Matthias gave a hollow laugh at the irony of the man being named after an angel. Well, one day a real angel would judge him.

The door opened and Artemas came in carrying The Book. "Get up off your knees, Matthias, we have the girl! She came to us and offered to sell us the scroll. She has it hidden, she says nearby, but will not tell us where without money."

Matthias got to his feet and looked at The Book underneath the Cavalier's arm. "Bring her in and let Dantalion talk to her. She will tell us what we need to know."

Artemas nodded, "My thoughts exactly," he said, not managing to hide a broad smile as he turned to the door.

Throwing himself back onto his knees, Matthias bent his head in a prayer of thanksgiving.

****

Ben was ravenous and attacked the bread and smoked ham with gusto. Tobias had filled a plate with selected morsels of food and taken it to Freya, having first informed them that it was advisable to leave the girl on her own for a time. Any excitement could be detrimental to her condition, he had said. The loss of blood would make her sleepy and sleep was the best medicine for now. They could resume their conversation over their meal and maybe talk to Freya later.

As Tobias had closed the door behind him, Gabriel poured them both some more ale. "He's a good physician; I trust him to do what is right for your friend."

"She's not really my friend," Ben explained, "I met her for the first time after I left your shop this morning. It was only because of her thieving that I got embroiled in all this.

"Ah," Gabriel sat back and sipped his drink, while looking at the boy. "It is I who am in part to blame. I had imagined the scroll would be secreted safely out from under Artemas' nose if I slipped it into your satchel. It never occurred to me that you would read it and thus draw him to you. I can only apologise."

"It doesn't matter, I understand why you did it," Ben said, seizing a hunk of cheese. They were both quiet for a few moments when suddenly, Gabriel slammed his mug down on to the table with a firmness that made Ben jump.

"I have been wondering, Benjamin, why it is that you could read the scroll and I could not."

Ben stopped pushing cheese into his mouth and thought about the question. "You could not? Well it was only some Latin and Greek words mixed up together, along with a few others I could not read ..." Ben's voice tailed away and he wondered why he had lied. He had read them. He had read them all, even though he had not understood some of the words.

Gabriel studied him as if he was some essay written by students at the school or maybe a work of art. It made Ben feel slightly uncomfortable. Did Gabriel know he had erred from the truth?

At length the bookseller shook his head. "No, they are more than that. I can read both languages and a number more

86

besides but I cannot read that scroll. This is because the Words of Power written upon it are of a realm I cannot use."

Ben frowned. "I don't understand." Something Gabriel had said earlier came back to him, "But earlier you spoke of spells. Do you mean real magic exists?"

"Benjamin, even the scholars at your school will admit that words have power. The study of rhetoric – that is of speech and of talking in such a way as to influence others – is still one of the main cornerstones of education just as it was for Caesar, Cato, Plato and Homer and countless others down the generations to the present day."

Thinking back to what he should have been doing today, Ben nodded, though he was not sure it was Busby's intention that he should be able to defeat demons or cast enchantments! He said as much to Gabriel and chuckled at the thought.

The bookseller took him seriously and did not smile. "No. I will allow that, but leaving demons aside for the moment, even normal words used together in the right way or at the right time can influence men and make them do extraordinary things. You have surely heard some of Shakespeare's *Henry the Fifth*, for example? Perhaps: '*Once more unto the breach dear friends,*' or '*And gentlemen in England now abed shall think themselves accursed they were not here.*' Stirring stuff don't you think?"

"I suppose so," Ben shrugged hiding a yawn, waiting for Gabriel to make his point.

"Words can be powerful. They can lead men to fight against extraordinary odds, defy evil, fight for good, defend a King - or defeat one, maybe. Words can make you draw on strengths you never knew you had. Even so, I am talking here of ordinary words spoken by ordinary, if occasionally inspired, men."

Gabriel sipped from his cup again, but did not take his gaze off Ben. "Then there are others that are more than just a collection of lines and shapes written on a page. Some words

87

seem to be an echo of yet more ancient tongues: angelic, divine or maybe demonic and infernal. These are words that our ancestors heard spoken in the deep past, in times more ancient than you can begin to imagine." His eyes became distant and he turned to stare into the embers of the kitchen fire. "Who were they?" he mused. "What remote primal fire did they sit round, and what stars wheeled overhead in the darkness when they first heard those words, do you suppose? Well, we have no way of knowing, but those words were heard by them and passed down and incorporated into the many languages of man. They were split up and divided for our own safety, but there were a few men who studied the ancient writings and were able to assemble some of them again."

"You are talking about the *Liberati*, to help them free the demons?" Ben asked.

"Yes, the *Liberati*, and also my Order, the *Praesidium*, so as to be able to oppose them - and others perhaps. However, it was not just a matter of assembling the words. It was also a matter of *who* spoke them. Even in our first ancestors' time this was the case. Only some could understand the words: only some could use the power in them."

"Why? The words are on a page. If a man can read why can he not use the words?" Ben asked and realised the same desire and hunger he had felt in the churchyard had returned to him, replacing his hunger for food. He dropped the bread he was holding back onto the plate and waited impatiently for Gabriel to respond.

"This is because each word belongs to a certain realm of power: a certain type of magic, if you prefer the term," the bookseller's voice suggested that he did not. "These words can manipulate the world about us in different ways like, for example, creating a type of energy such as light or heat, exerting force on an object, or changing something into something else, influencing the mind or confusing the senses –

there are in fact dozens of different realms. I have discovered that those of us who have the ability to use the words cannot use all of them or at least not to the same effect. I think it was not just the words that were divided, but the men also. Different races and types of people had different powers."

Ben scratched his head in thought. "So I could read the scroll but you could not. But on the other hand you did create that flash-bang in the warehouse, didn't you: the one that stunned and blinded everyone so you could rescue us, I mean?"

"Yes, I did that."

Ben's eyes glowed hungrily. "You said you'd tell me how. Could you teach it to me, do you think?"

Gabriel gave him a sharp look and Ben glanced away feeling oddly guilty and then stopped himself. He had done nothing wrong so why did he feel as if he had? He wondered if he was losing control here and becoming obsessed with acquiring the powers of which Gabriel spoke.

"Later perhaps," Gabriel said at length, his voice doubtful, "there are more urgent matters to attend to. Can you now recall which buildings stood up from the page in that map?"

"Yes," Ben nodded, "there were six of them."

"Very well, give me a moment." Gabriel got up and searching through a drawer in one end of the table, found a scrap of paper and a stub of charcoal. He sat down again and looked up expectantly at the boy. A moment later he frowned and tilted his head.

Ben became aware that Gabriel was staring at him. "What? What is it?"

"May I see that pendant you wear at your neck?"

"Why?"

"I will tell you in a moment. Let me see it, please."

Dropping his gaze, Ben pulled the pendant out from beneath his shirt and showed it to Gabriel, who studied the symbol for a moment.

"It is like the sign you have above your shop isn't it, and like the symbol on the parchment," Ben said.

The bookseller nodded and reaching to his own neck, he brought out his locket and flipped it over to reveal the image of a portcullis on its reverse.

Ben gaped in surprise. "It's the same as mine!"

Gabriel nodded and tapped it with his finger. "This is the symbol of the *Praesidium*. The parchment was made by one of my Order and so bears it, just as I use it on my shop as a beacon for any of my Order who survive. But what I want to know, Benjamin, is where did *you* get it from?"

Ben stared at his pendant and then closed his hand tight around it, remembering the night his parents died. He was being lowered on the rope from his bedroom window when the pendant had dropped from above, thrown clear of the flames by his father. His uncle had picked it up from the ground and later given it to Ben. It was all he had of his father and he treasured it, yet it had always seemed odd to Ben that it had been his father's dying act; that even as he perished in the fire, he had made that one last effort to throw his pendant to his son. The memory was too raw; too painful and as always, Ben blocked it and tucking the pendant back out of sight, said simply, "It was my father's."

Gabriel's eyes widened. "That is interesting."

"Why?"

"Only a *Praesidium* would have one. That means your father, or his ancestor was in my Order – at some point at least. That does explain something."

"What is that?" Ben asked as he absently traced the outline of the portcullis with his finger, an image of his father's face filling his mind.

"Remember I said that different races had different powers? What that means is that the powers were handed down over

90

the generations: inherited by son from father, daughter from mother," Gabriel said.

Ben nodded as this made sense.

"Well, the scroll was written by Cornelius after he had created the seals. He had hidden the slab itself in a secret location protected by another even more potent seal: The Last Seal. He was a genius. Beyond intelligent, he was unique and seemed to know and understand certain matters at almost a divine level. He used obscure Words of Power that only he could understand: only he and perhaps a direct descendant."

Feeling the intensity of the man's stare upon him Ben thought he could tell which way the conversation was going. He was filled with a sense of awe at the implications of what Gabriel was saying.

"Benjamin, Cornelius' surname was 'Silver'. Would that be your name too?"

Ben's jaw dropped open and he nodded numbly. "Yes, I am Benjamin Silver," he whispered.

Gabriel sat back and took a deep draught of the ale and then gave a contented smile. "Well now; that is more than just interesting: it is extraordinary in fact. We must study the scroll further." The stool scraped on the stone floor as he rose to his feet.

"So then, Master Silver, would you care to take another look at your inheritance?"

****

Twenty minutes after leaving the tavern on Cornhill, Freya had reached the Old Bull, entered and started scouring the room for Matthias, Artemas or any of his men. Before she had been there two minutes a firm hand had clapped down on her shoulder. She spun round, her dagger dropping from her sleeve into her palm as she did so. It was Artemas standing there, smiling nastily at her like a cat that has just cornered a fat mouse, and like a mouse, Freya was mesmerised.

"Well now, this is convenient, isn't it?" he drawled. "Nice of you to save me the bother of coming to find you!" he said.

"I have been looking for you," she said simply.

Taken aback, Artemas raised his eyebrow, "You have? Well now you've found me." His eyes narrowed and he gazed at her for a moment, "I wonder why – but perhaps I can guess," he sneered, "a falling out among thieves, eh?" Keeping hold of her shoulder, he propelled her forward, "Come this way." Under one arm he carried a huge leather-bound book.

He steered her towards a back room of the Tavern. "Wait there!" He nodded at the two men who stood guard on either side of the door. "Don't let her go," he snapped letting himself into the room. Freya, who had no intention of going anywhere, could hear the murmur of voices from within. She waited, eyeing the two guards; both ignored her. A moment later the door reopened and Artemas leaned out, grasped Freya by the elbow and pulled her inside, closing the door behind them.

The first thing she saw was Matthias. He was standing at a table upon which was the huge book Artemas had been carrying. Freya shivered; her head ached abominably and she couldn't think clearly. It dawned on her that she was now completely alone in the company of two men who not many hours before had tried to kill her. This was not quite going according to plan.

She looked around the room for other exits, but there were no doors. There was one window but its shutters were closed and latched. A fire burned low in a hearth but the opening was really too small to fit through and she had no idea how narrow the chimney would be above it. With a sinking feeling she realised there was no way out. She turned back to look at the man behind the table. He was staring at her with those disturbingly haunted eyes – a man so convinced he is right that everyone and everything else is unimportant. More than unimportant in fact: the things she had heard him say in the graveyard, together with what the merchant had told her about him, suggested he viewed her and most others as damned. His hand hovered over the book in front of him as he now addressed her.

"I need the scroll. You know where it is to be found, don't you? Is that why you came here? To offer it to us for money?"

"Yes," said Freya. She swung round to Artemas and back to the preacher, "Four pounds. He said he'd give me four pounds."

"Child of sorrow," Matthias said, "you have the effrontery to offer to sell it to us: the means of release of the Angel of Judgement and you barter with it as if it were a loaf of bread. You sin; your soul is black and corrupt. I offer you a chance to redeem it." His voice rose to a shriek, flecks of spittle spraying from his lips, "Give the scroll to me now!"

'He's mad,' Freya thought taking a step backwards, 'what have I got myself into? Gabriel believes it is the map of a prison for a demon and Matthias thinks it's the key to freeing an angel. They're all mad. This is stupid. It's just a piece of parchment, but, if I do this right, for me it means a better place to live, food to eat and some clothes to wear. I won't have to steal for months.'

Lost in a vision of unaccustomed luxury, Freya became aware that the preacher was waiting for an answer. "Sin or not," she shrugged, "that is what I am offering you. Give me the four pounds and you shall have your scroll."

Matthias' eyes bulged. He drew breath and opened his mouth showing his yellow teeth, but before he could speak Artemas butted in.

"How quickly could you get the scroll, girl?"

"Very quickly!"

"Indeed quickly, for you have it with you, don't you? It's no use denying it. It stands to reason you would not leave such an item of value to us out of your possession. Give it to me!" he shouted and moved towards her. Freya jumped over to the fire and pulling out the scroll with a flourish held it over the low flames.

"Stay away or it goes into the fire!" she threatened.

"Girl, give it to me now!" Artemas said, pulling out a pistol.

"I'm warning you. It burns if you take a step closer."

"Child, forgive me," Artemas wheedled. His voice was softer; it made her feel at ease and she found she was drawn to look into his eyes.

"I do not want to harm you," he smiled, pushing the pistol back into his belt, "and you need not burn the scroll. We can both profit from this. Put it on the table and I will put these coins there too." He pulled out several silver coins from his money bag, "Then you will take the coins and leave."

Freya nodded, surprising herself. She had not trusted this man a few moments before, yet now, something about his words calmed her. Not just the words he spoke, but the way he spoke them resonated in her head and without thinking she crossed the room and placed the scroll on the table.

Still smiling, Artemas walked over to her tossing the coins in the air and catching them as he did so. He placed the coins on the table. Freya reached over to take them and then, quick as a flash, he had grabbed her wrist. Suddenly the hypnotic calm she had felt was gone, replaced by panic. She struggled to get free but, like a vice, Artemas held on to her wrist. Then, he took the scroll with his other hand and looked at it. He frowned slightly and began reading.

"*Hostis hvmani generis,* " he recited, just as Ben had done, but looking down at it, Freya noticed none of the effects that had occurred when Ben read the words. Artemas frowned again. "*Ostendu!*" he shouted, but nothing happened. The map remained the same. "*Ostendu!*" he shouted again, and again nothing occurred.

Artemas hissed with disappointment, his hand scrunching the bones in Freya's wrist until she cried out in pain. "I think," he said at last to Matthias, "that we must take her before Dantalion and find out what she knows."

The preacher nodded.

"Let me go, you rat, I don't know anything, I don't!" Freya shouted kicking out at him as she fought to get free. Artemas cuffed her hard with his free hand so she tasted blood as it dripped from her lip. Her head pounded; the pain excruciating.

"Bastard!" she shouted, spitting at him, "I don't know anything!"

"Swear that you do not, swear it on this Bible," Artemas ordered and pointed at the book on the desk. Freya shook her head. She was a thief and a liar and had limited use for churches and bibles but there was no sense in offending the Almighty by lying under oath. Artemas, however, was too strong for her and, with a nasty grin, he pulled her hand over to the book and placed it palm down on the cover.

Freya felt a sudden burning sensation running up her arm, through her neck to her head. The room seemed to spin and then, a moment later, it had vanished from her sight and all she could see was a terrifying blackness.

Chapter 9
The Angel

London, Saturday 1ˢᵗ September, 1666: early evening

In the midst of the darkness there appeared a pinpoint of intense white light that rapidly expanded and – with a suddenness that made Freya cry out in alarm – she, Artemas and Matthias were standing in a sweetly perfumed sunlit glade in a peaceful wood. The ground was bedecked with the flowers and blossoms of spring and nearby a stream gurgled as it flowed over and around rocks and boulders. After the drought London had endured this summer, the coolness of the place was wonderful and refreshing.

Now, having recovered from her fright, Freya realised that of course she must be dreaming. She felt incredibly relaxed, but even so, the dream was so *real* that a part of her mind questioned where she was and how she had got there. She turned to Artemas, but before she could ask him anything she saw they were not alone in the glade and she gasped, awestruck.

The figure glowed with a deep white brilliance that was both blinding and wondrous to behold, transcending anything she had known before. It wore the shape of a man but seemed much more than just that. Over seven feet tall, he was clad in flowing white robes, had a stern but kindly face and bore glorious golden-coloured wings that reached out on either side in regal splendour. Freya glanced at Matthias and saw he was now kneeling and gazing up at the figure with a look of ecstatic adoration on his face.

The angel – for it could be nothing else – turned to the man and spoke to him. The sound was like the joyous pealing of bells. It reminded Freya of the day her mother had taken her to see the King returning from exile and the bells had been ringing out all over London.

"Faithful servant, you have done well and will be rewarded when I am free to walk the world at your side," the angel said. "Now go and pray while I talk to the girl alone. Let Artemas stay a moment as I wish to ask him something."

Matthias looked crestfallen, but then he bowed his head and was gone: vanishing from the glade just as swiftly as they had arrived. The angel turned to Freya and when she felt his gaze upon her it was almost unbearable, and yet at the same time irresistible; she could not look away. And then he broke eye contact to speak to Artemas and when that mesmerising gaze left her, Freya felt an aching sense of loss. She yearned for him to look at her again, and understood why Matthias had not wished to leave this place. She wondered how Gabriel could be so misguided as to believe this glorious creature was a demon. But, then again, the foolish man had never seen him in all this glory. Yet a small voice inside her head cautioned her not to be taken in by this weird dream, and in a daze, she listened to what Artemas was saying.

"My Lord Dantalion, we have the scroll. I cannot read it; can you, Lord?" Artemas offered up the scroll.

Dantalion did not take it but just shook his head, "Accursed work of an old foe that is. I can tell it has been read by our enemies and nothing we do will reveal its secrets to us. Only its owner or his heir could understand what is written now. We must find out what they saw when they read it."

"The girl was with them and may have heard without being aware of it the secrets we need to know," Artemis stared at her, his eyes narrowed.

The angel nodded and turned back to Freya. "Child, you have wandered alone for many years through the dark of the city around us. Let me comfort you and take away your sorrows."

Basking once again in his gentle yet penetrating gaze, Freya felt no fear. She nodded, "What must I do, Sir?"

"Open yourself to me. Allow me to look into your mind and your soul and purge them of sin and then you can serve me. Will you do that, my child?"

Freya nodded again, but, as he removed his gaze, a slight worm of doubt wriggled into her mind. 'What is it now?' she asked herself irritably. For once in her life she had felt happy, more than happy: almost ecstatic. Here was a chance for a purpose and joy and peace, so why did she have this lingering feeling that something was not right? She screwed up her eyes and looked inward for a moment - and then she put her finger on it: she was a child of the streets. She made a living as best as she could by using her wits and her agility, but more than that, it was her intuition. She was a more accomplished liar than anyone she knew and she could weave a yarn and tell a tale like a master storyteller to get a few coins out of some gullible young nobleman. And that was the point: she was so good at deceiving others she could tell when someone was attempting to deceive her.

Maybe it was after all the echoes of Gabriel's voice talking about demons that had laid the seeds of this doubt; or perhaps a hint of deception in the eyes of the angel – her mother had always said to look someone in the eyes if you thought they were lying - or it could simply be her suspicion that nothing could really be this perfect. Whatever the cause, Freya's sense that something was not right grew stronger. She had survived in the past by trusting her feelings - the instincts that told her when someone was spinning her a tale - and suddenly she knew beyond doubt that Dantalion was doing just that to her, right now. He was good, very good in fact, but not *quite* good enough. And somehow that knowledge diminished his power over her.

"Well?" he demanded.

"I don't think so," she said, stepping back a pace.

"What say you?" Dantalion thundered, a frown appearing on that perfect face, the voice sounding more like a cracked bell now.

Freya flinched, but stood her ground. "I don't believe you can be trusted and I certainly will not open my mind to you. All this is very impressive," she said, and with a sweep of her arm took in the blossom-strewn glade, "but it's just an illusion. It is clever and convincing: good enough to fool Matthias obviously, but not me."

Dantalion laughed and as he did so the glade vanished and they were standing in the streets of London: on Cornhill in fact. Around them the crowds thronged about their business apparently oblivious of their presence. Dantalion had changed too and was no longer an angel, but a tall, attractive man in a striking black leather tunic. Gone were the perfumed scents of the spring blossoms although, as Dantalion stepped closer to her, the usual stench of the city was disguised by his own seductive fragrance. His eyes, which gazed intensely into her own, no longer burned with a holy light but smouldered darkly, drawing her in, and now he spoke in a voice that was low, soft and, oh ... so very sensual.

"I can see you are clever and resourceful and that there is no fooling you. Yes, I am the demon, Dantalion. I am powerful and that power will soon be felt on this street and many others.

100

My enemies will learn to fear me, but I am generous to those who show loyalty. See now," he said, and with a flick of his fingers, Freya's rags and dirt were taken away and she wore a beautiful and expensive silk dress such as the noblest ladies of the court might wear. She looked down at it in wonder and Dantalion nodded. "See how I will make you rich, beautiful and powerful if you will serve me."

Freya was tempted. She was convinced by now that she was trapped in an enchantment, but what did that matter? Here at last was the chance of a lifetime: the wealth of nations could be hers. No more the ragged tramp folk spat on when they passed. No more the pitiable hand-to-mouth existence. All she desired she would have. And yet ... would they *really* be hers? When, in the guise of an angel, this creature had promised ecstatic bliss and her soul's redemption, she'd had doubts. Now this handsome suitor's gift was of unimaginable wealth and power and as before, Freya realised Dantalion was stringing her along. She felt neither fear nor anger; if anything her feeling was one of disappointment.

She shook her head. "You are lying. You will take what you need and then you will kill me."

Dantalion frowned and at once his eyes flared red as if deep within him a fire was burning; his face darkened to a ruddy brown and as he snarled at her his teeth became long, sharp and fearsome. The demon grew swiftly in size: seven feet became ten, a dozen and then fifteen. His shoulders broadened and the muscles bulged and tensed. He pointed one finger at Freya and as she craned her neck to look up at him, the nail became a talon and the hand a claw.

The beast roared at her and Freya's courage faltered. With a cry of fear she fell to the ground and lay there quivering in terror. The curtain had been drawn back, the veil torn asunder and all pretence was gone: there was no redemption on offer here, no salvation, no wealth and no seduction. Dantalion was revealed as he truly was: Gabriel had been right after all. And as the beast bent over her, Freya saw only death.

"There is a third choice. I will take what I need from you and then I will show you what I will do to your precious city," Dantalion growled in fury and reached down to grasp her head. At once a piercing agony stabbed down through Freya's skull and she felt the world spin about her. In her mind she could feel the presence of Dantalion breaking down her barriers, thrusting aside her resistance and sifting through her memories. Most he rejected with derision as soon as he considered them.

At last though, he found what he was looking for and suddenly they were not in the London street anymore, but standing with Artemas in the corner of Doctor Janssen's study. Freya gave a gasp as she saw herself lying on the couch, head bandaged apparently asleep, though in fact she had been eavesdropping on the conversation at the desk.

Now, she, Dantalion and Artemas, listened again as Gabriel talked about the scroll, the journal and the Words of Power, and Freya, the demon's hand still clutching her head, could tell Dantalion was pleased with what he heard.

Suddenly, Ben looked up and stared around the room and for a split second he seemed to look right through her. "Help me!" she cried out, but he did not respond; indeed no one in the study reacted.

"Foolish girl, they cannot hear you because we are simply revisiting what has already been, and you are but a shade," Dantalion said, forcing her to watch until the moment when she had picked up the scroll and left with it. Then he frowned and said, "You did not see the map here, however," his hand tightened on her head, "ah, but now there is the memory ...."

Freya pitted her will against the pressure of the demon's hand, tried everything she knew to blank her mind and close it to his probing, but in vain. She could not fight him. The scene

102

shifted and they were again in the graveyard. Ben was standing there and was speaking the Words of Power, gazing in awe as the map lit up and ghostly images of buildings arose from the parchment. The view moved nearer just as, earlier in the day, Freya had leaned in to have a closer look.

Watching the scene unfold, Artemas rubbed his hands with glee and Dantalion laughed out loud. Fascinated, Freya again saw one of the buildings clearly, and the roads nearby, a few letters marking its name. Saw herself reaching out to see if she could touch them. Then, the view shifted to focus more on Ben and away from the map.

Dantalion's eyes seemed to burn with a fierce fire as he too concentrated on the schoolboy. "I see you took more notice of this boy than the scroll. I would dismiss it as human weakness and desire, but this boy awakens some deep memory I cannot place. What is it?" The demon seemed momentarily distracted. "Artemas, you will have him watched. Do not kill him yet, I must know more of him."

"Yes, my Lord," Artemas bowed.

Then Dantalion laughed even louder, and as he did the scene shifted again and Freya felt her throat tighten in fear as she found herself looking down from the highest point of St Paul's Cathedral, right on the top of the huge square tower. Beneath her was a black abyss. It was night time; the city was lit dimly by starlight, enough for her to recognise the main thoroughfares. She could see the distant Thames, a ribbon of mist rising eerily from its waters. She swayed, gripped by terror.

The demon released her head and stood looming over her. As he lifted his hand, the pain subsided. The dull ache in her wounded temple seemed irrelevant now. Freya felt numb; her mind violated. Repelled, she stared up at Dantalion, her eyes wide open as she awaited his next move.

Still laughing, he extended his arms. "Behold: the depraved, stinking metropolis that men call London. For three hundred years it has been my prison – but no longer. It is you, selfish child, who has given me the means to break free. If you had not come to us, we would not know where the first seal is, nor the secrets of the pernicious *Praesidium*. Now though, because of you, we have enough information to locate them."

"But Lord – we have only one seal. We know roughly where the other five are, but not well enough to find them," Artemas said, his face creasing with anxiety.

The fire in Dantalion's eyes had dimmed to an amber glow of contentment. Almost he seemed to purr. He smiled at Artemas, "One will be enough. Destroy it in the way I will show you and the others will follow. Now, both of you; observe how I will avenge myself on this place."

Below them the city of London slept. A few houses pricked with candlelight, but in these small hours most folk were in bed and at peace, ignorant of the horror about to strike them. Freya watched in helpless anguish as Dantalion spread his arms to encompass the view.

Then, a fair way away to the south and east, a column of fire sprang up like a beacon warning of invasion. It was seemingly swiftly answered for all around it greedy flames were licking at dry timber and in no time at all, London was dotted with fires. Sparks exploded in the air, setting light to other buildings and turning the sky black with billowing clouds of evil smelling smoke. Soon the city was illuminated by an inferno, its peace shattered as in their teeming thousands London's inhabitants streamed out of their houses and took to the streets to escape the blaze. They came closer and closer. Freya could hear them screaming now and see their terrified faces; faces that turned frequently as people looked back to gauge the speed of the fire pursuing them.

The blaze soon raged in a great arc from the Royal Exchange in the east to the Temple in the west and now Freya could feel its heat. She turned away, unable to look as her city burnt, but Dantalion seized her by the hair and tugged at it viciously so her head was pulled back and she was forced to look on this vision of Hell. The spires of churches erupted in flame and fell, crashing into the devastation around them, houses in their thousands were obliterated, the great trading halls were consumed too, along with the warehouses lining the river – some, filled with combustible materials, exploded and left great gaping chasms in the earth's surface as London died.

"See your city burn, girl, and know I will do it for real very soon," Dantalion taunted.

The smoke was acrid and blown by the wind into their faces, Dantalion's grip on her hair was painful and tears now stung her eyes; they were not due to the smoke, nor the pain, but from seeing the city she loved turn to ash. She watched a family below them, one of many, leading a cart loaded with all their belongings, a terrified horse blindfolded between the shafts. They were careering down Watling Street towards St Paul's churchyard when suddenly a blast of fire shot down the street and engulfed them. The cart was incinerated in a moment, but the husband, his wife and their three children burned for longer, as did the horse, screaming in pitiful agony until finally the oncoming fire consumed them all.

"Make it stop, please!" Freya pleaded, weeping, but Dantalion ignored her.

St Paul's itself was now ablaze and she could feel the roaring, burning heat soaring up through the ancient building, weakening the structure. The roof of the east transept caved in and fell into the flames with a great boom and still the fire came on until it reached the tower they stood on. The tower creaked and groaned, then suddenly it collapsed and they all tumbled downwards into the hungry flames. With a cry of horror Freya closed her eyes and waited for searing agony and death.

Death did not come. She opened her eyes and saw she was back in the room in the Old Bull Tavern. Matthias was kneeling and praying on the other side of the table, his eyes closed in rapture. Artemas, who was examining the scroll, glanced up at her. Freya expected to see some sign of shock and horror at what he had just witnessed, but his face showed only acceptance of the price the city would pay for his master's freedom. Somehow his selfish and coldhearted approach chilled her almost as much as the demon's malevolence. The demon? She looked around expecting to see Dantalion's ominous form towering over her. Where was he? Had it all been some kind of horrific nightmare? The last thing she remembered before it started was touching Mathias' great book. As Freya struggled to understand what had happened, what was real, what imagined, she felt a great weakness come over her and slumped on to her knees.

Rolling up the scroll and placing it carefully inside his coat Artemas crossed to the door and opened it. He shouted a word Freya did not hear clearly. There was a murmur of voices and a shadow at the door revealed another man standing there, talking to Artemas. Their conversation was muffled at first and only as her head cleared and the pain subsided did Freya hear what the Cavalier was saying.

"Are you sure you want to involve them, your colleagues are not brethren? Still, I guess it will keep Gabriel occupied and unable to stop us. Very well, be careful what you say to them, but do it tonight. We need the *Praesidium* pinned down and unable to intervene, for a few hours at least. Go now!"

Artemas came back into the room and closed the door. At the noise, Matthias opened his eyes and grasping the table, pulled himself onto his feet, not bothering to look at the girl. "It is time, Artemas. Do you know now where we must make a start?"

"Yes, Matthias, I do."

"Then let us depart," he glanced then at Freya. "Bring the girl along. She may still be useful. You shall see the angel arise, my dear," he said, now fixing his gaze on her and pointing a shaking finger, "and you shall see that your part in this was pivotal and find joy in that."

"He is a demon not an angel, idiot," Freya taunted, "you're mad; you know that, don't you?"

Matthias' face grew dark, "Or perhaps you will be the first victim of his judgement. Bring her along," he repeated to Artemas. "I will gather the faithful; this is the day we have waited and prayed for." Picking up the book from the table, he tucked it under his arm and left the room. The two guards followed, and with Artemas bringing up the rear dragging Freya behind him, they went to destroy the seals and free their 'Angel of Judgement': an ancient demon whose name was 'Dantalion'.

****

Gabriel pushed open the door to Tobias' study and then stopped so suddenly that Ben almost ran into the back of him. Looking over the older man's shoulders he saw what had caused him to pause. Tobias was sitting at his writing desk, but the desk itself, which should have been covered by the scroll, was instead host to a pair of pistols, a gunpowder horn and a small pile of shot. Of the scroll there was no sign. Tobias was cleaning one of the pistols with a cloth.

Gabriel recovered and bustled into the room and over to the desk. "Where is it?" he burst out, voice shaking with panic.

"Where is what?" Tobias said vaguely, not looking up from his work.

"Tobias, the scroll: where is it?"

Ben glanced over towards the couch where Freya had been lying. "Erm ... where is Freya?" he asked, pulling Gabriel's sleeve.

Spinning round, Gabriel took in the empty couch, and then turned back to glare at Tobias. "What have you done?" he asked, a hint of rising anger edging his voice.

Putting down the cloth, Tobias at last looked up at them and raising a quizzical eyebrow leant back in his seat. "What do you think I have done? You know I do not believe in this obsession you and my father wasted your lives on. Because of it my father is dead and my one concern is to find his killer and have my revenge."

He cocked the pistol and pulled the trigger, looking with one eye down the sight. The flint sprang forward striking against the frizzen and producing a small shower of sparks. Tobias nodded to himself as if satisfied and started pouring gunpowder into the barrel. His eyes flicked up again to survey Gabriel.

"You said yourself that Artemas would pay for the scroll, so I had our little thief friend go and find him for me. Once I know where he is I will kill him."

Ben could not believe what he was hearing. "You sent her to be killed, did you think of that?" he snarled.

"She didn't need much persuading and I don't think they will kill her. All they want is that scroll. If she sells it to them they have no reason not to let her go."

"You are a fool, Tobias, if you think it is as easy as that," Gabriel said coldly. "If they find out we know about more than just the scroll - and they soon will if Freya overheard our conversation earlier - they will force that information out of her. You are a fine one to talk of obsessions, Tobias. What you have done here proves - if I did not know it already – that it is you who is obsessed: obsessed with finding Artemas at whatever the cost. Freya could come to harm because of it."

Tobias paused for a moment and seemed to think about that, but soon hefted the pistol, picked up a ball of shot and popped it in the barrel.

"You don't care, do you?" Ben demanded. "She is just a 'gawping tramp' and hardly worth your time: that's the way you see her, the scum of society with no value or importance. Providing she gets you to Artemas that is all that bothers you. "

"That's hardly fair, young man! All I saw was that Freya had something Artemas wanted which I could use to get to him. Besides, as I said, she was keen to get her hands on the money. I did not think I was putting her at any real risk."

"Didn't you? Are you sure about that or is it more the case that you thought nobody would miss her?" Gabriel asked.

"Certainly not – but why are you so bothered about her anyway, Gabriel? You only met her today as did the boy. A chance meeting with a thief: that is all it was. Had she the opportunity, she would rob you blind. Why then are you now so bothered?"

Gabriel shook his head sadly, "There was a time, from what I have heard, when Tobias Janssen was considered one of the most caring and considerate of men, dedicated to his vocation and trying to do his best for others. Your father spoke about it often, despite you and he falling out. 'My son is doing his bit to save the world' is how he put it. What happened, Tobias?"

The doctor's shoulders slumped at the mention of his father. "Lately the world does not seem much worth saving." He looked and sounded depressed.

"This is because your father was killed, isn't it?" Gabriel said. "You gave up on the world because of what happened to him – and you are riddled with guilt. Does that seem fair? If Freya dies will that make everything better? I don't think so!"

"What do I have to feel guilty about? It wasn't my fault Father ..." Tobias' voice tailed away and he gazed down at the desk as though unable to meet Gabriel's eyes. After a moment he gave a big sigh and looked up at them both. "The good Lord save me from mad booksellers and altruistic schoolboys! Oh, very well, let's go and rescue her then." He stood up and taking both pistols pushed them into his belt then, pulling a coat from a hook behind the door, shrugged it over his shoulders adjusting the folds to cover his weapons. "But I warn you," he said, "if we see Artemas I will deal with him myself."

"Where will we begin to look for them? London is big place and it's already after eight o'clock," Ben said.

Tobias opened the door, "Well, we can head first to the Royal Exchange," adding over his shoulder as he walked into the hall, "but you will not come with us, boy. You should be back at school safely away from all this."

"No! I won't go back there and you can't make me. Firstly, I feel a bit responsible for Freya. If I had not followed her into that graveyard she would not be involved. Secondly, I do not want to face my Headmaster yet if I can avoid it and finally, Gabriel needs me: out of those of us here, only I can read the scroll and find out where the seals are." He was about to add, but thought better of it, *I also want to know more about what is going on with this scroll and Dantalion, and most of all with these Words of Power Gabriel talks about.* When he had asked what words the bookseller had used to create the stunning flash in the warehouse, Gabriel had reacted strangely, so it seemed best he did not know what thoughts Ben was having on the subject. Not just thoughts, he acknowledged to himself, but desires and they were becoming increasingly urgent: he simply *had* to know more.

"Not that again you stubborn boy," Tobias waved his arms about in frustration, "Look, I keep telling you. There is no demon. The scroll is just a bit of parchment and there are no

110

seals. It's all just superstition. It's going to take more than a few ghost stories and a scrap of paper to convince me otherwise." Then, seeing Ben's determined expression and folded arms, Tobias rolled his eyes and added, resigned, "Come on then, if you must. Let's go."

He led the way along the hall, with Ben and Gabriel following on behind and was approaching the front door when there was a knock on it.

Tobias turned to the others. "See, told you she would be all right. Ah, Owen, there you are," he said as his manservant shuffled into view from the direction of the kitchen. "Let the young lady in would you?"

"At once, Doctor," said Owen and opened the door.

"Wait. Don't!" Gabriel shouted suddenly, but it was already too late. As the door was opened it flew inwards, propelled by the shoulder of a man, who knocked Owen to the ground and jumped over him, at the same time pulling a dagger out of his cloak and advancing on Tobias. Owen manoeuvred himself up to a crouch and seized the man's cloak. Then Ben heard a wet thump and the servant slumped to the ground. A second man was standing over him with a blackjack in one hand and a pistol in the other. Behind him, Ben could see two more men coming in, one with a musket and the other with a dragoon's long sword. The leader now looked at them and to Ben's surprise, he smiled.

"I would be grateful if you did not move!" His tone was polite, contrasting with the threat of the pistol currently levelled at Tobias' chest. "We would be much obliged if we could have a word with you, Doctor Jansenn." Tobias' hand twitched toward his coat, but the intruder saw the move and shook his head, "No, I really would advise against any sudden movements."

"Are these *Liberati*?" Ben whispered to Gabriel so that Tobias could hear.

Gabriel shrugged. If they are I have not seen them before," he answered.

"You boy, what are you saying there, eh? You wonder who we are perhaps. Well my name is Captain Gymer and I work for Lord Clarendon, who is Chancellor to the King, you know," he puffed up his chest.

Ben gawped; Tobias and Gabriel nodded vaguely at this information not knowing what the implications were. The Captain paused to study them and Ben took the moment to have a good look in return. Gymer was a short man, but looked strong in the arms and shoulders, a fact backed up by the splintered door hanging from one hinge. His cap had fallen off as he came through the door, revealing that he was quite bald. His skin was tanned and scarred as if he had travelled much in tropical places and fought a few battles. His clothing was practical and tough and lacked the elaborate frills and lace that Artemas wore. When the man continued speaking his voice was deep and slightly hoarse.

"Forgive me staring at you, you are wondering why I do perhaps? Well I was considering if you really are Dutch spies and saboteurs as my reports suggest."

"*Spies?*" Tobias' eyes widened in surprise, "What do you mean by that?"

"Well I do like to be right about these things." Gymer's eyes narrowed as his jovial face dropped into a threatening glare, "I would find it extremely distressing to hang you and find out later I was wrong!"

Chapter 10
The King and his Kingdom

London, Saturday 1st September, 1666: mid-evening

"**H**is skull is intact and there does not seem to be any palsy or concussion. He will live, no thanks to your thug," Tobias said, after Gymer had herded them back into Tobias' study and allowed the doctor to examine Owen. The valet recovered in a few minutes and sat groaning and holding his head. Ben and Gabriel were sitting back on their seats of earlier in the day, while Gymer himself had taken up residence in Tobias' own chair and was watching the practitioner at work. His other men were positioned at the door and windows.

"Fascinating subject medicine, I think," Gymer muttered, apparently ignoring the doctor's comments. Ben glanced over at the window where the man carrying the blackjack was staring up and down the street, and noted that he looked just as unaffected by what had occurred as his captain, who now continued to speak.

"I could not possibly comprehend most of what you have learnt in your books, my dear doctor, but leaving that aside our professions are not unalike, do you not agree?"

Tobias wandered back across the room, bringing with him another chair, put it down in front of the desk and then stood behind it, leaning on its back.

"I'm afraid, I do not agree. I don't know who you are, but the evidence so far is that you break into gentlemen's houses and assault their servants and then hold their guests prisoner. How is that similar to my vocation?" Although Tobias spoke softly, Ben could hear anger in the way his voice trembled.

"I meant that we both examine evidence and draw conclusions from it. So, just now you examine this man's eyes and head and decide he will live. Ironic is it not then that I have to examine your stories and decide if you will die."

Tobias said nothing, but just stared at the man. Gymer smiled again in response.

"You asked what I do, well I will tell you. The King needs his Kingdom keeping safe. There are enemies within and without and I must ensure it is kept safe from them. So, the question is, are you an enemy to the King or to his Kingdom?"

"I am a doctor, Gabriel here is a bookseller in the Royal Exchange and Benjamin is a scholar in Westminster. Does it look like we are enemy spies?"

"A curious conspiracy indeed," Gymer muttered, "but let me look at the evidence. Firstly, there is an explosion at a warehouse just behind the Royal Exchange, followed by the noise of pistol fire. A man and two youths, one of whom was bleeding from a head wound, were seen fleeing the area in a Hackney carriage. We found the driver and he told us where he had taken you. He also said one of the youths was a girl, or at least that is what he was told."

He paused and looked from Gabriel to Ben. "So, you two are the man and the boy and in which case, where is the girl?"

Neither spoke.

Gymer waited in silence, one eyebrow lifting as he studied their faces. At length he smiled. "I see. Well, let us proceed:

secondly, we have this on the table." He held up a finger and showed a few speckles of dust clinging to it, then licked at it and spat. "Gunpowder, I believe. Finally," he turned to Tobias, who had stopped leaning on the back of his chair and was perched on the edge of the seat, "it is still a warm night after a hot summer's day and yet, Doctor, you sit here indoors with a coat on. Would you care to take it off and remove your pistol? I am sure you will be more comfortable without it, don't you think? Just in case you are considering using it, I should warn you that Spencer and Marlowe at the door there are armed and both are excellent shots."

Glancing at Gymer's men, Ben gulped. Spencer, a short, shrew-faced man, whose eyes glinted with intelligence, was holding a pistol. Marlowe, in contrast was tall and massively built, rather like a wrestler. His eyes were dull and he seemed disinterested in anything apart from staring at Tobias, his tree-trunk arms cradling a huge firearm that looked more like a cannon than a musket.

Grimacing, Tobias shrugged out of his coat and revealed his two pistols, which he placed regretfully on the desk.

Gymer smiled at him. "Two pistols indeed! So then: we have a Dutchman living in London who is armed and harbouring two fugitives, who themselves are believed to have been involved in a bomb detonation. Is that a fair assessment of the situation, would you say?"

"This is complete nonsense, Captain," Tobias replied. "You really have no evidence at all apart from a few flimsy facts. I am English not Dutch, though granted my father was Dutch, but I was born in London. As for these two, they were attacked by some thugs in that warehouse. Probably a shot hit something explosive, but it was not a bomb they planted, right?" he raised his eyebrows at Gabriel and Ben who both nodded. "As for the girl, she was injured by a shot fired by the same thugs. Gabriel and Ben did the right thing and brought

115

her to me. She recovered quickly and went from here some hours ago. That is the truth: take it or leave it!"

Not the entire truth, thought Ben, but good enough. Not one of the three of them wanted to tell the whole truth. Tobias obviously wanted a chance to find Artemas and certainly did not want to mention his planned revenge; Gabriel's entire life was based around keeping a secret; and as for Ben himself, well he had no reason to talk about what was really going on either, primarily because he wanted to know more about it and did not need this Gymer interfering.

"I hope you will not take offence if I check a few further pieces of evidence. Spencer, come with me to search the house, you other two stay and watch them," Gymer ordered, and taking one of Tobias' two pistols he left the room.

Tobias leaned forward slightly towards the other pistol, but the click of a flintlock hammer being cocked behind him stopped him in his tracks and slowly he moved back against his chair.

****

"What time is it now, do you think?" Matthias asked. He and Artemas were standing in a dark alleyway observing a building on the other side of the road. The Cavalier held an unlit pitch-soaked torch under his arm and was reaching in his pocket for his tinderbox.

Freya, her hands tied together and her head still pounding was slumped down against the wall of a house and staring at the pair. For the moment they seemed to be ignoring her so she looked around considering escape, but the dozen or so followers Matthias had gathered on the way here were all standing in the alleyway, keeping a respectful distance from their master, but too close for Freya to evade them.

116

"Maybe half an hour after midnight, perhaps a little later," Artemas replied.

"Then it is time, I think. Everyone will be asleep. Where is the seal?"

"It is in the basement of that chandler's over there," Artemas said, pointing. "I had a quick look down through the trap doors. It's a well-built, stone-lined cellar, but it is filled with barrels of tar. Enough heat and fire will detonate them. Then either the heat or the explosion will destroy the seal."

"So we throw in a torch?"

Artemas' eyes widened. "No, Matthias, we could be unlucky and detonate the tar with us right on top. I suggest we start a fire nearby and let it spread. Let's say," he paused, glanced around, "ah, yes, there look, that baker's is just the place. A torch thrown in there should start a nice fire and the ovens are known to be a fire hazard. Perfect!"

"Artemas ...?" Matthias' voice was hesitant.

"Yes?"

"Do you suppose the Lord will forgive the murder we do tonight?"

Swinging round, Artemas studied the preacher for a moment before replying, as though choosing his words with care.

"You said yourself that the city is corrupt. Sacrifice must be made to burn that away and leave it reborn. You accept the need for sacrifice for the Lord's work, so I am sure He will forgive you."

Artemas spoke with apparent sincerity, but Freya thought she saw the edge of a smile come to his face as he turned away to light the torch. To her disgust the fanatical preacher seemed completely unaware of Artemas' blatant manipulation.

"Yes, you are right. Praise to Dantalion and to the Almighty!" His eyes bulging, hands raised high above his head, Matthias turned to his flock. "Come, gather closer. Now,

117

on this the second day of September in the year of our Lord, one thousand, six hundred and sixty-six, when according to God's holy word the end of mankind is nigh, let us beseech Lord Dantalion to come to us." His followers crowded around him, knelt and bowed their heads as the preacher spoke. Spittle was dribbling from his mouth, but on fire as he was with holy zeal, if Matthias noticed he did not care.

"Hear what the Psalmist wrote: '*At the wrath of the Lord of Hosts the land quakes and the people are like fuel for fire. No man spares his brother; each devours the flesh of his neighbour.*' So it was and so it shall be on this night. On this holy night: when the Lord God punishes the unrighteous and delivers his judgement with fire."

Above them, there was a creak and Freya glanced up to see that a shutter had opened. A man stuck his head out through the window and peered down at the cause of the commotion.

"Keep it down yer drunken rascals," he shouted, "don't you have any idea how late it is. Get off home!" He disappeared inside and slammed the shutters.

Matthias' flock ignored the interruption. "Amen. God's will be done," the followers intoned, their faces ecstatic and almost glowing with joy, oblivious to all but their master's resounding words.

Watching them, Freya felt sick. Moments before, the preacher had questioned what he and Artemas were doing, but now it seemed he was again committed to the task, all his doubts put away. His men appeared to be just as bad. "Mad, the lot of them," the little thief said to herself with a shake of her head. Glancing around, she knew there would be no better opportunity for escape. Scrambling to her feet she started to edge away down the alley.

Behind her, Artemas took the lighted torch and crossed the road to the bakery.

****

"What time is it now, do you think?" Ben asked, stifling a yawn and glancing at Gabriel, who was sleepily rubbing his eyes. Tobias, slumped in a chair beside him, was actually snoring softly. They were still being held in the study by Gymer's men. The Captain had been gone for some hours – or so it seemed - supposedly searching the house, though Ben could not imagine what was taking him so long. The guards had occasionally been changed about, but always one of them, armed with pistol or musket, would be in the room and they were completely alert. Walton, the third man of Gymer's group, stayed throughout and still held his blackjack, while the pistol was in reach on a small table near the window. He kept a disturbingly persistent watch on the trio, interrupted only by the flick of his blue eyes, which were barely visible under dark, bushy eyebrows, in order to glance out of the window. Hardly a word was said except once when Spencer had offered to get them a drink, but Walton had told him to leave them be.

"I'm only trying to make them a little more comfortable, Walton. They may be spies but it doesn't hurt to be civil, I always say," Spencer had said in a hurt tone, but Walton merely frowned and shook his head and silence returned. That was about thirty minutes ago, although Ben was finding it hard to keep track of the time since the sonorous tones of the Watch calling the hour had stopped some time ago.

"The time?" Gabriel responded. "I've no idea, getting on for midnight I would think, but ..." his voice tailed away as the door was flung open and Gymer reappeared. Ben nudged Tobias awake and all three turned with trepidation to look at the Captain.

"Spencer, Walton come!" Gymer barked out an order and without a word the men walked out of the door. Gymer alone remained. He tapped his fingers on the table and then he placed Tobias' pistol back there, next to its twin.

"I can find nothing to incriminate you, so I will wish you good night," he muttered and turning away he walked out into the hall.

Tobias jumped to his feet and went after him. "Wait there a moment. Is that all you are going to say? You hold us at gunpoint for hours on end and falsely accuse us of being spies, and then you just plan to go without a by your leave?"

Gymer stopped and turned to face him. He was not smiling and the grimness of his expression made Tobias take a step back.

"Let me make myself clear, Doctor. I am a loyal servant to the King. We are at war with your father's country and I have a city full of traders and merchants who are Dutch, as well as a half-Dutch doctor or two. Any of you could be spies. I will take such steps as I deem necessary to protect the King and his Kingdom. I very much advise that you three stay out of trouble and away from exploding barrels, pistols or runaway girls. I will be keeping an eye on you all." Stooping to retrieve his cap, which still lay on the floor by the splintered front door, he replaced it on his bald pate and with a brief touch to the brim, he left.

Tobias went back into the study and glanced at his manservant who was dozing on the couch. Apparently satisfied, he moved to his desk and brushed the gunpowder into his hand, tipping it into the flask at his belt. That done, he looked from Gabriel to Ben, his expression pensive, then, as if reaching a decision, he nodded. "You two had better stay here for the remainder of the night. You, Ben, I can take back to the school in the morning."

"What about Freya?" Ben asked, not wanting to think about what would happen to him when he finally faced up to Busby.

"It is far too late to find her now. All the taverns will have shut up for the night. We can start early in the ..." Tobias' voice tailed away and he tilted his head to the window.

"What is it?" Ben asked.

"Bells! Can you hear bells?"

They all listened.

"There are bells," Gabriel said, "well, one bell: a church bell, but sounding distant, maybe a mile or so away."

"Who'd be ringing a bell at this time of night? Sounds odd, doesn't it," Ben asked, cocking his head, as more bells began to chime, "like they are being rung wrongly or something?"

"Not wrongly, but backwards," Gabriel said, his face suddenly pale. "The timing is opposite to normal. It's the signal that a fire has broken out."

"Of course it is; I had forgotten. Are you all right, Gabriel?" Ben asked, concerned. The bookseller was gripping the back of a chair, his jaw clenched, knuckles white. "You look as though you've seen a ghost."

"No, not a ghost," he looked over Ben's head to where Tobias stood watching him. "It's just a hunch and I hope I'm wrong, but as a matter of urgency we need to know where the fire is."

"Why?" asked Tobias. When the bookseller did not reply he asked again, "Why? A fire is common enough; the Watch will soon put it out, same as always. What's the problem?"

Ignoring the question, Gabriel stepped towards the window and peered out at the city. He stiffened and muttered, "Oh God, no!"

"Gabriel, what *is* it?" Ben pleaded, his throat tightening with anxiety though he did not know why.

"Gabriel?"

Chapter 11
The Great Fire

London, Saturday 1ˢᵗ September, 1666: shortly before midnight

G abriel chewed his lip and continued to stare out of the window.

"Why do you need to know where the fire is? Answer me, Gabriel," Tobias insisted. At last, heaving a sigh, Gabriel turned into the room, his brow creased with anxiety.

"Intense fire is one of the things that can destroy the seals. I fear Artemas might have started it to get at them."

Ben gasped, "Surely even he wouldn't do anything so drastic?"

Dejected, Gabriel sat down heavily on the chair by the window and rubbed his tired eyes. "There's nothing he would not do to get at the seals, Benjamin. And if that's what he's done, he'll never control it; the city is as dry as dust. That won't matter to him, of course. Death and destruction will mean nothing if he has somehow found out where the seals are located and-"

"Oh, stop it!" Tobias shouted, cutting across him. "There you go again fantasising about non-existent seals. If I hear any more of that nonsense I swear I'll ... wait a moment; what did you say about Artemas? Will he be there?" Tobias, his tone suddenly animated, pushed the pistols into his belt and headed towards the hall. "If so, come on, let's go!"

Getting to his feet, Gabriel stared at him, "This is not about revenge, Tobias, yes indeed, let's go – but whatever you do don't just charge in and start shooting. I need to find out what has happened to the seals."

"And don't forget that Freya might be there as well," Ben chipped in.

"Yes, yes of course whatever you say," Tobias agreed nodding his head, but his voice was distant as if his thoughts were elsewhere. Ben caught the murderous look in his eyes; it was not hard to guess what those thoughts were.

Whatever Gabriel's worries, however, Ben was glad the doctor was coming along. Artemas and his men were killers and Tobias looked like he could handle himself in a fight. Moreover, Ben had felt a sudden tightness in his chest when the word fire had been mentioned and in his mind the echoes of his parents' screams of terror returned to haunt him. Despite the warmth of the house, he shivered as a sudden chill of fear passed through him: a fear of flames in the night and a fall into the dark. He felt dizzy and reached over to the table to steady himself.

"Are you unwell, Benjamin, you look pale?" Gabriel asked, peering into his face.

Ben swallowed hard and then nodded. "I'll be fine," he said, his voice unsteady. He coughed and in a stronger tone continued, "Come on, let's get on with it." He pushed past Gabriel and followed Tobias outside.

It was the dead of night now, some time after the taverns had closed, but long before the most dedicated churchgoers would rise for matins. As such the city was quiet and dark and as they rushed through Ludgate, across St Paul's Churchyard to Watling Street, they passed no one. At first they saw no sign

124

of the fire so allowed themselves to be guided by the distant sound of the bells, which were now growing in number as the lonely voice of the one church's peal was joined by others further afield, all ringing out the alarm. Even so, the noise still seemed very distant and the sounds of Gabriel wheezing slightly, as well as the clatter of their shoes on the street, were far louder in Ben's ears.

For a while, as they passed the dark shape of All Hallows Church, the mood of the city about them appeared calm and tranquil and yet it seemed to Ben that a sudden tension had sprung into the air: impalpable and invisible, but there. It was as though London were holding its breath, waiting for something extraordinary, something magnificent - or something horrific - to happen.

'CLANG!' The sudden sound made Ben jump. It rang out from a church tower only yards away and as the noise of the bell reverberated around them a flurry of startled pigeons soared from their roost into the starlit sky.

"Good Lord, that thing scared me half to death!" Gabriel exclaimed in fright, clutching at his chest and shouting

Like a wave passing across still water, the sound of pealing bells rippled outwards in a rapidly expanding circle and now the city was in uproar. As the alarm calls spread to still more churches, people started spilling out of their houses, befuddled, afraid; looking around them, some still in their nightgowns; some crying out in fear, others dashing back indoors to rouse their children and gather belongings.

Pushing through the press, Gabriel in the lead with Ben and Tobias at his heels, they ran along a lengthy curve of the road and emerged at last on Cannon Street. In the same instant, as the road straightened out, all three of them stopped running and gaped at the sight now revealed to them.

"Oh, my God!" Tobias cried, "Will you look at that!"

They did look and Ben let out an involuntary shout of fear. The memory of the fire that killed his parents was vague and dim in his mind, but nevertheless disturbing - and that had been just the one house. Some two hundred yards ahead of them, at least thirty houses were ablaze. Bright yellow and orange flames stabbed up at the night sky, their light reflecting off the clouds of smoke and hanging above the devastation as an angry red glow. Even at this distance they could hear the roar of the fire and the crackling and splintering of timbers.

Ben put his hands over his ears to shut out the terrible sounds that filled him with blind panic. Concerned, Gabriel turned to him, "Are you sure you'll be all right? You look terrible."

Gasping for breath, his throat tight with fear, Ben managed to nod, and not wanting to discuss the cause of his anxiety further he started off towards the fire. Gabriel and Tobias leapt after him. The glow in the night sky was spreading with every minute and it soon became apparent that this was no small fire, but a blaze that was a serious threat to the city. It was also obvious that Ben and his companions were not the only ones to have realised this. Streets that not long before had been empty were suddenly – and chaotically – alive with people.

"Look out!" came the words of warning and just in time Ben jumped out of the road as a wagon appeared out of the gloom to their rear and hurtled by them, bouncing up and down on the uneven road surface, as the driver used his whip to urge the sweating, terrified pair of blinkered horses on towards the fire. Ahead of them, half a dozen members of the trained band, carrying fire hooks and preparing to use them to pull down houses nearby, were blowing whistles to summon more militia to the scene.

"Move over, coming through!"

Another warning: this time from up ahead at a road junction. Travelling at a more sedate pace, a cart turned towards them from out of Fish Street, swerved around Gabriel and Tobias, and rattled on past Ben. This one was carrying boxes and chests and was piled high with bedding, a rolled up rug and half a dozen chairs. Husband and wife were up front, the latter cradling her sleeping baby, while five other children and an elderly grandparent were perched anywhere they could find in the cart. Two of the youngest children turned their soot-stained faces to the fire and gazed at it through tear-filled eyes. While Ben was watching the cart, the dwellings on either side of the road where he stood emptied of their occupants, who now streamed out onto the street and milled around in confusion. Everywhere he looked, the scene was being repeated and all the while the blaze was gaining in ferocity.

"Fire!" an old crone cried, pointing with her walking stick and rather stating the obvious.

"Fetch the Mayor!" her husband called.

"He's no bloody use," answered a neighbour, dressed in striped bed socks, shirt and nightcap. "Turned up a while back and took one look at the fire then said that a woman could put it out by pissing on it, and went back to bed. Bloody fool: anyone can see this one's a big 'un."

"It certainly is a 'big 'un'," Ben muttered to Gabriel as they crossed the road junction and saw the blaze more clearly. Flames leapt up from houses lining a lane just behind Fish Street, silhouetting the dwellings that stood on the main road. Smoke ascended in spiralling columns, coalescing into a dense cloud that blotted out the night sky for hundreds of yards around. Ash rose with the smoke and then fell like rain in all directions. The acrid smell of burning tar and the shower of ash polluted the air, which now stuck in Ben's throat, choking him. He coughed and then spat out phlegm. Next to him Gabriel was wheezing more now, as smoke clogged his lungs.

"Are you sure you'll be all right?" Ben asked, echoing Gabriel's earlier question to him. The bookseller seemed to have weak lungs and was obviously struggling with his breathing, but he just nodded and moved onwards.

There was no direct route through to the flames from where they stood, so they carried on along East Cheap looking for access to the lane that was the heart of the fire. A hundred yards further on, they reached the top end and peered down it the heat now searing their faces.

"Where are we?" Ben asked Gabriel.

"Top of Pudding Lane," gasped the bookseller, leaning one hand against a wall while he caught his breath.

Next to them, the bells in the church of St Leonard at the top of the lane were still pealing a desperate plea for help, but further down, those of St Margaret's had fallen silent forever: one of the first to be engulfed by flames, the old church had perished. The dwellings in the city were for the most part built of wood and the long days of summer had dried even the dampest of timbers. Like logs set aside for a Guy Fawkes bonfire, the houses were ready-made funeral pyres just waiting for a spark, such as those now flying up the street and, like a tinderbox, igniting the buildings all around them.

The local people were trying desperately to fight the fire, but for every man or woman with a bucket there were four or five who had chosen to empty their houses and run away. It was a hopeless fight and, with apparent contempt for the efforts to extinguish it, the fire moved on to destroy another house and then another: indifferent to the tears of their owners, it was like a living thing, venomous and spiteful.

Ben spotted a group who were not fighting fire but were huddled in an alleyway running off Pudding Lane to the east. His eyes widened with recognition as he saw Artemas and Matthias staring across the lane towards a building that had now all but burnt to the ground. As Ben watched in horror the roof collapsed and fell crashing down into the flames. Doubling over, he gasped as in a momentary flash of memory he saw his own parents' house tumble to the ground.

Artemas seemed unperturbed by the destruction; quite the contrary, he was laughing. Ben could hardly believe what he was seeing. A surge of anger rose in him so strong it obliterated both the memory and his fear. With his anger came the conviction: *'Gabriel was right; Artemas did start the fire!'*

He was about to warn Gabriel and Tobias, when the Cavalier happened to glance up the lane and his gaze fell upon Ben. For an instant his face froze in recognition and he stood perfectly still, as though contemplating what to do about him, but then Artemas relaxed and smiled, raising his hand to point at something behind Ben and his companions.

Swinging round, Ben saw Captain Gymer and his men standing at the top of the lane, wearing expressions more appropriate to the farmer who has just caught a fox in his chicken coop.

"Well now, this is interesting, Doctor Janssen," Gymer said, "How very kind of you. How so you ask? Well I will tell you. There was I with no evidence against you and here you are returned to the scene of the crime, so to speak. I must congratulate you on the scheme. What better way to disturb our war efforts against your Dutch masters than to burn down our capital city, eh?"

Tobias and Gabriel turned to face Clarendon's agent. "What on earth are you talking about, Gymer? We heard the church bells ringing just like half of London and came to see what was going on." Tobias stepped towards him bristling with indignation, but Gymer wasn't impressed and shaking his head he stood his ground.

"No, that does not quite ring true I am afraid." Laughing at his own pun he turned to see if his men appreciated the joke, as if he had all the time in the world; as if there was no fire raging a short distance away and hoards of milling, screaming people rushing past.

"No, Doctor," he continued, "there you were in your very comfortable house and you expect me to believe you ran across the city at the sound of the alarm for purely altruistic reasons? I find that hard to accept," Gymer moved closer, his now grim face reflecting the dancing flames behind Tobias. "And what I find hard to believe I naturally suspect. It is a time of war and an emergency is going on in our city. Would the King object, do you suppose, if I shot you here and now?" His face broke into a smile again and he added, "I can apologise later if I am wrong."

As he was speaking something about the gleeful expression on Artemas' face clicked into place in Ben's brain. He shot a glance towards Gabriel, desperate to voice his growing suspicion that it was the Cavalier and not the King who was behind this man's activities and that they'd been set up. But if that was so, was it best to go along with it for now? Hesitating with indecision, Ben's thoughts were interrupted by Spencer.

"Captain, I think we should take them in for questioning and find out who they are working for," he suggested in his squeaky, high-pitched voice. "We can shoot them afterwards if you like." Marlowe nodded in silent agreement while Walton said nothing either way, but studied the fire-fighters with apparent indifference to their fate.

"Yes, you are probably right," Gymer said with a touch of reluctance. "Well gentlemen, it appears at least some of my lads wish for your company a little longer. You will accompany us to White Hall."

"Gymer, you fool," Ben blurted out, his anger getting the better of him. Trembling with pent up frustration he pointed down the lane at the alleyway, "As you know full well it's not us who started the fire, its Artemas and Matthias there!"

Hearing Artemas' name, Tobias gave a shout of rage and dived towards the passage, pulling out a pistol as he did so. He stopped abruptly; looked back at Ben, uncertain.

"The good doctor appears as puzzled as I am," Gymer said. "So where are these phantom arsonists then, boy?"

Ben looked again. The alleyway entrance was empty. Maybe, though, the *Liberati* had merely withdrawn out of sight. With that thought, Ben moved towards the alleyway himself, craning his neck to look round the corner.

"Both of you will stop right there and turn around slowly," ordered Gymer, "and you, Doctor, will drop that pistol to the ground and-"

He never completed the sentence. With a boom louder than thunder and a flash brighter than lightning, there was a sudden violent uprising of the street for fifty yards in all directions. Everyone in the immediate vicinity was knocked off his feet and stunned by the force of the detonation.

Ben could see nothing but blackness, nor hear a sound and for a moment he thought Gabriel had used his flash-bang attack again, though this time the smell was different: a pungent, acrid stench that caught in his throat and made him cough and retch at the same time. Finally, his vision began to clear and blinking he looked about him. To his side Tobias was pulling himself to his feet and clearing dust from his eyes. Gabriel was lying on his back and groaning. Gymer appeared to be knocked out and his three companions were staring blankly about them. Walton was the first to recover. He took a few steps towards the source of the explosion, his dark eyes wide and agitated. Still numb, Ben turned to follow his gaze.

The cracked and blackened cobbles of the street about ten yards from where Ben stood suddenly exploded upwards, sending chunks of stone high up into the air, from where they came spinning back to earth to smash into fragments on the street. One hit Walton on the shin and with a yelp of pain he collapsed again.

The eruption had thrown up a cloud of dust and released thick fumes from the cellars beneath the street. As a result, Ben could not see much for a few moments, but gradually the dust cloud settled and the smoke dispersed to join the black clouds given off by the fires around them. Through this smog, Ben perceived a dark shape standing in the lane. It was indistinct and hazy at first but, as visibility improved, its features came sharply into view. As he saw the horror revealed, Ben stepped back and cried out in terror.

Seven feet tall, the creature stood upright on two legs, but otherwise was utterly inhuman in appearance. Ben saw that its limbs, thorax and abdomen were covered in a hideous black-green external skeleton, much like an insect or spider. Behind it flapped bat-like wings, the skin stretched between thick ridges of bone that ended in long sharp spines. Its monstrous head bore needle-sharp teeth that were black, as was the tongue, which now flicked in and out. Its jaws were open and from them a brown liquid drooled and dripped on to the ground. Pale, pupil-less eyes gazed around the lane and fixed themselves upon Ben. From its mouth an ear-piercing screech emerged as it advanced upon him, claws snapping open as the beast prepared to attack.

Numb with shock and disbelief, Ben was rooted to the spot. As the creature took three steps towards him he knew he should run, but was incapable of movement. Then, from the alleyway behind Ben, Artemas barked out three words at the creature and it paused before giving another screech, which this time sounded like frustrated anger. Artemas spoke again and the creature tilted its head as if in acknowledgment. It threw Ben a hungry glare and then, with a single leap and beat of its wings, it passed over his head and landed at the entrance to the alleyway.

Gabriel was suddenly at Ben's side and was rapidly reciting Words of Power and spinning his hands about each other until at last he had what seemed to be a ball of spitting, fizzing energy. With a grunt of effort, he threw it at the creature.

Artemas pointed his finger at the missile and just as rapidly swung his arm in an arc. A shimmering disc of pale blue light appeared in front of the beast and with an ear-splintering boom the ball of energy shattered on the disc and dispersed into a huge cloud of smoke.

When the smoke cleared both the creature and Artemas were gone. Ben became aware of terrified shrieks in the distance from those who had not been concussed by the explosion and had caught a glimpse of it. Around them the fire continued to rage.

"Was ... was that Dantalion?" Ben croaked.

Gabriel shook his head. "No, that was an avatar. It is a projection of the demon's will. He is propelling his mind into the world through the breach left by the destruction of the first seal. We still have a little time while the other five seals are intact before the *Liberati* can free the demon. But we can't stand here talking about it. We have to get away before Gymer and his men recover. Come on Tobias," he added taking the doctor by the arm.

The doctor's eyes were wide and his face pale. His legs were trembling and he was holding his pistol so tightly that his hand was shaking. "What in God's name just happened? That creature ... your hands ... those words you spoke ... what is going on?" he muttered, staring about him with unfocused eyes.

"Not now, Tobias, we can talk later. Come on, Benjamin, move," Gabriel shouted over his shoulder.

The three of them scuttled past Gymer, who was groaning and starting to come round. Nearby, Walton was moaning about his shin, holding it in both hands, his face creased with pain. He seemed oblivious to them, as did Marlowe and Spencer, who were staring blankly about them; neither reacted as Gabriel led Ben and Tobias at a run away from the scene, pushing their way through the panic stricken crowds.

They reached the top of the lane and turned along East Cheap in the direction of Cannon Street. The fire had already reached there and Gabriel headed on up towards Cornhill to avoid it. As they ran Ben looked quickly behind and was relieved to see no one was following. A few yards further on he glanced back again; this time he thought he saw something move in the deeper shadows cast by the fire. The shape seemed to duck back as he stared at it. He blinked, straining his eyes to see, but whatever it was, it had gone and Ben dismissed it as a trick of the light.

"Where are we going?" he panted to Gabriel, but the bookseller did not answer. They pushed past another cart stacked high with chests and furniture. On the back of the cart two scared children sat and stared back at him. A little girl, perhaps about three, was crying and her brother put his arm round her and held her. The expression on his face was bleak. Ben wondered if they should all turn back and help fight the fire. He suggested this course of action, but Gabriel shook his head.

"The fire is a possible danger to the city, but Dantalion is a certain and more terrible danger to the world. If he gets free the destruction of one city will seem trivial, believe me. There are one hundred thousand people within a mile of where we stand. Any of them can fight the fire and three more won't make any difference to that, but three of us might prevent Dantalion from rising."

Ben could not see how, but he repeated his original question. "Where are we going?"

This time Gabriel stopped and turned to look at him. Tobias, his face still showing shock and disbelief, tottered to a halt behind him.

"I don't know," Gabriel admitted with a shrug, "Both Gymer and Artemas know where all three of us live or can find out easily enough in the morning. We need a place to hide and think, away from both of them. Any ideas?"

"I can suggest a place," said a familiar voice from behind them.

"Freya! I knew I'd seen something," Ben laughed with relief. "It was you." The thief was standing there bold as brass, right in front of his eyes, a fresh layer of soot now mixing with the dirt on her face and clothes.

"Although it's a bit basic compared to the Doc's place." She gave Ben a weak smile, "Yes, it was me."

Tobias glanced at her vaguely and then a moment later his eyes widened in recognition. "Oh, my girl, I am sorry if I put you in danger, I didn't think I had. Then again, I didn't believe what Gabriel had said about demons, but now I have seen that monster, I realise I should not have suggested stealing that scroll ..." he tailed off again and stared at her. He seemed utterly confused and unusually timid.

"What's his problem, then?" Freya asked of the other two, with a jerk of her thumb towards the doctor.

"Oh, we just saw a demon and it came as a bit of a shock," Ben said.

"Well I had one in my head, so top that!" Freya said cheerfully, but Ben saw the smile fade fast and knew she was putting on a brave face.

"Hmm; what with demons and stolen scrolls," Gabriel said, emphasising the last bit with a stare at Freya, "it does seem that we have a lot to talk about. But first we must get somewhere off the streets and away from the fire."

"I have a loft. It's over stables up near Cripplegate, if that's any good to you," Freya said, adding, "assuming the fire doesn't reach that far. And if it does we might as well throw ourselves in the Thames."

"God forbid! Stables sounds good, let's go," muttered Tobias, shivering. Gabriel nodded and they started to walk quickly northwards as a feeling of gloom descended upon them.

"You know, I skipped school today to find something more interesting to do," Ben murmured as they walked along. "All this makes me wish I'd gone to that Latin lesson now."

Gabriel let out a humourless bark of laughter, "Yes, it's all turning out a bit grim, isn't it? My secret society, which has for three hundred years protected the seals that keep a dangerous demon imprisoned under the city, today failed in that duty and the first seal is destroyed."

"The King's agent and his gang think I am a master conspirator working for an enemy government," muttered Tobias, "and the man who killed my father is still out there."

"And my bloody city is on fire and earlier a horrible demon was inside my head," Freya said.

"So then," Ben mused, grinning despite himself; "what shall we do tomorrow?"

Chapter 12
Nightmares

London, Sunday 2nd September, 1666: dawn

"*B*en! Ben you must wake up!" *The voice sounded strained and agitated. Groggy with sleep Ben was aware of the door to his room being flung open. A figure stood there silhouetted against a red and yellow glow. The smell of burning caught in his nostrils. He struggled to sit up, staring around him, blinking in confusion as he recognised his mother. Eyes wide with panic she was rushing towards him. He felt her fingers close around his arm and tug.'*

"Wha ... wha ... what is it?" he stammered as she stood over him.

"It's a fire, lad. The house is on fire, come on," she said again, "we must get out."

"Fire ... but I ... how?" he said as he tumbled to his feet.

"Come on, Ben! There is no time ... you must get to the window quickly," she insisted, pulling him by the hand. She opened the shutters and leant out to look below. Ben looked down as well, and saw a number of men there, struggling to contain the fire that was now consuming the ground floor of his house. As he watched them, he felt something being tied round his waist. Was it a rope or a sheet? In the confusion he was not sure. He tried to move, to protest, but his legs were like lumps of lead and his head was filled with smoke. He became aware of someone else in the room: his father now stood beside

137

him, the other end of a rope in his hands. Urging him to hasten, both parents gazed at him, the calm assurance of their love holding back his rising panic.

"We can't get down the stairs, son, so I am going to lower you gently," his father was saying, "you'll be all right."

"Father, I must tell you something," Ben said suddenly, but his mother let out a gasp of fright and Ben saw that smoke was pouring into the room and that the flickering of flames had now reached his doorway. His father saw this too and shook his head.

"There is no time now. You must get down and we will follow. You can tell me later, whatever it is."

His father pushed him to the window and, before he knew what was happening, Ben had climbed over the sill and was being lowered towards the cluster of figures below. Suddenly, overhead there was a roar and a boom and flames erupted out of the window. He heard a cry and then, without warning, the rope was let go and he tumbled the dozen feet to the ground thumping his head hard on a stone.

"Ben! Ben!" he heard his mother scream above him.

"Mother! Father!" he screamed back, and then once again, "Ma!"

There was no answer, just the angry roaring of fire: the last sound he heard as darkness overtook him.

****

"Ben! Ben wake up!" said a familiar voice, but now sounding distant: a voice from a different time and another place. He opened his eyes and lay for a moment staring at the dark roof above him, wondering where he was and what had disturbed him.

"Ben?" the voice said, louder now. "Are you all right?"

He came fully awake and sat up, staring wildly around him.

"Ben, it's all right," Freya said, "you were dreaming that's all. You kept screaming and tossing about."

He stared at her for a long moment until, all at once, everything came into focus: the dark loft above the stable, light from the early hint of dawn seeping through the gaps in the roof; the smell of horses through the trap door below and the snoring of Tobias next to him on the straw.

"Freya?" he said. "Sorry; I had a dream."

"More like a nightmare I would say," Gabriel muttered from a corner of the loft where he was sitting on a sack of oats, smoking a pipe and watching Ben, who nodded.

"I was dreaming of the night my parents died in a fire," he paused, screwing up his face, shaking his head. "It's odd because I can hardly recall it when I am awake, although it was only six months ago. They say I must have bumped my head in the fall. Every so often I get a flashback, but this dream was so vivid," Ben ran his fingers through his hair. "I guess ... I guess it was the fire last night. It brought it all back." He gulped hard; inside he felt all twisted and knotted up.

"You can tell us about it if you want," Gabriel said, leaning forward.

Irritated by the avid curiosity sparking in the bookseller's eyes, Ben's usual anger surged back blocking out the pain. "Mind your own business: why should I tell you anything!" he shouted.

Sliding off the sack, Gabriel stepped quickly towards him and laid a hand on Ben's own, "Benjamin, it's all right, lad. There is no need to be afraid: there is no fire here today. As for the one we saw last night, well fires are two a penny in London. By now I imagine it should have been put out."

"I'm not afraid. I had a bad dream, that's all. Ben shook off Gabriel's hand, "What time is it?" he asked, turning away and wanting to change the subject.

"A little while before seven I would say," Gabriel answered, leaving Ben and picking his way through the straw to the shuttered window at the end of the loft, brushing bits off his robe as he went.

"Anything for breakfast?" Ben looked hopefully at Freya.

She turned her mouth down and shook her head. "No; sorry."

"I will buy us some food in a while when there is some place open," Gabriel said over his shoulder, opening the shutters to peer outside. "They shouldn't be long. I'll take a look down the street ...," his voice sank to a whisper.

"What is it?" Ben asked, getting to his feet and walking over to look. From their elevated position they could see across the rooftops of the city to where, in the distance beyond row upon row of houses and past dozens of church spires, they could see a tall column of smoke climbing skyward from a blaze that very clearly was not yet extinguished. It was the best part of a mile from Freya's loft in Cripplegate to Pudding Lane where they had been last night, but the fire and smoke were clearly visible even so.

"It's still burning!" Ben gasped.

Half asleep, Tobias pushed himself onto his elbow and yawned, "You would have thought they would have had that out by now." He rolled off his makeshift mattress of straw and got to his feet. "Aren't they supposed to organise bucket chains, fire drills and so forth for these emergencies?"

"That only works if the people stay and fight the fire and if there is someone in charge who knows what they are doing. Even were that so, there is another factor." Gabriel said, stooping to pick up a handful of straw and throwing it in the air. Caught by a breeze it flew swiftly across the stable. "As I thought," he murmured, "the wind is strong and getting stronger, blowing north and west and spreading the fire. A cruel chance ... or *is* it chance, I wonder?"

Ben's eyes widened, "You mean *Dantalion's* affecting the wind?"

"Well, the avatar projecting Dantalion's will is, anyway," Gabriel said.

"You mentioned this avatar last night," said Tobias. "What did you mean by it?"

"I'd like to know more about that too," Ben nodded.

Freya looked from one to the other, "Avatar? What's that?"

Moving away from the window, Gabriel settled back down on his sack. Tapping the spent plug of tobacco out of his pipe onto the heel of his hand, he peered into the bowl then wiped his fingers on his breeches and slid the pipe into his pocket. He appeared to be lost in thought. In the stable beneath came the sounds of restless hooves, horses snorting and chomping hay. Ben sat down in the straw near to Gabriel's feet and waited, looking up at him. After a moment the other two followed suit and Gabriel, seeing their expectant faces, cleared his throat and began to speak.

"The demon is imprisoned beneath the city trapped by powerful sorcery and then also shielded by the seals. It cannot communicate with or reach our world. Now though, the first seal is gone and there is a window through which Dantalion can project a little of his will and power. It is enough to create weaker versions of himself in our city and he can use these to attack his enemies, maybe find the other seals or track down more knowledge about his prison. We must be cautious. I drove the avatar off last night, but it was weak then, having only just spawned. Its powers will grow with time and more so if the other seals are destroyed. We must assume Dantalion now knows where all the seals are."

"No, he doesn't," Freya contradicted. "You're wrong about that and you're wrong about him not being able to talk to folk here too. He can; he talked to me."

They all stared at her, mouths agape. Gabriel frowned, "What do you mean?"

"When I went to see Artemas about the scroll I'd, er, borrowed," she flashed a guilty look at Gabriel, "that stinking rat tricked me into putting my hand on this bloomin' great

141

book. Next thing I know I am somewhere else talking to this angel, only it wasn't an angel it was a demon and-"

"Hold on," Gabriel held up his hand to stop her in mid-flow, "slow down a minute. After you took the scroll – and by the way I want to talk to you about that matter later – what did you do? Tell us from the beginning."

Taking a deep breath, Freya told her story from the moment she had left Tobias' house until her escape from Artemas and Matthias near the bakery in the alley on Pudding Lane. "It wasn't easy with my hands tied, but they never thought to see if I had a knife," she gave a triumphant smile, "so after I got away I managed to cut through the rope and then I ran, and that's when I saw you, so I followed."

When she had finished, Gabriel was silent for many moments as he thought about Freya's story. Eventually he nodded and said, "So they do not know where the other seals are, but they do know they are mostly within the old city of London – the city within the walls. From what you are saying, Freya, you recalled that much from your glimpse of the map, but you only saw one of the locations clearly. We can assume, therefore, that it was the same for Dantalion, since it was your memory he was seeing. Searching for the others would take years, but they don't need to: intense fire will destroy the seals. Dantalion is aware of that, which is why Artemas torched the bakery. There has been no rain for months and with the scorching summers we've had, both this year and last, London is like a tinder box; the fire will burn intensely. With a strong enough wind the whole city will burn." Gabriel shook his head in despair, "And as I said, the wind is already strong and now I think the avatar is making it stronger."

There was a stunned silence until Tobias stood up and stretched, "So, you're saying that if we stop the fire we beat them, and we stop Dantalion rising? Then that's what we must do."

Everyone looked at him in surprise. He shrugged. "I owe you an apology, Gabriel. I did not sleep much last night. What I saw in Pudding Lane stunned me and I had to think about it. Finally I realise I was wrong: that much is obvious. Dantalion *does* exist and everything I thought was nonsense is true. If that is so, it changes things, doesn't it?" He looked around at them, but still no one said anything.

"My father: I thought he had died a fool believing in superstitious rubbish. I was angry at him for that. And at you, Gabriel, and all you damn zealots. You were right, I was obsessed: all I wanted was to kill Artemas, it was as though revenge was all I had to live for. Last night changed all that. I now know I was wrong; my father died a hero fighting for what he believed in to keep the city and the world safe."

He walked over to the window and stared out at the distant burning city for a moment before continuing. "I have to live with the guilt of how we parted, but I can make amends now. Oh, make no mistake, I still want to see Artemas dead, but I can do as you want me to, Gabriel. I can take over my father's role to protect this city from Dantalion and his kind. I can become *Praesidium*," he said with a sudden nod of decision and turned to look at Gabriel. "What must we do?"

Gabriel pulled out his pipe and stuck it between his teeth, chewing on the stem as he studied Tobias. At length he said, "Are you sure you want to do this? It will be dangerous."

"For the last year you have been trying to persuade me to take on my father's role when at the time I did not believe in Dantalion. Now that I know he exists and I am willing, you are suddenly hesitant. Why? It makes no sense."

"Things have become a lot more dangerous in the last twenty-four hours," Gabriel shrugged. "Last year I was trying to get you to help watch a few buildings – now there is a serious risk of having to fight a demon, and I am not sure you are fully aware of the danger. It will not be as easy as you make it sound; far from it."

Tobias laughed, "After last night I think we all are starting to get the idea! But what about the two young ones?" He pointed at Freya and Ben, "Perhaps they should get out of London and to safety. You and I have a reason to be here, but they don't."

Freya shook her head firmly. "Nothing doing, I've got nowhere else to go; aside from which this is *my* city and I'm not letting that misbegotten demon loose in it. Besides, I owe the bastard for getting into my head," she declared, punching her clenched fist into her palm to show she meant it.

"That's the spirit!" Ben grinned.

"Yes, well, if it weren't for me ..." she faltered, blushing.

"Stop looking so guilty, Freya," Ben chuckled, "it doesn't suit you."

"You don't understand," she muttered. "Matthias was right when he said I had given the demon what he needed to escape. It's all my fault and I've got to do something to put it right." An expression of surprise flitted across the little thief's face, as though she was taken aback by her own words.

Despite the seriousness of her confession, Ben couldn't help laughing at her. From what he knew of Freya she wasn't one to worry about her actions as a rule. "Then you'd best make amends by fighting the avatar singlehanded," he teased, "but get me some breakfast before you do, eh?"

For once Freya did not retaliate. She looked down at the straw, one finger toying with the frayed and filthy bandage that still clung to her head."

"Don't blame yourself entirely, Freya," Gabriel said. "Artemas is clever; he would have found a way with or without your help. It was wrong of you to take the scroll, but I know you were encouraged to do so," he shot a pointed look at Tobias.

Quickly changing the subject, his face flushing a dull red, Tobias gestured at Ben, "What about him? The boy should be at school."

"No," said Ben. Before he could say any more, Gabriel answered for him.

"No, Tobias. Benjamin is a direct descendant of Cornelius Silver and he looks to have inherited the man's talent with the Words of Power, those used to bind Dantalion and create the seals. From what Freya has told us, the demon senses some of this and Benjamin is in danger from Dantalion and his servants. We cannot send him away. On his own he would be at terrible risk. More than that, we need him; I think his talents must be used if we are to prevail."

Ben gave an emphatic nod agreeing with everything Gabriel had said. There was more, however, that he did not want to admit to. This new world of Words of Power and demons was frightening, but above all it was seductive, exciting and so very tempting. He felt it could fill the space inside him that was suffering: the space he poured his anger into to block out the pain caused by ... but no, he did not want to even think about that. He just knew he wanted the power and that was enough for now.

"I see," said Tobias. "Very well, what are we to do then?"

Stowing away his pipe again, Gabriel retrieved and opened his locket, took out the parchment and examined it. "Cornelius speaks of the seventh seal and its location being recorded in his journal, which I believe will be at Sir Robert de Windley's estate near Badersley Compton. The de Windleys still own the land and the house. We must go and get the journal from there and bring it back. However, we must also try to protect the seals here in London. Ben here has given me a list of their locations." He rummaged in his robes and retrieved the list, together with a blank piece of paper, a small corked bottle of ink and a quill, which he handed to Ben. "Would you make a copy for Tobias, please Benjamin?"

"What else do you keep in those robes, Gabriel?" Ben grinned at the bookseller, who tapped the side of his nose with his finger and winked. Everyone laughed; it was a welcome release of tension for them all.

"So we must divide our efforts," Tobias suggested, glancing at the list after Ben had blown the ink dry. Gabriel nodded.

"I suggest Ben and I go and get the journal and you two do everything you can to delay the destruction of the seals. It's a tall order, Tobias, but do the best you can. Freya: use your skill to follow Artemas' every move – but whatever happens, stay out of sight. Oh, and keep a look out for Captain Gymer too; he is on our trail. Ben and I will travel as quickly as we can. We will aim to return by tomorrow night and meet you back here. Does everyone agree?"

They all nodded.

"Good, let's begin then, and may God protect us."

"Amen to that," Ben muttered under his breath.

****

At the same moment, half a mile away in the Old Bull Tavern, Matthias and Artemas were having an argument. After withdrawing from the alleyway, having soundly berated the preacher for letting the girl escape, Artemas had called in the avatar and thrown a blanket around it to hide its appearance from anyone they passed. Even with the chaotic scenes on the streets and the distraction of the expanding fire, someone would surely have seen the creature and Artemas did not wish for that to happen; not yet. For just a little longer concealment was necessary.

They had pushed their way through the fleeing crowds and returned to the inn and then the three of them: Matthias,

Artemas and the avatar, had come into the locked chamber in which they kept the great book: 'The Tome of Dantalion'. As they entered the room, the avatar at once rushed over to it and stood in front of it with a posture and attitude the Cavalier could only describe as prayerful. The contrast to the bestial ferocity it had revealed in Pudding Lane was striking, and even the cynical Artemas could feel the reverence the beast was exhibiting now. Perhaps it was this that Matthias saw and which, in combination with his stubborn blind faith, enabled him to ignore the infernal appearance of the creature and see in it something holy. Something he now wanted to show the world.

"No, Matthias, not yet!" Artemas replied, fighting an urge to strike the fool. When Matthias voiced this thought, the Cavalier had been sitting in a chair near the fireplace examining the map on the scroll, trying to estimate how fast the fire would spread. He now jumped up, crossed the room in two strides and threw the scroll down on the table.

"We can't reveal the, ah ... messenger yet."

Matthias was standing beside the avatar, hands clasped in prayer. He now opened his eyes and cast a wild look at Artemas.

"But why not, Artemas? Surely the sinful and the lost should be given this one last chance to repent. Let us show them the angel's messenger and they will believe." He was preaching now, his arms raised, his body shaking with zealous fervour. "I will take him to the Royal Exchange and down Cornhill and Cheapside to show the unfaithful and the unbeliever what the Lord of Hosts has done this night. When they see him and see the holy fire we have unleashed, they will believe."

'*They would hang us, gut us and throw our bodies in the river,*' Artemas thought, staring at Matthias. Only a few hours ago the preacher had expressed doubts about starting the fire, and now the fool was again convinced they were doing God's will. It

147

always amazed Artemas how people found ways to justify their actions. Still, he did not care what the preacher thought, providing he did what was needed. Right now that meant staying out of sight until the seals were destroyed. London was paranoid enough with the war going on; the fire would only make that worse. Artemas could only imagine the effect it would have on people if they saw the avatar at a time like this! The thought of it brought a smile to his lips, but he had to keep the creature safe until there was no more need for secrecy. Yet, he still needed Matthias. He forced himself to calm down and then walked round the table to put a hand on the preacher's shoulder.

'Matthias, I too burn for the day when Dantalion is released," Artemas said, for once not lying, "but you must trust me. You know I work in all things to fulfil the Lord's will." Again no lie, he thought, it was just a matter of which lord you were speaking about.

The old preacher frowned. "Are you sure we should not bear witness to Dantalion's gift to us?"

"We will very soon, I promise you. Come, let us talk to the angel and he will give us our instructions," Artemas pointed at the Tome. Matthias nodded and they both reached over and touched the book.

Even now Artemas did not fully understand all the secrets of the ancient artefact he and the preacher used to communicate with Dantalion, but he appreciated that in some way the demon and this book were linked. The book provided a channel or portal through the seals the Praesidium had created, and on into the mind of its master. Within the prison Cornelius Silver had made, Dantalion was able to create whole illusory worlds in which to reside. Yet, he always met Matthias in the blissful woodland glade beside the stream and always in the form of the angel: tall, beautiful and magnificent. Matthias as ever fell to the ground in reverence.

"You have done well," Dantalion said to the kneeling preacher, who looked up at the angel in surprise.

"Yes, I know what has occurred, Matthias," Dantalion said in response. "Now that the first seal is destroyed I can witness what you do through the messenger. I am pleased, but there is still work to be done. Once light returns in the morning, you must take him to the river and he will call in a powerful wind to fan the flames. The wind will blow and the fire will spread and one by one the seals will be consumed and soon – oh so very soon now – it will be time for my rising."

"I pray each day for that moment, Lord," Matthias said, his eyes bright with joy.

"You will not wait long now, beloved servant: but I need you to be patient. I will entrust the messenger to you, but you must keep its identity secret for a little longer. Will you do that for me?"

His chest puffed out with pride Matthias nodded eagerly, "Of course, my Lord!"

Dantalion smiled at him and the preacher gazed back in adoration.

"Now, go and sleep, Matthias. You have earned a few hours' rest. I must tell Artemas of another task I need him to do when morning comes."

Matthias hesitated, looked sharply at the Cavalier and for a moment a hint of jealousy flashed across his face, as though he was about to ask why Artemas spent more time in the presence of the Lord Dantalion than he did, but after a moment he shrugged, bowed his head, and was gone.

As soon as the preacher had departed, Dantalion turned to look at Artemas and as he did so his appearance altered. His body grew in size and height, his skin tone changed and became a red-brown colour, teeth gaining a razor sharp edge and nails elongating into talons. In moments, Dantalion, the Great demon Lord, stood before the Cavalier. Artemas bowed and then looked around him at the glade, which was altering rapidly as he watched. The trees erupted into flames and fell into heaps of ash. The stream boiled away in clouds of steam that then evaporated into the sky above them: a sky that was changing from bright clear blue to a dirty, smoke-filled brown. Artemas staggered slightly as, with a surge, the land on which the pair stood rose up as a pillar of rock. The pillar altered shape and expanded about them, gaining definition and form until, at last, they stood on the top of St Paul's Cathedral looking down on the city of London and the fire, which was presently consuming the area around Pudding Lane. In the real world outside this illusion, the avatar was witnessing the scenes and the demon was seeing them through its eyes and recreating the images here.

"Soon, Artemas, soon I will be released. See the pathetic city burn below us. That fool preacher talks of serving his God! See what I have done. Imagine the wrath I will pour on this city. Let me show you what I will do when I am free."

Dantalion spread out his arms and roared like a wild animal. He then held out one clawed hand and a ball of fire appeared in it. He threw it far across the city so that it slammed hard into the Tower of London, a mile away on the far side of London Bridge. The fire detonated the barrels of gunpowder stored there and the whole building erupted in a devastating explosion, leaving a huge crater where the ancient fort had stood. Dantalion now turned his head to look at the River Thames. Boats and ferry craft plied the water, rescuing the citizens and taking them to safety. The beast laughed and he threw another ball, this time at the river. It passed over five river craft, incinerating them all instantly, and slammed into a large transport crammed with refugees. These now screamed as the ship burst into flames and men, women and children threw themselves into the water, many on fire themselves. Some never made it but were dragged down along with the sinking

150

vessel to drown in the filthy water. From the air, there came a terrible screeching cry and there, in full flight, was an avatar. It bowed at Dantalion and then swooped down over the rooftops to water level, seized in its claws a screaming man, plucking him out of the river and climbing high into the sky before letting him fall a thousand feet to his death.

Again Dantalion roared and from his open mouth a huge, cone-shaped plume of flame burst forth. Like a dragon from mythology he breathed fire across the stricken city blasting away hundreds of houses in a moment. Turning to Artemas, the demon appeared even more massive, more terrifying.

Shaking in awe, the Cavalier dropped to his knees and bowed deeply in worship. This was not the worship a weak fool like Matthias would understand. The preacher adored the purity and holiness he saw in the 'Angel Dantalion'. Artemas knew it was all a sham. He saw the truth and worshipped the power and strength of evil that stood before him. "Lord," he murmured, "I am yours to command."

"Am I not a god, Artemas?" Dantalion asked and the kneeling figure nodded.

"Yes, Master."

"Then stand by me now," Dantalion ordered.

Artemas got up from his knees and looked down on the city. From up here he felt like a god himself. He revelled in the power he felt when he was alone with Dantalion. Just a few more days now and the power would be real. They stood for a while enjoying the devastation below.

After a moment the beast frowned and turned to his lieutenant. "Matthias seems to be asking too many questions. I can sense our control is not as strong as it was earlier. Are you quite certain his beliefs and zeal will not harm me?"

"It will be fine, Lord. He will do what we need for more days yet." Artemas pursed his lips, "We don't need him for much longer."

Dantalion fixed Artemas with a piercing gaze, which as ever dug down through the layers of the Cavalier's mind, painfully stripping away his deceptions and lies. He knew the demon was reading his thoughts and was aware how ruthless he could be, and nevertheless still used him despite - or maybe because of - that ruthlessness.

Today, Dantalion seemed satisfied and he grunted and dropped his gaze. "Very well, Artemas. But be aware that my kind does not take failure well. There is little forgiveness in me." As he spoke, fire flared again in his eyes. Artemas nodded fearfully and the demon smiled. "Good. Now, I must instruct you what to do next. The six seals will fall to the inferno. Now the avatar has come it will be no ordinary fire; mere water and sand will not extinguish it. The intense blaze will incinerate this rat-infested city. What I have shown you is how it will be within hours."

With a snap of his talons, Dantalion stopped the illusion so that what they saw below them was an image of the city as it was now. They both looked again at the panorama of London spread out before them. The damage thus far was trivial compared to what Dantalion dreamed he would do. Yet, as they watched, to the south of them, a spray of molten ash was flung into the air to the west of Fish Street and then arched up high to be carried by a sudden gust of wind over three more streets. Sparks fell upon a church spire where hungry flames soon appeared and moved rapidly down to the body of the holy place. Dantalion smiled as he watched and, sighing in contentment, stood for a long moment watching the fire gut the church. When it was done he turned back to face Artemas, a lust for destruction shining in his eyes.

"There is more that must be done," the demon spoke at last. "We need to find the Last Seal. We need the journal of Cornelius Silver and thanks to the memories of that girl thief we know where it is to be found. You will take men you can trust, find it and bring it to me. Ride with haste, as soon as you can in the morning."

Artemas nodded then a question occurred to him. "Lord, even with the journal and the location of the Last Seal, we still cannot destroy your prison. From what we saw and heard, the parchment in Gabriel's possession speaks of words that are needed to free you, but it seems there is no way of discovering what they are. What are we to do?"

Dantalion laughed and as he did so the ground trembled, the city around them shook and Artemas, despite knowing it was just an illusion, cried out in fear and held on to the tower. In a moment the laughter and the shaking subsided and Dantalion turned to his ashen-faced lieutenant. "Listen carefully, and I will tell you how to find the words that will free me forever."

And as he did so, Artemas' fear fell away and he smiled.

Chapter 13
London Bridge

London, Sunday 2nd September, 1666: early morning

"The de Windley's estate is just outside Badersley Compton, which is a village twenty or so miles to the south. We will have to cross the river and then try to get a horse or a coach if we are to get there and back as quickly as we can," Gabriel said. He had gone out as promised and purchased some bread to eat and beer to drink and now the four of them were sitting above the stables, eating breakfast and making plans.

"Why not 'borrow' a couple of horses from the stable?" Freya suggested.

"No, I don't think so," Gabriel frowned. "Don't want to start a hue and a cry by stealing horses. We need to avoid trouble with the Watch – we can't afford any delays."

Freya looked thoughtful. "Then, you must leave at once," she said. "The fire cannot be far from the bridge and that will be the easiest way across the river. Otherwise you will have to go by boat. I think Tobias and I should come with you as far as the bridge. I can find a way quickly through the streets avoiding the traffic and the people."

"I'm not so sure." Gabriel frowned. "Gymer is still looking for us all and Tobias is the man he has latched on to out of all of us. We can't afford to run into him – there would be too many questions we can't answer."

"I know some very narrow passageways most folk don't know exist. I will get you to the river all right, with a lot more chance of remaining hidden than you lot blundering along the main roads," Freya insisted and with such an intense, indignant glare at Gabriel that he just held up his hands and nodded. He turned and made his way to the ladder and climbed down to the ground floor. Ben picked up his satchel and followed, the others bringing up the rear.

With a reluctant glance at the horses, Freya set off at a run. The little thief hadn't been lying: she was familiar with routes none of the others had known existed. In the heart of the great city they zigzagged through alleyways and scuttled along gloomy passages, barely encountering a main road as they crossed London. It was still early, only just past dawn and it was odd to think that all around them a hundred thousand souls slept on, most as yet ignorant of the blaze in the south of the city and the demon that threatened their lives; unaware too of the group of four desperate people, who fled past their homes racing the fire to London Bridge. After only a few minutes, Ben had lost all sense of direction as he hurried along behind Freya, but the girl navigated the route without pause or hesitation.

Eventually they emerged on Thames Street. Looking east along it towards Pudding Lane, they froze in their tracks as they gazed upon a scene of utter chaos. Pudding Lane and Fish Street were lost in the fury of flames that rose a hundred feet skyward, vomiting up great plumes of smoke and ash. The blaze, though still two hundred yards distant, was moving west towards them on either side of the street, throwing the inhabitants into frantic activity. Some were stacking carts high

156

with their belongings and pushing them up Thames Street. Others were running down the alleyways to the river, filling buckets and bringing them back to fling at the fire before returning for more. Still more were preparing to use great long fire hooks to pull down the timbered houses that lay in the fire's path, in an attempt to stall or halt its spread, but the residents of each house argued bitterly against this latter course until they realised their own houses were aflame and that it was now too late. On this Sunday morning there appeared to be no trace of any organisation, no leadership and no strategy for fighting the fire.

"So much for fire drills and bucket chains, eh Tobias?" Freya muttered.

He nodded glumly. "Should we help, do you think?"

Gabriel shook his head firmly just as he had the previous night. "This will be as nothing if we can't stop Dantalion. We must go on."

Freya led them quickly across the street and they plunged into another cut-through. Ben saw the name painted on the corner of a house: Black Raven Alley. It connected with a tiny courtyard off which a dozen doorways led to pathetic wooden shanties and shacks, where lived the poorest of the city, a score or more souls crammed into each house. Freya glanced at them as she passed. She was poor indeed, but her loft was not so bad compared to these terrible places. Further west was a similar courtyard where she had lived with her mother and where the plague had spread as it had here, wiping out whole families in a few days. When she escaped the prison her house had become, she had quickly left the narrow passageways, craving the solitude and space her loft now gave her. She smiled slightly to herself: the fact it was rent-free helped too. Its previous occupant had died in the plague and the innkeeper who owned it allowed her to live there in return for sweeping out the yard each week. It was a mutually beneficial arrangement.

She turned to make sure everyone was still following and noticed that Ben had dropped back. "Hurry up, rich boy," she called, "stop gawping!"

Ben had slowed down to stare at the rat-infested warrens they passed by: that people could live in such places beggared belief. Before it was destroyed by fire, his parents' house could have swallowed ten of these hovels, as could his uncle's. Even his room at Westminster, sparse as it was, seemed like a palace compared to this place. At Freya's call, he looked up, gave a quick wave and put on a spurt to catch up. They moved on down the alleys until they finally emerged breathless on the waterfront. Ben let out a deep breath, unaware he had been holding it in.

Despite the early hour, the river was already busy with boats and barges, ferrying Londoners and their belongings to Southwark on the far side. Some of those who owned warehouses along the river, worried about the approaching fire, were opening the doors and dragging out barrels and crates, trying to find passage for them on boats to get them away from the flames.

"This way: quickly," Freya shouted and turned east along the waterfront. They passed the Old Swan Tavern and the huge stone-fronted Fishmongers' Hall, after which they could finally see the northern end of London Bridge.

"Oh snoggers!" Freya gasped, one hand moving up to cover her mouth. The other hand was shaking as she pointed at the bridge. "Look! We're too late!"

The other three joined her and they all stared in horror. London Bridge had been a wonder to behold when Ben had first laid eyes upon it, arriving at the school four years ago. The bridge was like nothing he had seen before. Made of stone, with a dozen and more arches, it was impressive enough, but upon it an entire town had been built. Dozens of houses, shops and taverns of timber and stone crammed upon either side and soared three or more stories high. At either end was a fortress-like gatehouse that was locked at dusk and opened each dawn. The southern gate bore a grizzly display of the severed heads of more than a dozen criminals and traitors which, after their execution, were impaled on spikes as a warning to all who saw them. That gatehouse was still untouched on the far side of the river, but here, on the north side, its twin had been incinerated and all the buildings, some thirty or more houses, had fallen into the river. The fire had died out before it could cross further, saving the rest of the bridge and the city south of the river, but that didn't help Ben and his companions.

Dismayed, Ben surveyed the devastation. The fire must have surged down Fish Street while they slept, and now, as Freya had grimly pointed out, they were too late: it had cut off their means of passage to the south. He looked back at the billowing clouds of smoke, quick to realise why the fire had progressed only halfway across the bridge before dying down: the wind had changed direction and was now blowing strongly west and north, driving the fire away from the bridge and along Thames Street, through the small alleyways and passages, such as those Ben and his friends had come through just a few minutes before. What he also saw was that the fire, in its full terrifying fury, was already surging past them.

"Oh God!" Ben shrieked, as only yards away the flames drew level to where they stood, destroying forever the shanty town of the poor and breaking with avarice into the first of the great trade halls. Ben's throat tightened with fear and – panicking now – he screamed, "My God, the fire is moving too fast, we're going to get cut off!"

A determined look sprang into Freya's face. She seized Ben by the elbow and pulled him back along the waterfront.

"Bloody demon's not won yet. Come on, we have to move fast!"

She shoved past Tobias and Gabriel, who were still gawping at the tidal wave of fire flooding past them, and shouted over her shoulder for them to follow. Tobias blinked and then tugged at Gabriel, who was rooted to the spot. "Gabriel, come ON!" he shouted.

They staggered back to the Fishmongers' Hall. The front of the hall was stone: insulation for a time against the elemental force that was only yards away from them. They sheltered in its shadow, catching their breath for a moment.

"What do we do now?" Ben asked, his voice trembling. "We can't cross the bridge."

"We must find another way to get across the river - and quickly." Gabriel stared at the crackling flames, "With the speed the fire is moving I would say we have only two or three days at most before all the seals are destroyed." He gestured towards the few soldiers of the militia who were trying to bring some sort of order to the haphazard fire fighting around them. "I cannot see them putting it out before it reaches the old city."

Their eyes red and streaming from the smoke, they all looked at Freya. Shrugging, she pointed at the quay in front of Fishmongers' Hall. There at the water's edge was a wherry, already filling up with people escaping from the hovels. More bewildered folk were on the quayside standing as close to the water as they could, trying to secure passage across the crowded Thames and turning to gaze anxiously at the flames now flickering through the front of the trade hall just yards away.

"This way," Freya said, and ignoring the queue barged her way through to the front.

"What the hell are you doing? I was here first. I get on this boat," yelled a scrawny man with wild grey hair. He carried a bulging sack in one hand and clung to a small, snotty-nosed

160

boy with the other. From the look of the pair of them, it was not hard to guess the sack contained his few pathetic belongings.

"I told you: no one gets on my boat without five shillings!" the boatman shouted. He was a burly fellow standing like a guard in front of his boat, eyeing up the crowd and holding in one hand a heavy-looking hatchet, the other outstretched for his fee.

"Five shillings! That's daylight robbery," the first man spat at him. There was a chorus of angry agreement.

"Five shillings each or I cast off and we start rowing!" the boatman said again.

"Please, the fire is getting closer!" a woman cried, "I beg you to take my children if you won't take me."

As if to emphasise the point there was a crash from behind and everyone turned to witness the doors of Fishmongers' Hall falling in, tumbling away from them and into the waiting flames now raging inside. The woman looked again at the boatman, pleading and panic-stricken, she screamed, "For God's sake, help us!"

He stood his ground. "I'm not taking anyone without five shillings each."

"I will pay you five pounds if you take all of them and my two friends here!" Tobias shouted. Just go NOW!"

"God bless you, Sir," the mother cried, her face streaming with tears of relief.

The boatman looked stunned and then did his sums quickly. A moment later he smiled and stood to one side to let the crowd pass, the wherry rocking alarmingly as it rapidly filled up. More people were running along the quay towards them.

"That's it; no more or we'll all land in the river!" the boatman cried, holding up his hatchet to keep back the flow of desperate Londoners while Gabriel and Ben, one hand firmly on his satchel, pushed past and climbed on board.

"Good luck!" Tobias called, tossing his money pouch to the boatman who seized it in mid-air. He tipped a few coins out and they glittered in his hand as he counted them. After a moment he grinned at his crew and sliding the coins back into the pouch, turned and boarded his vessel.

"Good luck yourself!" Gabriel shouted back to Tobias as the boatman pushed off with a pole and his crew started rowing. The wherry moved out into the river, threading its way through the dozens of craft similarly crammed with refugees fleeing to Southwark.

Tobias and Freya watched them leave and then turned away. Suddenly, Freya screamed and pointed at the west end of Fishmongers' Hall. The fire had emerged and now leapt across to the Old Swan Inn, threatening to reach the waterfront and cut them off entirely. She started racing down the quay and Tobias, breathing hard, followed her.

Running flat out now, Freya passed the Old Swan. Moments later the fire ignited the spirits inside and a fireball erupted from the front and leapt thirty feet out over the water. She turned round, wide eyed, searching for Tobias then gasped when she saw the doctor was trapped on the far side of the firestorm now consuming the tavern. There was a huge crunch and behind him the entire front of Fishmongers' Hall crumbled, throwing red hot brickwork tumbling onto the quay where she had been standing only moments before. With a groan part of the quay collapsed into the river, sending up billowing clouds of steam into the air. Freya could just see Tobias through the steam. He was stuck on the other side of the chasm that had opened up in the quay, looking all around him in despair, his face grim with the realisation that there was no escape route to be had. Freya hesitated, uncertain what to do.

Suddenly, Tobias smiled and waved at her. As she watched, he backed off a few feet and then ran headlong towards the river and jumped. He soared over the disintegrating quay and landed on a wooden crate bobbing at the water's edge. He stumbled, lost his balance and almost fell backwards into the river where the red hot stones were still boiling the waters of the Thames. Throwing his body forward, he managed to right himself then jumped again, landing beside Freya before tumbling to the ground, panting hard.

"How ... was ... that for an amateur ... thief?" Tobias gasped, grinning up at her, his teeth glinting white in his soot-grimed face.

"So-so," she tilted her hand left and right then grinned back at him. "Not bad; you're learning." Not giving him a moment to recover, Freya dragged Tobias to his feet and pulled him onwards.

"Come on, Doc, got to keep moving. Stop panting: you need more exercise! How was THAT for medical advice?"

"*Touché,*" Tobias grimaced.

"Toosh what?" Freya asked, urging him along.

"Never mind," the doctor said, still panting.

They ran along the water's edge a while, then turned north into the alleys. Moments later the fire cut behind them, blocking any hope of escape back to the river. Freya kept them moving swiftly, but then she stopped so suddenly that Tobias barged into the back of her.

"What is it?" he asked, peering past her, he was in time to see the fire surge across the alleyway in front of them. To the left was a door. She opened it and moved inside. The hovel was empty – its inhabitants having abandoned it only moments before, as evidenced by the kettle boiling on the hearth. They moved through the room to another door, which led out into a passage at the back. Freya looked left and right, her brow creased in concentration. They could hear the fire breaking through walls close by, roofs falling in with ear-splitting crashes and all around them the panicked screams of men, women and children fighting to get free of the warren that had been their home and now might well be their tomb. Freya hesitated, for once uncertain which way to turn.

"Are you lost?" Tobias said, trying to keep calm, but his voice was high pitched with fear. Freya looked at him and nodded. The alleyway was filling with smoke now and they were both choking.

"Just trust your luck, girl: it's kept you alive so far," Tobias spluttered.

So, abandoning memory and relying on instinct, Freya turned right. Moments later, Tobias let out a cry of fear as the fire burst out of the doorway behind them. They ran on to another junction, turned west and then north through the endless maze until, suddenly, and much to Tobias' intense relief, they emerged onto what seemed like a highway. They were on Thames Street a few hundred yards west of where they had first left it.

Leaning against a wall to catch her breath, Freya slid to her haunches, coughing to clear her lungs of the fumes that had gathered in those terrible passageways. Wheezing, Tobias slumped down next to her and closed his eyes. After a few moments he opened them again, glanced over at her and smiled.

"Well, your luck held out, girl. Remind me to take your advice next time I hazard a few shillings at whist, eh?" It was a poor effort at humour, but it made her smile.

"The problem with luck, Doc, is you never know when it might run out."

"The young lady has a point about luck; do you not agree, Doctor Janssen?"

They looked up into the smiling face of Captain Gymer. Short of breath as they were, and with the roaring of the fire in their ears and the pounding of their hearts, they had not heard the shuffle of feet approaching. "Oh snoggers," Freya muttered, "it just did!"

"Well anyway, I am certainly feeling lucky in managing to find you again, Doctor, after thinking I might not see you for a while!" Gymer said. He was standing in the road and his man Walton had just stepped out from an alleyway a few yards distant. Pulling a pistol out of his coat the dark-haired, sour-faced man limped over to stand beside Freya. Gymer stepped closer and leaned over the hapless pair as they dragged themselves to their feet.

Tobias tensed ready to make a dash for it, looked up and down the street, but seeing no possibility of escape he stared sullenly at Gymer's sneering face.

"This is the young lady, I assume," the captain glanced at Freya, "delighted to meet you, my dear. I hope you have recovered from your injury? Now then, Doctor, we can continue our conversation from last night." He smiled, "What was it, you ask? Well let me remind you: I do believe we were discussing my theory that you and your friends are Dutch spies." Gymer's smile dropped from his face as he added, "To which it now seems we can add the charge of arson!"

Chapter 14
The Cavalier

South of the River, Sunday 2nd September, 1666: mid-morning

A ccompanied by three of his men, Artemas had ridden his
horse out of the city soon after nine o'clock. Having taken
a look at the spreading fire around dawn, he had quickly
realised that the bridge was blocked and that boat transport
between the city and Southwark was chaotic at best, so he had
turned away and headed towards Westminster. In any event he
first had a stop to make in the west of the city, under
Dantalion's orders.

Sometime later, his mission accomplished, Artemas
found a boat near White Hall to take him, his men and his
horses across the river. Now, riding with a loose rein, he
wondered idly how far Gabriel and the boy were ahead of him.
That they were was certain. They too wanted to know where
the Last Seal was hidden. The path he now rode led to the
village and manor house that he surmised they, like he, needed
to reach in order to find out.

Artemas shrugged, his detour might have put him
behind them, but it had been worth it. He was not in any
particular hurry; not now he had the words to set his master

free. Dantalion had told him where to look and as always, had been right. Artemas had found them exactly where his master had said they would be, and had written them down. Pulling the sheet of paper out of his saddlebag he looked down at the words. It occurred to him then that he should have tried to destroy their source, but Dantalion had not so instructed him. Besides, it would have been difficult as well as time consuming. So he had left them where he had found them. Not that it mattered: the way the fire was going, it would surely do his work for him. He stowed the parchment back in his saddlebag and contemplated the task ahead.

Soon he would have wealth and power: he was so close to his goals now that he could almost taste them. He was aware that some men risked their lives for great things: for a country they loved, a King they served, a God they worshipped or a cause they felt worthy of sacrifice. In contrast, Artemas had been raised to believe in one cause only: the elevation of self and the domination of others. It never occurred to him to question this; after all, wasn't everyone the same? All men were out to get what they wanted for themselves and the few who were not were fools.

He vaguely recalled a time when his father had shown him affection: when he could toddle up to the man and be hoisted on to his knee and bounced like he was a rider on a galloping horse. His father would tell him stories of heroic knights defeating ravaging dragons and then read him fairy stories or sing folk songs. Then, when he was about five, it had all changed. His grandfather had just died and soon afterwards his father started locking himself away in his room for hours on end. That was when he had started drinking. If Artemas had tried to see him, the boy was sent away with a flea in his ear. There were no more stories: just cold silence or, when his father did speak to him, there was no further talk of heroes and good causes. Instead, bit by bit and week by week, he was taught to think of his own interests, to take advantage of others and gain what he could for himself. The world was weak, his father said. There was no great good worth fighting for, only one's self. Money, land and power: they were all that mattered. Too young to question the change in his father, Artemis had absorbed everything he was told.

Once, when Artemas was ten, his father in a drunken stupour had told him of a great secret, one that enabled him to have all he ever desired. It was a secret he promised one day to share with his son. When his father had woken the next day, bad tempered and suffering the effects of too much red wine, Artemas asked about this secret. All that got him was a slap that sent him spinning across the room, and banishment to the old barn for the day.

As the years passed, Artemas had all but forgotten his father's rather vague promise. With no trace of the love he had felt as a young child, he had grown into an arrogant young nobleman: just as compassion had been extinguished in him, so he had none left to offer others. He was seventeen when King Charles had raised his standard at Nottingham and summoned loyal followers to join him in his war against Parliament. Artemas had gone, leaving his family estate in Norfolk, not because he felt loyal or because he believed the King was in the right, or even for the adventure, but because in war there is always the chance for personal gain. He had fought bravely enough when circumstance called for it, but inevitably managed to place himself where there was a chance for plunder or where, with the minimum of risk, he could be seen to be acting heroically.

At Edgehill, he had ridden with Prince Rupert's cavalry as it charged and routed the enemy horse and then went on to ransack the baggage train. The Prince should have got his men back to the field where their presence might have won the day for the King, but Rupert had lost control of his exuberant troopers and instead they helped themselves to the enemy's pay chest, and while they robbed and caroused, the battle was lost. Not that Artemas had cared either way, of course. Edgehill might have been a poor result for the King, but not for him. The same pattern repeated itself at too many battles for Artemas to remember. In the end Cromwell's superior forces had cost King Charles the war and eventually his head, but Artemas was left unscathed – and a very rich man.

It should have all gone wrong for him then. As supporters of the King, Artemas' family were seen as traitors by Cromwell and his generals. As such, along with many other nobles, their lands should have been confiscated together with any wealth they owned. All around the country others suffered this fate, and yet his father's land, as well as that of a number of his father's closest friends, had been safe from this retribution. Artemas knew enough not to question his luck and planned to enjoy his money. However, England, now rigidly Puritan, became an extremely dull place for the next ten years: playhouses and many taverns were closed; gambling was banned - even Christmas festivities were outlawed. There was no fun to be had, so Artemas left the country for a while and travelled around the Continent. Within two years he had lost most of his ill-gotten gains on wine, cards and women. When the money ran out, rather than return home he earned his living as a soldier of fortune in a variety of wars across Europe. Finally, in 1660, when he had been away for the best part of ten years, he heard news that Cromwell was dead and the country had called Prince Charles back from exile. The new King returned in triumph as Charles II. Artemas returned too and went home to Norfolk, where he learned that his father was dying and wanted to see him.

He found the old man sitting wrapped in a blanket, shaking and shivering with fever beside a fire. Next to his chair was a huge brass-bound chest. As Artemas entered the room his father slammed the lid shut and then looked his son up and down. Feeling like a child again, Artemas waited for him to speak.

"You and I have never been close, son. We care too much for wealth and ourselves to have wasted much time on love or affection," the old man spoke harshly, his breath coming in short gasps.

Artemas shrugged: love and affection? He had observed both in other families, but such emotions had been seen as sentimental and weak by his father for so long now it had rubbed off on him. A long-forgotten image flashed into his mind of his father talking about heroic deeds. It vanished just as quickly, to be replaced by another: the old man saying to him, 'If you have enough gold you don't need love'. Artemas had lived his life thus far with this as his motto. So he said nothing; what was there to say?

"Still," his father paused, his voice sounded less harsh and Artemas thought he could almost detect regret in the dry tone. "You are my son and heir, my flesh and blood and I am now dying, so I must pass on to you a secret that will give you riches and authority and might make you the most powerful man who ever lived." The old man broke off, coughing and wiping his mouth with a bloodstained handkerchief before continuing.

Thinking back to it now, Artemas felt again the awe that his father's words had inspired in him on that day. In the next ten minutes, he had learnt the most important fact in his life: he was descended from a man who, three centuries before, had bound the family to the fate of a powerful demon. Wealth and power, life and death: all depended on that service. His family had nurtured this secret through the years, passing it from one generation to the next. Only as each head of the family approached death could he tell his heir about his inheritance: a

171

destiny bound up with Dantalion which granted unimaginable power and wealth.

Believing the old man was raving Artemas had listened with increasing scepticism as his father had told him of their ancestor, Stephen Blake, and had spoken of demons and of the great Tome of Dantalion. Finally, he had told of Cornelius Silver, the demon's arch enemy, who had imprisoned him in stone. Only when his father retrieved a key from round his neck and passed it to his son, did Artemas, with burgeoning excitement, begin to believe what he was hearing.

"Put these on, son," his father had handed him a pair of gloves. "Go on, do as I say," he'd said as Artemas hesitated. "Now open the chest."

Always in the past this chest had been hidden away in his father's room. As a child, Artemas had often looked at it with curiosity, but had never been permitted see inside. He fitted the key in the lock, turned it and lifted the lid. It contained a huge book, larger than a family bible and bound with leather and iron. Artemas opened it and saw words he did not recognise, which seemed to blur and move on the page.

"Study the book and learn its secrets," his father had said. "If you want wealth and power, you must commit to Dantalion's service and in return he will grant you both - and maybe much more."

The old man had paused, his skeletal hand clutching Artemas and drawing him close, his foul breath whistling through his rotted teeth. "But on pain of terrible death, you *must* keep the secret safe. I have discovered an enchantment to reveal the demon's prison. In a few years I believe it will be possible to free him. I had hoped to live till then," his head sank to his chest, his voice dying to a whisper, "but I will not see the day. So it will be your task to restore honour and domination to our family."

Within a day, the old man was dead. Artemas had obeyed his father's dying wish and studied the book hard. That had been in 1661; five years ago.

Now, riding towards his destiny, he mused on all that had happened since. His father had been correct. There was an enchantment he could use to reveal the location of the demon's prison, but he needed help to gather the necessary physical components – such as rare metals, spices from remote locations and symbols of obscure, long dead religions: for this was old magic developed in ancient times and it needed old items to carry it through. In that, as he had learned, the *Liberati* would help, for his father was not the only man to know the secret; his was not the only family Stephen Blake had recruited to Dantalion's cause. And the largesse of the demon extended to all who promised him service. Other families had passed on this knowledge and over the years had become wealthy and powerful. When the King had been executed, they had survived Cromwell's revenge - and now Artemas knew why.

The Tome of Dantalion was more than a book of power. It also enabled him to talk to the demon. The first time he had done so, it was terrifying. He had read the book without wearing the gloves the day after his father died, and had screamed with terror as he found himself in front of the demon. Dantalion had explored his mind causing Artemas great pain, but what the demon discovered had pleased him and Artemas knew he had found the greed and thirst for power that burned within him. He had only to serve Dantalion and he would gain his reward, the demon had told him. Further, if Artemas could set him free from Cornelius Silver's prison, together they would rule the world.

As Blake's heir, Artemas was the head of the *Liberati*. He had summoned them to help him: first in gathering the components and then to complete the ritual to reveal the location of the seal. They had attempted it last year, but had been attacked by those zealots from the *Praesidium*. What kind of men were they? Artemas wondered idly. Men like Gabriel and the late Janssen, who foolishly served some ideal, aiming to protect their city and its ungrateful masses from Dantalion. What motivated them? What reward did they hope for? Nobody did anything for nothing, as he well knew.

In the battle that had followed, gunpowder and steel clashed with sorcery in an engagement that destroyed both organisations. Only Artemas and the three men he rode with remained from the *Liberati*. Gabriel alone had survived from the *Praesidium*; he had run away from the battle when he could perhaps have saved that old fool Janssen. Was Janssen's son aware of that, Artemas wondered? Maybe he should let the doctor know that little titbit of information. He smiled to himself; no harm to divide those two men; perhaps win Tobias to Dantalion's side?

Then his smile dropped as he recalled that the ritual had been in vain. The enchantment had failed because the Last Seal was protected by some shield emanating from other points around the city of London. With the seals intact he could not find the Last Seal. He had actually considered Dantalion's solution before the demon had suggested it: a great fire to destroy the city, but without knowing exactly where the seals were, it would have been pure luck to destroy even one of them before the fire was put out. Now, with the knowledge they had gleaned from the thief, they had destroyed the first seal and the avatar would help spread the fire to the others.

The avatar: before leaving the creature with Matthias, Artemas had hesitated, but he could not be in two places at once and clearly he was the one to go and find Silver's journal. Matthias was wild and unpredictable, but Artemas was sure he would be able destroy the seals with the avatar at his disposal, if only he continued to believe the creature was a messenger from God! Dantalion had questioned his decision to recruit the preacher, but Artemas had won that argument. Firstly, he had needed manpower to find Gabriel, who had been searching for the scroll they needed. The *Liberati* may be destroyed, but London was full of resentful, easily-led fools cast adrift by an uncaring society, which, in the past twenty years had changed and changed again, but each time had been equally indifferent to the lower orders, whatever those in power professed to the contrary.

It had not taken much to convince Matthias that he was serving an angel. His mind was already so fragile that by arranging an encounter with the demon it had tipped him over the brink into a kind of controlled insanity, which Artemas could use. Matthias had recruited followers and they now served Dantalion, although they believed they were serving God through his angel. Some would call it cruel, but Artemas laughed again at how naive some men were. There was another reason he needed the fanatical preacher and his followers, but he and Dantalion had kept that very secret. Matthias would discover it soon enough.

Artemas shook his head to clear his drifting mind and concentrated on the task ahead. He looked up at the sun climbing into a clear blue sky, heralding another scorching day, and wiped away the sweat that was already heavy on his brow then, calculating the distance remaining to his destination, he dug in his heels. Behind him his men followed his example and as the four horses left the city far to their rear, the easterly wind fanning the flames blew harder and London burned.

****

"Are these the men who think you're a spy?" Freya asked. Seeing Tobias' nod, she turned to Gymer, "You're a bunch of idiots," she said in a voice filled with contempt, "you know

175

that, don't you? He'd be hopeless as a spy. Anyway, we don't have time for this right now."

Without warning, Freya, a child of the streets who survived by her wits and sly, rough fighting, kicked her foot forward against Gymer's shin, hooked his foot from under him and at the same time swung a sharply pointed elbow into Walton's belly. Gymer let out a curse as he fell back onto his behind and Walton gave a muffled cry of pain as the wind rushed out of his lungs and he crumpled into a crouch, dropping his weapon with a clatter.

Tugging Tobias by his coat, Freya started off down Thames Street and away from the fire, but she had only got a few yards before a man stepped out into the road and fumbling inside his jacket, pulled out a pistol.

"Spencer!" Tobias shouted, pointing. With a choice curse, Freya led Tobias back the other way, easily dodging Gymer who had got back to his feet and had lunged at her with both arms flailing, but then stumbling as Walton jumped forward from the crouch to grab her ankle. She screamed and slammed her other foot down hard on his wrist, breaking the grip and, judging from Walton's, piercing shriek, maybe some bones.

The pair fled, but now they were running directly towards the fire, which Freya realised was not a tenable situation. This was doubly the case because she had just spotted Gymer's third man. Marlowe, the huge brute with the blunderbuss who was actually at present armed not with his usual weapon, but with a fire hook. He was helping a group of residents manoeuvre the fifteen-foot pole up to the top floor of a house that was already catching fire. When the hook had taken hold they began to tug hard. Another group got their hook up as well and with a dozen men pulling at each, the wooden structure began to give out great groans and creaks as it tilted forward.

"Pull again!" Marlowe boomed. They did and the building buckled as it fought the strain. Marlowe glanced down the

176

street and his eyes widened in recognition of Tobias. He looked quickly across to where he had leant his blunderbuss against another house.

"Freya, its Marlowe!" Tobias shouted. Freya stared at the big man, who had now abandoned his position at the hook and was running over to retrieve his weapon.

"Right," she said and checked behind her. Walton, still nursing his wrist, was glaring at them with murder in his eyes and was now only a dozen yards away. Gymer and Spencer, both now armed with pistols, were close behind him.

"You can't get away you know!" Gymer called, "Give it up."

Freya hesitated; any moment they might take aim and fire, but she had not dodged the city Watch, not to mention vengeful shop owners on more occasions than she could recall, without learning a thing or two. Shouting at Tobias to follow her, she ran straight towards the fire.

He stumbled after her for a few feet then shouted "Where the hell are you going?"

"Shut up and follow me, I told you I would get you across the city."

Despairing, Tobias increased his speed to keep up with the thief as she continued running towards the fire, which now filled the street ahead of her, surging outwards between the blazing buildings until it seemed she and Tobias would be engulfed in the blaze. Then – at the last moment – she turned away from the flames and ran straight into the same buckling building, which shortly before, Marlowe had been helping to pull down. Tobias hesitated a moment and then, half-closing his eyes he leapt after her. The building was already burning and was full of smoke and fumes. He ran a few paces inside the house and then stopped.

With panic in his voice he called out, "Freya! Freya, where are you? I can't see you!" The thief grabbed his ankle.

177

"Down here, man! The air is clearer, get down!" Freya urged him and he dropped on to all fours. She was already crawling away towards the rear of the house and he followed her.

Above them, there was a huge splintering sound and then a thunderous crash as the building lurched and started to collapse. Tobias gave a cry of panic and stopped moving. Freya turned back to help him, but seeing this, the doctor shook his head and crawled forward again, although he looked terrified, scampering along like a little dog. The fumes were getting thicker and both were gasping and coughing as they crawled through the debris. Freya felt her lungs burning and now she too began to panic until, all at once, she tumbled out of the rear door of the house and found she was in a back yard.

She spun round to search for Tobias, who crawled out of the smoke and crumpled onto his stomach just outside the door, where he lay wheezing and coughing violently. Freya beckoned him towards her, gesticulating wildly at the building, her face taut with fear.

Sighing, Tobias dragged himself to his feet. He had only got a few yards when the house shuddered, gave another lurch and collapsed in on itself sending fumes, dust and embers skyward in a huge black cloud. The belch of smoke out of the back of the house forced him, once more, onto his knees. Freya came over to help him up and they stared at the smouldering ruins in stunned silence, then the thief moved away to the rear fence and finding a loose plank, pulled it to one side creating a narrow exit.

"Come on, we must keep moving before ..."

"Before what?"

"Before Gymer's men come through the next house along and find us here!"

178

Chapter 15
The Manor

South of the River, Sunday 2nd September, 1666: late-morning

Motivated by the need for speed, soon after they had landed in Southwark on the other side of the river, Gabriel and Ben tried to buy a horse. It was hopeless: word of the fire had spread and it seemed that every available horse and cart had been hired out, and at extortionate prices, their owners looking to make a quick profit. Folk were so desperate they paid the premium just to get a means of moving their possessions away from the fire.

Ben suggested a stage coach, but when they enquired there were none heading towards the Badersley Compton area until Tuesday at the earliest. Gabriel despaired of finding any transport until at last they came across a farmer going their way. He had carted sacks of grain into the city the previous day and having stayed the night in a Southwark tavern was now preparing to head home. He was a bald, fat man with dirty clothes reeking of sweat and the ale he had drunk too much of the night before, but his cart was empty.

"For a couple of shillings each, I can get you fairly close to where you want to go," he said. "You'll still have five miles to walk but it's better than twenty, eh?" He gave a loud belch and the smell of stale beer and fried bacon on the man's breath made Ben's stomach heave.

"Beggars can't be choosers," muttered Gabriel, deciding that smelly transport was better than none. He paid the man and the two of them climbed up onto the rear of the cart and with a jerk they were away. The carthorse moved at a leisurely pace, not much more than a fast walk, but at least they could rest. Disturbed by his nightmares, Ben had not slept at all well the night before and was tired from their traumatic journey to the river. Now, with the cart swaying gently from side to side and the heat of the day increasing as the sun climbed in the sky, he was finding it hard to keep his eyes open. He fought the feeling of drowsiness, but eventually he surrendered to it, drifting off to sleep and praying he would be spared the recurring dream.

Ben had lied to the others when he said it was only seeing the fire in London that had brought back memories of his parents' death. The truth was it had simply made them worse, more vivid perhaps, but for months now, his nights had more often than not been disturbed by the dream. He had lost count of how many times he had stayed awake trying not to fall asleep and how many mornings he had woken early, screaming.

His prayer went unanswered and as he slept, the cart moving slowly south and London falling behind them, the dream came to him once again. It always started in the same way, with him being woken by his mother and father and then being lowered to the ground. It always ended the same too, with him crying out in anguish, shock and grief. Except this time there was another feeling, one which his mind had fought against acknowledging: an overwhelming sense of guilt. *"You shouldn't have saved me. I should have died, not you. It is all my fault. Father, Father, I wanted to tell you that I'm sorry. I'm so very sorry ..."*

Ben woke with a start. Guilt: he felt it in every inch of his body. His eyes snapped open and he gazed unseeing and uncomprehending at the cart, the back of the farmer's head and finally, the stout man in dusty academic robes, who sat opposite and was staring at him. Ben could see that he was speaking, his kindly face creased with concern.

Gradually, Ben became aware of where he was and realised he was panting hard. He forced himself to take slow, deep breaths.

"I said are you all right?" the man asked.

"I am not sure. I ..." Ben's voice tailed away and he wiped the sweat from his face. His thoughts were still confused and he struggled to sort them out. It was the dream of course, but this time it was different. That last part of the dream was new, he realised that, and he also knew he did not like it. He usually woke when he had shouted for his mother and father and heard them screaming. This time he was aware of new feelings he had not felt in all the dreams before. He shook his head, trying to clear his mind.

"You were dreaming about your parents dying, weren't you?"

Suddenly, the man's features clicked into focus and Ben knew who it was. "Forget it, Gabriel, please don't ask."

"You were shouting that you were sorry. Do you want to talk about it?" Gabriel persisted, moving over to Ben's side of the cart and placing a hand on his wrist.

Ben pulled his arm away quickly. "Gabriel, please, just leave it."

"You don't have to feel guilty because they died and you didn't, you know. It's common enough to feel like that. Nothing you could have done would have made any difference."

"I said leave it!" Ben bellowed. The farmer turned in his seat and glared for a moment then he muttered something about noisy Londoners before turning back to stare blankly at the fields they were passing. Ben felt ashamed.

"Gabriel, I'm sorry. I didn't mean to shout. I just don't want to talk about it right now."

Looking slightly hurt, Gabriel nodded. "Sorry if I pushed too hard. Let's change the subject," he suggested, and then he smiled.

Relieved, Ben nodded. "Tell me more about the Words of Power. If I can read them and use them I need to know more," he said, eager now to rid his mind of sad emotions and feelings of guilt and replace them with new thoughts and ideas.

Gabriel said nothing at first, but chewed at his lower lip for a moment. "It can be a danger knowing too much, you know," he said eventually.

"Why?"

"Our ancestors had their reasons for dividing the Words across the languages and through the races. Keeping them united, they knew, would allow men to use them and not necessarily for good."

"I thought the idea was to use the power to defeat the demons they were fighting against?"

"Well, yes, that was exactly the idea and they learnt enough of the infernal language to use it against them. In the end they were able to force the demons away from our world into the void outside it. That is when the troubles really began."

"Troubles, what troubles?" Ben asked.

"Men, Benjamin: they were the trouble. Our race always strives for what it does not have, always struggles for wealth, power and dominion over others. How many wars have been fought in the last two or three thousand years do you think?"

His hand straying to his satchel in which he still carried the book about the Punic wars, Ben thought of all the works of history he had read. "Hundreds, I guess," he answered with a shrug.

"Many hundreds indeed - and thousands more in the uncountable years before - man is a creature of strife and struggle. Some men believe it is inevitable, that in struggle and through war our race advances and develops. They say that all the great discoveries have come about because of it. Artemas would no doubt say that kind of thing."

"What do you think?" Ben asked. Gabriel shrugged and then rubbed the unshaven stubble on his chin.

"I hope he would be wrong, but I fear he might have a point. Anyway, whatever the truth, there is no denying there are many men who will use any edge to their advantage. It has ever been so, and our ancestors knew this. After the forces of evil were defeated there was a war between those who wanted to use the demons' power to rule others and those who wanted to live in peace. That war divided the races. You have heard the tale of the Tower of Babel?"

Ben nodded, "It's in the Bible. Men were trying to reach heaven by building a huge tower."

"That's right; the story goes that God sent his angels to cast down the tower they were building and then confused their languages so they could not try it again. I guess you could say those men were trying to become gods and using the power of the Words to do it. There was a huge battle and in the end the men who became the *Praesidium* overcame the others. Perhaps they did succeed in building a tower and it was destroyed, we'll never know, it was all too long ago."

"You seem to know a lot though, Gabriel. How do you come to be so knowledgeable?"

"I told you: I was the Record Keeper. I read books, you know, as well as selling them. The bookseller disguise was a useful way of owning a library of manuscripts handed down through the years. The knowledge is kept secret, but it is there for those who know where to look."

"So, after the war, what happened then?"

183

"Like I said, the Words were divided and incorporated into the many languages of man. So it was they were kept alive in order that we might know them, but separated so men would not easily discover and be tempted to use them. Only in times of great need are we supposed to reunite the Words. Use them too often and it becomes hard to stop. They are like the strongest drug or the finest wine only much more so, and as with wine it is easy to drink too much and then each day to drink a little more, until you can't do without it. Because of that, they are also far more dangerous ..." Gabriel's voice tailed away and he stared out over the fields, his eyes distant.

The cart stopped suddenly and turning to look at Gabriel, the farmer belched. "That way is where you need to go now." He pointed down a lane that dipped beneath overhanging oak and beech trees, their leaves just starting to turn brown with the coming autumn. "You've got about five miles to go from here."

"Thank you kindly," said Gabriel as he and Ben jumped down stiffly and waved the farmer off. As they started out on foot, the sun was now high overhead.

"Come on, Benjamin, we have a couple of hours' walk ahead." Gabriel looked at Ben for a long moment then said, "I guess we should use the time to teach you some of the Words in case you need to defend yourself. I am not keen to, but you are mixed up in all of this and there is no telling what might happen in these next few days."

Ben tried not to smile, but he felt a jolt of excitement at the prospect, desperate as he was to know more. Gabriel was clearly worried about him learning too much, so he hid his eagerness and just nodded.

"Very well," Gabriel began, "I will start with the 'flash–bang', as you call it; the device I used yesterday afternoon to rescue you and Freya from the warehouse."

For almost two hours they followed the meandering lane, passing through a dark forest, walking by occasional hamlets and farmsteads, without seeing a soul. It was a warm, sleepy, Sunday afternoon. Most of the folk in the area would have been to church earlier in the day and now would be enjoying the pleasant day's rest before the week started. They would be unaware of the inferno consuming the city only twenty miles away; oblivious of the existence of the creature and the fight against it that had brought Ben and Gabriel to their quiet part of the world.

Gabriel was still talking when they reached the village of Badersley Compton, and finally found some sign of human life when a local man staggered out of the only inn in the village, directly into their path. Staring at them in an unfocused way when they stopped him to ask for directions, he pointed up a lane.

"That's the way you want. Just you be careful of the warlock, mind," he slurred and wobbled on down the street.

"Warlock?" Gabriel muttered and looked at Ben who just shrugged.

Since a local, drunk or sober, was likely to know the area better than they did, they decided to give the lane a try. They went along it for a couple of hundred yards and then came to a fork. They were just wondering which way to turn when a labourer strolled into view carrying a scythe over his shoulder.

"Can you tell us the way to the Manor House?" Gabriel asked politely.

The man stared at them suspiciously for a few moments, lowered his scythe and directed a gobbet of spit on to the road before answering. "You witch hunters or something?"

"I'm a tradesman and this is my apprentice. The lord of the Manor asked us to visit to take an order for, er, cloth. But what do you mean by witch hunters?"

"You haven't heard?"

185

"About what?"

"I don't know anything," the man shuffled his feet, uncomfortable under Gabriel's scrutiny, "leastways only what I hear."

"And what is that?"

"Folk do say a few years back, during Cromwell's time, the Squire was overheard by some of his servants reading a spell book. He was in that there library place of his, and next thing you know there is clap of thunder and one of them servants falls dead and the rest runs off screaming. There was a big fuss of course, and we all thought they would string the Squire up on account of him being a warlock and all, but he swore blind he was innocent. Quick as you know it, we had Roundhead soldiers all over the place searching everywhere they could, but they never found no spell book and in the end they shoved off and left us to it."

Ben exchanged a glance with Gabriel. From the labourer's tone it sounded as if he had been disappointed at missing out on a public hanging. The man eyed them for a moment then added with a shrug, "So we keep away. Up to you, but I'd be careful up there," he finished and pointed to the left hand fork.

Gabriel nodded and he and Ben carried on up the lane, conscious that the labourer was still standing in the road, leaning on his scythe and watching their backs.

"What do you make of that then?" Ben murmured when they had gone a few yards and were out of earshot.

"I'm not sure, but I'm worried the Squire found the journal. There must be more in it than just the location of the Last Seal. Cornelius must have written down some Words of Power and the Squire had the ability to read a few of them, maybe."

"Well, it suggests the journal is here at least," Ben said.

"Perhaps," Gabriel shrugged, "unless he burnt it to save it from incriminating him," he muttered, chewing on his lip again. "Come on, let's press on."

186

The sound of distant gunfire stopped them in their tracks.

"It must be coming from the Manor. Come on!" Gabriel said. They broke into a run. The road they were following skirted a small beech wood. Beyond it the tops of tall chimneys gradually came into view. They heard more shots, a scream of pain and the crash of breaking glass. Someone shouted an order: "That's the last of them. Get round the back, Morris, the rest of you, in the door!" The voice rang out clearly and with a familiar tone.

"Artemas!" Ben hissed. Gabriel nodded and led Ben into the woods. Crouching low behind a beech tree, they peered out and saw the manor house. It was barely thirty yards away on the other side of a moat that ran round the entire building, but due to the summer heat had all but dried out, apart from a layer of muddy water and reeds at its bottom. A path leading from the road crossed the moat by way of a single bridge made of red stone, which ended in an archway over a fortified gatehouse and led into a courtyard beyond.

With no expectation of an attack on this quiet Sunday afternoon, the front gate was open. Ben and Gabriel tiptoed to the bridge, crossed it and sidled up to the archway. Four horses were tied to a fence on the far side of the moat.

"Those must belong to Artemas and his men," Ben whispered, "they must have taken the Squire by surprise, moved quickly across the bridge and into the courtyard before being challenged and then a fight broke out."

Gabriel nodded and signalled with a finger on his lips for Ben to keep quiet. They peered into the courtyard around which rose a range of stone buildings: the three-storey manor house, a stable block, buttery and coach house. On the far side of the courtyard one of Artemas' men was kneeling beside a comrade and wrapping strips of torn cloth around his arm. He was bleeding, but clearly was not seriously wounded as he got back on his feet as soon as the bandage was in place. Artemas himself was standing pointing a pistol at the house, while his third man covered the open front door with his musket. Two bodies lay in the open courtyard and there was a broken window on the first floor.

As Artemas and his men entered the house, there was more screaming and another crack of pistol fire. Straining to see, Ben and Gabriel ducked hurriedly back into the shadows under the archway as the Squire's terrified servants ran out of the door. They were herded at gunpoint across the courtyard and locked in the stables, whereupon Artemas and his men returned to the main house.

There followed a long silence; it seemed to go on for a full hour and more. Ben knew they dare not try to enter the house. Similarly, if they moved back to the shelter of the trees they might be spotted. So they stayed where they were and waited. Once, Ben tapped Gabriel on the shoulder and wiggled his fingers at the house, suggesting he might use Words of Power. Gabriel rubbed his chin and peered at the windows, but after a moment shook his head and they continued waiting. Ben's legs were getting stiff and he started to shiver slightly, for despite the heat of the day, here in the shadow of the archway it was cool.

At long last Artemas and his men emerged and walked across the courtyard. Gabriel tapped Ben on the shoulder and they slipped back from the archway, slithered down the near slope of the moat and squelched under the bridge. They were only just in time. A moment later they heard feet clattering above them as the men walked across the bridge and on towards their horses. Ben scuttled to the side of the moat and risked a peep over the top. Artemas and his men were glaring back at the house; their stony faces told that they were angry.

"They have not found the journal!" Ben hissed. "Do you think it's still there?"

"Who knows? Let's go and see," whispered Gabriel, joining Ben to watch Artemas' men mount up. Clearly they were in a temper: tugging on the reins and mercilessly spurring their horses into a gallop, away down the path to the road.

Gabriel waited a moment and then waved Ben forward. They climbed up out of the moat and entered the courtyard. Ben tried not to look at the bodies lying there, but he could not avoid it. "They were soldiers judging by their bandoliers," he said.

"Yes, the Squire here employed old veterans from the wars as guards," Gabriel said, also inspecting the men. "The last twenty years have not been safe, what with Cromwell's lot taking down their enemies and then, after the King returned, the Royalists taking their revenge. With thousands of soldiers from both sides looking for employment, many found the work they knew best: fighting."

"Should we let the servants out of the stables?"

"No, I think best not just now. Come on, boy!" Gabriel urged.

They ran on into the house, searching through the rooms on the ground floor, which included a kitchen, parlour and a richly appointed hall, before moving up to the first floor where they found the room they were looking for: the library. The Squire used the room as a study and his desk was strewn with financial papers, lists of tenants and their rent as well as bills of sale for livestock and crops. Gabriel glanced at these and turned away. From the shambolic state of the rest of the room, it was clear that Artemas and his men had ransacked the library looking for the journal. Books, parchments and papers had been thrown everywhere in their vain search.

Noticing the window was smashed, Ben realised this was the room Artemas had fired off a shot at. He glanced at the floor: there was blood there; just a few drops, not yet dry. There was another and another, then one or two more. The trail led away from the window, past the desk to a door. Ben pushed it open and gave a cry of shock as he found another body.

Gabriel came running in, stopped when he saw the corpse. "That labourer will be happy," he said, his expression grim, "I think that's his 'warlock'."

"The Squire?"

"I'm afraid so."

The man was lying face down with his feet towards the door and with a hand and arm outstretched, as if reaching for something. Ben looked about. At first glance the room appeared to be a garderobe, for there were open clothes chests and a linen press, its doors wrenched off. Artemas' men had been thorough: items of clothing hung out of drawers and were scattered haphazard on the floor. The Squire seemed to be reaching for the hinged wooden box built over the stone shaft of the privy, not only to provide comfort when taking one's ease, but also to suppress the inevitably unpleasant smells that came up it. The shaft must drop directly down through the house to exit into the moat.

Acting on instinct, Ben stepped over the dead man and pulled at the wooden box. It swung out easily, revealing the top of the open shaft. He looked down it and then, grinning, turned to Gabriel, "Come and look at this."

The bookseller frowned, but glanced into the shaft. They both gazed at the metal ladder leading down into the darkness, and Gabriel, knowing the average privy shaft does not contain a ladder, realised at once what it was.

"Clever boy," he said, "it's a priest hole disguised as a privy."

"I guessed as much," Ben said, remembering Gabriel's story about the de Windleys being devout Catholics. Everyone knew that when Queen Elizabeth's government had passed laws banning Catholic priests, the families who refused to give up the old religion had hidden itinerant priests and celebrated

Mass in their houses. To do this was treason and the penalty was severe if they were caught, so many families built secret compartments and hidey holes for the priests to run to in case the Queen's men arrived looking for them. It made sense that the manor house might have such a place. But right now there was no serious persecution of Catholics: Cromwell and his cronies had done all that again ten and more years before. Which, of course, raised a question: "Why should the Squire be desperate to get to this priest hole?" Ben gave a wry smile, "I doubt he is hiding a priest. Do you think he might be hiding something else down there?"

His eyes glittering with hope, Gabriel's feet were already on the ladder. "Let's go and find out!"

This was no ordinary privy sewer: the shaft dropped down through the ground floor to basement level and then it branched into two, one continuing out to the moat, the other turning at right angles into a passage leading to a narrow, confined space: perhaps large enough at a pinch for three or four men. It was furnished with a bench and a candlestick holder. The candle was low, but still burning and it cast a flickering light around the passageway. "He must have been down here before Artemas arrived," said Ben. "Pity the poor fellow didn't stay hidden." Beyond the bench he made out a patch of darker shadow; a small opening? A tunnel maybe? It was too dark to see. As Ben's eyes adjusted to the gloom his attention was taken by something else. There, at the end of the bench, was a book. He turned to Gabriel and saw, from the excitement in the man's eyes, that he had seen it too.

Gabriel pushed past Ben to get to the book then, to Ben's surprise, he did not immediately pick it up, but instead stood over it, fingers twitching nervously, as if afraid to find out if this was or was not what they sought. After a moment he reached down and took hold of the book with both hands and lifted it up. He then turned, sat on the bench and with great care, laid it on his lap.

The book had a plain leather cover, which gave no clue about its contents, so he opened it up. The loosely bound collection of parchments crackled and creaked as he did so. When he turned the cover, the bookseller gasped, for on the inside it bore a beautifully illuminated but disturbing image of a demon trapped behind bars. At the bottom was written a single name: *Cornelius.*

Gabriel's hands shook and he closed his eyes for a moment before looking up at Ben. "I have found it, Benjamin, at last I have found it." His voice shook with emotion, but at the same time was full of reverence. Ben gave him an indulgent smile: in many ways Gabriel was like a child with a new toy. Still, Ben would admit that he too was keen to look inside this book. This was the journal of his ancestor, a man who had fought demons and who had also passed on to his descendants his talents and powers. This book was as much a link to the man as was the pendant Ben wore: more so, for it contained Cornelius Silver's thoughts.

"Can I look?" Ben said.

Gabriel nodded and tucking the book into his robes got off the bench to walk past him and back to the ladder. "Yes, but come, we must take it up into the light and read it," he said and started climbing. As he did so a couple of loose pages fluttered out and fell to the ground. Gabriel was by now several rungs up the ladder and so Ben scooped the pages up and popped them into his satchel before starting the climb.

When they reached the top, Gabriel opened the book on the desk and flicked through it, Ben peering eagerly over his shoulder.

"So, can you see it?" he asked.

"Hmm?" asked the bookseller absently, lost in thought as he turned the brown, fragile pages.

"Can you see where the Last Seal is supposed to be?"

Gabriel did not answer because at that moment from the doorway there was the creaking of a floorboard shifting under the weight of a man's boot. Man and boy looked up to see Artemas standing there. Behind him were his men. A musket was pointing over Artemas' shoulder at Gabriel.

"Indeed, Benjamin," purred the honeyed tones, "that is a question we would all like to know the answer to!"

Chapter 16
Priest Hole

Badersley Compton, Sunday 2nd September, 1666:
mid-afternoon

"Artemas! But we saw you ride off!"Gabriel gasped. The Cavalier sniggered in response.

"Yes you did: that was clever of me, don't you think? I, um, get these ideas occasionally. Inspiration and improvisation, they say, they are the signs of true genius."

"Who says?" Ben's voice was mocking. Artemas hesitated for a moment and then just shrugged.

"Well, I do anyway. Actually, boy, I am not being entirely truthful with you. Morris here spotted you hiding in the ditch and I decided to let you do the work for us. That was the improvisation bit."

"Go on - and the inspiration part?"

"Well that was you, dear boy: it was inspired of you discovering that priest hole. Still, I guess that makes you half a genius," Artemas smiled.

"Whilst I guess it makes you a total-"

Ben's intended insult was cut off by Artemas. "Watch your language boy! Have you no respect for your elders and betters?"

"Betters?"

"Indeed. In fact I only have your true interest at heart, Benjamin. The Master wants to know more about you. He knows you have talents to read the words that others cannot: that you have the power. He and I can teach you how to use that power if you want it?"

This took Ben by surprise and although he still glared at the man, his interest must have shown on his face because Artemas' eyebrows went up and he smiled, "Ah, I see that you do."

Gabriel frowned and with a small shake of his head, turned to look at Ben, but the Cavalier just laughed. "I also see that Gabriel does not approve. Perhaps the meek fool does not appreciate what he has found. The Master knew who you were: who your great ancestor was. 'Imagine, the blood of the man who imprisoned me,' he said to me just this morning, 'how potent that would be. How perfect the partnership between me, Dantalion, and the descendant of Cornelius. There is nothing we might not accomplish together. Rulers of this and every world: just imagine that!'"

Ben said nothing, but he did imagine and in his mind's eye he saw himself wielding the sort of powers his ancestors must have done, countless millennia before: powers that could defeat demons and dominate men. It was a temptation and he could see that Artemas knew it.

"Enough of this!" Gabriel said breaking the moment. "So then, Artemas, you want the journal. Well here it is," he pointed at the book on the table. Are you sure you want it?"

"Well, that was the general idea."

"You will take it back and use it to free your master and then you will rule through him. It is as simple as that?"

196

For the first time a hint of doubt crossed Artemas' features and Benjamin wondered what Gabriel was hoping to achieve.

"Yes, that is the plan," Artemas sounded wary, "unless you have some better offer in mind?"

Gabriel held the book up. "This was written by a man who defeated the demon. Just a *man*: think about that. Your plans will come to nothing while there are some of us left who oppose you. Are you sure that you want to start this battle? And do you really believe Dantalion will relinquish even a shred of his power once he has made use of you? Walk away now Artemas, while you still can, then you and your men can live. Better still, join us. Join us and we can defeat this demon once and for all."

Artemas paled, said nothing, but Morris laughed in derision. The sound brought the Cavalier to his senses and he too laughed, though it sounded forced. "I think Morris just summed it up well. Join you – you and your rag tag team?" He sneered, "A failed academic, a vengeance-ridden physician, a vicious little thief and a spotty schoolboy? Ha! You don't stand a chance, Gabriel. Dantalion will cut you to pieces and turn your mortal remains to ash."

"So that is that," Gabriel shrugged and lowered the book. "Well then, what now?"

"What?"

"What about us, he means," Ben scowled.

"What about you?"

"Well, aren't you going to kill us?" Gabriel asked, but Artemas shook his head.

"Ah, but we do just hate violence, don't we, boys?" Artemas looked round at his men. They stayed silent, although Morris grinned nastily. "Well, some of us do at any event, but no, not today. The Master's orders are specific: neither I nor any of my men should lay a hand on you or harm you – unless, of course, you give us no alternative. So, I will just take the book." He leant forward and seized it. As he did so, they all heard the distant sound of horses approaching.

"Ah, the cavalry is coming. Gosh, someone must have alerted the local sheriff that a pair of murderers is in the area matching your descriptions. Imagine that!" He burst out laughing.

"But you just said you were not to harm us!" Gabriel shouted.

"Oh, indeed those are my orders," Artemas said and looked downcast. "I must say I would so very much like to kill *you*, Benjamin Silver." He added, "You see, I do not intend Lord Dantalion to have as a partner anyone save me. But yet, while *I* cannot kill you, the Master said nothing about me not letting *others* harm you. Terrible misunderstanding of course and I am sure he will be upset when he finds out – but that won't help you will it. Good luck!"

Artemas turned and still carrying the journal, walked out of the door. Morris and his companions retreated more slowly with the musket still pointed at Gabriel and then, suddenly, the door was closed. A moment later there was a crash as something heavy was pushed against it.

Gabriel ran to try it, rattled the handle then leaned his weight against the door, but it was jammed shut. "Benjamin," he said over his shoulder, "quick, have a look out the window. Can you see them?"

Barely aware of his surroundings, Ben had not moved; he was staring into the distance, an image floating in his head of him as a sorcerer wielding unimaginable power.

"Benjamin! *Come on!*" Gabriel urged. "Check the window. Quickly; do it now!"

Ben blinked and shook his head. What had he been thinking of? He stirred himself and ran over to the window. He looked down and found that he could see the bridge over the moat and the figures of Artemas and his men running for the horses.

They reached them, mounted and spurred into a gallop, not towards the road, but across the fields and away, vanishing into the woods. A moment later, half a dozen soldiers mounted on sweat-stained horses galloped up to the house. The riders dismounted, their captain waving his men across the bridge and on under the archway, above which the library was housed. Ben and Gabriel heard the exclamations as they found the bodies in the courtyard. They also heard the captain's comments.

"Murderers! If they are still inside they will be swinging from the hanging tree outside the village at dawn tomorrow."

Ben exchanged an anxious glance with Gabriel. It was the second time in two days that someone had wanted to kill him for a crime he had not committed. It did not seem quite fair. "What are we going to do?" he gasped.

****

Tobias looked at the paper that listed the locations of the seals, which Ben had scribbled down before they left. Beside him, Freya nibbled at a currant cake and then sipped her tea. It was the first she had ever tasted, for such luxuries were expensive and beyond a simple thief's means. Still, she figured, Tobias was paying so why not try it out? They were sitting in a coffee house on Cornhill, safe, at least for now, from the fire burning a quarter of a mile to the south east. Up here on Cornhill there was as yet little worry about the flames reaching the shops, coffee houses and taverns, although even here a few residents were loading their more expensive possessions into carts and moving them out of the city, some even taking them to the Tower where they would be safe behind the ancient walls and moat.

Tobias glanced up at the thief and then began reading out the locations, pausing after each one for Freya's comments.

"So then, we have: the wine cellar belonging to the priest of St Margaret's church on Fish Hill."

"That cellar's on Pudding Lane just behind the church - what's left of it - must have been the priest's house once," Freya commented in a muffled voice, mouth full of cake, "'course we are going to have to watch that kind of thing: buildings changing owners, getting sold and so on. Might make this harder."

Tobias nodded and went on reading.

"Crypt below St Martin's Wintry, Thames Street: that one can't be far from the fire can it?" he asked and looked up. Freya swallowed her cake with a mouthful of tea before answering.

"No, we might want to check that one soon." She pushed another slice of cake in.

"St Andrew's in the Wardrobe is the third one that Ben wrote down. That's close to Blackfriars isn't it?"

"Yes, where my mam and I lived. Just a few streets away from our old place," she looked a bit distant at that thought, but then bit off some more cake and nodded at him to go on.

Raising his eyebrow in mock amazement at her voracious appetite, Tobias looked back at the list. "Next, we have St Sepulchre-without-Newgate. That's close to my house, just outside the wall and up a bit. The fire has a long way to go to reach there."

Freya nodded without commenting.

"Right, then we have St Alphage, Cripplegate. Again, that's a fair way north west of Pudding Lane, near your stables actually. Lastly we have St Peter's church, Threadneedle Street."

"That's just the other side of the Royal Exchange." Freya looked glum, "I tell you what; if Matthias and Artemas burn my Royal Exchange I will not be happy."

"*Your* Royal Exchange?" Tobias chuckled.

She scowled at him, "You know what I mean."

"Of course I do," he smiled. "Those six locations are spread far and wide across London and even outside the city walls. They are all, however, stone buildings built at least in part before the time of Cornelius Silver. So they still exist, as he intended. We are going to be hard pressed to defend them all."

"Got to try though, Doc, don't you think?" Wiping the cake off her face, the little thief stood up.

"Yes, we have to try. Maybe we don't need to save them all. Maybe we only have to protect one and the shield will still hold. I heard the chimes for two o'clock a while back so we had better get started. Right then, where to?"

"St Martin's Wintry on Thames Street, I think. It's about twenty minutes walk, so come on and keep an eye open for Gymer. Not sure you noticed, but I don't think he likes you!" She eyed his generous girth, "Can you keep up do you think?"

Tobias said nothing but just glared at her.

****

Matthias stood on Thames Street looking east towards the fire. It was still some distance away, but moving inexorably in his direction, spurring some local inhabitants to begin pulling down houses in its path in an attempt to slow it down. Others had given up hope an hour ago and had loaded up their belongings onto carts and wagons and then gone west towards the River Fleet and the city gates, trusting in the ancient city walls to hold back the fire, or north to St Paul's Cathedral. The huge stone building was surely immune to mere flames, they had said, and taken their carts there. As a result, the streets around the preacher were now deserted and oddly quiet, disturbed only by the distant roaring of the fire. They had come here with the messenger of the angel. The avatar did not speak, but it seemed to understand what was being said to it, and when asked had led Matthias and his men across the city to this alleyway and then had pointed at the church, so Matthias knew that the small church of St Martin's contained the next seal that needed to be destroyed.

Earlier, he had spotted that little thief accompanied by one of the men who had been in Pudding Lane last night. They had emerged from the stinking alleys along the river and then encountered the spymaster Gymer and his men. Matthias allowed himself a smile at the thought that the King's own organisation of spies, set up to protect this depraved decadent Kingdom, was infiltrated by one of his own men - well, Artemas' man anyway; a servant of Dantalion, dedicated to freeing the angel that would judge this King and his Kingdom. Artemas' men would keep the demon's enemies on their toes, unable to interfere.

He looked across into the alley next to the church. There were his men, dotted around in small groups talking quietly and occasionally casting fearful glances at the figure with whom they shared the alley. There – standing alone – was the angel's messenger. The blanket it wore to disguise its appearance barely covered its upper body and was distorted by the movement of its wings underneath. Its jaw jutted out from the hood, so that Matthias could see how the upper and lower mandibles ground against each other, producing a clattering noise, somewhat like that of a cricket only much louder and far more unnerving. Its claws were also visible, protruding from the blanket, which revealed a glimpse of those powerful arms clad in shiny, almost metallic armour, like a crab or a praying mantis. The creature's appearance had been striking enough in the shadows and smoke of the night before, but now, in broad daylight, it was more frightening. Perhaps this was because night is when man expects such beasts and terrors to be lurking in the darkness and is on guard for them. But to see it now, looking so out of place here on a London street, with the sun

202

high above them, was a shock and Matthias and his men were struggling to cope with it.

"Faith," Matthias muttered to himself. "The Almighty has trusted me with this commission. I am His instrument on earth. I must have faith. I must believe there is a reason why the angel sends such a creature."

The preacher considered the scriptures. He closed his eyes, his face screwed up in concentration. Verses from the Book of Revelations came to him. He sighed and smiling, recited them:

"... And he opened the bottomless pit; and there arose a smoke out of the pit, as the smoke of a great furnace; and the sun and the air were darkened by reason of the smoke of the pit. And there came out of the smoke locusts upon the earth: and unto them was given power, as the scorpions of the earth have power. And it was commanded them that they should not hurt the grass of the earth, neither any green thing, neither any tree; but only those men which have not the seal of God in their foreheads."

Matthias looked over at the messenger and continued.

"And they had breastplates, as it were breastplates of iron; and the sound of their wings was as the sound of chariots of many horses running to battle ..."

"Yes, Lord, I believe; I believe. Forgive me for my weakness." Matthias prayed and now his face was flushed with excitement. The part of him that doubted, the part the devil sent to mislead him, was cast out in the certainty of God's plan. "Send me a sign, Lord, so I will know Thou art with me."

In the alleyway opposite, the creature turned to face the south east and, reaching out one claw, made a swift grasping motion at something unseen in the air. It pulled the clawed arm back to its chest and thrust out with the other arm, repeating the movement and then starting again. It looked a little like a fisherman pulling in his nets, or a man swimming through water. As it continued the actions, it lifted its head and began to grind its jaws, making that clatter-clatter noise that set Matthias' teeth on edge.

At first nothing happened, but then a few strands of the preacher's hair blew across his face and he realised that a very gentle and pleasantly cool breeze had sprung up. The creature's movements became more vigorous and the clattering sound grew louder and along with it the breeze intensified, becoming gradually more powerful until a wind was blowing. It grew stronger and stronger until it was almost a gale and as it came on, so the flames surged forward, house by house and street by street. Matthias had heard that during the hours of darkness perhaps three hundred houses had burnt. With the messenger controlling the elemental power of wind surely a thousand more would perish before nightfall. The next seal, buried somewhere in this small church, would be destroyed within the next couple of hours and no effort by the people still labouring further along the street could prevent it.

"Praise be to the Lord of hosts!" Matthias, eyes closed in prayer, waited patiently.

****

"What are we going to do, Gabriel?" Ben repeated anxiously. "If these soldiers catch us with the dead Squire they might not wait to listen to our excuses," he paused, "not that we have one they would believe anyway."

Gabriel scratched his head in thought and then clicked his fingers. "The priest hole: come on, Benjamin, quickly!"

They ran through to the little room and Ben climbed down the ladder followed by Gabriel, who pulled the wooden box back into place. Just then they heard a crash as the door into the library was flung open and Gabriel froze just a few steps down from the opening. There was pounding on the floorboards as several pairs of booted feet entered the room. The footsteps came closer, on into the garderobe and then stumbled to a halt.

"Gods! The Squire is dead," someone – the captain? - said in a shocked voice. After a moment's pause he barked out an order, "Right, men, search the house: every inch of it! If they are still here I want them found!"

Clinging to the ladder, Gabriel heard the clatter of boots as the troopers stomped back into the library. He went to step down, letting out an involuntary cry of alarm as his foot slipped off the next rung. He stumbled down to the bottom of the shaft, knocking his elbow hard on the stone floor. Ben stared up the shaft in horror. Held his breath. Heard a trooper ask, "What was that, Sir?"

"Sounded like someone falling," the captain replied. "Quick man: get to the windows. You others: outside, fast!" Then the boots were pounding away to the top of the stairs.

Slowly letting out his breath, Ben crouched down and examined Gabriel. The bookseller looked up at him with a pained expression on his now pale face. There was blood in his hair trickling from a wound in his scalp and his left elbow was swelling. Gabriel tried to straighten it and winced with pain as he did so.

"Is it broken?" Ben hissed, attempting to keep his voice as soft as possible. Gabriel shook his head and managed to bend and flex the elbow a few times. He was in pain and his arm would not be much use for a few days, but his eyes were clear and focused, so the head wound was probably not too serious. Ben helped Gabriel to his feet and the two of them felt their way down the tunnel away from the shaft. The stub of candle was still burning; it provided the merest glimmer of light and would soon gutter out.

"What do we do now?" Ben asked, slumping down on the stone floor of the priest hole. He looked up, made a face that was somewhere between a grimace and a grin, "Gods, I hope none of them wants to use the privy!"

Gabriel managed a small smile. "Well, we can't get back out that way or we will be caught," he mumbled, "and I don't much fancy squeezing out into the moat." He looked beyond the boy to the dark tunnel leading away from the shaft, "What do you suppose is down there?"

Ben stared with foreboding at the uninviting passageway as if it were the opening to some ancient tomb. He sniffed, but it was not the decaying musty smell he always imagined in the tombs of pharaohs or Greek kings. This was the smell of the privy. That meant there would be another drain somewhere emptying into the moat. Ben shuffled away down the passageway, peering into the gloom. The walls and floor were just visible in the faint light coming from behind him.

"I have an idea," he said, adjusting the position of his satchel so it lay in the small of his back. "Can you manage to crawl with that elbow?"

"Do I have a choice?" said Gabriel, stooping down to peer along the tunnel.

"Not if you want to get out of here," Ben said. "Here, let me go first."

He could just make out the walls on either side of him as he crawled along, at least until he got to a corner in the passageway. The tunnel bent to the right, following the wall of the house, and when he went round it he was plunged suddenly into pitch black. His hand tore through a dense spider's web and he gave a cry of surprise.

"What is it?" Gabriel hissed from behind.

"Nothing," the boy whispered back, "but I do wish you were in front. Who knows what I might put my hand intoooooo!" Suddenly his words became a shout of panic as he put his hand down and found nothing there. There was a hole in the floor of the passage and with a scream he overbalanced and fell headlong into another shaft.

"Benjamin!" Gabriel shouted and then realising where he was, held his voice. If those soldiers were in the room beyond the wall they would surely hear it. From below him he heard a sudden splash and from the stench that wafted up he realised Ben had found the drain from another privy.

"Ben!" he hissed again, "are you all right?" There was silence for a moment and then a muffled groaning below him.

"I'm fine, my satchel broke my fall actually," Ben whispered up at him from maybe ten feet down. "You just don't want to know what I've landed in. I certainly don't want to know, anyway."

"Is there light down there? Can you see a way out?"

"Hang on a moment," Ben muttered. There followed the sound of squelching and then came the answer. "Yes, the tunnel tips steeply down just in front of me and I can see the moat and daylight out there. There's a metal grill over the opening, though."

"I'm coming down, Benjamin," Gabriel whispered. "You can't get back up here anyway." He squeezed himself round and slipped backwards over the edge of the hole, hung dangling for a moment by his one good arm and then dropped. He landed, as Ben had, in something soft and unpleasant, the stink catching in his throat, but at least it broke his fall. The squeaks and scampering of small feet told of the presence of disturbed rodents. There was just room for the two of them to stand in a semi-crouch.

"You hurt?" Ben asked and then in the half light saw Gabriel shaking his head, his expression pained.

"Not too bad; it's just this sprained elbow. What a nuisance."

"Could have been worse, you might have broken it. Think we can get that grill off?"

Gabriel peered down at it and then shrugged. "One way or another we have to. We can't go back up there," he tilted his head towards the shaft, "but we can't try it just now."

"Why?"

"Because it's still afternoon out there; the soldiers will see us. We will have to wait until it is dark, sneak out and make a run for it – and then try and get some clothes from somewhere. I am not walking back to London in these."

Ben glanced down. Even in the poor light he could tell his clothes were filthy. "I doubt anyone will give us a lift back, we must smell as ripe as this wretched sewer. Old Rusty is going to be very upset when he sees the state I am in. Still, not only did I play truant yesterday and not go home last night, but I then left the city. I am in so much trouble already I guess a set of dirty clothes can't make it much worse."

"No?" Gabriel smiled and they shared a moment's contemplation of just how much worse Ben's Headmaster could make things - expulsion for one. Ben sighed. School seemed a thousand miles away; another world, in fact.

"Unless we can get the journal off Artemis and stop Dantalion, that, I feel, will be the very least of your problems," Gabriel said dryly, his whisper sounding hollow in the confined space of the tunnel. "However, I am worried about one thing – beyond the state of our clothes that is."

"What's that?"

"The Squire is dead and his knowledge of the priest hole died with him, but just suppose, for a moment, that one of his servants or household knew of the hiding place as well."

Ben stared at him, eyes widening. They both fell silent, two pairs of ears straining for any scuffle or tap from the passageway above to suggest the soldiers had found the hole and were coming to get them.

"You realise how it'll look if they find us down here," said Gabriel. "They will never believe we are innocent. Whatever we say we will be branded as murderers, which, of course, is what Artemas is counting on. I'm afraid we can only pray the Squire never revealed his secret to a living soul."

Ben grunted and leaned back against the slimy wall to wait out the rest of the day, trying not to imagine how painful it would be to be strung up from the tree outside the village, the noose around his neck tightening, choking him slowly to death.

Chapter 17
Tobias and the Avatar

London, Sunday 2nd September, 1666: late-afternoon

Freya and Tobias had zigzagged across the city, keeping to the small lanes and alleyways where possible, hoping to avoid Gymer and his men who were sure to be looking for them. This had worked well for fifteen minutes, until Tobias came out of St Swithin's Lane onto Cannon Street and almost walked straight into Walton. He was leaning on the corner of a house, looking at the flames licking their way along the eastern part of the road. Freya was gratified to see his arm was in a sling.

Tobias stopped in time, but Walton heard the noise of the doctor's boots scuffing on the road and turned. His eyes widened in surprise at seeing his prey just three feet away from him, but before he could shout out, Tobias smacked him hard in the solar plexus and he crumpled forward with a whoosh as the air left his lungs. Tobias ran on past, followed by Freya who was looking as surprised as the felled Walton.

"They teach you that at medical school did they?" she panted, running at his side.

"You'd be surprised what you pick up on a Saturday night in Edinburgh," was the only response. Then the doctor drew himself up sharply again and Freya could see Gymer and the bulky form of Marlowe straight ahead and walking towards them. The spymaster had apparently not seen them yet, so Freya seized Tobias' coat and dragged him off Cannon Street south on to Dowgate Hill. She then led him immediately into the small church of John the Baptist. Its doors were wide open and, in company with fifty other churches across the city, a stream of folk were bustling about bringing their belongings into the nave, trusting in the stone walls and the firebreak provided by the small churchyard to protect them. Freya doubted it would be enough and seeing the frightened faces felt a wave of pity for them. The feeling surprised the hard-headed thief, used for so long to caring only about herself, and she wondered why she was taking these risks. Why was she not running away from London as far as she could get? Was it really just to protect her city because it was a good place for theft? Was it for revenge on Dantalion, or was there something else driving her? She shook her head to clear her thoughts and concentrated on the present danger.

At the end of the nave, next to the pulpit, was a door leading into a vestry. They went in and closed it behind them. A minute later, above the hubbub of people they heard Gymer's voice call out from the main door of the church.

"You sure it was them, Walton? You did say they took you by surprise."

"I'm not a blind fool," Walton spat irritably. "That doctor was standing right next to me when he hit me; of course it was him, Sir!"

Walton's reply came from within the church and Freya, panicking, crouched down behind a chair, though it would hardly have hidden her for long. She trembled with relief when she heard Gymer say, "Well, they are not here, come on, man, they can't have gone far, we will try further down the street."

Footsteps led away from the vestry and Tobias turned to lift an eyebrow at Freya, but the girl shook her head and raised a single finger signalling for him to keep quiet. They waited like that for several minutes until finally she crept over to the door and opened it a fraction of an inch to peer out. The church was now full of boxes and sacks of knickknacks, piles of furniture and even bottles of beer and wine. Her gaze fell on a basket of bread and a large wheel of cheese. Nobody was standing near; she smiled.

"Wait here, Doc," she ordered and scuttled out of the door, coming back a few moments later with a loaf of bread, a hunk of cheese and a couple of bottles of beer.

"That's stealing!" Tobias said, slightly shocked.

"Gosh, is it?" Freya threw her head back in mock horror then laughed, "Come on: have a bit of a bite, it's likely to be a long day."

"I'm surprised you've got room after all that cake," Tobias said, but he shrugged and took a swig from one of the bottles and then sat back on the vestry desk.

Ten minutes later they left the vestry, tiptoeing carefully around the piles of belongings and trying to blend into the crowd, stopping to glance up and down the lane before emerging from the church. Freya continued her usual erratic route, avoiding the main roads where possible and slipping into churches, shops and guild halls along the way if she wanted to hide, which they were forced to do several times when they spotted one or other of Gymer's men, or someone who looked like them. Thus it actually took a full two hours to cross from Cornhill to Thames Street, where it led past the church they were heading for.

Freya now took them through yet another alleyway: Elbow Lane. It had a right-angled bend in it, which Tobias suggested was the source of its name, and emerged into a side-street about fifty yards from St Martin's church, so they could look on it without – she hoped – being spotted.

"Damn!" she said, peering at the small church. Tobias looked over her shoulder as she pointed out Matthias. "It's that mad preacher who thinks he is serving an angel."

"Matthias – that's his name, right?" Tobias said staring at the wild looking man, "I did see him last night but I was focusing on Artemas."

Matthias and his men were standing in an alley behind the church. A few feet away from them was another, much taller figure, partially concealed from view by a large blanket that stretched over an apparently deformed body. The covering could not hide two shiny black-green arms, ending in talons, which were reaching out in the direction of the fire and seemed to be clawing at the air.

Freya, puzzled for a moment by the strange action, glanced behind her, back along Elbow Lane. A gust of wind blasted down the passageway throwing up a whirlwind of mildewed sacks, old news sheets and fragments from rotten packing cases. It was obvious to the little thief that the wind was fast strengthening to gale force. Further east she could see the flames flare up and move towards them and realised, from the speed they were moving westwards, that it would not be long now before the blaze arrived at the church. The avatar creature raised its head and seemed to sniff at the wind and as it did, the blanket slipped back revealing its head. There was something of smug satisfaction deep in those terrifying pale eyes. The beast opened its jaws and let out a screech full of fierce joy and then resumed the motions with its claws. Awestruck that any creature had the power to summon the wind, Freya's throat tightened with fear. She slapped a hand down on the doctor's shoulder.

"Tobias: we must do something quickly! Gabriel said that avatar *thing* is driving the fire on towards the seals."

"I agree, but what? There are a good dozen of the preacher's men and two of us. I don't think my experience of drunken fights in Scottish taverns is going to be much help to us now, do you?"

Freya pursed her lips. "Still got your pistols?" He nodded.

"Think you could hit that thing from here?"

Tobias looked across the street to the other alleyway. It was long range for a pistol, but he was a good shot and the avatar was a large target. He nodded. "Probably: if not with both most likely with one ball anyway."

She smiled at him. "Let's see how good you are then," and before he could stop her, she ran out onto the street, across it and past Matthias and his men, down the alley and out of sight. The preacher stared after her in surprise for a moment and then shouted, "Get her!" Matthias' men set off at once down the alley and for a moment the preacher was alone with the avatar. The creature had not moved and still stood, one hand reaching to the east, pulling the fire on.

Tobias stepped out into the road, aimed one pistol and fired. The flintlock barked and a moment later the avatar recoiled as the ball grazed its shoulder. Tobias cursed at the shot and brought the other firearm up to the level and discharged it. This time the creature was shot squarely in the chest and screeched in pain as it tumbled over backwards on to the ground. It lay there motionless, looking for all the world like a dead beetle. Matthias stared at it open-mouthed and then across at Tobias, who had reached into his pocket and pulled out a powder horn and a bag of shot.

Tobias worked quickly: pouring powder into the pistol, popping in the shot, ramming the barrel then raising his thumb to cock back the hammer. Suddenly he froze in the act of reloading and stared in surprise as the avatar dragged itself to its feet and started towards him. The blanket slipped to the ground revealing the scaly body and the creature, scowling in fury, came across the road, green lips rolled back from teeth that tapered to points like needles. It let out an angry squawk and unfurled its wings, which spread out on either side, huge, dark and black. With another screech it launched itself off the ground with a single flap of its wings and hurtled through the air towards the doctor.

Tobias took an involuntary step backwards before managing to react and fire the pistol again directly at the creature's chest. Once again it tumbled to the ground but only for a moment before it leapt forward, seized Tobias by the throat and began squeezing.

"Wait!" Matthias shouted, "The wind! We can kill him later. The wind is dropping."

The avatar raised its head and sniffed the air and then gave a snort of anger. It did not release Tobias, but dragged him by the neck across the road, the doctor choking and struggling for breath. Reaching the church, the avatar kicked the doors open and with a swing of its arm, tossed the man inside as if he was no heavier than an orange. Tobias' head smacked against the stone font and he did not get back up.

Matthias watched as the avatar stepped back into the alley and resumed its position. A moment later the wind picked up with a vengeance as if the act of violence itself gave the creature power. To the east, the fire surged forwards down Thames Street and towards the now setting sun. Matthias nodded to himself: it would not be long now. The few men who were still trying to hold back the flames were moving closer; they were currently struggling to pull down a building just five houses away and were silhouetted in orange and red by the blaze. Matthias had to admire their perseverance as they kept trying against the odds to halt the fire. One of them, looking exhausted by his efforts, stepped back from his work for a

216

moment and glanced towards the church, then took a second look as he spotted the avatar. The man shook his head and rubbed his eyes, perhaps believing the smoke and fumes were making him hallucinate. Matthias grabbed up the blanket and flung it back around the creature so that when the distant figure turned to look again, he just saw two men standing outside the church, one much taller than the other, but still a man. He shrugged before going back to his work.

Matthias' men returned soon afterwards from the pursuit of Freya, but they came back empty handed. "She got away, Sir," said one, a vacant looking lout with untidy red hair. Matthias nodded without emotion or surprise. The fools had flocked to his side when he preached, but he now recognised there was little intelligence in any of them. Matthias had seen Dantalion's cause as redemption for him – after rejection and betrayal by an uncaring, changing world that had left him behind – and had set to his task with zeal, relieved to have something to strive for again. His recruits, on the other hand, were drifters and easily led sheep who, while devout and committed to the cause, lacked a single spark of initiative between them. Well, maybe when the angel came they would be inspired to find hidden talents.

He turned to the one man of the twelve who had a modicum of intelligence: a scar-faced, dark-haired, grim looking fellow. "Close the church door, Valentine, and bar it shut. The unbeliever has attacked the angel's messenger and must pay for his blasphemy. He will burn with the church when the fire arrives." He glanced down the street. "Do it quickly, the fire will be here soon."

A smile of unholy glee flashed across the man's scarred face as he ran to block the church door. Matthias watched him go, certain that this man at least had no illusions about serving some greater good. He simply enjoyed killing.

217

As Valentine started to pull the door shut, he heard Tobias' voice from inside the church. He hesitated, glancing back at the preacher. Matthias walked over and peered through the gap. Tobias had dragged himself to his feet, but was slumped against a pew. Blood was running down his cheek from a wound on his head and he looked confused.

"Matthias, wait!" he shouted. "What are you doing? You're not locking me in, are you?"

"The wicked are like tares which are gathered and burned in the fire; so shall it be in the end of this world," Matthias recited. He did not hear Valentine snigger, but Tobias did and glared at him and then back at the preacher.

"Matthias, this is murder. You pretend to be a man of God; can't you see this is wrong?" He staggered a few steps towards them, unsteady from the blow to his head.

As he got closer, Valentine pulled out a pistol and cocked it, then pushing through the door, walked towards him. "Back off, you!" he growled.

Swaying, Tobias stopped and stared wide-eyed at the thug now threatening him. "Why are you doing this? You and the others? Do you believe in his 'Angel of Judgement' too?"

Valentine glanced back at Matthias, but the preacher's eyes were closed, his lips moving soundlessly in prayer. He shrugged and speaking quietly said, "I've seen many strange things since I heard him preach and that 'messenger' is real enough, no denying that. Maybe there is an angel behind it all. Some of them others believe it. Don't matter to me either way. The Watch want me on the end of a rope for a little, ahem, accident, when one of them ended up with a broken neck in the Thames."

"You killed him?"

"You could say so. Weren't my fault. The fellow took offence when he found me in Whitechapel with an armful of silver candlesticks I'd lifted from a shop in Cornhill. Had to sort 'im

218

out didn't I; only someone spotted me getting rid of the body. So I ran away with 'alf the city Watch after me. Let's just say this fool," he nodded at Matthias, "and 'is band of misfits were a good place to hide."

"What about the fire? Don't you think that's taking things too far?" Tobias demanded, his voice rising in panic. Valentine sniggered again.

"Not at all. Serve toffs like you right. Your sort aint done nothing for me 'cept scrape me off your boots like I was somethin' fetched up by the dog. Bit o' vengeance I calls it." He backed away to the doors and looked up the street. "I'd be bothered you would snitch on me, but the fire is 'ere and I think your time is up."

So saying, Valentine gently moved Matthias out of the way and started pulling the door closed again, still covering Tobias with his pistol. The doctor shook his head and held up a hand in a futile plea for mercy.

"Matthias," he shouted again, "let me out. You think you are serving an angel, but you are not. Just look at the avatar, your so-called messenger. Is that something an angel would send? Well, is it? Of course it isn't. Dantalion is a demon. You have been fooled!"

Matthias opened his eyes and stared at the church door as it closed, and for a moment doubt showed on his face. Then he shook his head and blinked, reciting a verse from holy scripture: "*The one who doubts is like the surf of the sea driven and tossed by the wind. Lord I believe and trust in you.*"

"Mad as a March hare," Valentine muttered, staring at him for a moment and then turning away. Tucked into his belt was a set of short metal rods bent into various shapes. Selecting one, he slid it into the lock and turned it a few times until there was a sharp click. He tried the door to be sure.

"Locked firm, Sir," he said to the preacher.

Nodding with satisfaction, Matthias saw that the messenger had stopped summoning the wind. For the moment its work was done. The fire, driven on by a fierce gale, had roared west from Pudding Lane destroying many hundreds of houses, churches and guild halls and now it had arrived here. In a short while it would incinerate the church and sweep on west and north towards the other seals. The doctor locked inside was a blasphemer, his words a fantasy; he deserved to die. He, Matthias, was God's instrument, bringing to this evil city the judgement it deserved.

The preacher rounded up his men, who stood in a wary huddle as far from the avatar as they could get. They walked a hundred yards to the north, away from the fire, to watch and wait for the second seal to perish.

Inside the church, Tobias could hear flames roaring, the crack and boom of buildings falling. He tried the front door but it was locked, as was the door to the vestry. The windows were high up and impossible to reach. The only other door was up to the bell tower, but that could hardly be an escape route. He was going to be burned alive in this church.

"Help!" he shouted desperately and then noticed a waft of smoke in the air from the roof above him, which was already starting to smoulder. Now he panicked even more and yelled again, "Help!" But there was no answer.

Chapter 18
Bell Tower

Near Badersley Compton, Sunday 2nd September, 1666:
late evening

At first Ben did not mind the cold tunnel. The long summer had seemed unending. Rain had not fallen on London for almost three months and there had been barely a cool breeze to break the insistent, suffocating heat. So down in the drain, surrounded by the cold rock that insulated them from the sun's warmth, it had felt – for a few minutes – refreshing. Then the terrible stench, draining past them into the sewer, flowing from the half dozen privies situated in the upper stories of the manor house, began to surround them. Within half an hour they had had enough, but there was nothing to be done except sit on as dry a spot as they could find and endure it in silence. Every so often they would hear muffled voices from a distant room, the sound bouncing down to them through the drainage shafts, and more than once a scuffle nearby that was probably just a rat, but which the imagination could make into the boots of a soldier exploring the tunnel above them.

Ben tried to think of a good excuse to give to the soldiers and then he and Gabriel could emerge and be away from this dreadful, throat-catching smell. Yet whatever they said, he knew they would not be believed. Found hiding in a house where three men had been murdered would be enough to confirm their guilt, and having heard the captain's tone, Ben did not feel encouraged to think him merciful. Moreover, even if they were first given the benefit of the doubt there would inevitably be questions, which they would find hard to answer. Any ensuing investigation would take some days – and Gabriel had said they had only three at best to find the Last Seal. Meanwhile, London was burning and the seals binding Dantalion were coming under attack one by one. It might be too late by the time they managed to get away.

'Too late for what?' Ben asked himself. With the journal already gone back to the city with Artemas, and the seals failing, what could he and the others do about it? He wanted to ask Gabriel, but whenever he started to speak the bookseller would frown and hush him into silence. He was right of course. The noise of conversation would carry along the shafts and drains or through the walls around them and betray their presence. So, such conversation would have to wait. Still, Ben could certainly ponder the problem: indeed there was little else to think about. He preferred not to dwell on the dreams he was having or look back to the night his parents died. In the early days after the fire he had tried to remember what had happened, but found that if ever he did, the memory was too painful. Before he got far into his recollections a terrible sense of foreboding would steer him away and always he would block the feeling with anger or reach out for another topic. In the last twenty-four hours that topic had become the enticing words he had read on the scroll and heard spoken by Gabriel. Words of Power that had unlocked a hidden talent within him: talents inherited from his ancestor, Cornelius, and by him from yet more distant predecessors, right back to the days when the words were first discovered and used to battle the demons in ancient times.

When Ben and Gabriel had been walking to the Manor, the bookseller had spoken of the Words of Power he had used to create the explosion and flash of light in the warehouse. "The demons that lived on Earth, when our ancestors were primitive and little more than animals, discovered that their minds contained the potential to influence the physical world around them," he had said. "All it needed was a focus to direct that potential from within them to the outside. They discovered that certain words could do it and in time we learnt from them and turned their own words against them. The words you speak must be in a certain combination, in a certain order and even sometimes with a certain cadence and tone. If spoken by the right person, by which I mean one who has both knowledge and aptitude, it can activate their potency. The words focus the raw power of the mind on the elements and allow you to manipulate them."

"Is it safe?" Ben had asked, but Gabriel had just shrugged.

"No it is not, that is the short answer. Human minds are infinitely complex and we really know so little of what they do. Once you start to meddle with these powers you are exposing your mind to unimaginable forces. The results can be unpredictable at best. Some men have gone mad, others have literally burned out their own brains." The bookseller had looked a little distant and running his fingers through his hair, had wiped his brow before saying softly, as though speaking to himself, "Almost all of us have developed some psychological side-effect or phobia."

Ben had looked at the bookseller and hesitated for a moment before asking the question. "Have you, Gabriel?"

"Have I what?"

"Well you know ... side-effects?"

He had not answered at first and they had walked on in silence for a while. Eventually Gabriel spoke up. "Benjamin," he had paused, waiting for a grunt of response before continuing. "I have not told anyone this before, but when we went to confront the *Liberati* last year and Tobias' father died in the battle, I did indeed bring his body home. I did not, however, tell Tobias the whole truth."

"You didn't?" Casting his mind back to the previous afternoon in the bookshop, Ben had recalled something Artemas had said to Gabriel: '*You thought you had run so fast we would never find you? You should know better than that.*' It had seemed a little odd at the time, but Ben, confused by the Cavalier's arrival and aggressive stance, had thought no more about it. Walking beside Gabriel through the woods, it dawned on him what Artemas had been hinting at. "You ran away?" he had asked tentatively.

Gabriel had dropped his gaze, embarrassed. Nodding miserably, he had stopped walking and sat down on a fallen tree trunk that lay beside the lane.

"I have spent all my life reading everything I could find about demons: tablets of stone from Mesopotamia; sketches of cave paintings from the south of France; records, scrolls and parchments from five thousand years of history. There is no man alive who knows more about demons than I, or anyone who knows more about the *Liberati*. Yet, when it came to opposing them, like the coward I am, I panicked and ran away. Markus Janssen was killed and I could have saved him."

"You don't know that for certain. If you had stayed you would have died too. Then, with no one to oppose him, Artemas would have been able to do anything he wanted. Anyway, you said yourself that it was not your fault. The powers you used made you afraid." Seeing Gabriel shaking his head, Ben had stumbled to a halt.

"No, Benjamin, that's the problem. I had not used the Words of Power before that day. I did not use them until after I had run away – to hide myself in fact. Cowardice is not a side-effect: a coward is what I am. One day I must tell Tobias, but I don't know how." He had looked up mournfully at Ben and sighed heavily.

"Gabriel, you saved Freya and me in that warehouse and you stood up to that avatar. I think that took courage."

Gabriel had thought about that for a moment. "I was terrified both times if truth be told."

"That makes you even less the coward in my eyes," Ben had said softly.

"Perhaps," was all Gabriel replied and then he had got to his feet again. "Come on, boy, enough of all this talk, we must get on."

"Gabriel, please show me the words you know. I must know them if we have to face Dantalion."

The bookseller had nodded, "Very well, but keep walking."

Now, squatting in the dank sewer, Ben recalled the words Gabriel had said and how he had spoken them, creating again the flash of light and ear-splintering bang.

"*Kipofu–Lumen–Glimt*," Gabriel had shouted and then had explained how the words usually combined the different components needed to make the power work.

"Firstly, there is always a word that represents the type of effect desired: perhaps to fire a projected bolt of energy, maybe influencing the mind, or altering the physical world. The word focuses the mind on the end result. Secondly, comes a word that summons the force or power that will actually be used to make it happen, such as fire or light, pressure or subtle hypnotic effects. Finally, another word actually triggers the effect, in much the same way that an officer shouting the command, 'Fire' to his men will result in them shooting at the enemy. As you learn the words you have to work out what part of the syntax or the grammar they are and then you can combine them to build up different phrases with wide-ranging effects."

"Like learning a language at school I guess," Ben had mused.

"Exactly the same really, so then, go ahead and try."

Benjamin had tried and found that not only could he master it, but the power and force he used were much more than Gabriel had produced. The older man had nodded appreciatively, but then looked anxious. Ben had tried to appear modest, but inside he had felt the raw power build up and channel through him. It was intoxicating. It took away the pain of his parents' death and replaced it with a giddy, exhilarating sensation. He had to learn more; he *must* know more.

He thought back now on Artemas' words in the library a few hours ago: "The Master knew who you were: who your great ancestor was. *'Imagine: the blood of the man who imprisoned me,'* he said to me just this morning, *'how potent that would be. How perfect the partnership between me, Dantalion, and the boy, the descendant of Cornelius. There is nothing we might not accomplish together. Rulers of this and every world: just imagine that.'"* And despite himself, Ben could not help but imagine it. Power: a temptation like none other.

"Benjamin," Gabriel hissed at him from the end of the drain, "it's getting dark. I think we can risk going now. Come on!" Ben blinked. He realised he had been thinking about Words of Power for hours. He nodded and shuffled along behind Gabriel. The older man reached the grating to the outside and pushed at it with his good hand. The metal of the bars flaked and left a red-brown discolouration on his fingers.

"It's very old and rusty. Let me try forcing it," Ben said.

He squeezed past Gabriel, braced himself and pushed hard against the grating. At first nothing happened, but after a

226

moment it budged slightly. He drew breath, pushed again and this time the ancient brickwork around the grating cracked and crumbled and suddenly the metalwork fell forward into the water with a splash. They both froze, expecting at any moment someone would come and search for the source of the noise. No one did, though, and after a minute or two they crawled through the hole and crept out on to a narrow ledge that ran along the base of the wall. Above them, the fortified manor house rose through three storeys, its dark bulk outlined against the starlit sky. Away in the distance the ghostly sound of an owl shivered on the air. Ben looked around him and grimaced at what he saw. They had emerged at the back of the house and here the moat widened into a deep pond. Reflected in its still, inky surface, the clear black sky dotted with stars and the sliver of the moon. Ben shuddered; it looked dark and foreboding.

"Do we swim it?" Ben, unenthusiastic about crossing the filthy water, was grateful to see Gabriel shake his head.

"I can't swim." He pointed, "Come, there's a boat just there. You can row, can't you?" Ben nodded. Westminster kept a boathouse on the Thames and every boy was required to learn how to row. They shuffled along the ledge to the small row boat, which looked as if it had been long abandoned: the wood was rotten in places, but it was still floating and had both its oars intact.

They climbed into it and Ben rowed across to the far bank, the noise of the creaking rowlocks and splash of the oars seemed so loud that he expected at any moment to hear a cry of alarm or worse, a shot to ring out from the manor house. Reaching the other side, they scrambled out of the boat and ran. Beyond the pond were the woods they had hidden in earlier. Only when they were once more under the thick canopy of trees did Ben feel a wave of relief and with it, a feeling of extreme tiredness. Yawning, he adjusted his satchel on his hip and stumbled along behind Gabriel towards the village.

Country folk retire early it seemed, and the family who lived in the farmhouse beyond the woods were no exception. In the morning they would doubtless wonder who had taken the clothes the goodwife had fortuitously left hanging on a line outside, but by then there would be no sign of the thieves. The farmer might curse his two old, deaf hounds for not rousing him, perhaps until he found by the back door the small pile of silver coins, far more than the stolen breeches and smocks were worth. He would probably never miss the empty sack Ben had found in which to carry his and Gabriel's stinking clothes back to London, having first swilled off the worst of the muck in the stew pond. Ben's satchel, too, he attempted to clean. The leather and straps were caked with ordure; he dared not look to see if his books were ruined.

Feeling slightly more comfortable, they moved on to another farm a mile nearer to London, before finding an isolated barn and collapsing exhausted into sleep.

Ben was lost in peaceful oblivion until shortly before dawn, but then, as he had feared it would, the dream came again. This time, however, the vivid images were of the day before the fire, and even as he slipped into the dream, the part of him that was aware recoiled from revisiting the hours he would now be forced to live again.

The day dawned bright and warm, full of the promise of spring, the sparkling winter snow lying thick on the ground beginning to melt. His father suggested they walk to the local market and Ben eagerly agreed. After buying their food, the three of them, full of laughter, cooked his father's favourite dish of roasted partridge. It was the first time Ben had helped with the cooking and he was pleased with his efforts, even more so when his father enjoyed the meal. Ben felt the warmth of his approval and beamed with pleasure at his praise.

Then his father spoilt it all by talking of Ben's future. It was an ongoing argument between them: Ben wanted to try for a scholarship to Oxford, but his father meant him to leave Westminster School, insisting he be apprenticed to a master draper; learn the trade and eventually gain membership to the Draper's Guild. "Then one day, son, you will be able to take over the business," his father said, smiling with satisfaction.

"I don't want to be a damn draper," Ben sneered. "I can't abide the thought of it!"

"How dare you belittle my trade; our business," his father roared, offended, accusing him of, among other things, having his head in the clouds. Ben stormed out, ran to the orchard behind the house and hid. As the day wore on, the sun disappeared and the snow began to freeze. Shivering, Ben hugged his arms around his chest and nursed his resentment until dark.

His mother found him in the end and brought him inside. He apologised, as was expected of him, but he did not feel sorry, just angry and frustrated. His father, with a curt nod, said they would discuss it all in the morning. His parents went off to bed then, leaving Ben with orders to make sure the fires were out before he came up.

He stayed downstairs for hours, shivering with the cold, grumpily feeding and stoking the flames before, half asleep, he stomped upstairs to bed. Belatedly he remembered he had forgotten to damp down the fires, but now he was warm and comfortable. He turned over and pulled up the covers, thought sulkily, 'Let the damn fires burn out by themselves!' He was fed up with his father; fed up with following his parents' orders all the time.

Vaguely aware he was dreaming, Ben stirred in his sleep, tried to wake himself up, but as always he failed. His dream turned into the recurring nightmare, taking him through the tortured images of waking to his mother's urgent summons, of being lowered to safety and of his parents' sacrifice for his sake; he who had so wilfully caused the blaze. Now came again the horrifying feeling of guilt as he stood below the burning house screaming that he was sorry.

Tossing and turning, Ben emerged from the nightmare rigid with despair, feeling sick. Never until now had he allowed himself to acknowledge the horrifying truth. Since the day after the fire, he had recalled nothing before he had hit his head and lost consciousness, other than being woken and saved by his parents. Overlying it all, night after night, the overwhelming sense of guilt, which he had never understood before, had suffocated him. Now, finally, he realised why: it was not, as Gabriel had suggested, because his mother and father had died and he had lived. No. His guilt was because their death had been his fault. Lost in self-absorbed pity, he had failed to make sure the fires were out and, as an open fire could so easily do, it had spat out a spark. Always a risk in a wood-and-thatch-built house, the spark had caught and rapidly spread. In effect, Ben was guilty of murder: his selfish, childish resentment had killed the two people he loved best, and for as long as he lived, he would never be able to forgive himself.

Ben's eyes snapped open and he sat suddenly upright, sweat pouring from him and his heart pounding. So, then, this was the secret his mind had rejected as being too painful to recall. The head injury had affected his memory and his unconscious mind had buried it deep inside: locked away where even he would not look at it. Yet he had known there was some reason to feel guilty. There was something he did not like about himself. So the bright, enthusiastic student had suddenly become the sulky schoolboy, who did not give a damn anymore. He hated himself and reflected that hate, which only anger could assuage, out on to everything and everybody because he did not want to face the truth.

Shaking in anguish, he realised he could not face it even now. The pain was too raw and too terrible. But he knew what could take it away and make it feel better. His lips started moving as he recited the Words of Power Gabriel had taught him. Inside he felt the power well up and take away the sorrow and guilt, just as a draught of poppy juice eases a man's physical pain.

So, then, how far could he go? Could he erase the guilt and pain completely and forever if he poured more and more of himself into the power tracking through him? He smiled at the wonderful feeling of joy and did not notice Gabriel standing over him, his face full of terror.

"Benjamin! Benjamin, please stop! You are killing yourself!" Gabriel shouted, but Ben ignored him. The words passed quicker and quicker over his lips and now all around them a blaze of electrical energy lit up the hayloft like a firework display on bonfire night. Ben could not now feel his body, could see nothing – all he could feel was the raw energy coursing through him. It was perfection. He was not even aware he was laughing.

"Ben! Please stop!" Gabriel implored again in desperation, but Ben had passed beyond hearing. Could see nothing now other than an intense blue light as the wondrous feeling of exultation overwhelmed him. Then the intensity grew, so that he felt he would burst into flames. The sensation became pain and the pain exquisite. He screamed now, although he could not hear it. He tried to stop but could not. Then there was a blinding flash of white light and he slipped into oblivion.

****

"Matthias, you murderer, let me out!" Tobias shouted once again in desperation, but he knew it was futile.

From very close by, just outside the church, Tobias could hear the roaring of the flames. The heat in the building was rising fast and his clothes were soon drenched with sweat. His eyes were stinging; smoke making him cough and retch. He wiped his forehead and then cried out in alarm when, with a crash, a neighbouring house collapsed and fell against the side of the building. The whole structure shook violently. Tobias ducked for cover under the stone altar. This was it then; this was the end of his miserable life. So be it. On his knees, he started to pray.

From the moment his father died, Tobias had spent little time in churches. Hatred and revenge had become the twin pillars of his new faith. Yet, now he prayed. There seemed little else to do: he was certain he would die here and he knew that calling out would do no good, for there was no one left to listen to his pleas. Matthias and his followers, the local inhabitants and even Freya had fled because the fire had come at last.

The walls of the church were smouldering now and as he looked up, part of the roof suddenly gave way and fell crashing down around him, pulverising the font, which stood only a few feet away, showering him with glowing embers that burned and scorched his skin. Still praying, he abandoned his shelter and scuttled towards the bell tower door. Opening it, he started towards the stairs, but before he reached the bottom step a voice came to him from above.

Not an angel, but Freya.

Standing half way up the stairs looking down on him with a cheeky smile, "Hi, Doc, fancy getting out of here?"

Staring up at her through red-rimmed eyes, he was aware his mouth had just dropped open. He shut it, said simply, "Yes please," and staggered up to her. "How on *earth* did you get in here?"

"From the alleyway down there," she pointed. "I was able to swing up to the church roof and then walk along the top of it to the window."

Looking where she pointed, Tobias could see that the tower had a window in it half way up its length and that from it there was access out on to the roof.

"Stop gawping," Freya tugged at him, "or it will all be for nothing and we'll both be incinerated instead of just you, and if it's all the same with you, I am not ready to die just yet!"

Tobias almost laughed. He hurried to the window and poked his head out, surprised to find that night had fallen and that the brightness came only from the fire. He looked down on the roof and felt the blood drain from his face. The fire now raged all around the church, which stood like a small island in a sea of flame. The island was under attack though and could not last long. The wooden roof and doors were ablaze and soon the stones would crack and collapse.

"The roof has caved in, Freya. I don't think I can get down that way – but you might," he added, noticing an intact beam running the length of the roof. If she could crawl along that she might be able to get down from it to the alleyway.

Freya looked over his shoulder and then shook her head. "I might be able to manage it but even for me it's tough and anyway I don't intend leaving you."

"God, Freya, you're the bravest person I know, but there is no need or sense in us both dying."

"There is no need for either of us to die. This is a bell tower remember?"

"It's no good ringing the bells. No one will come: the place is surrounded now."

"I don't plan to ring the bells. I plan to use the ropes," she said walking to the hollow interior of the tower where the ropes from the bells above them dangled down to the floor below. She pulled them over to the side, handed him one and took the other.

Tobias smiled; this might just work! His admiration for the little thief rendered him speechless. They took the ropes to the window, threw them out and let them fall away to the ground, the other end still secured to the bells above them. Then Freya climbed out of the window and took one of the ropes with both hands. She manoeuvred round to the side of the tower – the stonework was getting hot but was still intact – braced her feet against it and then leant away, letting herself fall down the tower in small jumps, each time lifting her hands to let the rope slide through them before grasping it again. Above her Tobias was watching her descent, grimacing at the ear splitting clanging of the bells that swung wildly with her every jump. Anyone who heard them must think it a hopeless plea for help. If so, nobody ventured near. He could not blame them. After a moment he lowered himself out through the window and copying Freya's technique proceeded down the side of the tower. A few minutes later they were both standing side by side in the street, panting hard.

Around them the flames were incinerating everything and were streaming across the road. The heat was incredible, but they huddled together, kept their heads low and scuttled along Thames Street. Fifty yards further west they emerged from the suffocating fumes on to a street beyond the edge of the fire. Freya ducked up Garlic Hill before leading Tobias into a side alley where they collapsed, coughing up black-stained sputum and breathing deeply.

Tobias dragged himself to his feet, looked down at the girl's soot-smeared face, scorched hands and bloodshot eyes. "I don't know how to thank you; you saved my life, but we can't stay here. We will have to risk my house. We will get a change of clothes for us both and clean up. I must also take a look at your head wound; it's filthy.

Freya frowned slightly. "My head's all right now, Doc, and I ain't taking no charity from anyone, not even you," she said.

"If it helps you could steal the clothes from me?" Tobias suggested dryly.

Giggling, Freya brightened up at the prospect of clean clothes. Getting to her feet, she let out a gasp of pain, winced and held her side. Tobias rolled up her tunic and shirt a few inches and pursed his lips as he studied the nasty burn. He shook his head.

"That decides it. We need to dress that before it gets infected. Come on, quickly," he ordered sternly, and for once Freya nodded and followed him.

Suddenly there was an enormous explosion from the direction of the church and even from this distance they felt the ground shake from the detonation.

"That's the second seal gone, I reckon," Freya suggested and Tobias nodded, his face showing his disappointment.

"I failed, Freya," he said.

She frowned at that. "*We* failed; it was both of us. Anyway I don't think you could have done more: you almost died."

Tobias shrugged. "Maybe you're right, I ..."

He was interrupted by a monstrous sound from the direction of the church: something between a roar and a shriek that curdled the blood.

"Oh my God!" Tobias whispered as a moment later they heard the flapping of wings and saw a shadow rise into the sky. They watched open-mouthed as it moved away towards the north east.

Freya's eyes widened and she stared at her companion. "You don't think ... it can't be ... can it?"

"I am afraid so. It seems a second avatar is born. Gabriel never warned us about that!"

"Two of them! We couldn't kill *one*," Freya gasped. "Tobias, what are we going to do?"

The doctor shrugged. He really had no idea at all. He looked up at the sky. Stars, planets and the moon alike were obscured by a thick pall of acrid smoke from the fire, which now covered a vast swathe of the heart of the city. Tobias reckoned it was now past midnight, which meant the fire had been burning for twenty-four hours. He wondered if anything could stop it now. Suddenly he yawned and realised he felt exhausted. He needed rest, food and preferably a cold bucket of water to stick his head into, but not necessarily in that order.

"Come on," he said softly, "let's go."

Chapter 19
Hang 'Em

Near Badersley Compton, Monday 3rd September, 1666: daybreak

"**B**enjamin! Benjamin, wake up! Now, Benjamin, please!" A voice called from a great distance as if through a tunnel, but muffled, as though it was coming from the other side of a wall. How long had he been unconscious? It felt like forever but, as Ben opened his eyes and the concerned face of Gabriel came into focus, he saw from the half light that it was not yet fully dawn. He was lying on the straw in the barn loft where they had spent the night. He sat up and a sudden sharp pain shot through his head, triggering an attack of vertigo. As the room spun he flopped back again, on to the straw.

"Easy there, lad, take your time."

"What ...?" Ben started to say, but his mouth was dry and he coughed. A flask of something strong tasting was pressed to his lips and he choked on it. He suspected it was brandy, which he had never drunk and he was not sure he wanted to again, but at least it wet his mouth. "What happened?" he asked, blinking to clear his vision and trying to focus on the bookseller crouched down beside him.

"Don't you remember?" Gabriel asked and frowned when Ben shook his head.

"Well, about an hour ago you woke up raging: shouting and shaking and yelling that you were sorry. Then you started reciting the incantation for the Blinding Light. You drew far too much power through yourself and you lost control of the words you were saying. If I had not been here to stun you ... well, you would be dead now," Gabriel said gravely.

"I don't remember. Why don't I remember?" Ben said panicking now. The older man put a hand on his shoulder to calm him.

"It's all right. You will be fine in a while," then he glanced out of the barn door at the faint light, "look, it's practically dawn. We need to get started if we're to reach London today. It's a long way and we are tired. Do you think you can walk?"

Ben nodded and got to his feet. His head felt clearer now and the pain had faded. "How's your arm?" he asked, looking down at Gabriel's swollen, bruised elbow and smiling slightly at the man's ill-fitting smock and breeches.

"It'll do," said Gabriel shortly.

"Well I'll carry those," Ben picked up the sack of clothes, wrinkling his nose at the smell that still clung to them. His satchel too looked the worse for wear, but he shrugged the strap over his head and settled it comfortably on his hip. They climbed down into the interior of the barn and set off across the fields to the nearest road. As they walked, Gabriel did not say much, but kept studying him when he thought Ben was not looking, and glancing quickly away when Ben met his gaze. The bookseller's expression was anxious – almost fearful - and Ben's thoughts raced. What had he been dreaming about that had disturbed him so much he had lost control and almost killed himself? Alarmed, he asked Gabriel to describe again what had happened.

"Like I said, you woke up suddenly reciting Words of Power, interrupted by crying and saying you were sorry."

"Sorry about what?"

Gabriel stopped walking and turned to look at him.

"Well, I would think it was your parents' death you were recalling again."

Shocked, Ben came to a standstill and stared blankly at the bookseller. "My parents are dead?" he asked at length.

Now it was Gabriel's turn to stare. "You know that, boy, you told me yourself. You live with your uncle now. Keep walking, Benjamin, we don't have time to stop."

Placing one foot in front of the other, Ben plodded forward, his mind reeling. Why could he not remember this? He tried to think back over the days and months, but could not recall much beyond faint, blurred memories of the last few days at school, meeting Freya and running for his life from the Exchange. Not until the moment he had read the scroll in the graveyard did everything come suddenly and sharply into focus in his mind. It was as if all that had happened before that moment was meaningless, little more than a succession of grey images in his memory and only events from that instant onwards were bright, colourful and vibrant: and the most vibrant of all were those moments when he had felt the power pulsating though him. He could recall each exhilarating second of that feeling and yearned for more, but the thought occurred to him that it might have been that very power that had lost him his memories. Was the price worth paying? Ben was not sure.

Gabriel was still staring at him, looking alarmed now. "Benjamin? Don't you remember?"

Ben realised he needed time to think about what had happened: that meant keeping quiet, for the moment, about the loss of memory. He nodded and smiled at Gabriel.

"Sure I remember all that. Sorry if I'm a bit dim-witted this morning: I think I'm still tired. Let's get moving, as you say, we need to reach the city today," he answered and increased his pace, but when he glanced behind he saw the bookseller following along after him, a thoughtful and concerned look on his face. Ben smiled again and waved at Gabriel to catch up. Secretly, though, he was worried too. If the Words of Power had made him lose his memory, did this mean using sorcery was too dangerous for him? If so and he needed to use it against Dantalion or Artemas, what would he do? Dare he risk losing control again? He needed to know what Gabriel thought.

"Gabriel, about the journal and Dantalion, what am I, er, we, going to do?" he asked. There was thoughtful pause before the bookseller answered.

"We go back to the city and find the others and come up with a plan, but ..."

"But right now you have no idea, do you?"

Gabriel said nothing. He did not need to.

They plodded on in gloomy silence as the sun rose, dispersing the ground mist and warming the air around them. As they walked, both were aware they had twenty miles to cover, and that when they got to London it would still be burning, for there was not a rain cloud in the sky and only a miracle would quench those fierce flames now.

****

It had been a long night for Matthias. After its birth, the second avatar had homed in on the first and now the two of them stood side by side in the road. Their movements appeared effortlessly synchronised, so that the clawing motions they made had become, to him, rather like a strangely hypnotic ballet. Each thrust and pull of their arms drew on the now powerful winds, driving the blaze onwards to yet more destruction. As the fire expanded it took up an increasing frontage and the citizens of London, the trained bands and the Horse Guard regiments under the command of the King's brother, James, Duke of York, were increasingly pressed to contain it. Even the King himself had spent some time that morning helping the fire fighters.

Matthias stood on Watling Street and as the fire moved towards him he suddenly yawned. He had not slept much for days and was aware he must rest soon or collapse with fatigue. Then again, he knew that today, Monday, was the critical day for Dantalion's plans. This was the day when Matthias and the avatars needed to expand the fire even more than they had yesterday.

Two seals had perished, but four more remained in addition to the Last Seal. He thought about Artemas a moment and wondered if he had found the journal of that warlock, Cornelius, along with the secret that would finally free Dantalion. So much still remained to be done; for each yard that the fire had advanced, it needed to move another five. The whole of the mediaeval heart of the city would have to burn. Maybe fifteen thousand houses along with the Lord knew how many churches and trading halls must be sacrificed. How many people's homes must go: fifty thousand? One hundred thousand? How many livelihoods and how many life's savings? How many lives? He thought about that for a moment and was surprised that he wasted time on it.

Down the street a small church collapsed into the maelstrom with a crack and a boom. Nearby, a small boy separated from his family wept in despair. As Matthias watched, the boy's mother emerged from the milling crowds and ran towards her son. Her relief was plain to see and, witnessing her joy, the preacher felt a moment's pleasure. He smiled at her and for an instant their gazes locked and she smiled back at him. Then he frowned. Why did he care? About her, or any of these lost

241

souls? This city was decadent and sinful and the purging of its filth was the best thing that could happen. That is what he believed. Why then did he suddenly feel so sad?

He yawned again and felt his eyes, heavy with fatigue, start to droop. He was tired, that was all: a few hours' sleep and his mind would be clear again. He looked back at the fire approaching up the street and nodded. The progress was fine here. He would move on to the Royal Exchange and spread the fire northwards now. There was little chance of anyone stopping the flames for no one would be attacking the main force behind it - the avatars - unless somehow the doctor had survived or that troublesome girl. But it was unlikely; he had heard St Martin's bells clanging in discordant despair and then suddenly cease. Dr Janssen was certainly dead, if not the girl. Perhaps, when Artemas got back, he would arrange for Gymer and his men to pay a visit to the doctor's house in case she had returned there. Artemas: where was he? He should be here by now.

"My word, Matthias, you have, ah ... been busy!" Artemas' sarcastic drawl broke into his thoughts, making the preacher jump. Spinning round he saw the Cavalier standing behind him.

"Talk of the Devil! I was just this minute thinking about you," the preacher said.

"You were? Well here I am."

Matthias raised his eyebrows in silent question and looked pointedly at the leather-bound book Artemas was carrying.

"Yes, here it is, Matthias: Cornelius' journal," Artemas patted the book. "With this and what I found in the Cathedral I know everything. Everything, I tell you: where the Last Seal is, how to unveil it and the words and ritual that will finally release Dantalion." He grinned and Matthias sighed with relief.

"So when can we do it?"

"As soon as the six seals are destroyed, when do you think that will be?"

Matthias thought about it for a moment, calculating the rate of the fire's spread and then replied. "Tuesday – tomorrow I mean - quite late in the day."

"Then at midnight tomorrow, Dantalion rises!"

****

Tobias yawned, sipped at his coffee and munched on some toast. He and Freya had got back to his house without incident in the early hours of the morning. The girl was all but asleep on her feet, but he had insisted on dressing her burns before showing her to a guest bedroom. He had rummaged in the room of his housekeeper - Owen's sister, who always went home at weekends and would not be back until later - and borrowed a nightgown, an assortment of clean clothes and a pair of shoes. These, along with a bowl of warm water and a towel, he had taken to Freya, and helped her to clean off the soot and smoke from the fire. Then he had left her to sleep. His opinion of the little thief had altered radically since she had first arrived in Gabriel's arms, and Tobias was surprised that not only had he found much to admire in her cheery indomitable spirit and native intelligence - without which he would of certainty have fried in St Martin's church - but that he had actually grown to like her.

Before allowing himself to relax, he had checked on Owen. The valet was fast asleep in his own room and seemed well enough, though his face was swollen and badly bruised. Tobias decided that in the morning he would send him home to convalesce for a few days. His family lived in Westminster, which was well away from the fire. Tobias could not imagine it would get that far; the militia had been mobilised and would surely succeed in putting it out soon.

Finally, he had collapsed into his own bed and slept for several hours. Emerging blearily from his room soon after noon, he had prepared some food and left a tray outside the girl's door, giving a few gentle taps to wake her before taking his own toast and coffee into the study.

Half an hour later, he had just helped himself to another slice of buttered toast when there was a polite knock at the study door and, almost bashfully, Freya entered. The doctor stared at her in silence for a moment. It was the first time he had seen her in a woman's garb. Her dress was a practical garment such as housemaids and craftswomen wore: lightweight and lacking the frills and heavy skirts of a noblewoman's attire, but it suited her nonetheless. Over a plain white cotton shift, Freya wore a dark green jacket-like bodice that had three-quarter length sleeves, pleated at shoulder and cuff. It was worn with a matching skirt and an embroidered lace cap. On her feet a pair of thick-heeled shoes with square toes were a distinct improvement on the disintegrating boots she had previously owned. It was fortuitous that Owen's sister was much of a size with Freya; the clothes seemed a good fit. Her skin, now clean, was smattered with light freckles and her copper-coloured hair, still wet, was curling into natural ringlets.

Tobias gaped, realised his mouth was open, pulled himself quickly together and smiled at her: the little thief was in fact a quite beautiful young woman.

"Good Lord! You are a girl after all," he teased to cover his confusion.

"What you mean by that?" she replied.

"Well, now that you have changed and cleaned off all that soot and dirt I hardly recognise you." He gave an exaggerated sniff, "You even smell like a girl and not like, er ..."

She edged closer and her eyes narrowed dangerously. "Like what?" He could see that a small knife had suddenly appeared in her hand.

"Well, you have slept in that stable a long time and I, oh ... never mind." He smiled weakly, "Is that one of my kitchen knives?"

Freya shrugged. "Possibly, is there a problem?

"No, not at all. Look, I did not mean to offend you. You really are quite pretty; that's all I meant. Maybe you have not been told that enough?" He raised his hands defensively as her eyes narrowed again, "Don't worry. I'm not going to try anything. Were I Ben's age I might have difficulty in keeping my hands off you," he grinned, "but you are only fifteen and I am a little more than twice your age. Even so, you ought to try wearing a dress more often, it suits you."

She shook her head, slid the knife away out of sight and considered him for a moment before grinning back at him.

"London's a dangerous place, you know," she said. "You might not realise it here in your nice house, but only a few streets away girls my age have been prostitutes for three years. I didn't want to end up like that. I made my way the best that I could and it was easier if no one knew I was a girl."

"I'm sorry. You've had it tough, I can see that."

"First Ben and now you: that's two of you who've said 'I'm sorry'. Why do you say that? Why does everyone say that? You did not cause the plague or kill my mother. It just happened. Crying about it don't help, nor being sorry."

He nodded and then to change the subject pointed at her side. "How's the burn?"

"Better now you dressed it. Thanks for doing that and for the food. What do I owe you?"

He looked surprised again. "Freya, you astound me. You are a thief and a vagabond. You steal a few trinkets and the odd knife from me without blinking and yet you worry about paying me for treatment. You saved my life in that church – it is payment enough many times over."

Again she shrugged, but he noticed the relief flitting through her eyes before she looked down to conceal it.

"Tell me, girl, why are you still involved in this business? You don't need to be. You can leave. I will give you a little money and you can get out of the city and find a job somewhere. As you say, it's a dangerous place to live – and getting more so now!"

"Oh, I'm not leaving. That Dantalion hurt me and I owe him for that, and my city is still burning because of Matthias and Artemas. There's going to be a reckoning and I want to be there when it happens."

Tobias finished his coffee. "Well then, what should we do? It seems impossible to beat those avatars." After a moment he added, "Maybe we should ..." He was interrupted by a loud knocking at the front door and stopped speaking, alarm flaring in his eyes.

Freya slipped over to the window and peered around the curtains. Suddenly she darted back, the freckles standing out on her suddenly pallid skin. "It's Gymer with a couple of his men," she whispered.

Tobias was on his feet and pushing his pistols into his tunic pocket he beckoned Freya. "Quickly, follow me. We will go out the back way."

They scuttled out into the hall and through the kitchen. A door led outside into a yard at the rear. As they pulled the back door closed, they heard the one at the front burst open as Gymer's men forced their way in.

"Search the house. Walton," Gymer shouted, "back door. Now!"

Freya and Tobias ran through the yard towards the gate. It opened into a narrow passageway between the doctor's house and the one next door. Freya came to an abrupt halt as she

246

opened the gate, for Marlowe was standing in the alleyway, his huge musket cradled in his arms, the lighted match smoking in his fingers. He looked just as surprised to see them as they were to see him, but he recovered faster.

"Stop right there," he said dully, "or I fire."

He stared at Freya, the barrel of his musket dropping slightly as he gazed lasciviously at her bodice. She jumped forward, scraped her heeled shoe down his shin and stamped hard on his foot. Marlowe shouted out in rage and pulled the trigger involuntarily. The huge boom, echoed down the alleyway deafening them all and the bright flash half-blinded them, but the shot flew wide. Tobias swung a fist and felt it connect with the giant's chin sending him sprawling backwards against the wall, which he slid down to end up in a heap at its base.

"Ouch, that hurt," Tobias shook his hand and winced. "Brute's got a jaw like an elephant. Come on, quick – they will have heard the shot."

"You seen an elephant then?"

"Only in pictures – come ON Freya!"

They ran down the alleyway to the street and turned up Old Bailey in the direction of Pie Corner, intending to enter the city through Newgate and hide in Freya's stables. They didn't get far before they found themselves in a traffic jam. Just about every cart, hackney carriage and sedan chair in London seemed to be trying to exit through the gates and out towards Holborn. There was panic in the air and the crowd was bad tempered and angry. This was not helped by a troop of the Duke of York's soldiers, who were pushing the common folk out of the street, fighting against the tide to get into the city with their wagonloads of fire fighting equipment.

As Tobias and Freya ground to a halt, the doctor looked back down Old Bailey towards his house and gave a sudden cry of alarm. Gymer and his men were moving up the road towards them. He didn't think he and Freya had been spotted yet, disguised as they were amongst the crowds and with their change of clothes perhaps a source of confusion, but it couldn't be long before Gymer had them in his sights.

"Got to get moving, Freya." He turned to look ahead up the road, then let out a yelp of surprise as he found he was looking straight into the eyes of Artemas. Tobias reached into his coat for a pistol, but the Cavalier shook his head.

"No Doctor, I would ah ... advise against that," he said softly, his head tilting slightly to the side. One of his cronies was there. Tobias could see from the bulge beneath the man's coat that, unnoticed by the crowd milling around them, he held a firearm at the ready. Tobias relaxed his hand slowly, bringing it away from his pistol.

"That's better. Be a shame to cause a scene here. The crowd is on the edge of hysteria as it is, but Morris does have such a quick trigger finger and I have to try so hard to control him."

"I bet you do," Freya hissed, glaring at Artemas' companion.

"Can this be our little thief?" Artemas purred, looking Freya up and down, "My word; what a change! Bedded her have you, Doctor?"

Humiliated, the girl snarled, her face flushed scarlet. Knife in hand, she tensed ready to spring.

Moving quickly between Artemas and Freya before she did something silly and got herself shot, Tobias growled, "What do you want, *murderer*?"

"Murderer?" Artemas raised his eyebrows. "Oh, of course. You must be referring to your dear departed father, Markus Janssen. The fool died trying to stop us."

"He succeeded, with Gabriel's help. You did not raise the demon last year and we will stop you again this year. Soon we will have discovered more."

"Perhaps you refer to this?" Artemas taunted, pulling an ancient book out of his coat. "The journal of Cornelius Silver,"

248

he laughed, "Benjamin and Gabriel did well to find it. Or I did well letting them do the work for me before taking it from them. We have not quite decided what was more brilliant, have we, Morris?" Morris said nothing, just stared at them.

"What did you do to them?" Freya asked between gritted teeth.

"Do? I did nothing. When I left them they were unhurt. Mind you, what the local sheriff will do when he finds them in a house full of dead bodies is a different matter," Artemas added with a grin, "so you see we have everything we need. Well, almost everything. Now, though, the Master would like something from you."

His eyes narrowing with suspicion, Tobias held the Cavalier's gaze. "What are you talking about, Artemas?"

"Well, he is sure that the young lad and Gabriel will find a way out of their predicament, and he wa-"

Tobias cut across him, "If anything happens to them you will regret it!" he threatened, face flushed with anger.

"Why are you so bothered about Gabriel?" Artemas frowned.

"I owe him. He was with my father in the last fight."

"He abandoned your father in the last fight, you mean. That's why Dr Janssen died. Your friend, the cowardly bookseller, ran away and left him to fight alone. Did he not tell you? No, I suppose not."

"What? You lie!" Tobias shouted and now several people in the crowd pushing past turned their heads to stare at them.

"Why? Why would I lie?" Artemas went on in his soft voice. "You must ask him if you see him again, but there is the point. You have no reason to be loyal to the man who abandoned your father. Likewise, my dear young thief," he added turning to Freya, "what reason do you have to help the snobby schoolboy who would not normally look twice at you in the street. Will he pay you anything?"

"I don't care about money!"

Artemas' snort cut across her. "Balderdash. You are a thief; of course you care about money. Would you care about a hundred pounds? It can be yours if you bring Benjamin and Gabriel to me."

"A *hundred* ..." her eyes wide, Freya's mouth dropped open. She swallowed, shook her head, spat out the words, "Get lost, I'm no traitor."

Next to her, Tobias nodded, although his eyes were distant, still wondering about the truth of what the Cavalier had said. It explained something about Gabriel that had always puzzled him.

"Where's the betrayal?" Artemas smiled. "You only met them two days ago. One hundred pounds for the boy seems like a bargain to me. You'd never have to thieve again. And for you," he said to Tobias, "well, you get revenge on the man who betrayed your father. You talk about betrayal – Gabriel is the traitor here."

He studied them both for a moment. "So, what do you say?"

"Go to the devil and be damned, Artemas!" Freya shouted. Tobias nodded firmly, his eyes clearer now.

"Well then, you leave me no choice. Do you remember my saying the crowd was on the edge of hysteria? It is true. Just look at them. There is a story going round that a bunch of foreigners started the fire: French maybe, or more likely Dutch. What do you have to say about that Doctor *Janssen*?" he shouted the last words. The crowd suddenly fell silent and stared at the little huddle in their midst.

"That's right everyone: this is Doctor Tobias Janssen. His father was a Dutch merchant. I believe he smuggled combustibles into the country and the good doctor here set them off and started the fire. What shall we do about it?"

Tobias' eyes widened in fear, "Now just you wait a moment, I am English!"

"No, you are DUTCH," Artemas shouted, slipping back into the crowd, "What shall we do about it?"

"Hang him!" shouted Morris with a gleam in his eye. It was like setting match to kindling: one moment a spark and the next a roaring fire.

As one, the crowd surged forward shouting, "Hang him! Hang him from Newgate!" Several hands lunged at Tobias. He struggled and pulled out a pistol. That was a mistake.

"Watch out: he is armed. It proves he is guilty. Hang him now!"

Suddenly the world around Freya and Tobias was full of a raging mass of humanity, tugging, punching and raking at them. Tobias was lifted up in the air and he shouted to be let down. "I'm as English as you are!" he yelled. But it did no good. He craned his neck and saw that Freya was also being borne aloft.

"Leave her alone! She is innocent!"

Now though, the din was terrible. Nobody wanted to listen. Three thousand voices were all baying for his death as he and Freya were carried to Newgate.

There, above the ancient city gates, Tobias could see a man was lowering a rope with a noose on the end.

"Hang them! They started the fire," the people shouted. "Hang them now!"

"Oh my God!" Tobias muttered.

Chapter 20
Newgate

London, Monday 3rd September, 1666: late-afternoon

"Hang them!" the crowd implored and Tobias, still struggling and fighting to get free, was forced round so his head could be thrust through the noose.

"Leave him alone!" Freya shouted. One of the men carrying her leaned over and brought his pockmarked face so close to her she could smell the stale wine and tobacco on his breath.

"Save yer breath, deary, you'll be struggling fer it soon enough," he hissed in her ear, spraying spittle on her face. She turned away in revulsion then horror as she saw a second rope being lowered from the gate: a rope intended for her.

"Oh *snoggers*!" she swore.

Close by, the loud boom of first one musket, then another, cut through the baying din and the rabble fell suddenly silent, twisting their necks to the left and right in an attempt to see who had fired the shots. There was a commotion at the edge of the crowd and it parted, allowing Gymer, Marlowe and Spencer to stride into their midst. Walton came limping behind, his arm still in a sling. Each man was armed with pistol and musket and, although outnumbered and now surrounded by the angry and vengeful crowd, the spymaster walked confidently up to the men holding Tobias and Freya aloft.

"Let them down," he ordered simply.

"Why should we?" A voice shouted from on top of the gateway, "And what gives you the right to order us about anyway?"

Freya craned her neck so she could now see that the voice belonged to a weasel-faced man, who was standing high up on the gatehouse glaring down at them all, his arms crossed in defiance. Gymer stared up at the man for a moment and then dramatically pulled a parchment from his tunic. Holding it aloft in one hand he then turned slowly in a circle so everyone near him could see the elaborate seal emblazoned upon it.

"See here: I bear the King's authority. This warrant grants me that right, so – I say again – release them." Still, however, no one moved.

"I said RELEASE them!" Gymer bellowed, levelling his pistol.

Grudgingly the men holding up Tobias and Freya dumped them unceremoniously on the ground. They both sat stunned, rubbing their sore limbs while anxiously watching the mob. Faced with Gymer's authority and his men's levelled muskets, people slowly and reluctantly began to disperse.

When the crowds had surged off westwards towards Smithfield, Gymer walked over to the sorry pair and looked down at them. Tobias frowned back at him, his eyes narrowed. "Why did you do that? Are you expecting gratitude?"

Gymer gave a humourless bark of laughter. "Hardly, Doctor. Oh, don't be mistaken: I wasn't saving you for your own good. I know you started the fire. I just need to prove it. Then, Doctor, and you, Miss, you will both hang. But first I want to know who you work with and what their plan is. Only when I am sure the King and his Kingdom are safe will you die."

"I'm not working with anyone," Tobias protested. "I'm innocent I tell you. It's all a mistake."

"Lock them away!" Gymer said, ignoring him and turning to Marlowe. "We will make them talk."

The giant seized them both roughly by their arms, and dragging them to their feet manhandled them across to the gatehouse. Freya was gratified to see that, like Walton, he was walking with a slight limp due to her recent handiwork, and nursing a sizeable swelling on his face from Tobias' fist.

Spencer stepped past Marlow and hammered on a sturdy oak door that led into the gatehouse on one side of the roadway. When it opened he spoke to the doorman, who glanced sharply at Freya and Tobias and then nodded before stepping to one side. Marlowe dragged the pair inside and down a few steps.

The light was faint at first, but as her eyes adjusted, Freya realised where she was. She was inside Newgate lockup! A place she had always imagined she would end up in if they caught her thieving. Now, dammit, through no fault of her own, here she was.

They were pushed into a cell and the metal-barred door locked behind them. Gymer spoke to the jailer and after a moment came over to address them through the bars. "I'm making arrangements for you to be transferred to White Hall later. I have ... well, I have equipment there that will assist in this process and make it all so much easier. Meanwhile, enjoy your night in this fine guest house," he added and behind him, Walton sniggered. Gymer and his men then departed.

"What does he mean by 'equipment'?" Freya asked in a strangled voice as their footsteps receded.

"I fear it means he intends to put us to torture." Tobias sat down heavily on a wooden bench along one side of the cell. Freya walked to the other side and looked up to the top of the wall. There was a barred window up there. Through the bars she could see people's feet as the crowds hurried past on their exodus from London and the fire. It dawned on her that it was the window at which prisoners begged for food, thrusting their hands through the bars at passersby on their way through the city gate; the same window where, not so long ago, she had bent to drop copper coins into an outstretched palm. She had never imagined that she would be sitting on the other side of the bars just two days later. The place stank of damp and ordure, the walls crawling with lice. In the mucky straw at their feet fleas were already jumping to fasten onto new flesh.

Scratching, Freya sat down against the wall and stared dully at Tobias.

"You all right?" he asked after a moment.

Colour was slowly returning to his face, which a few minutes before had been so very pale. Freya suddenly shivered as the full horror of what had almost happened to them washed over her. Running her hand through her hair, she wished she was not wearing a stupid dress; it felt damnably uncomfortable and she could feel things crawling up her legs. She grimaced, shrugged at Tobias.

"These last few days just keep getting better and better, don't they, Doc? Any ideas on how to get out of here?"

Tobias shook his head. "I'd rather hoped you would have a few thoughts about that, actually."

The little thief examined the locked and very solid looking cell door, and then the sturdy iron bars of the window and shook her head.

"Oh well, I wonder if Ben and Gabriel survived," she murmured after a long silence.

****

"My God, Gabriel, look at it," Ben said, his voice shaking. They had been walking all day through meandering lanes, gradually getting closer to London. Now they had come to the top of a small hill and could see the city just a few miles away. Southwark was off to their right and directly north, hardly visible in the late evening haze, were the shapes of White Hall, Westminster Abbey and other buildings. Somewhere amongst them was Ben's school. Trying to make it out, Ben, whose memory was gradually returning, wondered idly what mood Busby would be in when he finally got back – if he ever did! Ben smiled wryly to himself: it was pretty certain he was in serious trouble; he'd been gone for more than two days. The Headmaster had probably contacted his uncle by now. Had they begun a search? When the fire started in Pudding Lane, did they fear he had perished? He knew he should be terrified of Busby's reaction, or at least concerned about the worry his absence would be causing his uncle, who might be a bit stiff, but had always shown Ben kindness. It did seem unfair to leave him wondering what had happened to his nephew. Somehow, though, Ben did not feel as concerned as he should. He had an insistent feeling that something more significant was happening to him. There was Dantalion, of course, but even the prospect of an ancient demon did not seem really all that important. The odd thing was, Ben could not quite put a finger on what actually *was* important, but he was sure it was something he should remember. His head had felt muzzy since Gabriel had woken him that morning and he had a kind of disconnected feeling, almost as though he was not really here.

Shrugging, Ben turned his gaze away from Westminster and looked north and east towards the city. Even at this distance he could see the huge plume of black smoke billowing up from the fire that was consuming thousands of houses. Eerily, the sky was blood red and the city itself seemed lost in bright orange light. It was hard to avoid the conclusion that London was dying.

"We must pick up the pace, Benjamin," Gabriel said urgently, his eyes wide with alarm at the extent of the blaze. "Matthias and his avatars have spread the fire even faster than I had feared."

"Avatars?" said Ben. "There's only one, isn't there?"

"Each time a seal is destroyed, Dantalion will spawn another avatar. We can't tell from this distance, but from the size of that inferno surely half the seals at least are lost. There could be three or even four of the creatures by now."

"Then what's the point in hurrying? What can we do when we get there?"

The bookseller looked grim, fearful – terrified even – but something else: something more than all that. Whether it was what Ben had said yesterday about Gabriel's courage, or some internal change he had gone through while they were hiding in the sewer, Ben did not know, but whatever it was, the man looked more determined than he had before.

"We can fight, Benjamin. We can face Dantalion and try to find a way to bring him down."

"Maybe we should just warn the King, or maybe we should find Freya and Tobias and get away from London while we still can."

"No!" Gabriel snapped, "I won't run." There was a long pause before he added, "Not again."

"You are thinking that if you sacrifice yourself you will make up for running away from the fight a year ago?" Ben suggested. Gabriel said nothing but glared at him.

"Gabriel, I don't think you are thinking straight. Let me say this ..." but before he could finish, the bookseller turned away.

"Enough talking: come on, let's go!" Gabriel muttered and started off down the hill. Ben hurried after him, gesticulating wildly in exasperation.

"Wait! You're not listening. I'm trying to tell you something."

"Not now! Come on."

"Damn it all then. Have it your own way!" Ben shouted and stomped after him.

With night rapidly falling, they marched on in angry silence, their mood seemingly mirroring that of the smouldering inferno consuming the city they walked towards. Over the next hour they got closer and closer to the river, until finally arriving at the bank opposite White Hall and there they took a boat across. Most folk wanted to be going in the opposite direction today, the boatman told them, his face alight with curiosity, but they did not enlighten him. Grumpily, he deposited them on the steps close to the government buildings. Gabriel paid him off then led the way, navigating a series of passageways to get to the main road. They emerged, to Ben's alarm, directly opposite his school.

Despite the lateness of the hour, the scene outside the gates was nothing short of chaos, matching similar activity along the roads around White Hall. Linkboys scuttled hither and thither holding up flaring torches. Carts and carriages of every size were parked along the wide thoroughfare: outside the Abbey; the school; the Palace of Westminster, and White Hall itself. Priests and acolytes, tutors and pupils, flunkies and officials were all busy pulling boxes and cases of papers, books, files and furniture out of the buildings and loading them into carts. To Ben's and Gabriel's right, the glow of the fire did not seem so far distant and although it must still be more than a mile away, the decision had clearly been made to start evacuating Westminster.

Suddenly, a hand slapped down hard on Ben's shoulder and as he turned to see who it was, his mouth fell open in dismay. Standing there in the middle of the road, his face a mask of indignant fury, was Dr Busby, Headmaster of Westminster School.

Just then, the hubbub of the city around them was drowned by the nearby Abbey bells chiming eight o'clock. Busby glanced towards the sound and then back down at Ben, a look of vicious triumph replacing the fury.

"It's time we had a conversation, Master Silver!"

Chapter 21
City of Ash

London, Monday 3rd September, 1666: mid-evening

"Silver, perhaps you will explain where you have been for the last three days?" Busby wrinkled his nose as he stared down at Ben. "Whatever is that you are wearing? And where is your mortar board? How dare you go gallivanting around London dressed like a peasant! What do you have to say for yourself, boy?"

"I ... that is ..." Ben started to reply, but Busby held up his hand to stop him babbling.

"Wait! I don't care, boy. Nothing will excuse your disobedience of my direct orders." His hand twitched and he looked down at it, as if surprised to find he was not holding his cane. Unable to punish the miscreant immediately he wagged his finger under Ben's nose. "You are suspended. I will inform your uncle and have you removed from the school forthwith. For now you can have some influence on whether that suspension becomes expulsion by helping load the carts. We are transporting the books out to a safer location, and you will help. Then, boy, you will be caned as you deserve."

Busby pointed at the cart and Ben, his heart sinking, moved to obey, but turned back when he heard Gabriel address the Headmaster.

"Sir, I have to confess it is my fault the boy has been absent."

Busby stared at him, as if noticing the bookseller for the first time. Drawing himself up to his full height, his eyebrows bristling, he stared down his nose at Gabriel, as if the bookseller was a pupil who had just reported to his study having failed an exam.

"Whom am I addressing?"

"Gabriel Barlow, Sir."

Busby leaned closer to Gabriel and peered at him with intensity for a moment.

"Barlow? Barlow? Don't I know you? Did I not have you for Latin some years ago?" Gabriel nodded and Busby snorted, "Ah ... yes, I do remember you. What became of you then?"

"I own a bookshop in the Exchange."

"Eh, where's that?" Busby asked.

"The Royal Exchange, Sir," Gabriel replied, shuffling his feet and speaking in a deferential tone, as if the years were stripped away and he was a fourteen-year-old schoolboy again.

"Had you did, Sir, had you did!"

"I'm sorry?" Gabriel sounded both mystified and anxious. "What *do* you mean, Old R ... er, Sir?"

"Eh? Haven't you heard? Your shop is no more, Barlow. The Royal Exchange and all of Cornhill have gone up in smoke. The fire reached there not an hour ago."

There was a shocked silence from Gabriel.

"How do you know, Sir?" Ben ventured.

Busby's head whipped round, his expression becoming grim as he saw Ben had not yet moved towards the carts. "Unlike you, Silver, some of us take our responsibilities seriously. With y permission, the Dean led a party of the senior boys across the city to help fight the fire. The Duke of York sent them down to

St Dunstan's over near the Tower, and they passed the Exchange on the way. The Dean sent Monrose back to let me know where he was going, and the boy was able to report the extent of the conflagration. The Exchange, I am afraid to say, is a blazing ruin. Not that I feel obliged to explain this to you, boy!"

"No, Sir; sorry, Sir."

Gabriel looked crestfallen. Ben moved back and put a hand on his shoulder. "I'm sorry, Gabriel," he said, feeling it was inadequate – but what else was there to say?

"Yes, tragic indeed, Barlow," Busby said, and a slight hint of compassion touched his voice briefly, but was just as quickly gone. "However, none of this explains what this boy has been doing in your company for the past three days and what delayed his return." Gabriel, distracted, did not seem to hear the Headmaster.

Busby looked across at Ben. "Perhaps you can provide a satisfactory account, Silver?"

"Well he ... I," Ben stammered, but could still think of no explanation that would sound reasonable, "I got cut off when the fire started, Sir."

"That may be true, Silver; *may* be. But even if it is, it does not explain why you left the school in the first place and were in a position to be trapped by the fire, does it?"

"No, Sir," Ben mumbled.

"No, Sir, indeed!" Busby said and then his gaze fell upon Gabriel once more. "So, Mr Barlow, I thank you for bringing our errant schoolboy home. Rest assured his truancy will be punished. I am sure you have much to do, what with the tragedy that has befallen your business. I would not like to detain you any longer. I'll bid you good night, Sir." He turned away from Gabriel and addressed Ben, "And as for you boy, you will come with me!"

With a helpless glance at Gabriel, Ben had just started to walk across the road towards the cart, when one of the other tutors came running up to Busby.

"Headmaster, you must come quickly. Parsons fell and has injured himself carrying some books down the stairs from the library. I think he may have broken his leg."

"Tch! Parsons is a liability. That boy falls over even if he sneezes. You should not have got him carrying anything. Well, come on then, we had better see to him." Busby walked a few steps across the road and then shouted over his shoulder at Ben, "Silver, do as I say at once. Go to the carts and help them. We will continue this discussion later." Then he bustled away.

Watching him depart, Ben turned to Gabriel and laughed. The bookseller was standing in the road, his face pale and hands visibly trembling as he let out a long breath of relief.

"'The Royal Exchange, Sir'," Ben mimicked, in a fair imitation of Gabriel's voice, "'Struth! You looked more scared than I felt."

"Scared?" Gabriel smiled weakly, "I was terrified! Twenty years just fell away when he spoke to me. I was back in third period Latin again. Right now I would rather take on Artemas, Matthias, Dantalion and a gaggle of those avatars combined, than face Old Rusty again!"

Snorting with laughter, Ben glanced back at the school gates. "Come on, we had better be going." He set off at a fast walk towards the city, Gabriel hurrying to keep up.

"If he comes back and you are not here, he won't be very happy," Gabriel pointed out.

Ben nodded but kept on walking. "Come on! If Dantalion is free, expulsion from Westminster is the least of my worries." Ben stopped suddenly and turned to look at the bookseller, "I am truly sorry about the shop, though," he muttered, still unsure what to say to a man whose livelihood had just been destroyed.

Gabriel looked sad, but nodded his thanks. "I kept the most important *Praesidium* records at my house outside the city, but the books and documents at the shop were – in some cases – priceless," he admitted. "Still, as you say, if we don't deal with Dantalion, what does it matter? Let's go!"

They walked quickly to get away from the school, but also to approach the city as soon as possible. It would normally be full dark at this hour, but with the sky reflecting the glow of the fire it was almost as bright as day. Every stride brought them closer to the conflagration ahead and they walked on in apprehensive silence. Looking at the fire, Ben felt it had some deeper significance for him than for others, but he could not quite place what it was. Some memory stirred in the back of his mind, but it was intangible and transient and when he reached out for it, it flittered beyond his grasp. It was like walking towards the end of a rainbow: he could never quite reach it.

He had the feeling that somewhere deep inside he knew what it was that was so important and that it was linked with the fire. He also knew something had happened to him last night, some kind of dream, and that Gabriel had seen his reaction to it. But Gabriel would not discuss it. Each time Ben broached the subject, the bookseller would say only that it was too dangerous and he needed time to think. But Gabriel, it seemed, was too absorbed with his own worries to think about Ben's just now. Ironically, Ben *could* remember the bookseller's problems, if not his own. Gabriel had acted the coward, running away and abandoning Markus Janssen to his death, or so he believed. Furthermore, he now seemed set on confronting Dantalion to make amends, at whatever the cost.

Despite the brief moment of humour at the school, Gabriel had lapsed into depression again and resisted Ben's attempts at conversation as they hurried along. Lost in their own thoughts, neither of them noticed, until it was almost too late, a group of four horsemen riding towards them westwards along Holborn and away from the city.

Hearing the approaching hooves, Ben glanced up. The red glow of the fire ahead lit up the stern features of the leading horseman: it was Captain Gymer! At that very moment the spymaster also spotted Ben. A look of recognition crossed his face and he shouted to his men.

"There are the other two of them, my boys, come on let's get them!" Digging in their heels and giving a whoop as they charged, Gymer and his men rode down upon Ben and Gabriel.

****

"You did *what!*" Dantalion roared. His face contorted with rage and he launched himself across the roof of the Cathedral tower, landing with such an impact that the whole building shook. Artemas gave a startled cry as he was thrown to his knees. Dantalion seized him by the throat and dragged him to the edge.

"Master, I made a mistake!" Artemas whimpered as he was thrust face downwards off the top of St Paul's and then hung in the air, suspended by Dantalion's claw hooked into the back of the Cavalier's tunic. The collar of his shirt was tight around Artemas' throat and he started to choke. Under his weight, a button snapped off his tunic; he could feel the thread on the others stretching, the garment beginning to loosen. It was chilling to realise that all that was between him and oblivion were a few strands of cotton. His feet scrabbled in a vain attempt to find a purchase on the tower's lip. He stared down at the yawning gap beneath him and fought to ignore his rising panic; tried not to imagine what would happen if Dantalion let him go to tumble to his death several hundred feet below. Sweat drenched his clothes and he felt as if his heart would burst out through his chest it was pounding so hard. Only one thing kept Artemas from screaming for mercy; the one fact that kept him sane: Dantalion needed him.

He swallowed hard, difficult while choking, but he managed to speak. "I'm sorry, Master, I made a mistake." It came out as a weak croak.

"Mistake?" roared Dantalion, thrusting him out further and then letting him drop a couple of feet before yanking him violently back again. Another button popped off and Artemas' tunic gaped open, fastened now by only one remaining button. He tried to close his eyes, but Dantalion grasped the back of his head and tugged at his hair. He screamed in pain and was forced to stare through tear-filled eyes at the burning city beneath him. For the first time Artemas wondered if he had overestimated the demon's need of him. Was it possible he could die in this make-believe world – this mirage of the creature's febrile imagination? Was Dantalion's anger now out of control? Choking, terrified, Artemas wished he could turn the clock back. It was all the fault of that stupid boy, Benjamin Silver.

When Artemas had read Cornelius' journal on the journey back to the city from Badersley Compton, he had realised to his consternation that he had made a mistake at the Manor. He had allowed his natural penchant for cruelty, as well as his desire to rid himself of a potential rival for the demon's attention, to cloud his judgement. Dantalion had perceived something of the boy's importance that went beyond what Artemas had understood. The journal confirmed it: they needed the boy alive. Thus it was in some trepidation that on his return, Artemas had reported to his master.

As ever, when Artemas saw him alone, Dantalion had reverted to his true appearance as a demon lord, and these last couple of days when he did so, instead of conjuring the peaceful glade for their meetings, it was this illusion of London in flames. Or was it an illusion? Artemas began to wonder if this was happening in the real London right now; the reality every bit as horrifying as the scenes Dantalion projected so he could enjoy watching London die.

When, a few moments before, Artemas had confessed what he had done, his master had flown into such a violent rage that Artemas feared Dantalion would now simply kill him. "Please, Master, I can make amends," he gasped, his voice rising to a hoarse squeak. "Please, Master!" It was becoming harder to breathe now; his lungs were burning, his vision beginning to dim. Artemas truly believed he was about to die.

"Pah!" Dantalion suddenly spat, and dragging his lieutenant back swung him round and threw him down. Gasping, Artemas landed sprawled on top of the tower, a red mist in front of his eyes. His master stood glaring down at him, breathing heavily, claws clenching and unclenching, nostrils flaring. Artemas rubbed his neck and forced air through his painfully swollen throat as he lay and watched the demon above him, much as a mouse watches a cat about to pounce.

Gradually the demon's breaths slowed and the rage dissipated. When he finally spoke, his voice was angry but controlled. "I am most disappointed in you, Artemas," he growled. "You had the boy and the last of the *Praesidium* in your hands and not only did you let them get away from you, but you arranged for their certain deaths. I told you they were not to be harmed."

That was not strictly true, but Artemas thought better of pointing it out. "I'm sorry," he whined.

"You should have brought them to me as I ordered. If we fail because of this I will not be forgiving. I trust you know that."

After what had just occurred, Artemas had no doubts at all. He scrambled to his knees and bowed deeply to the demon.

"Master, I apologise, but I am sure we can find them. I have already ascertained that the Sheriff found neither the boy nor the man Gabriel in the house. Obviously they escaped and are on their way here. They will stop at nothing to retrieve the journal. We will find them and this time I will bring Silver before you, on my oath."

Dantalion studied him for a long time, the glare of his eyes boring into him and peeling away any deceit or secrets Artemas might still hide. At last the demon's gaze returned to the fire below. When he spoke again, his voice was controlled with no hint of the anger of moments before. "That error apart, you have done well, Artemas. We know where all six seals are and four are already destroyed. The other two will perish tomorrow. We know now where the Last Seal is located. We know the ritual to free me and what that involves and the Words that you must use. Tell me, does he suspect anything?"

Artemas knew to which 'he' Dantalion referred. Shaking his head, he dragged himself to his feet. "Matthias has grown sceptical over the last few days, but I think he is too far committed to his dream of the Angel of Judgement to turn aside now. He and his followers will see it through."

"Very well, we still need him for a few more hours, he and the others who act in my name. This time tomorrow his doubts will be irrelevant. In the morning you must go to the Last Seal and prepare the vault. Take Matthias, his twelve followers, my book and everything we need. Find and take the boy and then all will be ready for the Rite."

Artemas nodded and thought of the Rite they must enact: *The Rite of The Thirteen and The One.* His eyes glinted in anticipation. Tomorrow fourteen would die and one demon would rise! Himself! The world and everything in it would be within his grasp.

****

Ben froze in panic as sixteen steel-shod hooves pounded the road ahead. He had heard stories about Prince Rupert's cavalry charges and how terrifying they were; he could now see why. The horses surged towards them, their flaring nostrils flecked with spume, their riders holding blazing torches aloft. A family, who had been dragging a hand cart away from the city, screamed and scattered like a flock of birds as the horses thundered past. Ben's heart pounded. 'MOVE!' he said to himself. 'You *must* move!' Yet he could not; his legs were like lead and would not obey him. He let out a strangled cry as Gabriel grabbed his shirt and yanked him sideways.

"This way, Benjamin, follow me. Quickly!"

The two of them stumbled off Holborn into Fetter Lane. A few yards along, a dark and fetid alleyway led off the lane to pass the backs of the houses on Holborn. Not a moment too soon they dived down it into darkness, looking desperately for somewhere to hide while from behind them came the noise of galloping horses entering Fetter Lane. Ben spotted a pile of abandoned wooden crates and pulled Gabriel down behind them. They crouched low, panting for air, noses pressed to the rotting wood as they struggled to control their breathing.

The horses clattered to a stop, their hooves sliding on the cobbles. Gymer's shout rang out: "Dismount, lads. Bring those torches over here, we need light." There was a brief silence; Ben could smell the smoking pitch of the torches, see a glow of light at the end of the alleyway. He crouched down further, horribly aware that his right foot was going to sleep. He rubbed at it. Beside him, Gabriel breathed in his ear, "Hold steady, lad."

"Right then," Gymer's, voice came again, "spread out and search."

A few moments later, Ben heard the sound of boots stomping down the alleyway towards them. He felt Gabriel tense beside him, wondered if the bookseller would resort to Words of Power – tempted to do so himself. The boots stopped on the other side of the crates. A torch flared casting strange shadows on the wall behind them. The shadows changed shape. A man was moving around the crates. A moment later the light cast by the torch he carried illuminated Ben and Gabriel, and a shadowy figure came into view. Ben squinted to make out its features, but the light blinded him. He drew breath, opened his mouth to shout the Words, but at that instant the figure turned abruptly away and walked back to the lane. "Nothing down here," he called.

Hearts hammering, Ben and Gabriel stayed very still, hardly daring to breathe. From the lane, Gymer spoke again, "No one see them? Well forget it: we will find them soon enough. Then they will get what is coming to them – come on, mount up, they can't be far." This was followed by the sound of horses trotting off back to Holborn and then moving at a gallop on towards Westminster.

The pressure of Gabriel's hand on Ben's shoulder kept him crouched down for another couple of minutes before it was released and they finally stood up.

"What happened then?" Ben asked, amazed at their good luck and rubbing frantically at his leg to dispel pins and needles. "I mean he – whoever he was – must have seen us."

Gabriel scratched his chin thoughtfully, "Yes, he must have. Yet he said nothing. That is worrying or at least puzzling."

"So why ...?" Ben's voice tailed away.

"I have no idea."

"Who was it, Gymer or one of his men?"

The bookseller did not answer at first. Then he shrugged. "I couldn't tell. The torchlight blinded me – I don't think it was Marlowe, the man was not that massive, but it could have been any of the others." He sighed and continued, "Ah well, another mystery to add to the others. Come on let's get going. We should be able to get to the stable loft before too long."

"I hope the fire doesn't reach it and that we'll find Freya and Tobias are there," Ben said gloomily, not holding out much hope.

They walked on up Holborn, looking all around in case Gymer and his men returned and now also wary of running into Artemas. To their right was an ominous red glow; sparks shooting up through clouds of black smoke were visible even from here, and carried on the wind the acrid stench of the fire, overlaying the usual fetid smells of London. They passed dozens of folk leaving the city in what seemed a constant stream of people. As the fire spread and more houses were lost, more refugees were being created and Ben wondered where they would all go. Presumably some to relatives and friends in areas safe from the fire, but others not so fortunate would have to find somewhere. Maybe they would head for the open areas that lay all round the city; places like Smithfields near Newgate, turning them into shanty towns, camps and bivouacs for folk who had lost everything but their lives, and who, on this the third night of the fire, needed shelter. And what then? Their livelihoods and homes destroyed, where would they go? It would take forever to rebuild so many houses. Poverty already rife would become even worse. It was a disturbing thought. Suddenly, Ben let out a cry and slapped his hand against his thigh.

"What is it?" Gabriel asked, concerned.

"I've left our sack of clothes behind the crates in the alleyway. Sorry, I forgot."

"Well we can't risk going back for them. No matter, I doubt we would ever have got rid of the stink anyway, so maybe it's just as well."

"I'm not sure Old Rusty will agree with you!" Ben grinned, thinking he must now add his best school shirt and britches to the tally of his lost mortar board and gown. He looked down at the farmer's smock he was wearing and snorted with laughter at the thought of Busby's face, but Gabriel seemed too preoccupied to respond. Ben wondered what the bookseller would do after this business with Dantalion was over. Would he go back to selling books or would he find another trade? Ben laughed again, but this time without humour: would there be an "after Dantalion" for any of them? Right now it seemed unlikely.

As they got closer to the city wall, the traffic lightened into small scurrying groups of folk then dwindled to just ones and twos, and then it pretty much stopped altogether. London had emptied and what lay ahead of them was a city of ash, abandoned by all but the militia who continued to fight the fire.

Freya's stables lay up near Cripplegate on the other side of the city wall, so they headed for Newgate, planning to strike north after going through the wall. The gateway was deserted, but as they approached, Ben noticed two ropes, both with empty nooses, dangling down from the top of the gate. He pointed them out to Gabriel, who shrugged at them vaguely. Ben had not walked through Newgate before, but he knew from hearsay that low down on either side were the barred windows of the condemned prisoners' cells. Curious, he peered through the bars.

What he thought he saw brought him up short. He blinked, crouched down to peer more closely. It was dark in the cell, the glow from the sky barely reaching through the bars, but there was something about the two shapes that was familiar. They appeared to be asleep, sitting on a bench opposite the high window.

It couldn't be ... it was!

"Gabriel!" Ben yelled, jumping to his feet. "Look, here, quick!"

A couple of militia men walking through the gatehouse just behind them gave Ben a suspicious look and added a few choice curses as they swerved to avoid him. Gabriel pulled him over to the side and glared at him. "What are you doing?"

Mutely, Ben pointed into the cell and dropped to his knees. Crouching down beside him, Gabriel's jaw dropped as he too saw the occupants through the bars. "Tobias, Freya!" He called as loudly as he dared. "Wake up; it's us, Gabriel and Ben."

Freya opened one eye and stared blearily up at the window. Then both eyes snapped open and she smiled at them. A swift elbow into Tobias' ribs woke him.

"Wha ... what is it?" the doctor muttered sleepily, but then he too came fully awake. He rushed over to the window, "Thank God! You're alive. When Artemas came back and had the journal I feared the worst."

"Don't worry about us. What happened to you?" Ben hissed, looking warily around for the militia.

"Gymer caught us, and unless we can get out of here he is taking us to be tortured and executed. He still thinks I started the fire. Or at least he's determined to find out if I did. He thinks we're working for the Dutch and wants to know what is planned and ..."

Suddenly, as though remembering something, he stopped speaking and glared at the bookseller, drew a breath then said through gritted teeth, "Gabriel, we ran into Artemas and he said something I want to ask you about. It concerns what happened when my father died. Artemas said ..." Tobias paused, swallowed, "he said you abandoned my father and ran to save yourself. Is that true?"

Ben glanced at Gabriel's ashen face; saw him gaze through the bars at Tobias, then look away.

"I ... I ..." Gabriel stammered; lapsed into silence.

"So it is true!" Tobias hissed out an indrawn breath, his hands coming up to grip the bars, knuckles white, clearly fighting to control his anger. "Very well, I will leave that for now. We will talk later, and you will tell me exactly what occurred." He took another deep breath and went on, "I'm sorry, but Matthias has destroyed most of the seals. We tried to stop them, but he locked me in a burning church. I would have perished, but Freya here got me out and ... well anyway, those avatars are so tough and he has several of them now."

Ben listened, wide-eyed. Gabriel, though, his expression suddenly distant, made no reply. After a moment, Ben spoke into the awkward silence. "We did no better," he said, and gloomily explained how Artemas had ambushed them and taken the journal, and how they had escaped. There was another silence as they each absorbed the implications of all that had happened.

"So then, if I get this right, the situation is not good," Freya eventually piped up at Tobias' elbow. "Artemas has the journal, knows where all the seals are including the Last Seal. We on the other hand have no clue where that is, have no idea how to stop them raising Dantalion and even if we did ... "

"Even if we did we are both locked up in here by one of the King's agents who thinks we started the fire and who is probably searching for you even as we speak," Tobias finished. "Unless we can think of something fast, Artemas, Dantalion and Matthias will have won."

"Then an ancient demon of horrific power will be unleashed on to a defenceless world," Gabriel concluded, stirring at last.

Freya nodded. "What is worse, I'll be hanged!"

They all stared at her and she sighed. "Oh all right, I suppose the end of the world beats that, but from where I'm standing it is a matter of opinion!"

Chapter 22
Escape

London, Monday 3rd September, 1666: approaching midnight

N ot far away the great bells of St Paul's Cathedral sounded eleven times. Gabriel cursed under his breath and thumped the ground with his fist. "Time is running out fast. We have to get you out of there. Tobias, where is the guard?"

Tobias walked across to the cell door and glanced across at the guard's room along the corridor outside the cell. "Not here. I'm not sure where he is actually, perhaps ... "

"He's pushed off," Freya interrupted, "I heard him say earlier the fire was not going to get him, so he was off to clear his stuff and get out of the city. Presumably leaving us to burn.

"Well then, in that case," Gabriel said, standing up, "get away from the bars everyone," he ordered and then glanced both ways out of the gate house. An elderly couple pushing a wheelbarrow filled with their few belongings were coming out of the city. They looked cautiously at Ben and Gabriel, naturally suspicious of anyone hanging about a jail house at this time of night. Gabriel let the pair walk by and smiled at them as they passed, but all he got back was a dark scowl as they hurried on their way. He gave another quick glance and when he was certain the coast was clear, raised his hands and spoke.

"*Calamus Αστραπή Стрелять*," the words came quickly and with venom and he then pointed at the bars. A brilliant bolt of light jumped from his finger tips and arced across to them. Sparks flew off the bars and a little smoke appeared, but when that had dispersed the bars were still clearly intact.

Freya gasped, "How did you-"

"Damn!" Gabriel swore. Cutting across her amazement, he repeated the incantation. 'Crack!' went the bolts, but the bars held. Gabriel tried a third time, but with the same result. His shoulders slumped in disappointment and he turned to look at Ben.

"I can't do it. I am not strong enough." He studied the boy in silence for a moment then, sounding very reluctant, added, "You will have to do it, Benjamin."

"Me? Is that a good idea? Last night I lost control, I almost died and I did lose some of my memory."

"I know, but we have no choice, I can't do it. We must be quick. Dantalion ..."

Ben nodded at that. They could not face Dantalion alone: they needed help.

"Besides which," Gabriel went on, his eyes suddenly almost apologetic as they flicked to look at the doctor, "we can't leave Tobias and Freya here to the mercy of Gymer or to the danger of the fire spreading this way, as we know it must if it is to reach all the seals."

Ben nodded again and having swapped places with Gabriel, looked urgently at Freya's white face. "Get away from the bars, as far back as you can," he said and reached out a hand. The words he had heard Gabriel speak were now oddly familiar to him as if he had known them all this life. Just as before with the scroll he instantly understood the words, even those he had never heard before, as if a hidden part of his mind was being unlocked. *'Being unlocked!'* A spark of understanding flared in his mind: a thought process to follow through later perhaps. Yes later, because right now he filled his mind with those three words and felt as he had before. The exhilaration that came with the Words of Power surged through him. He thrust forward violently with his hand and shouted, *"Calamus Ἀστραπή Стрелять!"*

A tingling sensation took root in his neck and spread, slowly at first and then with a sudden rush down his arm and into his hand and finally was focused though his pointing finger. A blindingly bright bolt of light shot from the finger and crashed with a ferocious boom into the bar he was pointing at. There was a terrific explosion and he and Gabriel were flung back against the far side of the gatehouse, stunned.

When his vision cleared, Ben's mouth dropped open in astonishment as he took in the gaping hole where the bars and the surrounding brickwork had once been. Dust found its way into his throat and he coughed to clear it as he dragged himself back to his feet, extending a hand to Gabriel who was slumped on the ground wheezing and looking up at him, his face a mixture of irritation and awe. They rushed over to the cavity that had opened up into the prison cell and gazed inside.

"Freya? Tobias? Are you all right?" Gabriel shouted. Inside there were groans from Tobias, as well as cursing from Freya, as the other two also picked themselves up, coughing and spluttering.

"We are unharmed, although, Ben, I would be grateful if you pointed your finger at someone else in the future," the doctor replied drily, his lips lifting in a slight smile.

"Yes, not us anyway, save it for the demon, pal," Freya muttered, but she looked at Ben with considerably more respect than before. It occurred to him that there was something different about the little thief. It took him a moment to realise what it was; she was wearing a dress. Admittedly the

279

worse for wear, but she actually looked like a girl! He wrinkled his nose and grinned down at her, but she shot him a look of such disdain that he forbore to comment.

Gabriel and Ben now crouched and stretched their arms down into the cell. Freya was able to scramble up the wall, pulled up by the two of them. She rolled out of the way and Tobias dragged the bench over and clambered up on that so he could reach the lip of the hole and heave himself up and over.

"You there! Stay where you are!" An order barked out at them from the city side of Newgate. There, the red glow of the still distant fire moving along Cheapside illuminated a patrol of half a dozen militiamen walking towards them, armed mostly with pikes, although two had pistols. They were still fifty yards away: a long pistol shot.

"Run!" Tobias shouted, grabbing Freya's hand. And run they did: back out through the gates, turned right at Pie Corner and out on to the wide open space of Smithfield. There Ben discovered he had been right: as far as the eye could see the ground was covered in temporary shelters. People huddled beneath sailcloth, rugs and blankets, anything they could find, stretched over poles stuck into the ground; others were lying beneath carts, or simply sitting round fires trying to keep warm. Here, amongst the many scores of bivouacs, the four fugitives hid. Their pursuers searched the fields briefly, but in the dark among so many people and with the light from the camp fires casting confusing shadows, they soon gave up and went back to the city.

It was now very late – at least midnight – and although they discussed going to Freya's stable, everyone was so exhausted that they simply found a place by a fire, whose former occupants appeared to have retired to a nearby crudely constructed tent, made by throwing a blanket across a tree branch and weighing it down with bricks.

Almost instantly, the four friends were asleep.

****

Benjamin Silver was walking in a dark garden around a dark house. He knew there was something important about the house: something personally important. What had happened here? What had he done here? Why was he struggling to remember it? Above him the stars were bright and the night air crisp and cool. It was a beautiful night, but despite that he was not happy for some reason, but what was it? He moved towards the house and felt snow crunch under his feet. The sensation sent shivers of memory through him. Once before he had walked through a garden covered in snow like this and then something had happened that had changed everything.

He reached the door and saw a figure standing there. He moved closer and then stopped. It was not the person he was expecting to see. Who had he been expecting?

"I can't remember!" he said in exasperation.

"No, and that is the way it should stay. There is nothing here but pain for you," the figure said and then moved into the moonlight. Ben gasped for he was looking at himself. A hand shook his shoulder and he turned to see who it was.

"Benjamin? Benjamin?" Gabriel was calling.

"Gabriel, I can't remember: what should I do?" Ben asked, his mind still spinning and vision blurred.

"You should flippin' well get up, you lazy oaf!" Freya said and suddenly he was fully awake. He sat up and saw they were in Smithfield along with many hundreds of other Londoners who had slept here the night before.

To the southeast, the sky glowed with an ireful red colour, bearing witness to the impossible fury of the fire being driven towards them, carried on the wings of a wind powered by the might of a demon. Ben grimaced. He had hoped the fire fighters would have halted it by now, but he knew Dantalion needed the fire to destroy even more of the city so it could

281

reach the final seals and incinerate them. What chance did ordinary mortals stand against the demon's power?

The sun was already high overhead, so it must already be afternoon. Ben was shocked to find the others had let him sleep so long. Gabriel, Freya and Tobias were all sitting round the burnt-out camp fire eating apples. Tobias tossed one to Ben, but he fumbled the catch and it thumped into his stomach. Rubbing it against his smock he took a bite and stared round blearily.

Nearby, a family huddled around a cauldron they had managed to suspend over the flames of a fire. A woman was stirring the contents while a trio of dirty-faced, hungry looking children sat on a log, each cradling a bowl, faces hopeful and expectant. The steam wafted in Ben's direction and his stomach rumbled as he smelt ... was it rabbit stew? The wind changed for a moment and the aroma of frying sausages replaced the rabbit. Around them he caught a few words from a dozen conversations. For a moment, Ben eavesdropped: a grey-haired woman, huddled near another fire and looking worn and worried, was speaking to a lad of about his own age.

"Where is yer grandfather, Jeremiah? Have you seen 'im?"

The lad shook his head, "No, sorry, Grandma, I ain't seen 'im since we left Thames Street. Want me to go look fer 'im?"

Ben did not hear the old woman's answer because from behind him there was a sudden disturbance and a man shouted in outrage. "Let me look at them dice, friend." The voice belonged to a huge man - maybe a dock worker - crouched amidst a huddle of labourers playing dice on an old sack. When his opponent snatched up the dice the big man leapt forward and seized him round the neck and they rolled away into the crowd, with the rest of the group chasing after them cheering them on, a thin cur barking excitedly at their heels.

Wincing at the noise, Ben turned back to look at his friends. "Why did you not wake me?"

"To be honest, pal, we've not been awake that long ourselves," Freya answered. "We were all knackered. Tobias kicked me awake only a little while ago. We left you because you seemed so tired last night after you did that thing at the jail. How ...?"

"We should get moving, Ben," Tobias cut across her and then groaned as stiffly he stood up and stretched. He rubbed the stubble on his chin, "I would kill for a shave and change of clothes."

"*What*? You only changed them yesterday!" Freya exclaimed. "They'll be good for another week at least. I could do to get hold of a pair of britches, a shirt and a jerkin, though. No offense, Doc, but I don't feel right in this garb. Mind you," she mused, looking idly around to see if by chance there were any unprotected bundles of clothing in the vicinity, "the cutpurses must be having a field day in this chaos ..."

"Freya, no! You can stop that right there," Tobias reprimanded, wagging his finger at her.

"Anyway," Gabriel said, "we dare not go anywhere near your house, Tobias. Artemas, Gymer and half the city Watch will be after us today. We will have to keep away from the places they would be expecting us to go to."

"And do what?" Freya asked. They all looked expectantly at Gabriel. He sighed.

"Frankly, I have no idea," he answered gloomily and then yawned. His stomach rumbled, "I could do with something to eat. It might help me think."

"Fat chance," Freya retorted, "unless you let me see what I can find hereabouts?"

"No!" said Tobias and Gabriel simultaneously.

"Suit yourselves," she huffed.

After a moment, Gabriel said, "All we have is the location of the two remaining seals, but it sounds like the chances of saving them are low. We probably need to focus on the Last

Seal, but right now I am at a loss. I had hoped we would find a clue in the journal of Cornelius Silver, but Artemas has that and ..." his voice tailed away because Ben suddenly gave a violent exclamation and jumped to his feet.

"What's wrong with you? You got ants in your britches or something?" Freya said with a chuckle.

"I've been an idiot that's what. When Gabriel was climbing the ladder out of the priest hole, he was carrying the journal and two pages fell out. I picked them up and put them in my satchel and then, when Artemas appeared, I forgot all about them. They should be here." Ben rummaged in his satchel, which he had been using as a pillow. "Yes, here they are. I don't suppose they are any use, but ..."

He pulled the two pages out and passed them to Gabriel, whose eyes had just lit up in hope. The bookseller sat down on the grass and looked at the pages. He held up one of them so they could all see.

"This is just a picture. Looks like a woodcut: two men with a door or something between them."

"Weird; mean anything to you?" Freya asked.

Gabriel shook his head and with an air of disappointment went to push the page inside his smock. As he did so, Ben noticed there was writing on the back and said so. Gabriel turned the paper over and with Ben looking over his shoulder, examined what was written there. As Ben read the first few words they seemed to writhe and twist on the page, just as they had done on the scroll. Surprised, he glanced at Gabriel and saw him nodding: he had noticed it too.

"They are Words of Power, Benjamin. Cornelius has written something underneath them."

"What does he say?" Tobias leaned closer, "Read them out to us, Gabriel."

Clearing his throat Gabriel started to read:

"'The gateway of sacrifice can only be opened if and when Dantalion rises. If he is summoned there is one chance to destroy him: to send him back to the void. Opening a door to the Abyss is difficult and dangerous. Only the most powerful of us will be able to do it, and even for us there would be a price to be paid and a sacrifice to be made, in that the door cannot be shut by any means save one: only a soul who goes willingly to the Abyss will seal the door behind them.'

"So what is he saying? We can get rid of Dantalion, but we would lose one of you two?" Tobias asked pointing at Ben and Gabriel.

"These sorcerer guys are a bit strange if you ask me!" Freya said, and no one argued. "All that power and wisdom and then they go inventing spells that only work if you die. What's the point of that, eh?"

Gabriel shrugged. "Not Ben, me, it's my problem; my task. If all else fails I will take my chance," he said, but he looked pale and shaken by the thought.

Ben took the parchment and read it again to himself then he passed it back to Gabriel with a grunt. "All this supposes we could force Dantalion through the door. It hardly seems likely he is just going to volunteer does it? So what is on the other page?"

"It appears to be the last words Cornelius recorded in the journal," Gabriel said, looking down at the paper. "These were the last two pages and they were loose - not bound - which is why they fell out. Here, he is praying that God will keep the *Praesidium* safe. Ah ... now this is interesting. Taking a deep breath he started to read out the next passage.

"'I have acted as best as I can to protect the world from one of the great enemies of mankind. My strength is failing and I know I will die soon. So I must take steps to pass on to those who succeed me that which I know. Three secrets I leave that tell of the seals that bind Dantalion. The seals number six but a seventh and last there is. The seventh cannot be found while the six remain. The locations of the six

I leave on a map in the hands of the Archbishop who knows our secret. The location of the seventh I have recorded in this, my journal, which I leave here at the Priory. Finally, one secret remains and that is the words that free Dantalion. That secret I am loath to impart and I have decided to take it with me to my grave where I can watch it forever."

"I don't see how that helps," Tobias complained. "Those are the same words you have on your parchment. We have already used the scroll, the journal is lost and Cornelius died with the third secret."

Gabriel was shaking his head. "No, the words are not exactly the same," he observed, "some have changed and in particular that last part. It is still a clue. Cornelius did not go to the trouble of making the scroll and the journal just to not tell us the third part. How could that help his successors if they ever needed to know? The third part exists and did not die with him." Gabriel laughed a moment before going on, "He did take it to his grave, however: literally to his grave!"

"My God, can it be that simple?" The doctor exclaimed, incredulous.

"Will someone tell me what you are talking about?" Freya asked, but it was Ben who answered her.

"Wherever Cornelius is buried we will find a clue: in his tomb I mean."

"That's a bit creepy if you don't mind me saying so," the little thief said, "so it's back to the manor house, is it?"

Again, Gabriel shook his head. "Cornelius is not buried there. A few weeks before his death, he deposited the journal at the monastery and then left to visit Canterbury, supposedly to pray there for his soul. In reality it was to give the scroll to the Archbishop, who then granted him the right to be buried in a permanent tomb: a tomb that still exists today." Gabriel slapped himself angrily on the thigh, "What a fool I have been. I have seen the tomb and even touched it. To think the secret was inches away from me all this time."

The other three shared an exchange of impatient glances.

"Yes, well where is it?" Tobias asked at length. Gabriel looked at him in surprise.

"Oh, did I not say?"

His attentive audience shook their heads and Tobias gave him a harsh glare.

Gabriel stood up and brushed himself down before answering. "It's here: here in London. Cornelius was buried in the vault of St Paul's Cathedral!"

Chapter 23
St Paul's

London, Tuesday 4th September, 1666: early evening

M atthias stood in the centre of the dark room. His followers busied themselves lighting candles in sconces set into the broad stone pillars that supported the vaulted roof above them. Two others grunted as they brought in the Tome of Dantalion and lifted it up on to a lectern they had constructed. As a yellow glow from the candles illuminated his companions, the preacher turned to Artemas.

"We are sure this is the place?"

"Quite sure. The journal mentions it by name and records that this part of the building above us was completed just before Cornelius Silver died. The city was building this and other halls in stone to replace the rotten wooden ones and it all needed money, but the war with France had depleted the treasury," Artemas mused, looking up at the stonework. "I doubt the renovation of this great hall would have been completed were it not for an anonymous benefactor funding the foundations – but Cornelius shows how the funds were in fact provided by the *Praesidium* and that they brought in a master mason who was one of their order."

"The *Praesidium*?"

Artemas grimaced. *'Damn,'* he thought, annoyed with himself for letting that slip; he had not mentioned the Order to the preacher before.

"Oh, that was the name the warlock called his followers," he improvised quickly, "his guardians or something," Artemas shrugged, examining his fingernails to give the impression that it was of no importance.

Matthias nodded and then looked doubtfully around the pillared vault with its arched ceiling. "Where is the Last Seal then?"

"It is hidden until the six are destroyed. Above us the avatars drive the fire on quickly now. Today will eclipse the destruction of those before it. The city will be incinerated and in time the last of the six seals will perish. When they do we will see the Last Seal."

"Then Dantalion will come?"

"Indeed."

Matthias said nothing. Artemas frowned at that. The preacher would usually respond with a 'Praise be' or a 'Let the hour come swiftly' or other meaningless nonsense and Artemas would smile and agree. Now, though, Matthias looked worried. Artemas needed him to believe for just a little longer. Everything depended on that.

"You look troubled, Matthias. Is there anything wrong?"

The preacher's wild eyes swivelled to look at the Cavalier. He said nothing at first and seemed to be considering the best way to phrase things. At last he took a deep breath and spoke quickly, like a rushing torrent flooding a valley, perhaps wary of letting Artemas interrupt him, or maybe he was afraid to pause lest he lose the courage to say what he wanted to get off his chest. "It just seems different to how I expected everything to be. I have told myself that all is well, that there are reasons for things to be this way. I have found solace in the word of

God. But ..." Matthias stumbled to a halt and glanced over at the Tome of Dantalion.

Artemas followed his gaze and frowned. "But?"

"Let me ask you something, Artemas: does it not seem odd to you that the coming of an Angel of the Lord should be heralded by all this destruction. Does it not feel wrong that he sends ahead of him creatures of such nightmarish appearance?"

"Matthias, I think ..." Artemas began, but the preacher held up one hand to interrupt him.

"Let me finish please!" he said. "Finally, I have to ask you, are you comfortable with this use of what to me seems very like sorcery and witchcraft?" His eyes bulged slightly and he looked again at the Tome. "Well, are you?" he repeated.

Artemas thought quickly. They needed Matthias for what was to come and they needed him to believe – at least until midnight. A way had to be found to dispel the preacher's doubts for a little longer, but how? A thought struck him: '*Ah; now that's an idea.*' Artemas knew it was wrong, evil perhaps, but he had never had any delusions that what he did was anything other than evil, or at the very least selfish, and he did not care. He was too far committed to his path to have qualms now.

"I too have had these thoughts, Matthias, and then I realised they were temptations to stray from the path we have chosen, you and I." The preacher looked confused at that, so Artemas tried to put it differently. "The Lord God wants men of faith and a certain moral strength to serve his Angel of Judgement. This is a trial to see if we are that sort of men; to see if we can be trusted with the great commission he plans for us."

"Ah, so you are saying this is a test of faith?" The preacher nodded as though answering his own question, "Now that I can understand." As he spoke, the wildness returned to his eyes, but with a bright gleam of renewed passion.

Artemas concealed a sigh of relief: this was the zeal he had looked for, knowing even when he recruited Matthias that Dantalion needed willing servants ... willing victims. This was the burning belief they needed in order to complete the plan. Confident that he had reignited it in the preacher, Artemas knew he had only to keep it aflame till the end of the day. After that Matthias would no longer be his problem.

Turning to look at the Tome, Artemas thought about the Rite and frowned. He was not quite there yet. It still needed one last part to be complete – one last victim. *The Thirteen and the One.* Fourteen must die and one demon would rise. He had the thirteen; he just needed the one.

****

Ben had a stitch in his side and Gabriel was wheezing slightly, but they carried on jogging towards the Cathedral. It was later in the day. Earlier, exhausted, famished and filthy they had found a tavern in Holborn that was doing a roaring trade from refugees and weary fire fighters. They had joined the queue and bought a plate of chops and a loaf of bread between them, as well as a tankard of weak beer each. As they ate, they eavesdropped on the gossip around them: evidently the King had been giving out handfuls of silver coins that morning to encourage the efforts of anyone willing to help fight the fire. Good luck to them, Tobias had remarked dryly. He at least had got his wish and found a barber to give him a wash and a shave, though Freya, to her chagrin, having found no change of clothes was stuck in hampering skirts.

Finally, feeling more awake and refreshed, they had set out once again.

They soon passed down Old Bailey and could see to the south that the huge hospital at Bridewell Palace, where once King Henry had lived with Queen Katherine, the first of his six wives, was a blazing mass. Oddly, while the fire from the south was already there, the blaze coming from the east was still some way away, beyond the ancient city walls. The puzzle was answered a few moments later when a gust of wind lifted burning embers off the roof tops of houses in Blackfriars, high over the city walls and across the fetid stretch of the River Fleet to drop them on other buildings around the hospital.

"Artemas has the avatars driving the fires on hard," said Gabriel. "We should have come straight here. We must rush or the Cathedral will be destroyed before we find what we need. I have been a weak fool; I should not have suggested we stop to eat."

"Come on, man. No point blaming yourself. We were all fit to collapse through hunger," said Freya.

"Can't keep going without food, Gabriel, we need to keep our strength up," the doctor agreed.

"Let's just make sure we get the job done," said Freya, stepping up the pace.

The fire was now incomprehensively huge. By Ben's reckoning, some ten thousand houses were burnt or burning, along with dozens of trade halls and scores of churches. London – the London Freya and Tobias were born in, and he and Gabriel called home – was gone.

"I wonder what the King will do once the fire is put out," Ben murmured to Gabriel. "Will a new London emerge over the ashes of the old or will the houses just be rebuilt where they once stood?"

"Neither if we do not stop Dantalion!" said Gabriel shortly. "Stop talking, Benjamin, and conserve your energy."

They ran on in the direction of the fire, which raced towards the Cathedral from the east and south as quickly now as a man could run. Fire fighters were doing their best, but despite the King's generosity, it was a losing battle. As Ben and his friends passed through Ludgate, they could see the inferno was alarmingly close now. Cheapside, Watling Street and Trinity Lane were like dragons, belching out flames.

"If only it would rain," Ben gasped, the fire stirring a faint memory in his mind, but when he reached out for it, once again it flitted away. He swore softly and Freya, running at his side, heard him.

She raised her eyebrows, said, "You all right? The fire bothering you is it?" She hesitated, suddenly awkward, "I mean, with what happened to your father and mother an' all."

'What happened to your father and mother ...' Freya's words echoed in Ben's mind and he came to a dead stop. Tobias almost collided with him and had to side step swiftly.

"What are you doing, lad – almost killed me!" Tobias panted, then, seeing Ben's stricken expression, asked, "What is wrong, Ben?"

Gabriel stopped running and turned back. "Why've you all stopped? What's the problem?"

Standing, feet spread, fists clenched at his sides, Ben sounded tense and on the verge of tears. "What *did* happen to my father and my mother? Will somebody please tell me?"

The other three exchanged worried glances.

"Benjamin; not now! We don't have time for this. The fire is only just over there!" Gasping for breath, Gabriel pointed at the wall of flames approaching even now.

"I'm not moving until you tell me what happened!" Ben glared at him.

"Don't you remember?" Gabriel asked in a softer voice.

"If I could remember I wouldn't be asking!" Ben retorted.

"Are you serious, Benjamin? I mean, you only told me on Saturday that they died in a fire." Gabriel frowned, his face reflecting his deep concern, "And we talked about it again on Sunday, when we were on the back of that cart. Don't you remember that?"

Ben shook his head. "Died in a fire?" he repeated, the words rebounding around his mind. Feeling slightly dizzy he dropped to a crouch and closed his eyes for a moment. Then he looked up at them all, his face bleak with worry.

"I can't remember. I feel that I should, so why can't I? Why?"

Gabriel's expression was grim. "Benjamin, when you lost control on Sunday night I believe you caused yourself harm. I am concerned. This is bad, very bad. In fact, it is worse than I feared. If using your power has this effect it is best you refrain."

"What? You mad or something?" Freya stared at the bookseller in disbelief. "You saw what he did to that prison cell. We need him and his power."

"The point is," said Gabriel, visibly striving for patience, "should we trust the outcome of confronting Dantalion solely to reliance on Benjamin? Maybe we should get him away from here?"

"No, Gabriel. We can't do it without him," said the doctor.

"But even if he succeeds, Tobias - and there is no guarantee that he will - the harm to Benjamin may be irreversible."

"Look, I've *seen* the demon," Freya shouted. "I know how tough he is and a fat bookseller who can only fire damp squibs, and a doctor who only might be a good shot, just 'aint going to cut it. I'm telling you, we need Ben!"

Gabriel and Tobias both frowned at her and she dropped her gaze, murmured defiantly, "Well we do!"

"Are you forgetting," said Tobias, "that the harm to us *all* will be irreversible if he doesn't succeed?"

As they argued about him, a sudden wave of nausea and vertigo broke over Ben, his vision blurred and he slumped onto the ground. Holding his hands over his ears to block out the sound of their voices, he reached into his mind for a memory of the fire, of his parents, but all he found was a blank and he could not recall what had happened to them. He felt a desperate longing for something to fill the void. Should he use the Words of Power? But, if he did and Gabriel was right, would he lose more of himself; more of his past? No, he must fill the void with activity: anything to keep him from thinking, from trying to remember. With an act of will he dragged himself to his feet and blinked until his vision cleared. Knowing he had to keep his mind occupied he clapped his hands together loudly to get his companions' attention.

"We must go on," Ben said abruptly, "there is time for this later - if there is a later," he added, striding towards the Cathedral. "Come on!"

Startled into silence, the others exchanged another concerned glance before running after him.

They exited Ludgate Hill into St Paul's churchyard. The open space around the ancient Cathedral was crammed with the carts and wagons of Londoners, all hoping that by bringing their belongings away from their houses and out into the open they might be saved. Others, realising the approaching fire would not spare carts left outside, were pushing them inside the vast building, joining the stacks of goods already stored there by fellow citizens, shop owners and church officials who, like them, were trusting in the thick stone walls to keep them safe. Bolts of cloth lay beside barrels of ale rescued from taverns across the city. Carts loaded with tables and chairs were pushed between heaps of clothing and crates of smoked meats and cheeses. To add to the confusion, animals were being driven into the Cathedral interior: a braying donkey, a bellowing cow and someone's pig - the latter snorting and snuffling amongst the debris for food. Chickens were squawking, dogs barking, people shouting, children crying; the noise was overwhelming.

As Ben and his companions turned to enter the Cathedral's great doors, they looked back at the approaching flames. The fire spilled out of the many avenues and roads like tributaries of a great river and now, having coalesced into a single torrent, divided again to pass around the churchyard to the north and south, like hands reaching out to cup a goblet of wine. The danger was obvious: if these wings of fire were to pass by the Cathedral and reunite on the west side, those inside would be cut off like so many shipwrecked sailors marooned on their own island amidst an ocean of flame. Ben, still numb, felt a curious sense of detachment as he saw the vast banks of flame sweep past them in two great arcs. Tobias said nothing and just stared stony-faced at the devastation. Freya, who was usually so flippant, shuddered and looked small, vulnerable and scared. Gabriel's face was pale with terror, but it was he who first turned his back on the fire and led them through the doors.

Inside the Cathedral, the heat of the late summer afternoon was augmented by that of the fire outside and was oppressive. Gabriel led the way, pushing and squeezing past the crowd, along the nave to a small wooden door, which he opened and then, glancing back to check the others were following, he entered. The door opened on a staircase leading down from the body of the church into the vault beneath. It was really quite a relief to enter the coolness of this chamber: the last resting place of kings and bishops, dukes and saints. Their effigies lined the room, each lying as if asleep, their sightless eyes directed at the ceiling; stone hands clasped together on their breasts in everlasting prayer.

Gabriel led them past these memorials to a plain tomb hidden away in a dark corner. It bore no great statue or elaborate scroll work, but was simply engraved with the words: *HIC IACET CORNELIUS SILVER QUI OBIIT DUODECIM KALENDARUM IUNII ANNO DOMINI MCCCCXX.*

"Here lies Cornelius Silver, who died 12th June 1420," Ben read out, almost in a whisper.

Tobias had suggested returning to his house as they passed by it to fetch tools lest they need to prise the tomb open, but Gabriel had overruled him, saying it was too dangerous. As it happened the tools were not needed to access this sarcophagus: it had been recently opened and the stone slab that should seal it was laid loosely on top.

"No prizes for guessing whose work this is," Gabriel said in a worried tone and they all knew the source of his concern. If Artemas had destroyed whatever evidence was here, what then would they do? Tobias and Gabriel gently lifted the slab off the tomb and Ben, not sure what to expect, stepped nervously forward and feeling a strange respect, looked down on the corpse of his ancestor.

There was no whiff of corruption, just a stale, earthy smell. The body was wrapped in a shroud, but it was partially disintegrated and they could see that beneath it the flesh was gone, leaving just the bones. The skull was intact and the eye sockets seemed to regard Ben solemnly. He was surprised to feel a sudden compulsion to show he was up to the task of carrying on Cornelius' work, as though in some strange way his ancestor was communicating this to him.

"What's that stuff there?" Freya asked pointing at the inside wall of the sarcophagus. Ben followed the line of her finger. Focusing as he had been on the body of Cornelius, he had not at first noticed the engraving on the inside of the tomb. A few inches below the lip of the coffin the stone had been carved into a script. He leaned closer and read the first words. Suddenly the letters swam in front of him and he realised that he was once again looking at a long incantation of Words of Power. As before, he did not recognise some of the language used, but the words seemed to pop into his mind clearly, as if he had always known them, unlocked as it might be from a hidden part of his brain.

He continued reading the words, bending his neck this way and that so as to see round the four walls of the sarcophagus. As he reached the end he felt the blood drain from his face and, suddenly dizzy, he staggered back against Tobias.

"Steady there, Ben, what is it? What did you read?"

Ben did not answer. His mind was spinning with what the words had said. Gabriel now also leant over and read the script then glanced sharply at Ben.

"Well, what is it?" Freya asked. "Will one of you two tell us mere mortals what it says?"

Gabriel pulled out a now soot-stained handkerchief and wiped sweat off his forehead. Then, staring at Ben, he spoke.

"The script contains, as we suspected, the incantation and ritual to free Dantalion," the bookseller said, his voice catching in his throat as he spoke. "The mason must've been one of the *Praesidium*, or Cornelius would never have trusted him with the words he wanted carved into his tomb. Essentially, they explain what he had discovered about the nature of the ancient Babylonian tablet he used to entrap the demon, and what would reverse the process. The ritual speaks of the *Rite of the Thirteen and the One*. The ancient sorcerers wanted to prevent the easy release of those they sought to imprison and in fact made it virtually impossible, but they recorded on the tablet a procedure that would work – the only one that would work in fact – never imagining, I am sure, that anyone would succeed in creating the conditions necessary. I can't help wondering why Cornelius did not destroy it instead of leaving it here for others to find, but perhaps he too felt it was impossible to achieve."

Freya and Tobias were listening as if in a trance. Ben was looking blankly at the skeleton of his ancestor as if waiting for the answer to a question. Gabriel continued.

"The 'Thirteen' refers to thirteen followers of Dantalion who would gather to free him and then ..." his voice tailed into

299

silence. The muffled cries of terrified people in the Cathedral above them drifted down to this cold chamber of the dead. Tobias cracked his knuckles, making Freya wince. Ben shivered.

"Then *what*?" Freya asked, losing patience.

"If the 'Thirteen' gather in a circle around the tablet, which is the Last Seal, and promise their lives to Dantalion, then the demon will appear. However, he is still bound by the seal and unable to leave that circle. To free himself he must break the circle. Literally."

"You mean ..." Tobias said and then tailed off as the implication hit him.

Gabriel nodded. "Yes, thirteen who swear allegiance to him will be slain. That will free him from the circle."

"Matthias and his followers number thirteen, if you don't count Artemas and his little band. Freya said quietly. "Are they all to die?"

"That is what the Rite involves, yes."

"What of the 'One' then? You have mentioned the 'Thirteen', but not the 'One'."

"I may be wrong, but ..." Gabriel hesitated.

"It's me," Ben said, not taking his gaze off the corpse.

"What do you mean, it's you?" Freya said.

Ben walked forward again and touched some of the words. "It's as Gabriel says. If thirteen gather and swear allegiance around the Last Seal the demon is summoned from within the tablet. Then, to be freed from the tablet and walk again on the earth, the demon must kill the thirteen. The Rite talks of a 'Soul for a Soul'. The soul of the demon is only truly freed to roam our world if another soul takes its place. That soul must be taken violently by the demon – and only by him - from the 'flesh, bone and blood' that imprisoned him."

"Well, that's all right then!" Tobias laughed with relief. The others looked askance at him. "What?" he said. "Don't you

300

see?" Cornelius here imprisoned him and he is dead these almost three hundred years. Wherever his soul is now, I think it is safe from Dantalion."

Both Gabriel and Ben shook their heads. Looking from one to the other of them, Tobias added hesitantly, "Ah ... not safe then?"

"Cornelius is dead, *his* soul is safe, but I am alive and my soul is not," Ben muttered.

"I don't understand," Freya said, shaking her head, confused.

"Nor me," said Tobias.

"I am a Silver; a direct descendant of Cornelius. I am of his flesh, bone and blood," Ben explained dully.

Freya gasped, her eyes widening in alarm. "Then, to be free, Dantalion must kill *you*?"

Ben nodded. "I'm frightened," was all he said.

Chapter 24
Traitor

London, Tuesday 4th September, 1666: mid-evening

"You must get away, Ben," Freya urged, "out of harm's way, away from the city."

"She's right," Gabriel agreed, nodding his head. "If Dantalion does not have you, he can't be free. To sever the link with the Last Seal you must die at his hands to take his place in the tablet. So, we get you out of the city before he can find you; first we run and *then* we think of a plan."

At that moment, there was a squeak of boot leather on the stone steps behind them and as one they turned to look. There was a moment's horrified silence. Gymer stood on the bottom step; at his back was Walton, no longer wearing his sling. Both men were armed, their pistols pointing steadily at Tobias and Freya.

"I'm afraid there will be no running and no hiding this time. It's plain to anyone with eyes to see that you two got out of that cell using gunpowder – no doubt supplied by your accomplices here. If I had any previous doubts, that little scene up at Newgate has convinced me my instincts were quite correct. So then, shall we all go from here, and I'll take you back to a stronger cell." Gymer smirked, added, "All four of you."

"Captain Gymer, you have to let us go," Gabriel said, his voice rising in desperation. "This is far more serious than just a fire, albeit the worst we've ever seen, but if we don't get the boy to safety the whole city will suffer, indeed, the whole Kingdom!"

The spymaster's eyes narrowed. "Is that a threat?"

"Dammit, Gymer, but you are a fool!" Tobias shouted, moving towards the spymaster.

Gymer's pistol barked and the doctor spun backwards giving a cry of agony and grasping his arm. "What the hell did you do that for, God rot you!"

Walton pulled from his belt another pistol and passed it to Gymer, while still aiming his first at Gabriel. Tobias groaned and examined his arm. The shot had only grazed him, but it must have nicked a vein for he was losing quite a bit of blood. Gabriel offered him a somewhat grubby handkerchief and Tobias, with a grimace of thanks, pressed it to the wound to staunch the flow. Then he glared back at Gymer, "There was no need for that, you stupid man."

"That, Doctor, was a warning. It will be your last," Gymer said. "Any more false moves and one of you will die. Now, do please come with me."

They climbed back up the steps, Gymer leading the way and Walton coming up behind. Marlowe and Spencer were standing in the nave craning their necks to look anxiously at the high vaulted ceiling far above them.

"What are you two gawping at?" Gymer asked. Marlowe pointed and they all looked upwards.

"Oh my God!" Tobias muttered, for the roof over the south transept directly above them was on fire. St Paul's had been built of stone, with huge pillars, majestic arches and walls that in places were fifteen feet thick, it should have been fire proof.

There was, however, a problem or more precisely, three problems, which Gabriel, looking around, quickly identified. Firstly, the panicked citizens of the doomed city had piled their carts and wagons of goods in St Paul's churchyard, right up against the outside walls. Furniture, clothes and bedding stacked up in great heaps made an excellent tinder base for the fire. Then there was the problem of the repair work to the roof. The years under the rule of Cromwell's Commonwealth, which had despised bishops and cathedrals, had not been kind to the church. They had not maintained the place, had even, so it was said, stabled horses in it. Thus, when the roof had suffered storm damage it had been repaired, not with expensive lead tiles, but with timber: timber which would ignite from a spark. Finally, folk had deposited even more combustible goods inside the church, so that if the fire did penetrate the building, it had a ready supply of fuel for its own funeral pyre. All it had needed was that one spark to start the chain of events.

Surmising that while he and his friends were in the crypt, the rooftops of the buildings along the edges of the churchyard had collapsed, Gabriel imagined the scene: a cloud of burning embers billowing up into the air like a flock of pigeons startled by a gunshot; a great gust of wind blowing the embers high in the sky and then abandoning them to fall like rain upon St Paul's. He shook his head in despair. This beautiful, ancient building – the very beating heart of the city - was in its death agonies; or soon would be. This day, Tuesday 4th September, 1666, would go down in history as a day of great evil, he thought sadly. Assuming anyone survived to record it!

The embers had already ignited the wooden roof sections and the piles of flammable goods. Now, the third problem was about to deliver the final blow. As Ben and the others watched, the roof started falling away: falling upon them, in fact. Timbers, burning embers, ash and molten lead rained down upon the bolts of cloth that had been left in heaps in the pews and, in an instant, they burst into flames. Twin walls of fire rushed towards the far door. Above them the roof swayed and creaked and then, with a loud crack, began to tumble to the floor.

As one, the terrified people let out a cry of alarm. Most simply abandoned their goods to the fire and ran towards the exit. Some, though, moved back towards their belongings and in desperation tried to pull them out of harm's way. With a crunch a large section of timbers and roof tiles landed on an unfortunate couple who were struggling with a hand cart laden with barrels of fine wine. There was a scream of agony and then silence. A blend of red wine and blood trickled out from under the smoking rubble. For a moment everyone in the building stared in paralysed horror at the scene: seemingly unable to tear their gaze away.

"Everybody run!" Tobias bellowed and stirred into action neither Gymer nor anyone else argued. They fled between the burning pews, down the avenue of fire that was the aisle, towards the main doors. Walton reached them first and exited. Freya was next quickest and reached the doors just ahead of Ben. Tobias and Gabriel close behind. At that moment, there was a crash as another huge section of the roof fell to earth. Gymer gave a cry of pain and Ben turned just in time to see him knocked to the ground by a long timber beam that pinned him to the spot. The spymaster groaned as he futilely struggled to get free. Nearby, Spencer had been caught a glancing blow and was sitting back on the floor looking dazed, his ankle trapped by the same beam. Marlowe leant over and heaved on it, but it would not budge. None in the terrified stream of people fleeing in panic for the doors stopped to help him and Marlowe turned his face toward Tobias, an expression of mute appeal on his huge features.

"We should leave them both; really we should," Freya urged the others, but she did not sound as convinced as she might have done a few days before, though could not have said why. Gabriel seemed rooted to the spot, his gaze constantly scanning the interior of the Cathedral. Ben bit his lip in indecision: these were the men who had imprisoned Freya and the doctor, threatened them with torture or worse, and believed they were all four involved in a conspiracy to burn down London. Now they had a chance to escape. If they freed Gymer they would be prisoners, but to not do so would condemn him – and Spencer - to an agonising death as the fire took them.

While Ben wavered, Tobias did not hesitate. He joined Marlowe and gave him a quick nod before taking his place at the beam. "On the count of three," he shouted: "one, two, three, LIFT!" Faces red, eyes bulging, they both heaved, but the beam was too heavy and despite the effort that showed on their foreheads as rivulets of sweat, they were beaten. The doctor turned to Ben with a meaningful stare and a flick of his eyes at the boy's fingers.

Ben understood the signal, but hesitated, unsure what to do. Dared he risk using the Words? Above them more tiles tumbled to the ground and smashed on the flagstones nearby. Ben grimaced; teetered, then nodded and moved forward.

"NO!" shouted Gabriel. "It's too dangerous for the boy. He cannot use the Words."

"Gabriel, I MUST. We can't leave them!"

Freya attempted to hold Ben back, but he shook her off, took another step forward and pointed a finger at the rafter. Rapidly he spoke the words, "*Calamus Αστραπή Стрелять!*" and with a clap of thunder a burst of lightning leapt from his hand and cracked the wood in between the two trapped men.

Gymer gave a huge roar, pushed the timber off his legs and scrambled to his feet to help Marlowe and Tobias free Spencer. Only then, his eyes narrowing in disbelief, did the spymaster turn and stare at Ben.

"A curious thing, that there thunderclap. Be that *witchcraft*, boy?"

"He just saved your life, Captain, so I suggest you leave him be." The doctor cast an anxious glance up at the burning roof, "We don't have much time."

Still staring at Ben, Gymer ignored Tobias. "That's another curious thing: why did you do that? To impress us? Leaving us to die would have solved your problems better and would have left fewer questions to answer, don't you think? So why, eh? What's going on here?"

"COME ON, Gymer! We can talk later; move, NOW!" Tobias shouted and pulled Spencer to his feet. Together they all tumbled along the littered nave and out of the doors into the blazing inferno of the graveyard.

There amongst the gravestones, carts, wagons and heaps of smouldering belongings a mass of humanity was huddled together like frightened lambs sheltering close to their mother. A child cried for her parents, but no answer came. A dog howled as an ember floating through the air landed on its flank, but no one took any notice. They all seemed to be staring the same way, transfixed by something in front of them; too horrified to scream lest it draw attention to them.

"What the devil's going on here?" Limping along, Gymer pushed through the crowd. "Out of the way!" he bellowed as he elbowed a fat merchant to one side and emerged at the front of the crowd - where Walton stood, a pistol in each hand, both primed and pointing at Gymer's chest.

He was flanked by a pair of avatars and at his back, grinning with triumph were Morris and the other two of Artemas' men. "My master would like a word with you all, and especially the boy!" Walton hissed. "Please don't struggle. I would hate to lose anyone, but if you try to escape or cause trouble I will maim the boy and kill the rest of you!"

Artemas and Matthias were once again in the presence of Dantalion. The Cavalier was resting against a boulder that stood by the edge of the stream, enjoying the refreshing coolness of the breeze that blew across the water. Matthias, meanwhile, was kneeling on the grass of the clearing at the feet of the 'angel', his head bowed and hands clasped together. Artemas could hear the preacher reciting psalms and calling on his God to grant him strength. Dantalion stood before them in angelic form. Artemas wondered about that shape. Were the legends true that demons were fallen angels? If so, was this the shape Dantalion had worn before he and his kind had rebelled against the Almighty in a war they had lost? Or perhaps, just like men, were demons creatures from this world, but higher beings with infinitely more power? Artemas was not sure. He speculated idly what form Dantalion would use when he was finally free; then he sniffed, dismissing the thought. It did not matter really, for by then he, Artemas Blake, would be ruling the world under the demon. He pursed his lips in anticipation of the power and riches that would soon be his. Not long now; not long.

He looked over at the preacher. He had to admit that Matthias had become much calmer since this morning when he had seemed so wild and had expressed such doubts. His eyes were closed in prayer, his scarred face glowing with faith and belief. Let him pray, Artemas thought. Just let him keep his faith for a little while longer. Dantalion had been standing still, head raised slightly as if he were sniffing the air. Like Matthias, his eyes were closed in apparent concentration. He had stood like this for a full three hours as his acolytes had come and gone. Artemas knew that through the eyes of his avatars, now located far and wide across the city, Dantalion had been watching them bend to his will, driving the fire on towards the remaining seals.

Suddenly his eyes flicked open and his gaze fixed on the pair in front of him. "At last!" the demon's voice rumbled in relief, "The seals are destroyed. It is time to reveal the Last Seal and free me."

"But Lord, we do not have the boy yet."

"You are wrong, Artemas. We do have him – both him and his companions. Your men have done well. He comes even now. It is time: prepare yourselves."

Artemas smiled and glanced at Matthias, who had opened his eyes and scrambled to his feet.

"Praise be!" the preacher said. "Come to us, Lord Dantalion and judge us."

The angelic visage regarded the old man without emotion, but all Matthias could see was the golden white light shining from the eyes of an angel. Artemas could see it too; he knew it was intended to fool Matthias into believing that he saw a reflection of the glory of heaven. Artemas, however, knew the light shone instead with a burning lust for the murder they must do this night. Whereas he saw the deaths as merely necessary to complete the Rite, Dantalion longed for them with unmitigated passion, slavering at the thought of the kill. Committed as he was to the plan, Artemas nevertheless felt an involuntary shiver passing down his spine. For, in that terrible gaze, words unspoken passed between them: *fourteen must die and one will rise.*

****

Ben glanced around at the crowd. The appearance of the avatars had stopped them in their tracks and they stared with uncomprehending horror at the creatures with their insectoid bodies, great bat-like wings and drooling maws. The first to recover was an aged priest near the front. He lifted his hands above his head and then fell to his knees.

"It is the end of the world, brothers and sisters. Pray for forgiveness from the Lord of Hosts to spare us His wrath; for as it is written in the Book of Revelations, the beast has come and sent forth dragons to make war upon us and upon the Almighty."

Walton smirked and then nodded. "It is indeed the end of your world, old man. Flee now: all of you! Run for your lives, such as you value them!"

No one moved at first, not until the avatars took a step forward and opening their jaws let forth a blood curdling screech. Then there was pandemonium. The people turned and fled. All belongings were abandoned: thrown to the ground regardless of their value. The priest leapt to his feet and clawed his way through the crowd. The child, still calling for her mother was knocked to her knees and then, seeing the avatars for the first time, she too screamed and turned to run. An old woman hobbling along by the aid of a stick, tripped over an upended hand cart and hit her head on a tomb stone, opening a huge gash on her forehead. Blood trickled down her face. She groaned, rolled over and lay still. Tobias moved towards her, but the avatars screeched again and he halted and glared at Walton.

"Leave her be!" Walton growled,

"But ... "

"I said leave her!"

"Walton, just what the hell do you think you are playing at?" Gymer roared. "And what the blazes are those creatures? Can someone please tell me what on earth is going on?" Walton, Morris and the others had swiftly disarmed the captain and his men and rounded them all up.

Around them the fire had moved on, as they feared, to the west, breaching the ancient city walls and moving down

311

Ludgate Hill. The fleeing crowds had reached the old city gate and with several turning their heads for a last fearful glance back at the avatars, they fled through the gate and away. Watching them, Tobias strained his eyes in the direction of his house, a mournful expression on his face. Ben followed his gaze, but flames and smoke obscured the view and there was no way to tell if the buildings along Old Bailey still stood. With a sigh, Tobias turned back to look at Walton. His arm hurt like the devil and he was livid with anger, but he was also looking down the barrel of a pistol and there was nothing he could do about it. Walton, God rot him, was addressing his former employer.

"Oh dear, oh dear, Captain, you do seem to be behind with the plot. With just a few choice words and a false report from me, you have had us galloping around London searching for Dutch conspirators and French spies, when the real danger is worse; much, much worse; more so than you can imagine," he sneered at the quite bewildered looking Gymer.

"Well that explains that mystery anyway," Gabriel whispered out of the corner of his mouth to Ben. "It was Walton in Fetter Lane; he obviously had orders from Artemas to keep you alive. I fear they know who you are, Benjamin."

Freya clicked her fingers, "Ah, so it was Walton who Artemas was speaking to at the Old Bull tavern." She glanced up at Ben, who frowned at her in puzzlement, so she added by way of explanation, "Matthias and he agreed to have someone keep an eye on you. Now we know who."

"This way now, Captain!" Walton ordered, shouting to make himself heard and snapping his pistol over to the side. "I don't have time for explanations and we have to move quickly. I am sure the fool from the *Praesidium* or his companions will educate you on the way ... *Sir*," he added facetiously, "though you might be best advised not to ask. The knowledge would only upset you, and in any event will not do you any good."

312

He walked off leading the way with an avatar behind him. The other avatar, with Morris and the rest of Artemas' men herded everyone else along. Gymer was limping slightly and Tobias, walking beside him, glanced down at his leg.

"You have lost some blood, but at least it can't be broken," the doctor said.

"You telling me I should be thankful for small mercies?"

"Something like that."

Gymer looked at him, "Well?"

"Well what?"

"Are you going to tell me what is going on?"

"I am not sure you will believe me."

"Well, try me ..."

Behind them there was a huge boom and they all turned to stare as more of the vaulted roof of the Cathedral collapsed onto the burning remnants of the pews. Walton got them moving again and they left the great church to its death agonies and walked east through the glowing ruins of Watling Street.

Tobias proceeded to tell Gymer about his father, the *Praesidium* and, eventually, Dantalion, the story strangely disjointed as they hurried along. Ben, walking with Gabriel behind them, Freya at his heels, listened for a while but found his mind wandering. The inscription on the side of Cornelius' tomb had unnerved him more than he'd let on. What it threatened was worse than mere death - scary as that thought was - it meant his soul's imprisonment for eternity in a stone slab. Should he flee? Should he use the Words and blast Walton away and then run and never go near Dantalion. But to do that meant using more power and he was unsure what would happen: would he forget more of his past, become a vacant gibbering wreck? In which case what did anything matter? Maybe he could get away without using the Power? He could run and lose the pursuit in the ruins of London. He would just be one among the many thousands of displaced people, how would they ever find him? Yet, if he tried it he was certain not all of them would escape, certainly not Gymer and his men - who may be thugs, but they were only doing their job as they saw it - and probably not Gabriel, who was not exactly athletic. Well, so what? What did he care? Three days ago he'd have said 'nothing': for the past six months he had cared little about anyone or anything; would not have given a damn for the others. But that wasn't the real me, he thought. What had happened to the *real* Benjamin Silver - the one who cared about others and the world around him? Glancing surreptitiously at his three friends, Ben was surprised to find that actually he did care; not only that, but he knew they would do anything to help and protect him, and for the first time in what felt like a lifetime, a shred of warmth crept into his soul.

That decided him. He had to see this through, one way or the other. Very well, he thought, I will stay and face the demon. But, do I dare use the Words of Power again? Ben knew that to oppose Dantalion he would need to, but that same power was – Gabriel believed – putting him at great risk. It seemed a choice of burning his brain away or imprisonment forever. Neither were exactly appealing alternatives. It was Hobson's choice – no choice at all, in fact.

He was anxious about why he had lost his memory. He wanted to talk about it to Gabriel, but the bookseller was trudging despondently along at his side, lost in his own thoughts. Even as Ben thought about it, the stench and heat of London burning brought a wisp of remembrance drifting across his mind: the smell of fire; people screaming; no, not people, himself. He seemed to hear his own voice shouting out that he was sorry. He pushed harder – trying to force through the fog clouding his mind, to see the memory unveiled. Yet, it would not yield itself to him. He felt dizzy again and retreated from the attempt at recollection. Odd though, that shred of memory coming just now. Ben frowned: was it possible Gabriel was wrong, that the memory loss was not permanent? The more he thought about it, the more it seemed as if his using the Words in the Cathedral had brought back some of his memory, not taken it away. Maybe now that he had used the Power twice he could control it better. Yet, Gabriel had not thought so and Ben was not sure. Well, he would find out soon enough: Walton had stopped walking and was turning to face them.

Just behind Ben, Freya walked ashen-faced through the smouldering wreckage of London, staring grimly at the sheer scale of destruction around her. She had no house of her own, no wealth that had succumbed to the flames as it had for thousands of her fellow citizens. With the possible exception of the Captain of the Watch, who looked out for her, there was no one she cared about who might have perished. But she still mourned, because it was HER city that was gone. After her mother had died she'd had no one left to care about and had turned to crime to survive, happily robbing and swindling anyone and everyone. She had told herself that she was tough enough and did not need to care about anything. But she had been lying to herself. She cared about her city. She had wandered the streets each day, so that in time every alleyway, church, shop and house was familiar to her. The chiming of the city's bells had given her joy, the bustle and rumble of the Exchange, Cornhill and Ludgate had been her music and the candlelight at night glittering from a thousand houses had been her companion through the dark hours.

Now it was gone forever and that made her weep; it made her sad, but what was more, it made her angry.

"Bloody demon's going to pay," she growled and Walton turned to look at her quizzically. "You too, Walton, you two-faced claybrained clodpoll," she muttered under her breath.

Chapter 25
Gog and Magog

London, Tuesday 4th September, 1666: late evening

The course they took zigzagged along Watling Street, up Bread Street and across into St Lawrence Lane. The fire was raging in some buildings as they passed by, but in others it had died back, leaving smouldering piles of ash. On one occasion they had to stop suddenly because a house gave way in front of them and keeled over into the street, and on another they had to swerve to avoid a huge pit in the ground that gaped down into a cellar, open to the sky for the first time in two hundred years. Most of the people they passed hurried away as soon as they saw the armed guards and seemed too dazed to register the avatars; those who did ran screaming.

"We seem to be heading for the Guild Hall," Gabriel whispered to Ben, who swallowed, the fear balling in his stomach making him feel sick. He half turned to look back at Freya; she gave him a watery grin and a thumbs-up, showing him a glimpse of the knife concealed in her palm. Against the avatars it'd be about as much use as a pea shooter to kill a bear, but he nodded and smiled encouragement. He could see from the tear stains on her pale, dirty cheeks that she had been crying and was pretending to be brave for his sake.

At last they passed the church of St Lawrence and walked up the passageway between it and Blakewell Hall. The Guild Hall, now visible in front of them, looked untouched - for the moment at least. They passed some of Prince James's guards, who were leading the trained bands of the militia in fighting the fire that now threatened to destroy the church. As they entered Guild Hall Square there was a sudden roar from behind them. Morris at the rear gave a cry of alarm and they all turned to look. The fire was being channelled down the narrow passageway with the force of shot from a musket. It came rushing at them and they scattered left and right as the flume of fire erupted into the square and burst upon the front of Guild Hall. The guards and militia also ran for cover around the sides of the building. Only the avatars seemed oblivious to the danger. Seeing the creatures standing there, not trying to escape the full fury of the fiery blast, Ben was certain they would perish. Yet the demonic beasts appeared totally unharmed; indeed, they seemed to relax and wallow in the flames, raising their heads and letting out soft cries like the purring of contented cats.

"On your feet, all of you!" Walton ordered when the plume of fire had died back. He and Morris dragged everyone into a line and marched them towards the front gates of the Guild Hall. A guardsman, who had dived for cover behind a now steaming water butt, emerged and stepped up to Walton.

"You can't go in there, Sir. It's too dangerous. I-"

Without warning Walton aimed his pistol and fired at point blank range. With a cry of pain the guard fell back, his brains spilling out in a fountain of blood on to the ground. Ben stared in appalled fascination, the gorge rising in his throat; behind him he could hear Freya retching.

"You murderer, Walton, I swear I'll see you swing for that!" Gymer growled. Walton spun round and pulled another pistol out of his belt – Gymer's own in fact – and pointed it at him.

"Shut your mouth, Gymer. We need the boy; I have orders too to bring the *Praesidium* filth," he snarled, indicating Gabriel. He cast his gaze over Gymer's men, looked with contempt at Tobias and Freya, "The rest of you are not worth spit. Do as I say or I will kill you right here. Now, follow me."

With a screech, the avatars launched themselves into the air and hovered behind the party, flapping their hideous bat wings, creating a blast of air that pushed them all forward. The giant, Marlowe, bent to pick up a charred lump of brick and threw it hard at one of the creatures. He stared in disbelief as the brick ricocheted off its chest, hardly scratching the beast. The avatar swooped down upon him and swung a claw at his face gouging deep into his cheek. Marlowe screamed, stumbled to his knees, blood pouring down his neck.

Walton stepped back to him, seized the big man by his collar and dragged him through the doors. The avatars flapped their wings and sent forth another huge blast of air with the force of a hurricane that lifted the captives off their feet. As one, like rags in the wind, they tumbled through the already smouldering doors of the Guild Hall, were swept past the twin statues of the giants, Gog and Magog and on into the Great Hall, to fall sprawled in a tangled heap onto the tiled floor. Dazed, they lay for a moment catching their breath before Walton prodded them back on their feet and got them moving again, deeper into the hall.

Gabriel turned and looked back at the statues and then snapped his fingers. "Of course, I should have realised," he muttered.

"What?" Ben shot him a puzzled glance.

"Those woodcuts on that parchment were a reference to Gog and Magog," the bookseller grimaced. "They represent the

319

guardians of London. They have kept watch over the city for hundreds of years, and now they are doomed."

"So are we," said Ben. "Why are they significant?"

"Not them, Benjamin, the Guild Hall. It is one of the oldest of the stone buildings in the city. Cornelius could be certain it would stand for – well, if not forever, most certainly for centuries – and it has a stone cellar whose construction started in his lifetime: the perfect place. Why did I not think of it? What a fool I've been."

"I hope you are not saying what I think you are saying?"

"Yes, I am afraid this is where the Last Seal is, Benjamin."

"That means ..." Ben's voice tailed away as his throat constricted making speech impossible.

"Yes, Dantalion is indeed here. So it seems our choices are over. All that is left is the battle to come. Have courage, my boy," Gabriel said, but the quiver in his voice showed he was as scared as Ben.

The fire had begun to burn its way into the great building, consuming anything in its path that would burn. The prisoners were hurried through the hall to a doorway that opened on a flight of steps descending to the basement. Even as they were shoved down into the cool darkness underground, flames were already encroaching on the Great Hall.

"They're taking us into the vaults," Gabriel murmured in Ben's ear. "They're solid stone. In these chambers Mayors and Aldermen of the city have stored records and documents dating back to the time of the Norman kings, thinking they'd be safe enough down here even if all else was destroyed by fires ravaging above."

As they reached the bottom of the steps, Ben looked fearfully around at the vault. It was vast. Torches were stuck in wall sconces, casting flickering shadows on the huge arched ceiling, which was supported by pillars and decorated by elaborate scroll work. Doors led off to other chambers, but it was here in the central chamber that the *Liberati* awaited them. Dotted around the room were Matthias' twelve followers, including Valentine, who looked at them with cruel expectation on his scarred face. Others had a more serene expression as if this was the moment they had waited for. Matthias stood in their centre. Another four avatars were also in the room and these were gathered in a circle around Artemas, who was standing at a lectern upon which a huge book had been laid. He glanced up once, smiled with satisfaction when he saw Ben and his three friends huddled together, and cast a cold glance over Gymer and his men, who had been herded to one side of the vault and were being held there at pistol point by the murderous Walton. They all wore the same expression of stunned awe. Ignoring them, Artemas turned his attention back to the book that lay open in front of him.

"That's the book," Freya hissed, "the one they made me touch that whisked me away to God knows where."

"The Tome of Dantalion ... then it *does* exist," Gabriel said softly, an almost hungry look coming over his face.

"Somehow, I don't see you selling that in your shop, Gabriel," Tobias observed dryly in a weak attempt at humour.

Ben was staring transfixed at the floor. "Look down there, what is that the preacher is standing on?"

They followed his gaze and saw that Matthias was standing in the centre of a large design that seemed to be embossed in the stonework. It bore a gold rim edged with symbols of flame and at its heart was the gate-like image that Ben and Gabriel recognised instantly: it was the 'portcullis' etched on their pendants. They had all seen it before, on the scroll and above Gabriel's bookshop. Behind the gate was the visage of a raging beast: the face of the demon. The face of Dantalion.

"The Last Seal is revealed," Gabriel said hollowly. A touch of failure edged his voice and his shoulders sagged, "They have all they need. We are finished."

321

Artemas stepped forward. "Welcome, Benjamin, Gabriel, Tobias and Freya. Welcome to you too, Gymer, with your men. Seems we have all been ... ah dancing around each other these last few days. At last we are together. Shall we begin?"

"No!" Gabriel cried out. "Artemas, it is not too late. Do not do this; do not release Dantalion upon the world. He will kill millions and wreak havoc. You cannot want this!"

Artemas blinked and glanced at Walton and Morris. "Oh ... I think we do want this," he answered with a grin, then added in a grander tone, elevating his voice as if he were a preacher speaking his sermon, "do not try and turn us away from this course, for it is holy."

Freya, who was watching Artemas intently, noticed that he looked at Matthias as he spoke, as if his choice of words were for the preacher's benefit alone and, unlike a moment ago, his expression was not one of triumph, but anxiety. '*Interesting*,' she thought to herself.

"Matthias!" Freya shouted. "Do *you* want this? And you others? You want a *demon* released on the world? How can this be holy? I ..."

Before she could go on, Walton lunged over to her and cuffed her across the mouth splitting her lip. "Shut it ... I am warning you," he snarled, sneering as she cried out, blood pouring down her chin.

Then Matthias spoke and his voice was calm and strong. "I am beyond your temptation now, child of sorrow. I am the servant of the Angel, Lord Dantalion, who comes to judge this city. We will sit at his right hand and redemption will be ours."

"You are all going to die! Don't you realise that you fools?" Tobias shouted, but Walton spun round and pointed his pistol at him.

"Time for you to shut it too, Doctor," he directed a pitiless glare at Tobias. "Speak again and you die."

"I'm going to die anyway; we all are. Can't you see that you imbecile? It is time to ..." Whatever Tobias had intended to say it was drowned out by Artemas.

"Indeed it is time. Time to free Dantalion," he boomed, his voice bouncing off the vaulted ceiling and echoing around the chamber. Everyone turned to look at him and he smiled back at them all, revelling in their attention. This was his moment: the moment when he rose above his ancestors and achieved power and glory in reward for service to the Old Masters. Just as his line had once ruled much of the ancient world under the demons, he now would achieve a measure of immortality in Dantalion's service. This was indeed his moment and he relished every second.

On the lectern was the Tome of Dantalion, now opened to an incantation blessing the chamber. Artemas turned to Matthias and his followers and spoke to them. "This ceremony is to free the, er, Angel. Dantalion requires that you, his followers, are pure in heart and determined in your mind. To free him you must be willing to swear fealty to him and turn your lives over to his service."

Keeping her head down, Freya peeped under her lashes at the faces of Matthias' followers: all but one glowed with ecstatic faith, eyes closed in prayer. Matthias himself looked straight back at Artemas, his face calm, his head nodding from time to time as he listened. Freya looked again at the one wide-eyed, sceptical face. This was Valentine, who, of all Matthias's followers seemed out of place; a misfit. Freya recognised the type. She was not so very different; he too was a thief and they both lived as a law unto themselves. She dropped her gaze as Valentine stared in her direction.

Artemas noticed the man as well and frowned slightly. This was a source of concern. He needed thirteen to be committed to this for the ritual to work. If one of the preacher's followers did not do what he wanted, all was lost. Followers? They acted more like disciples. 'Ah, yes,' Artemas murmured softly to himself, 'that is the point is it not? Eleven true disciples there were ... and one corrupt, whose name was Judas. Perhaps I must phrase this a little differently.'

Raising his voice so all could hear, he said, "I will ask you in a moment to swear that you will do this. That you will make this sacrifice. Swear that you will and you will stand with the Master as he judges this city and this world. Above all men you will be blessed and honoured; all that you desire will be yours. Will you do this?"

Artemas saw Valentine's face flash with greed: the same greed for power he felt himself. Shame he could not have got to know the man earlier, for he could have recruited him to the *Liberati*. It was clearly not devotion to a higher cause that drove Valentine. No, this was a villain who enjoyed the thought of standing by and lording it over others as they suffered Dantalion's wrath. As it was, he would have to die to free the demon. Pity!

Aware of Artemas' gaze on him, Valentine now adopted a serene expression in imitation of his companions. The transition was so comical that Artemas almost laughed. It did not matter what expression the man adopted. Providing he made the promise and believed in it - for whatever reason - it was enough.

"This is a test of faith, my brethren," Matthias intoned. "You must commit yourselves to the task ahead. It is time to decide to do what you believe is right."

Artemas nodded with relief. Matthias' voice rang with faith and commitment again, the doubts of the morning apparently put aside. The 'test of faith' idea had been a good one. The Cavalier took a deep breath and asked the question.

"Will you swear now that you willingly commit your life in service to Dantalion, to do what he asks of you, and to give to him what he requests: life and death, blood and bone?"

"Life and death, blood and bone: we swear it," thirteen voices chanted the oath.

Ben could feel Gabriel trembling beside him. Tobias and Freya were staring at Artemas, as was everyone else. As before, Ben felt a strange kind of detachment, as if this was a dream and not happening to him at all. Yet, if what Gabriel had said was true, he, Benjamin Silver, was about to die – for he could not allow the demon to kill him and imprison his soul for eternity. There was only one sure way he could prevent Dantalion from being unleashed onto the world: it required an act of supreme sacrifice. He moved closer to Freya, his fingers sliding down her arm, seeking her knife.

She looked at him, startled, but reading the message in his eyes, shook her head. "No, Ben," she breathed, "that is not the way," and she switched the blade to her other hand out of his reach.

Walton, noticing the movement, stepped forward to face them. His eyes narrowed with suspicion and waving the pistol at Freya, he hissed, "What are you two hatching?"

"Nothing," said Freya, the knife once more concealed in her sleeve.

Defeated, Ben moved away.

Artemas now took the journal of Cornelius and laid it on top of the Tome. This gave precise instructions of the procedures that would break the seal and release Dantalion, but it referred to a Rite that was recorded elsewhere – the one Silver had taken to his grave. Artemas reached inside his tunic and unrolled a parchment. This was a rubbing he had made of the inscription in the sorceror's tomb; he had attached sections of it together so it read as a continuous script. Artemas glanced up at Matthias and his men, to make sure they all stood in a circle on the circumference of the Last Seal, and began reading.

As the words spilled from his lips he felt the exhilaration of power rising within him. When the flow of power passed out of

325

him and arced across to the Last Seal, he felt a connection with the beast imprisoned within it. Watching helpless from across the vault, Ben and Gabriel also heard and understood the words and they too felt the energies flowing. With Artemas they shared the moment as only the three of them could do, for only they understood the powers being wielded, but while Artemas felt joy and excitement the other two experienced a sensation of horror and terrifying anticipation, and because they were linked, each knew what the other was feeling.

Then, all three felt their consciousness shift as their minds were transported together, so they stood not in the vault, but somewhere else. Ben blinked in surprise as he realised they were on top of St Paul's Cathedral tower looking down on the fire destroying the city around them. Below them flames were gutting the ancient building. Paralysed with fear, Ben watched as lead tiles on the roof buckled and writhed, then melted and boiled under the incandescing heat. Finally, the lead poured off the roof, down into the churchyard and there became a river; a seething black mass that ran down Ludgate Hill to the gate and beyond. In that moment, Ben realised it was all an illusion. And that they were not alone.

Artemas stood a few yards away, his image still holding a scroll as he continued to recite the Rite, his words flowing and chanting like a psalm. Gabriel, his eyes wide and his face devoid of colour, watched the scene around them. But Ben now focussed on the fourth figure sharing the tower with them.

The creature was huge – as tall as a house, perhaps even taller and powerfully built with arms as thick as tree trunks that ended in long, sharp talons like daggers, which at present were interlaced as his huge hands clasped together. He was of human form, his skin a reddish brown, his great muscular body devoid of hair. He was standing on the very edge of the tower looking down at the destruction below.

Ben whimpered, a wave of terror rolling over him as he realised what he was looking at. Until now he had thought Dantalion would be somewhat like the avatars: repulsive and certainly frightening, but not invincible. Now he looked upon Dantalion and was made sharply aware just how much more terrifying was this demon lord. His insectoid servants were mere pussycats by comparison. The creature turned to stare at him and Ben recoiled as he felt the full force of the evil he now faced. It seemed to hang in the air between them as the demon's eyes, glowing with fire, gazed at him.

Dantalion studied him for a moment longer and then crooked one claw. Ben gave a yelp as some invisible force pulled him towards the beast. He dug in his heels and tried to resist, but when the demon growled the force grew much stronger and Ben found himself flying across the tower until Dantalion seized him by the neck. He brought Ben's head close to his own and proceeded to throttle him, a cruel smile playing across his face as the giant talons began to squeeze.

"It is finished, Silver," Dantalion growled. "You have lost."

On the other side of the tower, Artemas' words ran on, the pitch changing, becoming louder as they rose to a crescendo. The fires burning the city flared up and rose higher and higher, the roar of the flames becoming deafening, until it was as if the whole world was aflame. At last, Artemas lifted both arms in the air and cried the three final Words of Power.

"*Eleuthero Libertas Dantalion!*"

With Ben still clutched in his claws, Dantalion lifted his head skyward and howled out his triumph. "At last!" he bellowed.

Of a sudden St Paul's and the city were gone, and they stood once more in the vault beneath the Guild Hall. Shivering, Ben felt disorientated at the abrupt transition and although Dantalion's claws was no longer round his neck, he was still choking and gasping for air. The room seemed to lurch and spin and he could not focus his eyes. He heard Freya give a scream of terror, followed by cries of panic from some of the thirteen that stood around the Last Seal. Then came the sound of flapping wings as all six of the avatars launched into the air and hurtled around the room screeching in bestial exultation. Ben's heart seemed to freeze in his chest when something very close and very huge bellowed back at them.

When Ben's eyes finally cleared, he could see that a colossal figure stood in the centre of the Last Seal, its head almost touching the arched ceiling. Wearing the same cruel smile but looking, if anything, even more threatening, Dantalion, one of the Old Masters of the ancient world, opened his jaws wide and let forth a roar.

The noise rebounded off the arches and vaulted ceiling, and then vibrated across the stone floor so that Ben could feel the tremors through the soles of his feet and in his very bones. It was a noise that soared down to hell and up to the furthest heavens, challenging the Almighty to battle. It was a shout of victory and the herald of all their deaths.

"Oh snoggers!" said Freya.

Chapter 26
Dantalion Risen

London, Tuesday 4th September, 1666: midnight

M oving blindingly fast, the creature rushed forward and lashed out at one of Matthias' men. There was a brief cry of pain, a spurt of blood and the man lay dead on the ground, his blood staining the symbol etched on the stone. For a heartbeat no one moved, and then there was panic as Matthias, Valentine and the other ten men all tried to run away from the demon. They soon discovered to their undiluted horror that they could not get away. It was as if an invisible barrier was encircling the rim of the Last Seal blocking their escape, and try as they might they could not force their way through it. Some pushed at this unseen wall, while others collapsed to the ground and clawed at it in desperation. All their efforts were futile, the barrier was utterly impenetrable, and as they realised the peril they were in, a look of terror came upon their faces. They turned towards the lectern and started shouting for help. Artemas smiled.

"It is time to fulfil your promise. Life and death, blood and bone you promised: why I ah … I do believe he will have it all," he said, laughing.

Again the demon roared, launching himself into the air to hang there for a moment before crashing down, landing on another man's shoulders crushing him under his vast weight.

Helplessly, Ben watched Dantalion attack the Thirteen and knew soon it would be his turn. The Thirteen and the One must die to free the demon. He knew he should run, indeed, every instinct told him to. There was no helping the eleven men left in the seal – he knew that – so saving himself was the sensible course. Yet he could not just abandon them to their fates. These men were fools: mindless sheep for the most part, led by a gullible idiot who was leading them like lambs to the slaughter. Yes, they were fools, but did they deserve to die?

Dantalion, Ben noticed now, used no Words of Power. He was like a wild predator, leaping at his prey. He slashed at them with his claws, crushed them under him or snapped at them with his jaws. It was as if he chose to forego using power in favour of the hunt. The beast hurled one broken body to the side and advanced on Valentine. The murderer now screamed in terror and pulled another man in front of him. Dantalion reached over and simply tore off the man's head. As the body crumpled to the ground, Valentine made a dash towards the other side of seal and then cried out as he was knocked on to his back and pinned to the ground by a talon that pierced his throat. Blood gushed out of his mouth and he writhed in agony for a few moments before he finally lay still.

Ben had seen enough.

"Gabriel," he hissed softly.

The bookseller turned wide, horror-stricken eyes on Ben, his mouth working but no sound coming out. Amidst the roars and screams distracting Walton, Morris and the others, he alone heard Ben say, "We must do something now!"

Gabriel, his face frozen in an expression of dread, made no reply. It seemed as if terror had gripped him and would not let him go. A self-confessed coward; was this the moment his courage failed and he ran away as he had done the year before?

Within the seal a man was begging for his life and Ben, unsure of Gabriel, decided he must act alone. Grasping his friend by the shoulders he shook him gently and said, "Gabriel, I am going to use the Words!"

The bookseller blinked as though waking from a trance. "No, Benjamin, you can't risk it," he croaked. "The Words are too powerful for you to control."

Ben shook his head, "No, they are not. I can handle the power ... I think it is the sorrow I struggle with." He listened to himself in surprise. Where had that thought come from? Yet even as he spoke it, he knew he was right. His ancestor had fought this demon and now it was his turn. Seeing Gabriel's puzzled expression, Ben nodded, "Besides which, I have no choice, do I?"

"We have no choice, Benjamin - *we*." Visibly gathering his courage, Gabriel swallowed hard and stepping forward he shouted, "*Calamus Αστραπή Стрелять!*"

A flash of light burst across the room and hit the avatars knocking three of them down. They fell sprawling onto their backs like upturned beetles, a mess of waving wings and scaly legs.

There was a moment's silence as everyone, including Dantalion, turned to look at Gabriel, and then the demon roared again, baring his teeth at Artemas, who swung round and shouted to his men.

"Kill him!" Artemas pointed at Gabriel. "Kill them all – all except the boy!"

Walton nodded and turning fired his pistol at Gabriel. With a grunt the bookseller fell backwards, blood spurting from a wound to his chest. That was the signal for bedlam to begin. Marlowe swung a fist the size of a mace and connected with Morris's face. The *Liberati* member went flying sideways, a tooth cartwheeling out of his mouth. Gymer bellowed something incoherent and charged Walton, both of them collapsing in a tangle of arms and legs. Then Freya screamed because the three downed avatars were climbing to their feet, although they were staggering around and looking stunned. The other three were still circling in the air and as one they turned and gliding on outstretched wings, soared towards her, moving clockwise around the Last Seal to attack Freya and her friends.

On the far side, Artemas' other men were closing in on Spencer and Tobias. Meanwhile, within the seal, Dantalion had resumed his attack on Matthias' followers. The preacher was knocked to the floor by a massive blow and lay still while the demon cut down another of the Thirteen.

Ben knew he had to act fast, so summoning all his strength he shouted, as Gabriel had done: "*Calamus Αστραπή Στρελять!*" Searing light shot like a blast of lightning across the vault into the chest of one of the approaching avatars. The creature screeched as it was looped in a writhing, discharging surge of electrical power.

"Seize him, seize him now!" Artemas ordered and the other avatars closed on Ben.

Sinking to his knees, Ben tried to speak the words again, but he felt suddenly weakened and knew he needed time to recover. "I'm sorry ... I'm so sorry," he heard himself say, and then realised it was not the Ben, here in the vault fighting the avatars, who had spoken, but another Ben. For an instant in his mind he saw the image of a boy shouting up at a window, a window wreathed in flames. Where had that come from and why think about it now? He shook his head and the image was gone. Instead he saw the vulture-like faces of the avatars closing in on him, arms stretched and talons extended. One swung a claw and Ben screamed in pain as it ripped open his side, sending blood trickling down his leg.

"NO!" shouted Artemas, coming down from the lectern and carrying the Tome of Dantalion. "Capture him – don't kill him. The Lord Dantalion needs him alive!" The avatars screeched in frustration but came on again less aggressively.

Meanwhile, Freya had reached Gabriel and saw that he was still alive, but blood was pouring from a wound in his chest and he was coughing painfully as he breathed. Pressing down on the wound with her fingers to try and staunch the flow, she looked around in desperation for Tobias, but he was with Spencer, both occupied in fighting a now toothless Morris. Using her teeth, Freya ripped off the hem of his smock, folded it into a pad and pushed it hard against the wound.

Gymer and Walton struggled on the floor, rolling over and under each other, hands striving to find the other's throat. Walton had managed to pull yet another primed pistol from his belt and was trying to point it at the spymaster, but Gymer held his wrist tightly and shook it hard, attempting to dislodge the weapon. Walton's hand involuntarily tightened and with a loud crack, the pistol fired, deafening them both for a moment. The bullet ricocheted off one of the pillars and grazed Spencer's shoulder before burying itself in a wall. Cursing now, Walton dropped the pistol, shook off Gymer's hand and then reached down for his knife, bringing it back to point at the other man's throat. Gymer's eyes widened and he frantically twisted to get out of the blade's path as Walton thrust forward, a look of glee on his face.

Morris was now out of it; Spencer held one hand over his shoulder wound as he and Tobias approached the other two *Liberati*. Neither one of their opponents had pistols, but both carried long dirks, which they twisted expertly in their hands. From their apparent skill and the agile way they moved, they had clearly been soldiers once: perhaps Cavaliers alongside Artemas in the war twenty and more years before. Tobias, though, was in no mood to waste time with these small fry who

333

were barring his route to Artemas and his long awaited vengeance. He kicked one of the men hard in the shin and as his opponent collapsed to the ground kicked him again in the ribs. Then, out of the corner of his eye, he saw a glint of metal reflecting the candlelight and, with a cry of alarm, twisted to one side as the other *Liberati* stabbed at him with the blade, just missing him. Spencer then seized this man's wrist and the two of them fell to the ground, struggling for control of the weapon.

The first *Liberati* had dropped the dirk he carried when he fell. Tobias ran towards where it had fallen on the ancient flagstones not far from the Last Seal. He was reaching to pick it up when he felt a hand tighten round his ankle and lost his balance, falling to the ground with a grunt of pain. He flipped himself over as the man jumped on top of him and started punching him. Tobias brought his knee up hard, connecting with some unpleasant, sensitive spot and threw his enemy off him, but then he shouted in frustration as his opponent landed near the dirk. The *Liberati* gave a nasty grin as he now bent to pick it up, and then coming to his feet he jumped towards Tobias, swinging the weapon to the left and right as he did so.

The avatars had reached Ben, and as the leading three circled round to his right, the other three flew by on his left, threatening to surround him. Sweating with fear, his pulse racing, he wondered if he could manage to use the Words again, for he felt exhausted; he was also afraid of what the effect on him might be. If he used all his energy now, he would have nothing left with which to face the demon.

Another scream shrilled out from the within the force field encircling the Last Seal, and was cut off, gurgling to silence as Dantalion pounced again. How many was that, Ben wondered: five or six? Too many at any rate, it was time to act – he had to risk it, but how? The lightning bolts he had used had knocked the avatars down and partially disabled them, but it was only temporary; had not destroyed them. Perhaps the loathsome creatures had some protection or defence against it. So, should he conjure fire against them? But no; having seen the delight the pair of avatars had taken in the flames just before they had entered the Guild Hall, they were clearly impervious to that element. What, then? Ben thought hard. Ice? Yes ... maybe ice would do it.

He brought his hands together so that his thumbs touched. Then he extended his arms towards the approaching creatures, summoned his strength and shouted: "Κώνος, jää, décharge!"

A cone of ice shot out from his fingers and jumped across the room spreading out in the shape of a fan towards the avatars. Two of them took the full blast and were frozen stiff in an instant, keeling over backwards and hitting the ground with a sickening crunch. Another screeched in fury and suddenly the talons were back and it was lunging and stabbing at him. Ben should have moved: he knew he should, but for a moment he did not see the vault or the avatar, instead he stood in front of a house, and the house was on fire. "Mother! Father!" he heard himself screaming and a wave of horror and sorrow swept over him.

"Oh no," he said to himself, "I think I am remembering my parents' death. It's like every time I use the Words, a little piece of it comes back to me." Thrashing from side to side to avoid the talons, Ben's eyes cleared just in time to see the avatar's face twisting and snarling in rage as it jumped at him.

Out of nowhere Marlowe appeared. He charged into the beast shoulder first, putting his weight and power behind the rush and knocking the creature over. The other three avatars charged into the fray: one attacking Marlowe in a flurry of claws and razor sharp teeth. The big man swung his fist back and forth and was soon covered in cuts and dripping blood, but still he fought on. The other two moved in on Ben, talons retracted, but with an expression of grim determination on their dragon-like faces. They gave him no choice but to use the

Words: he staggered backwards yelling, "*Κῶνος, jää, décharge!*"
He flung another ice cloud blasting toward the creatures,
sending them reeling. A flash of memory passed across his
mind: the argument with his father on the night before the fire,
but he blinked hard to dispel it, with a supreme effort of will
focussing on the present. The avatars were still down, so he
risked a glance towards Dantalion.

He saw that the demon was closing in on a group of three
terrified men who were huddled up against the invisible
barrier around the seal. One of them was weeping, clawing
ineffectually at it.

"That will do you no good," Dantalion's voice rumbled
across the vault and the very earth seemed to shake beneath
their feet. "The promise you made bound you here as also I am
bound here. We cannot escape except by death: your death – or
mine."

The demon advanced again, arms held apart ready to sweep
the three of the dwindling Thirteen away. Suddenly, in a blur,
someone got up from the floor and moved in front of them to
stand between the demon and the men. It was Matthias and he
squared up to the giant monster, his eyes bright with anger.
Dantalion glared down at him and swept a claw towards the
preacher. Then, at the last moment he tugged it away and
roared in frustration.

"What is this? This is not right! Why are you not bound to
me?" Dantalion roared and then added in a frustrated tone, "I
need thirteen. Thirteen must die and then the One." The demon
shot an almost hungry look at Ben for a moment and then
glared back at the preacher. "What is this? This cannot be! You
took the oath ... you promised," he sounded almost hurt.

Matthias smiled, "I lied," came the simple answer.

Artemas, his face purple with rage, arrived at the seal with
the Tome of Dantalion under his arm and strode right through
the force field straight up to the preacher.

336

Ben's eyes narrowed. It appeared that although the invisible barrier prevented Matthias and his disciples from escaping the seal, it did not impede entry. If that were so, he or the others could get at Dantalion, maybe save some of the preacher's terrified followers and attack the demon himself. Ben grimaced: it was a tall order.

"What do you mean, you lied?" Artemas was shouting, casting wary glances at Dantalion. "You said only today that you understood what had to be done and that it was a test of faith."

The preacher nodded. "Yes it was a test, and I passed. I finally realised what my heart had been trying to tell me: that Dantalion is evil. He is no angel sent from the Lord, but a demon and I ... *we* have been used to destroy a city and murder innocents, and no matter how much I felt betrayed, what I did was wrong. I need redemption and tonight this is how I will achieve it."

"You old fool! You will die tonight. You know that, don't you?"

Matthias just nodded. "Yes I do, but you see you were right. It *was* a test of faith: my faith in my God. I knew that whatever happened I would die tonight. But in so doing I could deny that demon his freedom," he pointed at Dantalion.

"Matthias; Matthias," the creature pleaded, "You don't need to die; even now you can rule with me. Just promise to serve me. Bind yourself to me now. All you have to do is promise."

"Oh yes," Matthias snorted in derision, "you would like that wouldn't you. Another willing victim; I heard you just now. Thirteen you must slay to be free. What if there are only twelve, eh? What then will happen?"

Dantalion's glare grew furious and he reached out to Artemas for his book. The Cavalier handed it over and when he did so Dantalion almost sighed. He looked at the Tome with something approaching love and a deep longing.

To Ben, watching from outside the seal, it seemed that Dantalion grew a foot or two taller. Certainly the sense of menace pervading the vault increased, and around the seal there was silence, punctuated only by the grunts and groans from the fights still going on in the room. Dantalion flipped through a few pages and then looked up at the preacher.

"You will regret your choice. You see, although the man who made the seals separated me from my Tome, he neglected to retrieve it and it was found by Stephen Blake, one of my followers; an ancestor of this man here," he pointed at Artemas. "Cornelius Silver made one fatal mistake: he designed this ingenious trap - this prison that has been mine for the last three hundred years - assuming that I or my followers would only have access to items he knew of. He thought he had covered every possibility, but he did not appreciate that with my Tome I am invincible, nor did he foresee this day, this moment when I would be reunited with it. Fool that he was, he did not understand that with this all things become possible. With this, for instance," and he patted the book, "I can change the rules of Silver's little game."

He riffled through the pages, found the one he wanted, murmured an incantation, smiled and said, "And thus it is done. I now need but twelve victims and then the One. And so, preacher, your pitiful sacrifice is in vain." Effortlessly smashing Matthias to one side, the demon advanced on the trio cowering beyond him.

While he was thus distracted, Ben acted. From somewhere deep inside himself his courage welled into his chest and propelled him towards the seal, towards the demon, even though his heart was screaming at him to hold back. Without understanding why, his fear dropped suddenly away and he felt a strange calm. He stepped through the barrier, ignoring the slight tug of the magnetic force and stood squarely in front of Dantalion. Raising one hand to stop him, Ben said, "Leave them be, Dantalion, I'm warning you!"

"Get out of the way, Silver," Artemas snarled.

The demon paused to look down at Ben, his cruel face registering surprise followed swiftly by amusement. "Ah ... so, this is the descendant of Cornelius Silver. Well, you don't lack for courage, boy, I will give you that. I shall enjoy killing you when the time comes. But for now get out of my way," he said, advancing again, but Ben stood his ground and stared defiantly up at the creature.

"Why wait? Do it now, Dantalion!" Ben taunted. Dantalion hesitated and Ben laughed, "You can't can you. I am the One; if you kill me before the others die, the seal holds and you are trapped here forever."

Dantalion said nothing, but Artemas pulled out a pistol and advanced on Ben. The creature growled at him as he passed and shook his huge head. Artemas hesitated and then stepped back. Ben laughed again.

"I thought so. And seeing how that is the case, I also wonder about that Tome. I think it gives you many powers, but I don't believe Cornelius overlooked *anything*. I think you are lying: you still need thirteen willing victims. Matthias has thwarted you after all."

Frustrated, Dantalion's eyes burned red in fury. "You are right, Benjamin Silver. I do need thirteen and then you," he nodded his head and stepped towards Ben, talking as he did so. "But you are also right that the Tome gives me many powers: shall we see what I can do?" and without pausing he scooped up Benjamin and Matthias in one huge embrace along with his Tome.

An overwhelming, searing pain ran through Ben's body. He and Matthias gave involuntary cries of agony before blackness overtook them. On the edge of his consciousness, Ben heard Freya scream as he, Matthias and Dantalion vanished.

And above the vault, the Guild Hall continued to burn.

Chapter 27
Lead Us Not Into Temptation

London, Wednesday 5th September, 1666:
an hour after midnight

When Benjamin opened his eyes, he realised he was lying on his back looking up at the stars, which shone brightly in an inky black sky. He also realised that he felt very cold. His hand was holding something. He lifted it up and looked at it and was startled to find that it was full of snow. This was odd! Clearly he was not in the vault. Carefully raising his head he looked around him. He was in a snow-covered garden between an orchard at one end and a large house at the other. This was a familiar place somehow, but he could not remember why. However, he did have a horrible sense of foreboding. Something terrible had happened here once, but what? Now, though, he felt an odd feeling, as if this was all a dream. Dragging himself to his feet, he got up and walked towards the house. He was sure he had done this before ... or had he just dreamed that he had?

Ben knew there was something important about the house: something personally important. What had happened here? What had he done here? Why was he struggling to remember it? Above him the stars were bright and the air crisp and cool. It was a beautiful night, yet for some reason he was not happy. Why? He moved towards the house and felt snow crunch under his feet. The sensation sent shivers of memory through him. Once before he had walked through a garden covered in snow like this and then something had happened that had changed everything.

He reached the door and saw a figure standing there. He moved closer and then stopped, for it was not the person he was expecting to see. He paused as he wondered who he had been expecting.

"I can't remember!" he said in exasperation.

"No, and that is the way it should stay. There is nothing here but pain for you," the figure said and then moved into the moonlight.

Ben gasped for he was looking at himself: a doppelganger; another Ben, identical in every way to himself, stood there and gazed back at him. The feeling persisted that even this had happened before. If he had not been sure, now he was certain that he was dreaming, but as hard as he tried, he could not wake up.

"What? I don't understand," he said.

"There is nothing worth understanding here. You should go away and enjoy the power you have discovered inside you. Never return here. I can make it happen. I can bury this place deep inside you just like we did before."

"We did?"

The other Benjamin nodded. "Indeed, for it is too painful a place for us, so we blocked it out. We forced it away. Then the power awakened it again."

"But you just told me I should enjoy the power."

"Yes, you should now. For now the power has done more than we did before. You remember Sunday night when you slept in that barn and lost control of the power?"

342

Ben nodded, "But I can't remember why that happened."

"I did it; or rather we did it together," his doppelganger went on, "to blot out the memory of this terrible place forever. We used the power to burn it away. That is now how it should stay."

Ben nodded, "Yes, I remember that it was something terrible I had done: something I tried to forget. I had rejected it for it was too awful and I blocked it out with anger at the world and at everything, but the power awoke it even so: every time I used it, it awoke just a little more until I knew everything. Gabriel was wrong: I could control the power, what I could not control was the sorrow. I used the power until the sorrow was gone."

The duplicate Ben nodded. "Yes, we did that."

"No," Ben shook his head. "It did not work because I am remembering again. Each time I use the power I remember a little more. It did not work and it can't work, can it?"

"It can work," his doppelganger replied, "but it must be powerful words you use. I can give you those words and you will use them and you – we – can be free."

Ben squinted at his double suspiciously.

"Who are you?"

"I am you, you fool: the part that protects us from painful memories and from guilt. In other words the part that keeps us sane. So, do what I say now. Leave this place and never come here again."

Ben nodded and then noticed another figure standing behind his double. The second figure stepped out of the house and Ben gasped as he recognised who it was.

"Gabriel! What are you doing here?"

"I am not here, nor am I Gabriel. But your mind trusts Gabriel and you turn to him for knowledge and wisdom. I am here to say there is another course to get you through this."

"Don't listen to him," Ben's doppelganger said, but the man who was and yet was not Gabriel, ignored the interruption and went on talking.

"What I suggest is both simple and hard. You must enter the house. You must re-live the night you have blocked out all this time. That is the easy part. The hard part is that the pain you will encounter will tempt you to use the release of power to quench the anguish. Benjamin, you must NOT give in to temptation. Endure the pain and you will become strong."

Ben's double snorted, "If you do that you will go mad, but be my guest," he said and stepped to one side, "go inside and see what happened here."

Ben hesitated, but he must know, he realised, and he stepped inside the house and as he did the memory returned in full. He saw again that final blissful day with his parents, the argument with his father about his future; the angry fit of temper that had sent him rushing outside to spend hours skulking in the orchard, until his mother found him. He saw again how it had been his anger and resentment that had made him stoke up a roaring fire and then go to bed, forgetting to put out the flames; and how, when he remembered, he had sulkily turned over, pulled up the covers and done nothing about it, seeing this as an act of defiance: a small victory over his father.

Then he saw the victory turn sour as the fire destroyed the house and his parents perished in the act of saving him. He had escaped and in his terrible guilt he had screamed again and again at the window, "I'm so sorry."

Then he was back outside the house on the night before the fire, with his doppelganger and Gabriel still there, looking at him. The anguish flooded through him, awful in its intensity. "It is too terrible," Ben cried to himself. "What should I do?"

"Do what I say and be free of this place forever," his double replied, "use the words I give you."

"What words?" Ben blurted.

344

"You will command a man to do what you say and that command he cannot resist."

"What man?" Ben asked and saw that both Gabriel and the other Benjamin were pointing to where a man knelt in prayer.

Ben gaped. It was the preacher; it was ... "Matthias? What are you doing here in my memory? Wait! That means you ..." he turned back to the other Benjamin. "You're not me! You must be Dantalion!"

Everything came flooding back: the vault, the killing, standing up to the demon; pain so bad he had passed out. This, then, was another of Dantalion's illusions. But so *real*.

The other Benjamin nodded, as did Gabriel. The pair reached out and held hands and as they did so there was a flash of red light and in their place stood the demon Dantalion, looking down at him.

"So, this is all a trick," Ben said bitterly.

"No, it is not a trick," the demon smiled. "We both know this terrible place is what you fear the most. To remember what you did as a spoilt little brat; to know your action caused the death of your parents is terrible, is it not?"

"I did not kill them!" Ben shouted out, but Dantalion raised a finger to silence him.

"No? Yet, you believe that you did. You cannot live with that memory, so you bury it. I have brought it to light and I can leave you here in this place so that you will ever exist here, recalling afresh each day the sorrow, the guilt and the pain."

Ben's eyes widened. "No! No, please don't do that. What must I do to be free?"

The demon walked over to Matthias, who opened his eyes and glared up at the beast, his hands clasped in prayer.

Turning to Ben, Dantalion pointed at the preacher, "You will make this man believe in me; make him promise himself to me willingly. Then he will die and I will be free. Do it now, or I will leave you in this place for eternity."

Ben looked at Matthias then back at the demon. "But you still need me. You have to kill me to be free. Why should I do as you say?"

"It is your choice. Would you rather stay here living this moment over and over forever ... or take your chance against me in battle?"

"Once you are free I don't stand a chance."

"True, but it would be better than an eternity of this," and Dantalion clapped his hands. Above them the house burst into flames and Ben heard again his mother's screams.

Shuddering, his tears streaming down his face, he pressed his hands to his ears to block out the sound and dropped to his knees in the snow, crying out, "Make it stop! Please, Dantalion, make it stop!"

You want it to stop, boy; you want to be gone from this place? Then say the words I give you. Force Matthias to serve me and we will both be free."

"I can't stand it here ... but I can't let you be free. I don't know what to do!"

Dantalion folded his arms and leant back against the burning doorpost.

"Choose!"

Chapter 28
But Deliver Us From Evil

London, Wednesday 5th September, 1666:
two hours after midnight

T he house burned ferociously, and above them Ben could hear his mother screaming in agony. Now he also heard his father's voice in torment added to her pleas for help. Dantalion leant against the doorpost, oblivious it seemed to the flames that flickered about him, he watched impassively as Ben struggled with his decision.

Unnoticed by either of them, Matthias opened his eyes and got up off his knees. He walked through the snow to stand between the boy and the demon and now both turned to look at him.

The preacher addressed Dantalion. "Let me ask you something, creature of Hell. Perhaps you can tell me, *Lord* Dantalion," Matthais said in a mocking tone, "perhaps you can indeed explain why, if you are so powerful and if that book you carry gives you so much power, why you need this boy to weave your little spell?"

Abruptly, the screaming above them stopped and the fire in the house went out; suddenly they were standing in the snow-covered garden, with the stars bright above them and the house unharmed nearby. Ben stared at the demon and was shocked to see that he was apparently lost for words.

Matthias pointed down at the snow: two small melted patches revealed bare grass where his knees had rested. "You see, I was kneeling there praying for guidance and it suddenly occurred to me that a being of such, supposedly almost *omnipotent* power, should surely not need a mere mortal boy, whatever his talents, to free him."

Ben cocked his head and narrowed his eyes. What was the preacher saying? Whatever it was, somewhere deep inside he began to feel a tiny spark of hope. He did not know where this was heading but he prayed it would continue.

"Unless ... unless in fact you are not so omnipotent? Not yet; even with your book of tricks and illusions. While you are held by the sorcery of this boy's ancestor you are not truly free. Not even when the Thirteen die will you be free."

Dantalion snarled and bared his teeth. "When the Thirteen die, *I* am free to leave the seal; *you*, old man, will never be."

Matthias smiled. "It is as I thought: 'When the Thirteen die I am free to leave the seal'. That is what you said, yes? Well then, tell me, Lord Dantalion," and again his tone was mocking, "if the killing of the Thirteen frees you, why then do you need the One?"

The demon stepped forward and slapped Matthias hard over the mouth so that his lips started bleeding. Matthias tumbled on to his back, but he was laughing, his blood spattering red on the snow.

"Quiet, fool!" The demon shouted, but Matthias spat out some more blood, wiped his mouth and started laughing again, and now he raised one hand and pointed it at Dantalion.

"Oh, I have been such a fool to be taken in by you and Artemas. But that does not excuse what I did. Because of me the city is in flames and men have died. My life is forfeit: I

348

know that, but for my soul's sake I will see you defeated. You will not silence me." Now he turned to Ben.

"Benjamin, don't you realise why he needs you? It is not to be free – he admits as much himself. No – it is to get back his powers. The book gives him some, but not enough. Cornelius Silver did not just lock away the demon in that Last Seal, but all his demonic powers – his very soul in fact. Only the blood of the One – one of the descendants of Cornelius himself – will free that: your soul to replace his. Without that he is what? A fifteen-foot-high killing machine: strong; ferocious and terrifying. Oh yes, all of those things, but NOT invincible."

Ben pushed himself up off his knees, planted his feet squarely in the snow and stood facing the demon. Fists clenched, he stared at him defiantly. "You need me to force Matthias to give his promise to you because you cannot make him do that yourself. You know what I think? I think I am stronger than you. You almost had me then. I did not even test all this ..." he swung his arms wide to encompass the scene around him, "this illusion of yours, to see if I could break free of it, so convinced was I by your evil trickery, but not any longer. I challenge you, Dantalion! Let's go back to the vault and finish this!"

"Wait, boy," Dantalion sounded desperate now, "I meant what I said: I can remove the memory of this place. You need feel neither sorrow nor guilt; it will be erased. We can find a way around the problem of the Last Seal without you dying. You can forget this place and we ... yes, we can rule this world together, you and I. What could we not do? Imagine that!"

It occurred to Ben that the creature was actually pleading with him. He stared at Dantalion, feeling not even a shred of temptation; nothing but loathing and contempt. He pushed past him and walked a few paces to look at the house he had grown up in. It had always been a place of joy and love and now also of sorrow, but whether joy or sorrow it was his own home, his own memory, and he would not lose it again.

"No," he said, "we will leave this place, but it will always be a part of me; a part of what I am. I must face up to what I did; admit to my uncle what happened here, for he took me in and he deserves to know why his brother died. No, I cannot escape the guilt and I cannot go back and change the past. However, although it might mean sacrifice, I *can* change the future and that," he said, clapping his hands together and then pointing at the demon, "means you, Dantalion."

Ben reached out one hand, almost clawing at the sky above him, as if he was trying to pull down a star, and shouted the words, "*Ostendu, Realität, núhwílum!*"

With a flash of brilliant light, the house and the snow-covered garden were gone and they stood back in the vault surrounded by the bodies of the men Dantalion had slain. The battle still raged outside the confines of the Last Seal and it seemed as if only moments had passed.

Swiftly, Ben took stock: Artemas stood, a pistol in each hand, covering the six members of the Thirteen who were still alive. They were huddled together just behind Ben and Matthias. Tobias and Spencer were still struggling with two of the *Liberati* although, as Ben watched, Tobias knocked his opponent's head hard down against the stone floor. The man went limp and the doctor, gasping for breath and with blood trickling from a wound on his forehead, got to his feet and looked around for Artemas. An ugly expression of revulsion crossed his face as he spotted the Cavalier. Keeping Artemas in his sights, he picked up a stray pistol and began loading it, fumbling for powder and shot in the leather pocket at his belt.

Near to him, Gabriel was now sitting up holding the bloody cloth to his chest, his pallid features scrunched with pain. Freya had moved away from him and was creeping inch by inch around the perimeter of the seal, the knife in her hand, a calculating look in her eyes.

Gymer was still struggling to keep Walton's blade away from his throat, and Marlowe was battling the three remaining avatars. Blood was running freely from a dozen talon wounds, but the big man had somehow managed to retrieve his blunderbuss from the pile of weapons seized by Artemas' men at St Paul's. Now, swinging the gun up, he pulled the trigger. There was a huge boom and one of the beasts collapsed with a hole the size of a dinner plate in its chest.

Turning back to the immediate problem, Ben saw that Dantalion was standing in the very centre of the seal and looking at him, his red eyes filled with venomous hatred.

"I give you one last chance, boy. Do what I ask and recite the Words of Power that will force Matthias to serve me."

Ben shook his head. "No, but I give *you* one last chance: one final chance to depart this world in peace and leave us alone. If you don't it will be the worse for you."

Dantalion laughed, loud and mocking and then rage contorted his face. In his left hand he still held the Tome; his right hand came forward, talons extended and snapping at Ben. "Very well, so be it. If I cannot be free I will take a city with me to the Abyss!" He spoke Words of Power and sparks played around his talons.

Well, this is it, thought Ben, time to find out if Matthias was right. He reached out a hand and began incanting his own Words of Power.

Dantalion had created a ball of shimmering electrical energy; he dragged his hand back and threw it straight at Ben's chest. Alarmed, Ben abandoned his intended incantation and in desperation he instead shouted out three words.

"*Contego, Aeris, Minä!*"

A silvery translucent dome appeared all around him and the ball of electrical death disintegrated on its surface. Dantalion shot at him again, this time with a searing flame. Ben reacted a fraction too late and was flung to the ground by the blow.

"You are running out of options, boy!" Dantalion turned to Artemas, "Kill the others!" he ordered.

"But, Lord, if they die by my hand you cannot be free."

Again the demon laughed and Ben was worried at the triumph within it. He dodged another bolt of fire and rolled over. As he did so, he saw Freya was now close by on one side of the seal, and Tobias, pistol at the ready, was approaching on the other.

"You have found the Thirteen once," Dantalion said to the Cavalier, "you can find another Thirteen. There will always be fools who will fall for your playacting."

Artemas shrugged. "Perhaps I can, but the One, Lord: if Silver dies before the Thirteen – whichever thirteen – you can never be free."

"Ah, but I can, there is another of Silver's blood. I did not know it, but the boy told me himself that he lives with his uncle; his father's brother. *He* will be the last of Silver's bloodline if the boy dies, and *he* will suffice to set me free. So you see, Artemas, I no longer need Benjamin Silver!"

"*No!*" Bellowing with rage at his own stupidity, Ben jumped to his feet and flung a ball of ice at Dantalion, who deflected it with his Tome as if it were a shield. Artemas nodded at Dantalion and moved past him to the right, levelling his two pistols at the cowering group of Matthias' followers. Then, before Ben had time to defend himself, Dantalion, his lips curled back in a snarl of triumph, pointed his finger at him.

Suddenly, Freya darted in from behind Dantalion. Unseen by Artemas and Dantalion, she had crept through the invisible barrier to within ten feet of them, moving so quickly and lightly that no one had noticed her until she appeared on the very edge of the seal.

Holding her knife by the blade, she threw it at the demon. It flew like a dart to its target, whether by luck or by judgement it penetrated a thinner portion of the creature's naturally armoured skin beneath his arm. It hardly wounded him – but it hurt. Distracted, his pointing finger wavered from its mark.

With a roar he spun round and his eyes found the little thief, who produced yet another dagger and flung it at him, but the demon beat this one aside as if it were a bothersome fly. Then it was Dantalion's turn to ready an attack, this time another ball of electricity. Before he could discharge it, Tobias, who had stepped up to the far side of the seal and was aiming his pistol at Artemas, changed his aim without hesitation and fired at the demon. The shot took Dantalion in the shoulder blade, but barely dented it. The beast roared again and flung his ball at Tobias, hitting the doctor squarely in the chest and sending him tumbling head first into a pillar where he slumped unconscious to the ground.

All this had taken only a few brief moments, but Ben had not been idle. Until now he had just been trying to survive, with no plan beyond staying alive, but when Dantalion had threatened his uncle it was as if the mists had cleared and he saw clearly what he must do. His parents had died to save him and he now knew he must make their sacrifice worthwhile. Many people who live when others die wish for that, but few have the chance. Ben had that chance now. He could save his uncle, but more than that, he could save the world. In that instant, he had decided to incant the words that invoked the Gateway of Sacrifice.

Three hundred years before, Cornelius had foreseen this moment and had provided for it such that, if ever Dantalion escaped from the Last Seal, there remained one last chance to open the portal and banish the demon to the void, back to the Abyss where his kind lived. Ben had found the words written on the back of one of the pages he had rescued from Cornelius' journal. Neither he nor Gabriel had taken much notice of them at the time; it had seemed certain that Dantalion would be too powerful to be forced through the Gateway, but Ben now knew the demon was not all powerful. He also knew there would be a price to pay; the price Cornelius had mentioned: *'a life given to the void to close the door'*. As a last resort, Cornelius had been willing to make that choice, to pay that price, and had assumed his descendants would do the same. Ben nodded to himself; his ancestor had been right: the cost was high, the cost was his life, but he would pay it now. Drawing in a deep breath, he faced Dantalion.

"*Ingang, Vácuo, Nepokriven,*" Ben boomed, summoning the mystical energies bound in the Words of Power: words divided from each other in the ancient past and then handed down in mankind's languages or passed on through something even stronger than that, in mankind's very blood; words that waited to be spoken again by the right tongue, at the right time, and in the right way. Today the words summoned a doorway: a door created by the blood of the man who had trapped the demon. A door to send him back to Hell!

At first there was nothing. Then, at the limits of his perception, almost beyond sight and sound, Ben felt something. To begin with it was just a sensation: a feeling that something had changed. Then the feeling became certainty and finally, a burning intolerable anticipation of what was about to happen. The hairs on Ben's arms and head stood up, goose pimples appeared on his skin – and then the sound began. A buzzing noise was what Ben heard first, like a swarm of wasps on a hot summer's day. It grew in volume and became a loud vibration that resonated through the stone vault, shaking everything and everyone.

Around the chamber the fight was suddenly forgotten as everyone turned, open mouthed, to stare at a shimmering red light which hung in the air, swirling and pulsating and then slowly transforming and gaining shape and form until it became a rectangular void: a black doorway, going nowhere, hanging in the air on the edge of the Last Seal.

The buzzing sound ceased and through the doorway Ben could now perceive distant shapes and forms moving about. Though hazy at first, after a moment it was if veil was lifted. The doorway led to a land like no other Ben had ever seen. The first thing he noticed was a red glow coming from a myriad of burning lava streams, which flowed around twisted rocky pillars, arches and outcroppings that resembled encrustations of coral amidst a fiery sea. The rocks contained hollows and caves and in them, and over the arches and pillars, a multitude of impossible nightmarish shapes writhed and flowed. The inhabitants of the Abyss: the race of demons. Hell.

Ben's skin crawled. Some of the creatures had claws and walked on two legs, a little like Dantalion, but there were a hundred other forms, all wailing and moaning in the inferno. One crawled on its belly like a snake, but wore feathers and had two vast bulging eyes. It was sliding past another, which appeared to be a giant crab in all aspects except its face, which was that of a man. It scuttled out of the path of a third creature, which was even more bizarre having a man's torso, the legs of a cockerel, a reptilian tail and the head of a bull. The creature looked straight into Ben's eyes and snarled at him. A moment later a hundred more heads turned to look towards the portal and then as one surged towards it.

Dantalion bellowed with laughter. "Fool! Do you know what you have done? You have opened the portal for an invasion. Is this all that the descendant of Cornelius Silver can do? Don't you realise there is nothing that can close that gate now it is open? All I need do is to wait for my brothers and together we will destroy your world. You have lost, Benjamin Silver, you are a fool and ..." the demon's voice faltered as he saw that Ben was calmly smiling.

"Ah, but you are wrong, Dantalion, there is a way to close it," Ben said softly. "Cornelius planned for this moment imagining it might be him. But it is me and I will force you through and then I will follow you. A soul who goes willingly to the Abyss will seal the door." As he was speaking, Ben raised his hands and began weaving a ball of ice out of the air. Ice: the one weapon Ben had at his disposal to counter the demon's fire and force him back through the Gateway. Ben looked round swiftly, took one last look at his friends then hefting the ice, stepped forward.

"NO!" Dantalion roared and there was more than anger in his voice, there was fear, "I will not go. Artemas, kill him!"

Artemas nodded and pointed both pistols at Ben, his fingers beginning to tighten on the triggers.

As Ben stared helplessly, unable to move, another dagger flew through the air, passed close to his ear and sailed on to knock a pistol out of Artemas' hand. It tumbled away, passed through the portal and vanished into the molten lava. From behind Ben, Gymer shouted triumphantly. He was now standing next to Walton, who was lying on the flagstones, arms tied behind him. Over him stood Gabriel, one hand still pressed to the wound in his chest, the other covering Walton with a pistol. Gymer's throw had spun Artemas round and before he could re-aim, Freya sprang up and grabbed the Cavalier's arm that held the remaining pistol. The two struggled in front of the portal and Freya, her skirts kilted up by a wide leather belt she had taken from a dead *Liberati,* was using all the tricks she had learned on the streets, her thumbs gouging at the Cavalier's eyes, her knee slamming into his groin, but he was so much stronger than the little thief and was bending her backwards, his hands at her throat.

A bolt of light from the demon shot back at Gymer, lifting him off his feet and slamming him into the struggling forms of Marlowe and the one surviving avatar. The three went down in

356

a heap and lay stunned. Now, only one of Gymer's men remained standing: Spencer. Having knocked his opponent unconscious to the ground he staggered forward, but then collapsed, blood gushing out of a neck wound. Ben grimaced in despair: no further help would come from outside the seal. Whatever was to be done, he had to do it alone.

Dantalion flicked a dismissive glance at Matthias, who was still knelt in prayer in front of what remained of his flock, and then brought his gaze back to Ben.

"So then, it looks as though it is down to you and me, boy," he sneered.

Ben nodded. "So let's get it over with, shall we?" So saying, he aimed the ball of ice at Dantalion's head. As before, the demon lifted the Tome, the source of his power, to use as a shield.

It was what Ben had counted on. The ice sphere slammed into the artefact knocking it heavily to the ground five yards behind Dantalion. Powerless without it, he cried out in dismay and spinning round to retrieve it, presented his back to Ben. And for that one brief moment, the demon was vulnerable.

Suddenly, before Ben could act, Matthias leapt to his feet, ran behind the demon and taking him completely by surprise, seized the book, picked it up and with both arms hauled it over to the shimmering gateway. He looked through it at the array of loathsome creatures moving like an army towards the portal, then he swayed forward.

"NO!" Dantalion screamed, lunging for the preacher. But he was too late.

Matthias had turned to look back at Ben, his face incandescent with faith. "Now, I pay for my sins for my soul's sake. Pray for me, Benjamin Silver." His arms still wrapped around the book, he jumped through the door, landed on a rocky island, teetered on its edge for a moment and then fell forward over the precipice. In a trice both he and the Tome were gone, vanished into the inferno.

Dantalion roared in an agony of frustration. Ben, reeling with shock, stared at the portal. Then he noticed it was getting smaller. The shapes and sounds in that sea of fire were fading and the doorway was becoming black again. Matthias had given his soul willingly to the Abyss; the price had been paid and the portal was starting to close.

Ben knew he must act quickly now. He flicked a glance at Freya; she and Artemas were still locked in mortal combat and Matthias' followers were weeping, weak with shock. He was on his own. Somehow he had to get the demon to drop his guard. Mustering a broad grin of triumph, he stepped towards Dantalion, another ball of ice growing between his hands.

"Shame when you lose something important to you, isn't it?" he taunted. "Because of you, half the city feels that way, and now you know why! Feel bad, do you, *Lord* Dantalion? Huh! Lost your book have you? What a weakling you are, after all: a great big lout, too fat to scratch his navel with his paw!"

Shaking with rage, Dantalion swung round and Ben braced himself. He could see that though deprived of his arcane powers and weaker than before, the demon was still a fearsome beast. Teeth bared, Dantalion charged straight at him, but Ben was ready. He flung everything into a huge blast of ice that threw the demon backwards. A second blast had him staggering just a few yards in front of the Gateway.

"You are not welcome in our world, Dantalion: just go!" Ben shouted and sent a third blast at the demon, knocking him into the very verge of the closing portal.

The demon held out one hand and began to plead, "Please, no. Stop, I beg you. If you send me there it will destroy me. My soul will stay trapped in the tablet forever. Let me go. I will not harm anyone, I promise."

"What do you take me for?" Ben gazed without pity at the grovelling creature, his expression showing no mercy. "I warned you it would be the worse for you if you resisted."

Arms clasped together, Dantalion fell to his knees, and Ben was amazed to see the creature's eyes were wet with ... yes, with tears! "Please; I will serve you. We can conquer the world you and I!" Dantalion screeched in desperation, but Ben said nothing further apart from repeating the Words of Power and, summoning all his remaining strength, he sent a final icy blast that hurled the demon screaming through the Gateway. As he toppled into the Abyss, one claw whipped out and yanked Artemas by the collar.

Still entangled with Freya, his fingers hooked into her belt, the Cavalier cried out; his eyes wide with terror as he was pulled into the portal by his master.

Freya screamed; her arms and legs flailing as she too was dragged towards the void.

"Help me!" she pleaded, "Ben ... please help me!"

Chapter 29
The *Praesidium*

London, Wednesday 5th September, 1666:
approaching dawn

Ben flung himself full length to the Gateway, looped both his arms around Freya's waist and held on firmly. Beyond the portal, the demon pulled at Artemas, who in turn tugged at the little thief. Ben stumbled forward a few steps as he fought against the immense strength of the creature in the void, unable to spare a hand either to unbuckle Freya's belt or unhook the Cavalier's gripping fingers.

Artemas suddenly re-emerged through the blackness of the diminishing doorway. Only his head was visible and he was glaring at Ben, his face red with fury. "You are coming with me, both of you!" he snarled.

Ben ignored him and just gritted his teeth. "Hold on, Freya," he shouted above the screeching of the portal. "Just a few moments more: it is closing!"

His shoes were sliding, skidding across the floor of the vault. He jammed his heel into the cracks between the ancient flagstones of the Last Seal, grateful that the stones - which his ancestor had laid to ensnare the demon almost three hundred years before - now played their part in helping to save him, Cornelius' descendant.

As he hung on, the black portal shrank towards the Cavalier's arm threatening to sever it. At the last moment, Artemas, with a piercing shriek of chagrin released Freya and vanished into the void just as the portal boomed shut.

And then at last there was silence.

Ben and Freya collapsed to the ground gasping for breath, Ben's arms around her, clutching her tightly against him.

After a moment, Freya giggled. "You can get your arms off me now, rich boy. I mean, is this *really* the time for that kind of thing?"

Blushing slightly, Ben disentangled himself and scrambled to his feet, the flush spreading from his neck to his face as he extended his hand to help the little thief up from the floor. They looked each other up and down, both were dishevelled and with burns, cuts and bruises, but otherwise unhurt.

Freya grinned under his scrutiny, "Later perhaps," she added with a wink, and Ben blushed some more. Then they both looked around the room.

Marlowe and Gymer were groaning as they pulled themselves to their feet. Around them the avatars had turned into petrified stone and were quite inert, as if their life force had gone the moment Dantalion was banished. On the other side of the vault, Tobias was coming round, blinking and rubbing several large bumps on his head. He glowered, got to his feet and stared at the spot where he had last seen Artemas.

"He's gone, Doc, gone to Hell and the Devil where he belongs!" Freya called.

Tobias's face cleared and he smiled at her then bent down to examine the body of Gymer's man next to him. His smile changed into a sad grimace, for Spencer was clearly dead, a knife wound having cut an artery in his neck. Of the original Thirteen, including Matthias, six now remained alive in the vault and these had found that the instant Dantalion had vanished into the void, the invisible barrier around the Last Seal had collapsed. They wandered around the vault in stunned silence, trying to work out what had just occurred.

Ben took a few steps into the Last Seal. There in the centre was the portcullis symbol, engraved on a stone that was its very heart. Ben crouched down and touched it. This was the stone tablet that his ancestor had used to capture Dantalion, and had later placed here when he created the network of seals that imprisoned the demon. A tiny thrill of power tingled through his fingers as he touched the stone. He thought back to the body of Cornelius lying beneath the charred ruins of the Cathedral. He had felt a desire to prove himself to the man and he had done so. In his heart now the anger had gone. Yes, there was guilt and sorrow, but also there was pride and joy. Ben thought it was enough, for the present.

He looked up and saw Gabriel was still guarding the trussed up form of Walton, sitting near the door of the chamber. The bookseller looked weak and pale from blood loss, but he smiled thinly back at Ben and gave a slight nod: a shared moment of satisfaction that the job was done. Ben hobbled over and slumped down beside him. "What now?" he asked, but the bookseller just shrugged.

"To be honest with you, Benjamin, I had not thought this far ahead."

A shadow fell upon the pair and looking up they saw that Gymer was standing over them. He looked like a man desperately trying to make sense of what he had just seen. Finally he appeared to give up trying and just shrugged.

"Well now, what am I going to do with you all?" he asked eventually, scratching his head.

****

363

By the time they had found a way out of the scorching ruins of the building above them, the fire had moved on and away from the Guild Hall. Gymer rounded everyone up, searched them, made sure all the wounded were treated - as much as they could be in the circumstances – then marched them out of what used to be the door, covered by Marlowe's huge musket. Not that it was necessary since not one of them had the energy to consider escape; even Marlowe looked faintly sheepish as he loaded and primed his weapon.

Once outside, they could see the enormity of the devastation: not only the Guild Hall but dozens of other houses in the area had also gone.

Ben quickly noticed something else. "The wind is dropping," he said.

"You're right, Benjamin," Gabriel croaked. "Thank God!" He was being supported on one side by Tobias and on the other by Ben. The doctor had been able to extract the shot, which had not penetrated far into the bookseller's chest, and bind the wound, but Gabriel, older and less fit than the other three, was exhausted and weak from loss of blood.

Scarred, wounded and covered in blood, they formed a striking, possibly alarming column as they marched, shuffled and limped across London. They were aware that huge swathes of the city were still ablaze, but the powerful wind that had driven the fire north and west had finally abated. It seemed that at last, after three and more days, the fire was coming under control.

"There is going to be hell to pay after this, you realise," Tobias pointed out, "they will want to know how it started and who started it."

"What do you think Gymer will say happened?" Freya whispered. She had got rid of the leather belt and tidied up her skirts, but like them all, looked the worse for wear.

They all shrugged. Somehow, after the enormity of the battle they had fought - and won - nothing Gymer intended to say or not say was of much concern. They were alive; the city – the Kingdom – had been saved from total destruction. And right now, they were all too tired to care.

As soon as they had picked their way from the immediate surroundings of the Guild Hall, Gymer had produced a special warrant which, when shown to a patrol of Prince James's Guards, had obliged them to provide an escort. So it was that as dawn rolled across the city they now approached Westminster, and there, his pristine and well-groomed appearance seeming so bizarre after the fire and ash they had left behind, Ben saw his Headmaster bustling across the road towards them with a face like a winter storm.

"Silver! Come here at once, boy. Never, in all my years as Headmaster of Westminster School have I had such a case as you. You, boy, will be thrashed and then expelled, and by God if ..."

Holding up his hand, Gymer stepped in front of him stopping his tirade in mid-flow. "Doctor Busby? My name is Captain Gymer and I work for the King."

"What? The *King* you say?"

Gymer nodded. "Yes indeed, Sir. I am investigating the circumstances of the beginning of the fire, which still ravages the city. I have today made several arrests and am on my way to see the King right now."

Busby eyes swivelled, taking in Ben, then all the others in the little party; widened as he registered the muskets of the escorting guards, and returned to Ben.

"Are you saying that this boy – one of my pupils – started the fire?" he asked in a shocked voice.

Ben's heart pounded in his chest. He had fought a demon and been through the horror of re-living his parents' death, and what for? It was bad enough to be harangued for skipping

365

school, but was he now about to be hanged for arson and treason or – God! - drawn and quartered as well? But then he caught sight of Gymer's face and was surprised to see that the spymaster was smiling at him.

"No, I am not saying that at all. He has helped us. How? Well, I will tell you how. He helped us to locate the villains who started the fire and he has saved the Kingdom. You should be proud of him. I am taking him now to meet the King and when he returns to you later today I trust you will honour him just as the King will."

Busby's face was a picture. His jaw dropped open and he just gawped, his mouth working, but no sound coming out. Finally he nodded.

"There now, Old Rusty, that's a good chap," Gymer said, patting him on the shoulder.

Chapter 30
A New Order

S ome three hours later, Ben and his friends, along with Marlowe and Gymer, stood in a Long Gallery in the Palace of Westminster. Walton and the few remaining of Matthias' followers had been taken away for questioning. Ben and the others had been made to bathe and given fresh clothes, and now Freya was staring open-mouthed at the splendour about her, much as she had done in Tobias' home, only more so. The Long Gallery was decorated with paintings and expensive tapestries that covered the walls from floor to ceiling. Dotted here and there were dozens of musical instruments, among them virginals and harpsichords and a very large harp. Ben was aware that he and his friends were being eyed warily by bewigged courtiers, who lounged about in their silks and satins, on plush, velvet-padded chairs. In the centre of the room was a fountain, whose gently tinkling water merged with the chatter of the courtiers, the singing of brightly coloured songbirds in gilded cages scattered around the room, and the ticking of dozens of ornate clocks.

"Oh *snoggers!*" was all the little thief could manage, giving up trying to calculate how much it was all worth in pounds, shillings and pence.

A courtier at the far end of the Long Gallery beckoned a lace-swathed wrist at them, and they set off, passing the musical fountain and the ogling lords and ladies of the court, and out of the room, which exited into a guard chamber. Here they walked through a patrol of royal guards, before finally arriving in the King's Presence Chamber.

There, sitting in a high-backed chair beneath a tasselled canopy at the far end of the room, deep in conversation with half-a-dozen smartly dressed gentlemen, was the King.

Freya thought he was a striking fellow; not handsome as such – quite ugly in fact – and he was what ... thirty-six? Old really. Yet there was something about him that made her catch her breath. He wore a flowing black wig with elaborate curls that fell beyond his shoulders. His legs were encased in white stockings and under a blue cloak, his ruffled white shirt frothed at neck and wrists with lace. "Now he *is* a fancy man," she whispered to Ben out of the corner of her mouth, which made him want to giggle.

The people called King Charles II the 'Merry Monarch' and Ben could see Freya had fallen under his spell. Stories of his womanising, along with his gambling and drinking, were rife in the taverns and coffee shops and had even reached the common rooms of Ben's school. All these tales were completely true, but it was also true that he was a heroic leader, and the same gossipmongers were now very happy to admit that he and his brother had been seen these last few days galloping around London, directing the fire fighting and even at times getting into line passing buckets of water. Such had been his bravery that Londoners had taken this King to their hearts.

He was now talking to a group of men, who stood with rolled up parchments, maps and plans under their arms, while one of their number pointed at a map of London that had been erected on an easel. A line had been drawn showing the extent of the fire damage.

"The wind is dying and the work of pulling down or blowing up houses and fighting the fire with water has finally paid dividends, your Majesty. The fire has not spread further since dawn and I do not think it will."

"Thank you, Mr Pepys. Do we know how much was destroyed, gentleman?" the King asked. Another man stepped forward.

"I estimate at least four hundred acres has succumbed to the fire, mostly that which lay inside the city walls. Within that space were perhaps more than twelve thousand houses, almost one hundred churches and chapels, four dozen guild halls, a prison and countless civic buildings. At least ten thousand men, women and children are homeless and camped out on Moorfields and other areas of common land, and a very great number have been ruined," he answered.

The King pondered this for a moment before asking another question. "How much money have we lost? How much is the cost to the city?"

The second man pulled out a hastily scribbled note and studied it for a moment before answering. "Sire, I believe the damages are close to eight million pounds in terms of the buildings, along with over two million in worth of goods; the heart of the city and its wealth is gone."

"Well gentlemen, we must rebuild it! Mr Pepys, Mr Wren, all of you: I thank you. Come back to see me on Friday and we will make our plans. Good day to you."

The men all bowed and retreated out of the door past Ben and his friends. The courtier accompanying Gymer moved forward and spoke quietly to the King, who looked sharply at him and then across at them all, taking in the huge form of

Marlowe and the petite shape of Freya, who looked quite striking in a clean linen dress.

Freya leant across to Ben and whispered, "Stap me! You hear that? Ten million burned up. I never knew there was so much money about. I need to up my game."

Tobias' hand found her shoulder and pushed down hard to get her attention. "Just don't go thieving anything here unless you want your head decorating Tower Bridge come the morning, there's a good girl," he hissed with a wink at Ben.

The courtier returned and they were led forward.

"Can everyone else withdraw and take refreshment," the King ordered, causing looks of curiosity on the faces of courtiers, who were standing around the audience chamber. "And you two," he said to the guards standing on either side of the throne. Seeing their worried stare he added with a half-smile, "Don't worry, I have Captain Gymer and Mr Marlowe here to protect me."

The guards bowed and vacated the room. The King waited until the doors had shut before waving Gymer and the others forward. "Captain Gymer came to see me this morning with an extraordinary tale: a tale of demons below my city, of sorcery and of a desperate fight beneath the Guild Hall. He witnessed it all and frankly he still did not believe it himself. The tale is, of course, preposterous is it not? Surely no one would believe it and would dismiss those who did as lunatics, do you not agree?" The King looked quizzically from one to the other of them, but no one answered. Ben's heart missed a beat and he feared that the gallows might be waiting for them after all.

"Indeed, most people would not believe it, but as it happens, I am privy to knowledge most people are not. When a King succeeds to the throne there are certain secrets that are passed on from his predecessor. In my case the secrets were hidden from the usurpers who murdered my father, and kept safe until I came to the throne. One of these secrets is a certain document written centuries ago, that revealed the existence of demons and told of a group who fought against them: a group called the *Praesidium*. The head of the *Praesidium* reported to the Monarch alone. So it was, that a year after I became King a certain Mr Janssen came to see me and introduced himself."

Tobias gasped at this and the King nodded. "Yes, Doctor, it was your father I believe. He was a charming man and I grew to anticipate his visits with pleasure. He would tell me terrifying tales, but I enjoyed them nonetheless, and so I was quite anxious and disappointed when he failed to return as we had arranged last year. At his insistence I knew no one in his organisation beyond himself, and did not know who to contact. So, I waited for news; news that never came until Gymer arrived here today and told me of you all. Of you, Doctor and how you took up your father's work despite reluctance. You wanted revenge on the man who killed your father?"

"Yes, Sire. I had him in my sights, but ..."

"But you chose to forego your shot on your enemy in order to attack this demon - this Dantalion - instead, and so saved your companion's life. A noble act indeed," the King said, nodding his head, "and what of your companions? Let's start with the life you saved. A common thief from all accounts, a vagabond indeed, yet one who seems to possess as great a love for the city as I do myself and fights to defend it."

Freya shrugged. "Your Honour, I had to. You see, in a way it was my fault. I stole the scroll and tried to sell it to Artemas. But I did not believe in Dantalion then. Once I had seen him and knew what he wanted to do to my city, I had to stop him, didn't I?"

"No, you did not. You could have run and hidden away somewhere but instead you stayed."

Freya blushed, unusually for her, lost for words. The King regarded her for a long moment and finally turned to look at Gabriel.

"Next, we have a bookseller who is all that was left of the *Praesidium* and who-"

"No, your Majesty," Gabriel interrupted. "I beg your pardon, Sire, but please stop: I am not worthy of any praise. I ... I am a coward who ran away and left his friend in danger," Gabriel mumbled and turned to Tobias.

"I am sorry, Tobias, but as you found out, I left Markus to die. I should have stayed and fought beside him, but I did not. I think I should leave, with your permission, Majesty," Gabriel said and backed away, but Tobias put his hand out to stop him.

Gabriel stared at him. "Are you not angry?"

"I would have been had I known of this before the last few days or if you had not gone back and retrieved my father's body. I certainly was angry when Artemas first told me, but now I have seen for myself the terror of Dantalion and the *Liberati*, how can I blame you? Maybe you made a mess of things last year, Gabriel, but despite your fear, you came back and tried to make things right. Then last night, when the fight began, you stayed and stood in harm's way."

The King nodded. "Yes indeed. Courage is not just standing and fighting, it is also turning back to try again when you realise you did wrong or when you failed. You struggled on alone and in the end you found the courage to stand up to the 'Great Enemy' as Markus Janssen would have put it. Only because of you doing that did we have any hope of defeating the demon. This victory belongs to you as much as to anyone."

Gabriel flushed under the gaze of the King, until Charles turned to Ben. "Finally, we have the enigma: the schoolboy with great powers of sorcery. He was the only one strong enough to defeat the demon: and yet had demons of his own to overcome, I gather."

"It seems Captain Gymer has learnt a lot about us, your Majesty," Ben said simply.

"Yes, he has, and he has informed me of much. I will need to know more before we are done, but that will wait. For today, though, there is just one question left that I must have answered."

"What is that, Sire?" Ben asked.

The King moved down from his throne to stand amongst them. He looked at them all in turn, including the giant Marlowe. It was a while before he spoke.

"As my spymaster, Gymer here is tasked with defending me and my Kingdom from threats, external and internal. Dutch and French, assassins and spies all need watching as my people and my ministers know full well. Gymer is, as you have found, tenacious and although he can make mistakes there is no one braver, more loyal and more determined to do his duty, save Marlowe here, perhaps," the King said with a nod at the big man, "for Marlowe's family have long served the Crown.

"Yet, there are areas with which they have little experience that I would have them fight against. This business with Dantalion has proven that there are greater dangers than mere mortals bring."

"Other dangers, Sire?" Tobias asked. "Other than Dantalion? I thought this ended with him."

Charles shook his head. "No, not by a long way is this fight over, not while other demons exist, and evil, power-hungry men like Artemas. Maybe there are still more dangers. The King and his Kingdom need protecting from them. I need the *Praesidium*. Will you all help establish it anew?"

They looked at each other in stunned silence and the King went on. "You must be secret; no one must know you exist. There will be dangers, but the city and the Kingdom, perhaps even the world needs the *Praesidium*. I can arrange a little pay. Not much money, but enough, I hope. So then ... will you take the job?"

Marlowe and Gymer were the King's men and agreed at once without thought. For Gabriel there was also little choice: he was already *Praesidium*, body and soul, and he readily agreed, but the others did have a choice. Ben could go back to his school and earn his scholarship to Oxford, one day inherit his uncle's wealth and live his life in security and comfort. Tobias had a medical practice and with Artemas possibly dead, and certainly no longer in this world, he had no more need for revenge. Freya could leave and disappear into the city streets to pick up where she had left off when, barely four days before, she had collided with Ben in the Royal Exchange.

Sometimes, thought Ben, men and women do not change much in a lifetime, but for him and his friends, four days had become a lifetime and all of them, in one way or another, had changed.

The four of them looked at each other and then at Marlowe and Gymer, and they knew in that moment that they had all made the same choice. One by one they nodded at the King, moving to stand side by side, for they were now the Guardians: they were now the new *Praesidium* Order.

There was a moment's silence before Freya broke it with a final question.

"Just how much money are we talking about, your Majesty?"

Words of Power

In The Last Seal, Gabriel, Artemas and Ben use Words of Power as weapons with which to fight, a means of defence and a method of summoning a demon. These were once words that the demons spoke in their infernal language and which held power. These same words found their way into our many languages, buried away in a thousand dialects, but both the *Liberati* and the *Praesidium* have discovered and combined the words and now they can use these words in their conflict. Here are some of these words that I used in this book. I have included here the words used and shown the languages they come from as well as a pronunciation guide.

Flash bang: "Kipofu–Lumen–Glimt"
Blind (Swahili Kipofu); Light (Latin Lumen); Flash (Norweigian Glimt)

Bolt of Lightning: "Calamus Αστραπή Стрелять"
Arrow (Latin calamus); Lightning (Greek astrapi); Shoot (Russian strelyat)

Rite of freeing Dantalion: "Eleuthero Libertas Dantalion"
Separate (Eleuthero Greek) Freedom (Liberats Latin) Dantalion (name of the demon)

Cone of Ice: "κώνος , jää , décharge!"
Cone (Greek Konus) Ice (Finish Yar); discharge (French daysharge)

Dismissing an Illusion: "Ostendu, Realität, núhwílum!"
Reveal (Latin ostendu) ; Reality (German realitate) ; Now (Old English newveelum)

Mystical Shield: "Contego,Aeris, Minä!"
Shield (Latin contego), Air (Latin airis), Myself (Finish mineh)

Opening the doorway to the Abyss "Ingang, Vácuo Nepokriven"

Entance (German ingank); Vacuum (Portuguese vaqwo) Open (Serbian nepocriven)

Historical Note

T he Last Seal is set in and around the events of the Great Fire of London. This cataclysmic event is fascinating. On the evening of 1st September, 1666, a careless baker in Pudding Lane, Thomas Farriner, forgot to put out his fire, which spread, creating an inferno that would destroy 13,000 houses and make 70,000 of London's 80,000 population homeless – although amazingly only eight to sixteen people are thought to have died.

The Lord Mayor, Sir Thomas Bloodworth failed to act and did indeed make some dubious comments about how a woman could put out the fire. It was down to the trained bands of militia led by King Charles, and in particular his brother, Prince James, and other worthies to fight the fire and finally put it out.

Another major factor was the prevailing wind which was ferocious, but suddenly dropped on Tuesday night, allowing the fire fighters to finally bring the inferno under control.

London did indeed need rebuilding by the likes of Christopher Wren. I can recommend *The Dreadful Judgement* by Neil Hanson and *By Permission of Heaven* by Adrian Tinswood as good sources for detailed accounts of the fire. Samuel Pepys (the 17th century diarist) also has much to say on the subject in his diaries.